I. D. Roberts was born in Australia in 1970 and moved to England when he was three. From a young age he developed an obsession with war comics, movies, Tintin and James Bond. For the past decade he has been the film writer for a national listings magazine. After living all over the country and buying a farmhouse by mistake in Ireland, he finally settled in the south-west and currently lives in rural Somerset with his wife Di and their chocolate labrador, Steed.

idroberts.com

By I. D. Roberts

Kingdom Lock
For Kingdom and Country

a&b

FOR KINGDOM
AND COUNTRY

I. D. ROBERTS

Allison & Busby Limited
12 Fitzroy Mews
London W1T 6DW
allisonandbusby.com

First published in Great Britain by Allison & Busby in 2015.
This paperback edition published by Allison & Busby in 2016.

A CIP catalogue record for this book is available from
the British Library.

10 9 8 7 6 5 4 3 2 1

ISBN 978-0-7490-1975-4

Typeset in 10.5/16 pt Adobe Garamond Pro by
Allison & Busby Ltd.

The paper used for this Allison & Busby publication
has been produced from trees that have been legally sourced
from well-managed and credibly certified forests.

Printed and bound by
CPI Group (UK) Ltd, Croydon, CR0 4YY

For Nathan, James and Nick. We band of brothers.

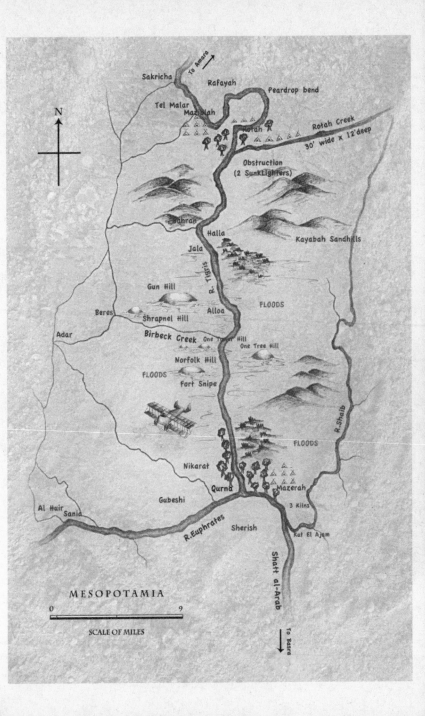

N

To Amara

Sakricha

Rafayah

Peardrop bend

Tel Malar

Maziblah

Nofah

Rotah Creek
30' wide X 12' deep

Obstruction
(2 Sunk Lighters)

Bahran

Halla

Kayabah Sandhills

Jala

Gun Hill

R. Tigris

Beras

Shrapnel Hill

Alloa

FLOODS

Adar

Birbeck Creek One Tower Hill

One Tree Hill

Norfolk Hill

FLOODS

Fort Snipe

R. Shaib

FLOODS

Nikarat

Qurna

Mazerah

Al Huir

Sanid

Gubeshi

3 Kilns

R. Euphrates

Sherish

Kut El Ajam

MESOPOTAMIA

Shatt al-Arab

To Basra

0   9

SCALE OF MILES

PROLOGUE

'Kingdom Lock, that bastard,' Wilhelm Wassmuss spat, shaking his head. 'I cannot believe this . . . *Scheißdreck.*'

The German agent was in a dark mood as he trotted along the length of the stinking, sweat-sour and dusty retreating column of Turkish troops and Arab irregulars. Once again he was dressed in the uniform of an Ottoman officer, but now as a cavalry *binbaşi*, a major. The Barjisiyah Woods were behind them and ahead, towards the setting sun, lay the small settlement of Nakheilah nestled on the banks of the fast-flowing and bloated Euphrates River. The soldiers paid little heed to the dishevelled mounted officer as he rode by, most just avoiding contact with the piercing blue eyes that glared down at them. These men were lost in their own thoughts, all glad to be leaving the carnage of the trees and the heat of the British guns behind.

It had been a hasty, panicked retreat. During the late

afternoon the Infidel British had suddenly charged forward, smashing into and overrunning the first line. The Turks had waited to see if the British would push on into the woods after seizing their trenches but, to their surprise, the Infidels had halted their advance. Many of the soldiers had worried that their officers would order a return to the woods and a reoccupation of the trenches but, Allah be praised, *Kaymakam* Süleyman Askerî Bey had ordered their complete withdrawal to Nasiriyeh on the far side of Hammar Lake.

The retreat was sounded quickly. Hundreds of white flags were raised by those too tired or too far behind, whilst the main body of troops turned and fled the trees, heading north-west for the river. There was confusion wherever one looked, with officers and soldiers moving as fast as they could without stopping. But it was worse for those stragglers at the rear, the exhausted and the wounded. They were suddenly set upon, not by the British, but from their own allies, the Marsh Arabs. They turned on their Turkish comrades like a pack of wolves, slaughtering any stragglers and stripping them bare, leaving their mutilated corpses for the vultures and flies.

At first the blood-curdling screams of the stragglers being picked off had made the panic all the more chaotic, but the NCOs and some of the more level-headed officers had formed the men into an orderly retreat, keeping them together and therefore less vulnerable to random attacks. The odd shout of anger and an occasional rifle shot could be heard at sporadic intervals until eventually a rhythmic, almost hypnotic state fell over the march. There would be hot food and warm fires waiting for them in the safety of the garrison, and it was those thoughts that kept them moving at a steady pace. Eventually the mud gave way to dry, rocky desert. But not a man shuffled or grumbled on that march back.

Wassmuss whipped his sweat-soaked horse with a crude crop made of reeds, urging it on. He was furious and desperate to catch up with Süleyman Askerî's litter at the head of the column. As he rode on, his mind was racing with questions. He could not understand why the troops were retreating. The Ottoman Forces outnumbered the British by at least five to one. Yet, why had Süleyman Askerî not used them to smash through to the fort at Shaiba and from there overwhelm Basra as had been planned? But after his run-in with Lock, he himself had been lucky to escape from the city, had been lucky to escape with his life.

'*Scheiße*,' Wassmuss spat again.

With his face cut and bleeding, he'd been unable to escape north up the Tigris to the Turkish lines at Amara and so had made his way to the south of the city. There he had sneaked past the British soldiers who were spread out along the shore, and made his way through the marsh towards Zubair and the fort of old Basra.

Along the way, he came across a Turkish patrol. But they were all dead, stripped naked, mutilated, and left to bloat and rot in the sun. A shifting miasma of flies engulfed most of the bodies, making them barely recognisable as human beings. And when Wassmuss approached, the insects swarmed around him, before settling back to do what they did in the great scheme of nature.

Wassmuss scoured the area, searching for something he could use. After ten minutes of fruitless exploring, he came across a missed corpse, that of an Ottoman cavalry officer, almost invisible and half-submerged in a reed-choked lagoon. He dragged the body on to dry land and was pleased to see that not only was the man not too tall, but that he was fully clothed. Wassmuss stripped the carcass and dressed in its muddy and drenched uniform. The tunic, with its silvery-grey collars, was a little loose across the shoulders, but the breeches, with their distinctive red stripe down the outside of each leg, could have been made for him. The larger than normal kabalak helmet with its upturned brim was a snug fit.

There were no horses, but he did find a saddlebag that contained a hunk of stale black bread and some dates, along with a battered brass telescope, a crude map of the surrounding area and some personal letters, which, when the need arose, he later used to wipe himself.

Wasting no time, Wassmuss moved on towards the old fort, now little more than a scattering of broken rocks and the remnants of walls, but was bitterly disappointed to find nothing but a group of Marsh Arabs camped there. He avoided contact with those natives, knowing that he would be set upon and killed as soon as they laid eyes upon him. So again he lay low, sheltering from the heat of the day and enduring the incessant pestering of flies, all the while listening to the guns shelling Shaiba with hope in his heart.

At nightfall he crept to the edge of the Arab camp and, with not so much as a second's hesitation, slit the throat of the young boy watching over the horses, and made off with the best mount, a tan mare with a frisky temper. The boy also had in his possession a gun tucked into his belt, a Mauser M.1910/14 pistol, with a full clip.

Wassmuss kept riding south and eventually hooked round to the west, where he planned to meet up with Askeri's army that was facing Shaiba. But instead, he was horrified to see a large British force marching on Barjisiyah Woods. Settling upon a mound within a copse of trees, he observed the battle through the battered telescope he'd found and watched as both sides pounded each other to the point of exhaustion. He saw with horror the British lightning strike on the Ottoman trenches, and cursed as the Turks fled into the woods.

The German stayed hidden on that mound in the copse, and cried bitter tears of anger when Askerî's troops abandoned their own positions and began to flee back towards Hammar Lake. But his disgust was multiplied when the British gave up their advantage and returned to the safety of their fort.

Wassmuss pushed his horse on towards the distant rooftops of the garrison town of Nasiriyeh. The beast's eyes rolled white as its heart pumped harder and harder, legs pounding past the line of troops. There was no sign of Askerî's litter and so Wassmuss cantered on, until the rocky desert gave way to scrub grass and then, passing through clusters of date palms, he finally hit a more established road that ran parallel to the nearby Euphrates River. At the end of a small row of mud-brick hovels was a checkpoint, its wooden barrier pole raised. Wassmuss passed by the sentry hut and rode on into the town following the string of telegraph poles and lamps that lined the street.

Wassmuss cantered by busy cafes, shopfronts and stalls, until he came to a junction. He turned left down a narrow side street, his horse's hooves echoing back from the surrounding buildings, and then right to emerge out onto a tree-lined square. The white-brick, flat-roofed buildings on two sides were of two storeys, with the ground floor being a series of open archways and the floor above one long, open terrace. The larger building over to the left was a grander affair of three storeys. Jutting out from the top of the latticed balcony on the second floor was a flagpole from which, flapping limply in the breeze, hung the red and white crescent moon and star of the Ottoman Empire. This marked out the building as Command Headquarters. The entrance was at the top of some stone steps. An ancient fig tree stood to one side, its canopy of leaves rustling in the warm breeze.

Wassmuss whipped his horse forward, crossing the square, until he reached the stone steps. He jumped from the saddle, threw the reins at the *Mehmetçik* on guard duty outside and bounded up the steps. Throwing open the large studded wooden doors, Wassmuss marched along the dark, cool inner corridor, his footsteps click-clicking a rhythmic, determined hatred. He had no idea where he was heading, but his anger drove him onwards. He must have made a terrifying sight to the young military clerks he passed, a thickset, stocky, short ball of fury, looking as ragged and enraged as he did, with a five-day beard, a face lacerated by tiny cuts, and his uniform crumpled and caked in mud and dust.

'Where is the lieutenant colonel? Where is *Kaymakam* Süleyman Askerî?' he growled at an alarmed-looking sergeant.

'The end of the corridor . . . turn right, *effendim*,' the *çavuş* offered, as Wassmuss stormed by without breaking stride.

Around the corner, the dapper naval lieutenant acting as Askerî's adjutant was not so intimidated, though. He stood, arms folded across the chest of his dark-blue uniform, blocking the way.

'*Effendim*, you cannot enter . . . Süleyman Askerî Bey is not at home to anyone today,' the *yüzbaşi* protested strongly.

But Wassmuss was in no mood for protocol. He roughly shoved the adjutant aside and forced himself into Askerî's office.

The room beyond the threshold looked more like a study belonging to some English stately home than the office of the leader of the Mesopotamian Area Command, such was the splendour of its heavy, dark decor and fine, plush furnishings. Süleyman Askerî was standing at the open French window at the far end, his back to the room, staring out onto the lengthening shadows in the gardens beyond. Beside him was a sparse desk, with nothing more than a single candlestick telephone and a cut-glass ashtray on the polished surface. There was a strong smell of jasmine wafting in from outside and the sound of the gentle chatter of songbirds bidding the day adieu. The distant clatter from the traffic on the river beyond was barely audible.

'*Effendim, effendim*, I protest!' the adjutant spluttered, chasing Wassmuss into the room.

Askerî slowly turned his head. His slim, studious face looked ashen and defeated. Even his large, carefully cultivated moustache drooped like a house plant deprived of water, and the usual sparkle of self-gratification was absent from the hazel eyes that peered back at Wassmuss through thin circular lenses.

'It is all right, *Yüzbaşi*,' Askerî said, his voice deflated. 'Fetch coffee, if you please. Welcome *Herr Doktor*? Or is it *Binbaşi*?' He frowned at Wassmuss's uniform. 'In the cavalry now? Well, no matter, it is good to see that you have survived.'

The adjutant glanced uneasily at Wassmuss, who remained motionless, standing in the middle of the room, then nodded and closed the door after him.

'Come, sit!' Askerî said affably, as he indicated to the chair opposite his desk.

But Wassmuss did not move. He just continued to glare back at Askerî. 'Did you order *Miralay* Daghistani to hold at Ahwaz?' he said.

The question clearly took Askerî by surprise. He blinked behind his glasses, and hesitated. And it was that hesitation that told Wassmuss all he needed to know. He knew then that Askerî had betrayed him. He knew then that Askerî was a coward.

In one swift movement he drew the Mauser pistol he had taken from the Marsh Arab boy, and pointed it at Akserî's head. Süleyman Askerî's eyes widened in horror and, as his hand fluttered up instinctively to protect his face, Wassmuss pulled the trigger.

The shot echoed round the room and out into the garden. The birds exploded from the trees, startled into flight.

Wassmuss quickly kicked over the chair Askerî had offered him a moment earlier, then turned the pistol and shot himself in the arm. He cried out in pain, fired two more shots towards the French window, dropped the gun, and collapsed heavily upon Askerî's desk.

'Assassin!' he screamed, just as the adjutant, with a pistol in his hand and two sentries close behind, burst into the room. There was a cloud of gunsmoke hanging in the air above the desk.

'Assassin!' Wassmuss gasped again, feebly indicating towards the French window. He then feigned blacking out and crumpled to the floor. It was a touch theatrical, but he hoped the confusion would mask his ruse.

'Quick, after him!' the adjutant shouted. 'Search the grounds!' The two sentries ran towards the open French window and burst out into the garden.

Wassmuss watched through hooded eyelids as the adjutant looked about the room. He spotted the bullet holes by the edge of the French window. Blood and matter were splattered up the wall and across the austere portrait of Enver Pasha that was hanging behind Askerî's desk. The adjutant stepped over Wassmuss's seemingly unconscious body and moved over to the desk. Wassmuss knew what he would see there. Süleyman Askerî was slumped like a broken doll behind it. The *kaymakam*'s left eye was half-open, and a look of shocked surprise was frozen upon his face. His right eye was no longer there. The lens of his glasses was pierced and splintered, the wound behind it small and black.

Wassmuss groaned as if coming to. The adjutant pulled the chair upright and helped Wassmuss into it. The German's arm was bleeding quite badly.

'What happened, *effendim*?' the adjutant asked. There was suspicion in his voice.

Wassmuss winced as he cradled his injured arm.

'An assassin . . . from the garden,' he gasped. 'I tried to warn Süleyman Askerî Bey . . . that is why I was in such a hurry . . . to get to his office . . . But I was too late.' He shook his head dejectedly and looked up at the adjutant. 'I fired a couple of shots . . . but he got me . . .'

The adjutant frowned. 'How did you know of this?' he asked.

Wassmuss coughed and winced again. 'I learnt of a plot . . . of an assassin . . . who had been employed by the Infidels. That is why I was desperate to get to the *kaymakam*.' He coughed again and shook his head. 'Is he . . . ?'

The adjutant nodded. 'Dead.'

Wassmuss let his body slump back in the chair. '*Dann habe ich versagt*,' he whispered. 'I have failed . . .'

The adjutant stood and watched Wassmuss closely, his hand all the while stroking his moustache like a man petting a cat.

'Do you know who the assassin is, *effendim*?' he asked eventually.

Wassmuss opened his eyes. 'Oh yes, that I do. An Australian officer . . . a dog and a spy for the British,' he spat. 'He is called Kingdom Lock, Lieutenant Kingdom Lock.'

CHAPTER ONE

Basra
One week later

It took Singh two days to track Kingdom Lock down, but he eventually caught up with him in a house in the north of the city that was situated near to one of the many picturesque canals. The house was like so many of the older properties in Basra, with large, arched latticed windows on the ground floor and the distinctive overhanging wooden balconies on the first. But it was what was behind the front door that made this house so different from the rest. It was a property frequented by officers and rich merchants. And it was known locally as '*Cennet*' or, to translate from Turkish, 'Paradise' . . . even 'Heaven'.

Once across the threshold, the visitor was immediately taken with the richness of his surroundings, not only visually but in smell, too. There were plush, elaborate materials from India and the Orient everywhere the eye fell: from the wall hangings to the carpets under one's feet, and to the chairs one sat on. The furniture was of the finest carved mahogany, and exotic plants were dotted in every corner. And, as Singh stood there drinking in the beauty of that place, his nostrils were filled with aromas that brought to mind the temples back home.

It wasn't long before the proprietor, a portly Arab with a large mole on his left cheek and mischief in his yellowing eyes, sidled up to Singh with barely a swish of his golden aba. He outstretched his sausage-fingered hands and beamed a smile of crooked teeth.

'Ah, a guest from the jewel that is India. Come, enter. I am Jalal Al-din Bahar and I bid you welcome.'

Singh nodded and stepped further into the foyer. His feet immediately sank into the thick carpet. He looked up to see, lounging on the chairs dotted about the room, about ten women in various stages of undress.

'You seek the pleasures of the house, my friend?' Jalal Al-din Bahar whispered, as the women rose to their feet and approached the tall, handsome Indian.

They were high-class prostitutes from all corners of the globe – Europe, Africa, Asia and the Far East. As they gathered around Singh they began to giggle, stroking his thick, black beard, his arms and his chest, and cooing over his strength and form.

'No, sahib, regretfully. I seek my officer.'

The Arab's charm melted away instantly. He clapped his hands angrily and the girls sulkily slipped away, back to their chairs, and their coquettish stares and whispered conversations.

'I know of no officers here,' Jalal Al-din Bahar said curtly. 'Please leave.' He made for the door, but Singh remained where he was.

'Tall and fair. An Australian officer with a bullet hole in the chest of his tunic, and . . . unusual eyes . . .' Singh mimed the description of Lock while he spoke, and pulled a gold coin from his pocket. He held it out to the Arab.

Jalal Al-din Bahar glared at Singh for a moment before snatching the coin from his grasp.

'He is upstairs, second room on the left.'

Then the Arab turned and scuttled away to the far side of the foyer, and exited through a doorway that was screened by an elaborately beaded curtain.

Singh watched him go, and his eyes fell upon an attractive, slender African girl reclining nearby. He grinned at her, then made his way to the foot of the thickly carpeted stairs. As he climbed, passing beautiful and intricately decorated tapestries that adorned the walls, he kept glancing back at the girl. Her dark, hypnotic eyes followed his ascent all the way to the landing at the top. Singh stopped and looked back down at the lounge. The African girl was no longer looking at him. A bald, plump British officer with a beetroot complexion had just come in from the street and, with a swish of the beaded curtain, Jalal Al-din Bahar had appeared again. Singh watched as the girls gathered around the blushing general, giggling as the Arab went through his salesman routine.

Singh turned away and walked along the corridor. It was lined with more tapestries and the occasional heavy, studded oak door. When he neared the first door, he stopped and listened. Muffled grunting was coming from the other side. He smiled and moved on to the second door. As with the first, he stopped and listened. There was no sound from the room beyond. He tried the handle. It was unlocked, so he pushed the door open and entered.

The room inside was again decorated to a high standard of

decadence. An opulent, dark Persian rug covered the polished oak floorboards and ran all the way over to a large wooden-slatted window that was open at the far end of the room. Next to the window was a dressing table adorned with perfume bottles, brushes and all the things that a woman uses to enhance her beauty. There was also a bowl of fruit and a plate with a half-eaten loaf of bread on top. A cloud of fruit flies hovered above the food. A number of liquor bottles littered the floor.

Strewn across a deep, leather armchair, which was pushed up against the dressing table, was Lock's uniform. The sweat-stained slouch hat and the tunic with the bullet hole were unmistakable, as was the prized Beholla 7.65 automatic that Lock had taken from the dead Turk officer in the trench at Barjisiyah Woods. Away from the window, beside a large hearth that, despite the heat outside, burnt gentle warmth into the room, was a tin bathtub full of milky water. Rose petals floated on its surface.

Opposite the door, taking up much of the room, was a large four-poster bed. It was enshrouded in mosquito nets that hung loosely open, like the curtains to a stage. On the bed were three bodies, entwined in an unconscious, drunken, post-coital stupor, such was their heady perfume of sweat, sex and alcohol. Singh moved forward and pulled the nets aside. Lock lay, head slumped on his chest, naked in the middle of the bed with a nude woman either side of him. One was milky-white, freckled and had long curled red hair; the other was a brunette with silky olive skin. Singh could not help but smile as he looked down on the slumbering trio.

After a moment's hesitation, he took hold of Lock's foot and shook it.

'Sahib! Wake up, sahib! It is I, Singh.' He shook Lock's foot again.

The redhead stirred and flopped over onto her back. Despite his best efforts, Singh felt his eyes magnetically drawn to her body.

'Sahib!' Singh called again, louder this time, and with a touch of embarrassed irritation.

Lock groaned.

'Sahib?'

With an immense effort Lock lifted his chin. He opened his eyes blearily and tried to focus.

'Sahib. It is I, Singh.'

Lock frowned and put the half-empty bottle of arrack he still held in his hand to his lips. He drank heavily and blinked back at Singh. 'Sid?' he slurred.

'Yes, sahib.'

'You wanna girl, Sid? Here . . .' He lifted the arm of the olive-skinned brunette. 'She's a bit of a minx though, I warn you.' He grinned stupidly and took another swig of arrack, belched loudly, and grimaced.

'No, sahib. I was sent to fetch you.'

Lock looked up hopefully. 'Amy?' he slurred.

Singh shook his head.

Lock's face fell again and he waved Singh away.

'Bloody Ross. Well, bugger him!' he said, and threw the bottle of arrack at the wall.

The bottle smashed, spraying glass and liquid over the floor, and both girls woke with a start. The redhead let out a yelp and pulled the sheets over her nakedness when she saw Singh towering over the bed. Her olive-skinned colleague merely groaned and turned over onto her belly. Lock pulled the redhead back down and put his arm protectively around her. She relaxed and let the sheet slip from her shoulders.

'Go away, Sid. Leave me be,' Lock whispered, and turned his gaze to the window.

'Sahib, if I may be permitted to saying so, this is not the way. You must get up now and come with me,' Singh said. 'The men need you, your men. They have a great respect for you, sahib, I have a great respect for you. I am proud you are my captain. But I am not proud to see you like this. You must take control of your heart, sahib, you must not let it ruin you. All is not lost, not yet. Perhaps Memsahib Amy will not marry that fool – forgive my bluntness, sahib, but a fool is what he is, this Sahib Bing Ham Smith. It is not over yet, sahib, not unless you wish it to be.

'You are a good man and a good officer, sahib,' he added. 'Do not throw all that away. Not like this, sahib. Not like this.'

Lock turned his bloodshot eyes back to Singh. He sat up and pushed the redhead away. 'But it is too late, Sid. She's gone, she said so herself, gone to that . . . slimy . . . pompous . . . buggering bastard, Bingham Bloody Smith.'

Lock's face was twisted with anger and hurt, and spittle was running down his chin as he spoke. He shook his head and winced, and pulled himself down to the end of the bed.

'What am I doing here? What am I doing wearing that bloody uniform?'

'You fight with us, sahib, to protect those we love, all that we hold most precious, from the evil Turk and the corrupt German.'

'Bollocks, Sid,' Lock said. 'What we fight for is a lie! It's all for greed, for money, for oil. For fucking oil, Sid. Sick black death . . . on our hands, on every man's hands. I cannot . . . I will not be a part of it. No more, Sid. No more.'

'But you are, sahib, and you have been. I know nothing of oil, sahib. But Major Ross wanted me to tell you that you are a true hero and that you have saved the reputation of the regiment by your actions at Barjisiyah Woods. He is very proud of you.'

'He's a using bastard, Sid, and well you know it,' Lock sniffed.

'Maybe that is so, sahib. But he is a good using bastard. Better than that monkey's arse, Lieutenant Colonel Godwinson. And we need men like you to keep men like Godwinson in . . . What is the term you like, from the chess, sahib? In check? Yes?'

Lock grunted and ran a hand through his matted hair. 'I've lost half the platoon, Sid. What can I do with so little? We're finished. We'll be swallowed up by that bloated aristocratic fart Godwinson and his bloody nephew. I'll lose my command, not that I really ever had one . . .' He fell silent for a moment. '*I'm* lost, Sid.'

Lock shook his head and pulled himself to his feet. He wobbled uneasily as he staggered over to the dressing table.

'No, sahib, you have not,' Singh replied earnestly, as he followed the naked Lock across the room. 'You have fought and won with much, much less. The platoon . . . it is still yours. That is why Major Ross wants to see you, why he sent me to find you, Captain sahib.'

But Lock didn't hear Singh's words as he leant down on the dressing table and stared back at his own reflection in the mirror. He looked truly awful. His face was sallow and rough, and his eyes were red and dull. He really did look as if he had been single-handedly fighting a war. He laughed suddenly and, pulling himself upright, he weaved his way unsteadily over to the bathtub. He hesitated, then stepped into the water and slumped down. He looked over at Singh, then closed his eyes and let himself slide under.

Singh watched as the air bubbles burst on the surface of the water. And just as it seemed that Lock had been under for too long, the fair-haired officer suddenly shot up again, gasping. Water sloshed and splashed over the edge of the tub, soaking the floor, and Lock shook the water from his hair like a dog. He groaned, squinted up at Singh, and rubbed his eyes.

'Sid! How are you?' he smiled affably and sniffed. 'What time is it?'

'It is getting late, sahib. The sun will be gone soon.'

Lock hauled his soaking body out of the bathtub and squelched over to the window. He pushed the shutters wide open and squinted at the setting sun.

'What does Ross want, Sid?'

'I do not know, sahib. Something to do with General Townshend, and the new election in Britain. Politics.' Singh shrugged, and looked over to the two girls that still slumbered in the bed. 'And she does too, sahib.'

Lock shivered. Goosebumps had broken out on his skin.

'She?' he asked, as he turned back and pulled a sheet from the bed, wrapped it around himself, and walked over to the fireplace. He crouched down and reached for a fresh log from the basket at the side.

'Memsahib Amy,' Singh replied quietly.

Lock threw another log onto the fire and stared silently down at the flames.

'All right, Sid. I'm up. I'm sober . . . well, conscious anyway. You go on ahead. I need to get dressed and settle my account here.'

'No, sahib,' Singh smiled wryly down at his friend, 'I am to accompany you. Major Ross's strict orders.'

Lock rose stiffly to his feet and walked over to the armchair. He let the soaked sheet slip from his body and began to dress. Sitting down to pull on his boots, he glanced over to the bed. The two girls had curled up together now. Lock looked to Singh. The big Indian must have read his thoughts for he shook his head firmly. Lock grinned and stood up. He bent down to the dressing table mirror and brushed his still damp hair back with his fingers.

'How do I look, Sid?'

'Very smart, Captain sahib.' Singh said, and opened the door.

Lock gave a final glance to the slumbering girls, sighed, and stepped out into the corridor. He hesitated, realising what Singh had just said.

'Yes, I'd forgotten that. My promotion, I mean. But I doubt Godwinson will stand for it.'

'But it is not up to him, Captain sahib, surely?'

Lock grunted, then they both made their way down the stairs and through the foyer towards the front door.

Jalal Al-din Bahar was waiting for them, and he bowed and smiled at Lock as the two men approached.

'I trust that your stay has been . . . refreshing, *effendim*?'

'Most. Here.' Lock handed the portly Arab a couple of coins. 'Right, come along then, Havildar!' Lock said, and slapped a bewildered Singh on the shoulder. 'If I'm to be a captain, Sid, then I insist that you're my new sergeant.'

'No, no, sahib, you cannot, please. What about the sergeant major?'

'Sod Underhill, Sid. I never wanted him as my number two, watching my back. That's like bedding down with a cobra. No, I want a friend at my side, and you're it.'

Before Singh could protest further, Lock opened the door to the street and stepped outside.

The sun had fallen behind the rooftops now and, despite the sky being an artist's palette of pinks and reds, the street was in darkness. For a moment, as the door closed behind them, it was difficult to see, coming as they had from the bright lights of the brothel out into the gloom of the street.

The two men paused in the doorway to let their eyes adjust, and Lock lit a cigarette. It was a quiet night. Only the insects broke the silence around them, and it was a relief not to hear the sound of distant guns. After a minute they turned and moved off in the direction of the canal. But, as they did so, a shadowy figure stepped out from the doorway opposite. There was a brief scuffle before two gunshots rang out, their cracks echoing off the surrounding buildings, and the muzzle flashes momentarily illuminating Lock and Singh's surprised faces. Then the street was enshrouded in gloom again. A body fell heavily to the floor as the sound of fleeing footsteps slowly diminished.

'Sahib,' Singh gasped weakly, before a second body slumped to the ground.

The echoing footsteps faded into the distance, until there was nothing, only silence and darkness . . .

CHAPTER TWO

Everything was white.

Too bright.

Kingdom Lock squeezed his eyes shut again. His thoughts and feelings were a tumble of confusion. He remembered a blinding flash of light and then nothing, just blackness and cold. He was no longer cold, though, no longer numb, but warm and somehow overwhelmed with a feeling of security, of safety, as if he was back in the womb. A part of his mind expected to feel pain, his body to ache, but there was nothing, only softness. He knew he should try and sit up, but found he hadn't the strength. So he lay still and listened. Nothing. No, there was . . . a gentle, rhythmic pulse. It was barely audible, yet he knew it was close. Then he felt his face flicker into a smile. His heart was still beating. He was alive.

Lock's nose twitched. A smell, faint, but there all the same, like a memory. Furniture polish and caustic soap. He opened his eyes once more, trying to focus through his bleached surroundings. He turned his head stiffly and a pain exploded inside his skull. He wanted to scream out, he wanted to vomit. But he lay still and waited for the wave of nausea to pass, for the pain inside his head to subside. His breathing slowed. Calm.

For the third time in what seemed as many hours, Lock opened his eyes. He was in a private room, clinical and white, lying on a bed, shrouded in starched cotton sheets. They were pulled up to his chest. His arms were free, stretched out either side of him with his palms facing down. Soft cotton pyjamas had replaced his uniform, but his head felt tight, encased, as if he still wore his slouch hat. Opposite the bed, daylight was streaming through a high window and Lock could make out the gnarly branches of a tree swaying in the breeze outside. He cautiously, should any sudden movement give him a relapse of nausea, turned his head. To his right was a door; to his left a small bedside cabinet. On top were a jug and a glass of clear water.

Lock licked his lips. They were chapped and sore. His throat was dry. He tried to reach for the glass. Sweat broke out on his brow. He could feel it prickling his skin. His heart started to race in his chest. A dull ache was building in his temple. His arm was trembling. It was barely off the bed. He stopped trying and felt the weight of his whole body sink back into the mattress.

A flurry of movement caught his attention. He moved his eyes. Three white-speckled bulbuls had landed on the nearest branch to the window. Lock could hear their loud chattering now, as if they were in disagreement about something. He frowned at the scene for a moment and tried to recall where he had been before, before the bed and the white room. He lost his focus and the birdsong melded into the voices of men talking.

Lock groaned in confusion. The voices were familiar, yet they sounded alien to his ear. He couldn't make out what they were saying.

'Speak up,' he said.

The voices ignored him and continued with their chatter. One said '*Kahve*'.

Lock grunted and relaxed. *Kahve* was Turkish for 'coffee'. Coffee would be nice. He'd like a cup, strong and bitter. Perhaps with a little sugar. He nodded.

'Yes, good idea,' he said.

Movement rocked the bed. Lock opened his eyes.

But he was no longer lying in bed, in the white room. He was sat upright, fully dressed in his old, brown corduroy suit, perched on the back of the ox cart he knew so well; the ox cart he had used for weeks at a time to lug telegraph poles and cables around the lonely roadways of eastern Anatolia. That was his job initially, and then his cover, putting up telephone lines for the Sultan. He recognised the man moving about next to him, rocking the cart. It was Bedros, the Armenian, a wiry fellow with pockmarked skin, who was always dressed in a worn, ragged blazer. He was part of the work detail Lock had assigned to him; one Armenian and eight Kurds.

'*I make coffee, effendim?*' Bedros said in Turkish, beaming a smile of broken, blackened teeth.

Lock nodded and noted that his head no longer throbbed with pain. '*Yes, good idea,*' he said in the same tongue, understanding perfectly.

He turned his attention to the main work detail a little way ahead.

The Kurds, despite being strong labourers, with rough hands and rougher manners, were struggling to lift a pole into a freshly

31

excavated hole. Two of them had even stopped working and were shading their eyes, staring off beyond the cart, into the distance.

Lock raised himself up and turned around.

Stretched out before him was a flat, grassy landscape dusted with snow. It ran all the way to the foot of the distant white peaks of three mountains to the north: Soli, Davutaga and Isik Dagi. To the right was the eastern shore of Lake Erçek, its azure waters sparkling in the afternoon sunshine. A road, little more than a dirt track, followed the length of the shore before hitting a crossroads, and it was here that Lock could see a large dust cloud rising up in the distance.

'*Strange. Nothing heavier than farm traffic usually passes along this stretch,*' Lock said.

'*Not farm traffic, effendim,*' Bedros said. '*They are . . . horsemen?*'

Lock turned back at the sound of running footsteps. The two Kurds who had been pointing off into the distance, a young man with bright, excitable eyes, called Mehmet, and an older, burly chap Lock knew as Fuat, were rapidly approaching.

'*What do you think it is?*' Fuat said.

'*I can't tell. I don't think they're coming this way,*' Lock said.

'*I go see,*' Mehmet said, lifting a pushbike from the far end of the ox cart.

'*Hey, no. We've work to—*' Lock started to argue, but the young Kurd had already pedalled off in a frenzy of pumping knees and creaking metal.

Lock shook his head irritably and jumped down from the cart. He gathered up a coil of cable and swung it over his shoulder.

'*Bedros is making coffee. Ten minutes, then I want the rest of those poles up before nightfall.*'

He pushed past Fuat and trudged towards the main work detail.

'Mister Lock? Mister Lock?' a soft voice called after him.

Lock turned about, but no one was there. The ox cart was empty and Bedros and Fuat had vanished. The dust cloud on the horizon had gone.

'Mister Lock?' the voice called again.

Lock dropped the cable and spun round. The main work detail had vanished. The road was deserted. He was alone. He shook his head and closed his eyes.

'Mister Lock?'

It was a woman's voice, gentle and speaking in English, tinged with a regional accent Lock couldn't quite place. Lancashire?

He looked up and started. Staring down at him through a blurred fog was a pair of wide, brown eyes.

'Mister Lock, I'm going to help you to sit up a little,' the voice belonging to the brown eyes said. 'I need to change your dressings.'

Lock felt himself nod as he was gently, but firmly, manhandled into a more upright position. The scent of strawberries tickled his nostrils. He stared until he could bring the woman into focus. She was a young nurse, in her early twenties, he guessed. Her face was as pale as milk and was framed by a white headscarf, which had a bright red cross emblazoned on its centre. A curl of brown hair was protruding from under the band. She had a delicate, small nose and beautiful, sensual lips. They were slightly open and Lock could see her tongue move across the tips of her teeth as she concentrated on what she was doing.

Lock knew her, remembered her, remembered the same act of concentration when she had . . . dressed his hand? . . . Yes, that was it, Nurse Owen. Molly? No, it was . . .

'Mary?'

'Here,' she said, and Lock felt the coolness of a glass of water touch his lips. He drank thirstily.

'Steady. Not too fast,' she said, pulling the glass away again.

'Thank you, Mary,' Lock croaked. 'It is Mary, isn't it?'

'Yes,' she smiled. 'It's a good sign that you remember me.'

Lock looked about the stark room. 'Where am I?'

Mary frowned. 'In the Officers' Hospital. A private room.'

'How . . . ?'

'Long?'

Lock nodded.

'A week now. You've been in a very bad way,' Mary said, while she fussed around, straightening out Lock's bedding.

'May I have some more water, Mary?' Lock smiled. 'My throat feels like it's full of sand.'

'Let me change your bandages first.'

Mary turned to the trolley at her side and picked up a pair of scissors and a roll of gauze.

'Now, let's take a look at your head.'

She leant forward and began to cut away and unravel the bandage wrapped around Lock's head. He hadn't notice the bandages were there before, but as they came away he could feel the pressure ease and the air rush to his itching scalp.

'We had to clip your hair very short to treat the wound,' she said. 'But it will grow back soon enough.'

As Mary worked, leaning close to him, her body heat radiating out, Lock's eyes fell on the swell of her bosom and he felt a sudden surge of desire. Had this girl not kissed him once?

'What is it?' Mary frowned, catching the look on his face, and standing back.

34

Lock's gaze moved to the soiled bandages in Mary's hands. He could see the dark stain of old blood. His blood.

'Nothing. I was just . . . thinking about Amy. Have you seen her?'

Mary looked down at him oddly for a moment, then picked up a fresh roll of bandages.

'No.'

She began to re-dress his head wound. Lock knew she was lying.

'I thought . . .' He squeezed his eyes shut, tensing, as a stab of pain rushed through his skull.

Mary hesitated. 'Are you all right?'

'A little dizzy. I . . .'

'Well, enough talking.'

'But—'

'No,' she said firmly. 'Be a good patient. Hush.'

She picked something up from the trolley.

'Here, take this.'

Lock felt a small pill pass his lips and touch his tongue. It tasted bitter and chalky. Mary pressed the glass of water to his mouth and he drank, swallowing the pill down. The bitterness remained coated on his tongue.

Lock lay in silence as Mary finished dressing his head, his thoughts a tumble of confusion. Where was Amy? Why wasn't she here, looking after him?

'Has she been to see me? Tell me that, can't you? Please, Mary.' He smiled weakly.

Mary gathered up the soiled bandages, ointments and scissors.

'I . . . don't know. I don't see her much any more, what with her wedding preparations . . .' She trailed off.

The wedding! Of course. Christ, he needed to see her, to get

35

out of here. But just the thought of trying to get up out of the bed made his head spin again.

'I need to see her, Mary.'

There was a distant banging and Lock saw a shadow at the window.

'Who's that?' he said nervously.

Mary glanced over her shoulder. 'Just the window cleaner. Do you want me to close the shutters?' She made to move over to the window.

Lock tried to shake his head. 'No, it's all right,' he whispered, feeling weaker as the seconds passed.

'I'll see what I can do. About Amy, I mean,' Mary said. 'Try to sleep now.'

She began to push the trolley towards the door.

Lock nodded and Mary left his field of vision. He heard her open the door and there was a sudden blast of chatter and comings-and-goings from the corridor outside. The door closed again and he was alone in silence once more.

As he lay there, he could see the top of the ladder resting against the outside sill, and watched as the window cleaner stretched up and began to meticulously wipe the highest pane in slow, circular movements, his damp cloth squeaking against the glass.

A shout came from Lock's left and he turned to see that Mehmet, the young Kurd, who had cycled off earlier, had returned from his scouting trip. He was standing in the corner of the hospital room and the rest of the work detail were gathered around him.

'*Effendim?*'

Lock glanced back at the window. But it wasn't a window any longer. It was a telegraph pole and at the top the man staring down at him wasn't the window cleaner, but another of the Kurds on his work detail.

'*All right, down you come,*' Lock said.

The Kurd grinned, shimmied quickly down the pole, and ran over to his comrades. Lock scratched his brow and passed his hand through his thick, shaggy hair. He pulled his fedora back down over his head, and slowly walked over to the chattering group of men.

The labourers were all extremely animated, talking excitedly at once.

'*What is this?*' Lock asked, rather bemused.

'*War!*' one of the Kurds blurted out.

'*I beg your pardon?*' Lock wasn't sure if he had heard right.

'*War, effendim,*' Mehmet confirmed. '*The dust plume . . . It is cavalry and soldiers. They are marching from Van to reinforce the garrison at Erçek.*'

'*War?*' Lock said, aghast. '*War with whom?*'

'*Britain, effend—*' Mehmet stopped and his face fell.

'*Turkey is at war with Britain? I don't believe it.*'

Mehmet shook his head. '*No, no, effendim, with Germany.*'

Lock was even more perplexed. Germany were strong allies of the Turks. '*I can't believe it. The Kaiser is a great friend of Enver Pasha.*'

Again Mehmet shook his head. '*Effendim, Germany is at war with Britain. It is therefore only a matter of moments before we, too, declare war on yo . . . on . . .*' He trailed off, embarrassed at his enthusiastic outburst.

'*Ah, I see,*' Lock said.

The labourers fell silent, each man staring back at him. Nobody said anything for what seemed like an age, until Fuat shifted on his feet and cleared his throat.

'*Work is over,*' he said, throwing down his pickaxe. '*The army will need us now.*'

'*But you can't,*' Lock stepped forward. '*The telephone lines need to be completed for the Sultan.*'

'*Curses to the telephone lines, Kedisi,*' Fuat snarled. '*We march for the Sultan. Come!*'

The Kurds downed their tools and gathered their belongings together from the back of the ox cart, and set off down the road towards the marching soldiers.

'*What about you?*' Lock asked, turning to Bedros.

He shrugged. '*Armenians are not really welcome in the Ottoman Empire, effendim. More so now there is war, I fear.*'

'*Then you'd best head back to the city and to your family. Take the ox cart.*'

'*And you, effendim?*'

'*I think I may have an appointment elsewhere, don't you?*' Lock flicked his stubbly chin back up the road.

A group of riders had left the main body of the march and were rapidly approaching. Lock imagined that most foreign nationals of the enemies of Germany would be put under house arrest sooner rather than later. He needed to get away and fast.

Bedros shifted nervously on his feet.

'*Go on,*' Lock snapped.

The Armenian began to gather up the discarded tools and pile them into the ox cart. Lock lit a cigarette and stood waiting for the riders. He could feel the ground rumble beneath his feet as they got nearer, and soon the sound of clumping hoofs filled his ears.

There were five horsemen, all smart in khaki uniforms with silver-grey collar patches, polished leather belts and riding boots. Leading them was a stiff officer with two stars on gold shoulder epaulettes and full silver-grey collars. He was sporting the obligatory upturned moustache favoured by the Young Turks. All the men rode typically tough, but small ponies that were adept at coping with harsh terrains.

With a jangle of bridle and bit, and a creak of saddle leather, the cavalry officer pulled up sharply and glared down at Lock. He waved his hand, indicating for his men to search the ox cart. The four riders with the officer dismounted, shoved Bedros aside, and clambered up onto the cart.

'*How can I help you?*' Lock said, exhaling tobacco smoke.

'*Papers,*' the officer demanded, holding out his hand expectantly.

Lock stalled by making a show of patting his pockets, until the officer snapped his fingers down at him irritably. Lock smiled and, pulling out his documents from his inside breast pocket, handed them up to the officer.

'*You are . . . Kedisi?*' the officer said, frowning.

Lock sighed. '*No. My name is Kingdom Lock. I—*'

'*You are German?*' the officer interrupted, leafing through Lock's documents.

'*No, British. Well, Australian actually.*'

The officer's piercing hazel eyes flicked up, and he scowled.

'*You can see, Yüzbaşi, that I am in charge of a work detail,*' Lock said, using the officer's correct rank of captain, '*laying telephone lines for the Société Ottomane des Téléphones.*'

The *yüzbaşi* leafed through more of the documents, and slowly shook his head.

'*The dates on these papers are invalid.*' He looked at Lock. '*You are a spy, a khafiyeh, and an enemy of the Sultan.*'

'*I am an engineer and have been working* for *the Sultan for nearly two years!*'

Lock was beginning to lose his patience. If there was one thing he hated more than bureaucrats, it was military bureaucrats.

The *yüzbaşi* folded the papers up and stuffed them in his tunic pocket, then opened his holster and drew his pistol.

'*Çavuş, place this man under arrest.*'

'*What?*' Lock protested, but he remained rooted to the spot. The *yüzbaşi* was pointing his gun directly at him.

The cavalryman with one band on his shoulder straps, indicating that he was a sergeant, jumped down from the ox cart and levelled his rifle at Lock.

'*Hands on your head!*' he ordered.

Lock glared up at the *yüzbaşi*. '*I am not a spy! Ask my men.*'

The *çavuş* jabbed Lock with the point of his rifle. '*Up!*'

Lock did as he was told.

'*Yüzbaşi, please, there is some mistake—*'

'*You are to be taken back to Van for questioning,*' the officer added. '*As for "your men", they are Mehmetçiks, soldiers, now. Except this one.*' He waved his pistol at Bedros, who had all this time been standing, frozen, watching wide-eyed as the cavalrymen ransacked the ox cart.

'*Armenian?*' the officer said.

Lock nodded. '*Yes, but wha—*'

A deafening crack cut him short.

Bedros didn't even have time to move as the *yüzbaşi* shot him dead.

'You bastard! You murd—' Lock screamed in English, dropping his hands and lunging towards the cavalry officer. But he didn't get more than two paces before a blow to the back of the head knocked him to the ground. A surge of pain shot down his spine and then he felt himself spinning and falling, deeper and deeper into a black pit of nothingness.

'Nurse, help me get him back into bed.'

Lock felt himself being lifted and laid gently back down again. Something was placed over his body up to the chest and then a sudden coolness enveloped his face.

'How long has he been like this, Nurse?'

'Most of the night, Doctor. Tossing and turning, calling out . . . Sometimes his eyes are open, but he doesn't see . . . He was calm for a while when I was reading to him, but—'

'Good, good. Well, keep bathing his forehead. We need to break the fever. I hope the wound isn't infected. He's strong, but we may have to operate again and I'm not so sure if he will survive the trauma to the brain.'

'. . . with the offer to abstain from alcohol in order to encourage armament workers to do the same.'

'Who's abstaining from alcohol?' Lock blearily opened his eyes. His vision was filled with Amy's face and it lifted his heart. She was sat in a chair next to his bed, reading from the *Daily Mirror*.

'His Majesty, King George.'

'Why on earth would he want to do that?'

Lock struggled to lift himself up. Amy folded the newspaper away and moved to help Lock sit up in bed.

'There's a belief that alcohol consumption slows down production,' she said.

'Bollocks.'

'You're clearly feeling better,' Amy said.

'I didn't think you would come.'

'Mary said you were asking after me.'

Lock studied Amy's face in silence. He enjoyed looking at her, he always had. Her face, framed by a ring of chestnut red hair just visible beneath her nurse's cap, was still as soft and as white as snow, if a little harder around the mouth. Her full lips were as moist and as sensual as when he had first seen her. Lips to kiss. Yet her eyes, her beautiful emerald eyes, had lost some of their defiant sparkle, a light Lock found so captivating, so inextricably drawn to. It was a light that illuminated his very being, brought brightness to his darkest moments. And that brought despair to his joy at being close to her again.

Amy sat back down.

'I'm glad,' Lock said.

'Glad?' Amy said.

'That you did.'

The room fell silent again.

'I miss you.'

'Don't.'

'What does "*kedisi*" mean?' she asked after a while. 'You kept mumbling the word in your sleep.'

Lock smiled. 'Do you remember me telling you about the cat in my prison cell? After I was arrested? When Britain declared war with Germany, and excitable panic broke out across Turkey?'

'No.'

'It used to climb in through the barred window looking for food.' Lock laughed softly, remembering. 'Funny little creatures – the type of cat, I mean. They're called *kedisi* and are native to Van. That's a city in Turkey, in eastern Anatolia.'

'I know.'

'Oh, yes, of course you do.'

'And?'

'Hmm?' Lock had drifted off momentarily, reaching back into his memory. 'Oh, well, the *kedisi* cat is known for three things: a love of water—'

'Really?' Amy raised a soft brown eyebrow.

'True. I saw one swimming once. For fun. It was trotting along beside a stream and just jumped in. Paddled about a bit, then got out again.' Lock smiled.

'*Non*. I do not believe you.'

Lock ignored her cynicism. 'They are always white and . . .' He paused, lifting his hand to his face, '. . . they have two different coloured eyes; one blue and one amber. So I was often referred to as "*Kedisi*".'

'But you have . . . a greyish blue one and . . . a green one,' Amy said, frowning and leaning forward as if to make sure.

Lock held her gaze and was filled with an overwhelming urge to kiss her. Whether she could sense what he was thinking, he didn't know, but she blushed and quickly sat back.

'Please don't,' she said.

'Why? Damn you, Amy. I love you and I bloody well know you love me. Stop lying to yourself. Ah—' Lock sucked in his teeth and squeezed his eyes shut, pressing his hand to his temple. The sudden burst of anger was making his head throb.

43

Amy got to her feet. '*Mon Dieu.* This is why I didn't want to come. I knew you would do this—'

'What? Tell the truth?'

'I don't love you, Kingdom. I love Casper. And we are going to be married. And I wish you could just be happy for me.'

Lock could see the tears welling up in her eyes as she spoke.

'Marry me, Amy. Marry me.'

'You just don't understand.'

'Understand what? That shit you spouted to me in front of your mother, about duty, tradition and honour? Where's the honour in marrying a coward like Bingham-Smith?'

Amy shook her head and a tear ran down her cheek. She wiped it away angrily.

'*Tu peux être un vrai salaud!*'

'There you go again, hiding behind your French ancestry when you can't explain yourself.'

'*Fils de pute!*' Amy spat, and stormed out of the room, slamming the door behind her.

Lock sat and stared after her, at the finality of the closed white door. The echo of her final insult faded and he was left with the silence of the now empty room once more.

'Bugger,' he sighed. 'I should never have left China.'

CHAPTER THREE

Lock paused in the doorway to let his eyes adjust to the gloom outside, and lit a cigarette. He thought with a mental shrug that to do so was a little stupid, for now all he could see was the flame of the match burnt onto his retina. The city was still, with only the insects protesting the silence. What a relief it was not to hear those damned guns booming in the distance. He gave a satisfactory sigh and, when the memory of the match flame faded, he turned to make his way towards the canal, its dank, mouldy, fetid stench a helpful guide to the right direction. But before he had taken more than two paces, a figure loomed out of the shadowy doorway opposite. Lock wasn't really concentrating on his surroundings and was slow to react, painfully slow. He put his hand up instinctively to ward off the expected blow, but then something exploded in the hand of the shadowy figure and a bolt of lightning slammed like a hammer into Lock's temple.

'Singh!'

'Easy there, laddie. Easy.'

Lock slowly felt the fog of his nightmare lift. He was drenched in sweat, his breath short and panting in his chest, which ached as if someone had been standing on it. He rubbed his wet eyes and relaxed as his mind adjusted to reality. He was in bed once more. It was dark outside the window now and a small lamp on top of the table in the corner threw a soft yellow light into the room. Sat by the side of his bed, leaning forward, a frown of concern across his dark, round face, was Major Ross.

Lock was inwardly pleased to see the Scots officer again, though he was surprised at the touch of grey dusting the major's thick chevron moustache. And were the bags under his hazel eyes a little larger, a little darker? Perhaps.

'It's nothing,' Lock said, easing himself gingerly up on his elbows.

'Didn't sound like nothing,' Ross said, settling back into his chair. He sat still, waiting for Lock to speak, his eyes just watching patiently.

'I keep reliving the moment when I was shot,' Lock said, 'over and over. Only . . . I just can't see the shooter's face.' He flashed the major a quick smile. 'The strange thing is, just now, in my dream, I was alone. Singh wasn't with me and . . .'

'Yes?'

Lock shook his head. 'I don't know . . . There was something familiar . . .'

Ross pulled out his pipe and knocked it against the metal bedframe with a dull, hollow clang. Then he began his methodical, familiar ritual of filling it. Lock found himself transfixed by the

46

major's fingers as they poked and prodded the sweet-smelling tobacco into the pipe bowl.

'Singh says the same. About the gunman.'

'How is he?'

'Better than you. The bullet grazed his rib. He'll mend.' Ross scratched the tip of his nose with a match. 'Well,' he said, 'the provosts have come up with nothing. No clues, no witnesses, not a dicky. Bingham-Smith and—'

'Bingham-Smith?' Lock said.

'Yes, he's leading the investigation.'

Lock scoffed. 'You *are* jesting?'

'I agree he's about as much use as an umbrella in a Zeppelin raid, but at least the provosts are stirring things up with their heavy-handedness. Shaking the cage, as it were, whilst Betty and myself sift through the crap that falls out of the bottom.'

'Betty?'

Ross struck a match and puffed his pipe into life.

'Hmm, you remember? My American girl? You met her a few weeks back at Command HQ . . . Pretty thing in a navy-blue uniform . . .'

Lock nodded and gave a wry smile. Betty was one of those girls who scared men. She was confident, as well as alluring. Her husky voice was one thing, her uniform another, but it was the way she held herself, the way she just . . . radiated sex appeal that Lock so vividly recalled. The polar opposite to Amy. Not that Amy wasn't attractive, wasn't desirable. But Betty was a different species altogether, a different kind of woman. She was grown up, whole, totally arousing, and fierce with it.

'Val. Yes, I remember her,' Lock said.

Ross scowled back at Lock. 'Not Val, Elizabeth. Elizabeth Boxer. *Petty Officer* Elizabeth Boxer. And don't you forget it. She's not one for fools, I can tell you. Or for fooling around. A good lass. Quick-witted and very intelligent. She'd beat you at chess, every time.'

The major paused, and puffed on his pipe.

Lock shrugged.

'She's doing what she can,' Ross said, 'and so far we have a few threads. Even Underhill is grudgingly impressed.'

'Underhill?'

Ross nodded. 'He's her . . . chaperone.'

'Pah!'

'Now, look here,' Ross snapped, jabbing his pipe at Lock's chest. 'I don't appreciate this ongoing feud. Bingham-Smith is one thing, I can understand that, what with everything you've been through with Amy Townshend, but Underhill is one of mine and you'd do well to remember that.'

Lock glowered back at Ross, but lacked the energy to argue. Yet, both names the major had mentioned, Bingham-Smith and Underhill, were on his list of suspects as to who pulled the trigger on him and Singh. And he wasn't forgetting about the rat in the White Tabs either. And the sergeant major was a sure bet for that little tag, too.

'Besides,' Ross said, 'we are pretty certain that it was Wassmuss behind the shootings.'

'He's dead.'

Ross tutted. 'You can't be sure. We never found a body, and the attack on you has got his signature all over it. The bullet removed from Singh's rib and the one Petty Officer Boxer dug out of the door frame of that . . . house you left . . .' The major smiled thinly, 'the one that bounced off of your skull, they're both 7.65 parabellum rounds. Those commonly used by the Luger semi-automatic. That's a German handgun.'

'I know it's a bloody German handgun,' Lock said, 'and it means nothing. Christ, do you know how many Lugers our boys use? The Webley may be able to blow an elephant off its feet, but it's a shitty, heavy and cumbersome gun.'

'Poppycock.'

'Poppycock nothing. I carry a Turkish handgun and the 7.65 is the same round I use. Or do you think that perhaps I shot Singh and then turned the gun on myself?'

Ross sat back in his seat and puffed on his pipe. 'I hadn't thought of that.'

The major narrowed his eyes and stared back at Lock, long and hard. Then he grinned.

'It's pretty nasty out there. Conditions, I mean. The city feels like an open cesspit. You're in the best place. Out there,' he nodded to the window, 'many of the streets are still flooded and with the temperatures rising . . . My God, the flies are out in force. It's unbearable at times. They get in everything.' He paused, grimacing at some recent memory.

'When Allah made hell,' Lock said, 'he did not find it bad enough, so he made Mesopotamia – and added flies.'

'Where did you hear that?'

'Thomas Cook and Son.'

Ross scoffed. 'Well,' he continued, 'there's overcrowding, poor sanitation and, by God, poor administration is compounding matters as well. The men are dropping ten to the dozen . . . Sickness is rife. The hospitals are overrun, bar this one. Seems the officer class has a better constitution.'

'Better sanitation and water, you mean,' Lock said.

Ross tut-tutted and sucked on his pipe. But he didn't disagree.

Lock shifted, wincing as he adjusted his position in bed.

'How's the shoulder, sir?'

Ross raised an eyebrow in surprise. 'Good of you to ask. A little stiff. Particularly when it rains.'

'It always rains.'

'There you go, then.'

Lock snorted. 'And how goes the war, sir?'

'Well,' the major said, clearing his throat, 'there's been an election back home, in Britain, and we have a new Secretary of State for India, chap called Austen Chamberlain. Seems he's a little bit more on the ball than Crewe was, though I did like His Lordship. Anyhow, Chamberlain is trying to get a grip on the situation here and has already telegrammed Hardinge and ruffled a few feathers.'

'In what way?'

'Oh, well, I'm paraphrasing, but he's insisting our generals grasp "their proper place in the perspective of the overall scheme of the war".'

'That amuses you, doesn't it?' Lock said, noting the sparkle in Ross's eyes.

The major shrugged. 'He's right though, isn't he? But more troops are on their way to help reinforce our presence here in Mesopotamia.'

Lock rubbed his eyes. He was feeling wearier by the minute.

'So what's next? Do we just hold the Turks off and sit tight and reinforce Basra? Stay in permanent check with them?'

Ross shook his head. 'No, laddie. Townshend's got the bit between the teeth and is itching to have a crack at Johnny, and Nixon and I have finally managed to convince London and Simla to push on and force the Turks further away from the oilfields.'

'Oh, good show, sir.'

Ross hesitated and gave Lock a withering look. Lock just smiled mischievously back.

'I can see your attitude is on the mend,' the major said. 'I told Lord Crewe way back in November that we should declare a permanent occupation of the Basra Vilayet . . .'

Lock raised a questioning eyebrow.

'The Basra Vilayet? Oh, historically it covered an area roughly stretching from Nasiriyeh and Amara in the north to Kuwait in the south. Where was I? Oh, yes, Crewe . . . He rejected the idea, of course, worrying about upsetting our entente allies when he'd promised there would be no acquisition of territories until the war was over. Ha! Silly man. He'd probably still be in the job if he wasn't such a cautious fool. So, now we're just waiting on the final say-so giving us the go-ahead to push on up the Tigris to Amara. Hopefully we'll get word by the end of the month.'

'Since when do you wait for the official go-ahead?' Lock said.

'I shall ignore that,' Ross said. 'Now, as for my own particular war . . . Well, I've been diligently working through the copies I made from Wassmuss's notebook before the blighter stole it back. Do you recall that rat mentioned in the White Tabs?'

Lock nodded, but didn't mention his own personal feelings on the matter.

'I believe,' the major continued, 'that it's all connected.

Wassmuss has a vast network of agents at work but,' and Ross clenched and squeezed his fist here to illustrate the point, 'I'm shutting his operations down, Lock, one by one.' He smiled and pulled himself to his feet with a grunt, then struck another match and relit his pipe. 'But don't concern yourself with it, just get on with recuperating and leave the investigating to us.'

'I'm sick of being in bed,' Lock said. 'I'm fine. I want to help.'

'Nonsense. You need rest. That's a nasty head wound and you're lucky,' Ross said. 'The doctor tells me your balance is still shaky and the headaches will be paralysing at times. That's no good to me out in the field.'

'Balls, sir. I'm feeling fitter every day,' Lock said.

'No. What possible use are you to me if you keep fainting like a damned young girl in too tight a corset? Just do as I say, and do as the M. O. says. You'll be back on your feet within a week or so. We'll manage until then.'

'And what about Amy?'

'What about her?'

'Oh, come on, sir. If what you say is true, about Wassmuss being loose about the city seeking revenge, then Amy's in danger,' Lock said. 'He knows what she means to me. Huh, he knows more than she does. Look, sir, I need to get out of here—'

Ross stepped forward, pressing Lock back down into bed.

'No you don't. You need to rest. We can manage. As for Amy, she's quite safe. I have people watching her. Besides, she's more than capable of looking after herself, isn't she?'

Lock grunted in agreement. He couldn't argue with that.

'She's distracted enough by her wedding preparations, anyway,' the major added.

Lock sighed heavily and relaxed back into his pillow. He'd quite forgotten about the wedding. 'Damn the girl,' he thought. He smiled up at Ross.

'Very well, Major, if you say so. I'll be a good little boy and take my medicine and wait for nurse to make me all better.'

Ross straightened up, a hurt look across his face.

'There's no need to be sarcastic.'

'It's why you love me.'

Ross snorted. 'You are impossible.' He gathered up his cap and cane and stepped towards the door. 'Well, take it easy, laddie. I'll be back in to see you in a few days. Let you know how we are getting along.'

Lock gave a soft nod of agreement, albeit an agreement he had no intention of sticking to. He had been laid low long enough. It was time for action.

'Before you go, Major . . .'

Ross paused at the threshold and inclined his head slightly.

'It's about Singh,' Lock said. 'Just before I . . . we were shot, I promoted him.'

'You did, did you?'

'To havildar . . . sergeant.'

'Didn't you mean to *naik*? Can't have him jumping two ranks. I think Corp—'

'Havildar,' Lock said. 'Sid deserves it.'

Ross pursed his lips. 'Hmm. We'll see.'

Then without any further comment he left, closing the door behind him.

Lock lay still after the major had gone and gave it a while longer should he return. When he judged that plenty of time had passed,

Lock threw back the covers and swung his legs over the edge of the bed and sat himself tentatively up. A wave of nausea forced him to pause and he pressed his hands to his head, and squeezed his eyes shut, waiting for the feeling to pass.

In his mind's eye Lock saw the Turkish cavalry officer who had accused him of being a spy – if only he had known how prophetic his accusation was – back when he was in charge of the work detail in Anatolia on the day that war was declared between Britain and Germany. Only now Lock couldn't make out the *yüzbaşi's* face. It was completely in shadow. Yet when the officer spoke, his voice was familiar to Lock. Only the more Lock tried to place it, the more it slipped away from him, like trying to grab hold of a handful of smoke. Lock opened his mouth to ask, but the shadowy officer was now standing in a darkened doorway opposite *Cennet*, his pistol raised. There was a flash and a loud bang.

Lock gasped. His cheek was cold and his left arm was on fire. He flickered his eyes open and the first thing he saw was the metal legs of his bed and a crescent moon of dust underneath where the cleaner's broom had swept lazily by. There was a cockroach scuttling along in the far corner and Lock watched its progress, while his brain began to fire up again.

He was on the floor.

'Christ, Kingdom, pull yourself together,' he muttered to himself as he groggily groped out. Using the bed as a support, he pulled himself shakily to his knees. He took a moment to assess himself, breathing heavily. Apart from a numb arm and what felt like a cut lip, he was still in one piece.

'Come on, you've been in worse states than this. Get on your feet and get yourself out of here.'

It took Lock the best part of ten minutes, drenched in the sweat of exertion, before he made it back up onto the bed. He sat wheezing, gathering his strength, then, on rubbery legs, staggered over to the far side of the room. Here, on top of a small table, there was a tepid bowl of water and a large jug with a cake of soap, a razor blade and a shaving brush all neatly lined up on a folded cloth.

Lock stripped naked and began to wash himself as best he could, careful to leave his bandaged head dry. Next to the table was a wardrobe. Inside he found his uniform, pressed and cleaned, with his new badges of rank – three brass pips for captain – already attached. As well as the sunburst badge and the three hills of the Mendips on each collar point, both arms bore the bronze 'Australia' title. The patches on the upper arms bore the plain block of purple for the 1st Div. Engineers, with an additional white square – for the White Tabs – in its centre. The bullet hole was still there, though, in the left breast, much to his pleasure. He pulled out the khaki shirt and the olive-drab necktie and began to dress.

Ten minutes later, standing in front of the mirror that was screwed to the inside of the wardrobe door, Lock gave his reflection a careful inspection. His face looked tired and slightly drawn, but the shave had made him feel younger, and there was a touch of colour in his cheeks. He looked from one eye to the other, from the green one to the blue one, and back again. They were watery and bright, if a little bloodshot. He shrugged, then tentatively began to unravel the bandage around his head. His sandy hair had been cropped very short, as Mary said, and was shaved around the wound high above his left eye. But already there was a thick growth of stubble there. The wound itself was covered with a patch

55

of cotton wool and gauze, a small spot of dark dried blood in its centre. Lock thought it best to leave it alone, so with delicacy, he pulled his brushed and cleaned slouch hat on.

'Right, Captain Lock,' he said to his reflection, 'there's some bastards that need a good kicking, a friend to drag out of his sick bed, and a girl in peril. Only this time it's a peril of her own choosing.'

He gave himself a wry smile.

'So what are you going to do about it then? Well?'

He nodded.

'Good. I agree. But, first thing's first. Let's go and fetch Sid.'

CHAPTER FOUR

'How the hell do you stand it, Sid?' Lock said, batting away at the flies circling his head.

He was standing with Singh in a claustrophobically hot alleyway, directly opposite a busy cafe on the main thoroughfare in the Ashar district of the city. Half of the alley was in shadow, the other in blinding sunlight, which bleached the bricks white and radiated such a heat that it reminded Lock of standing in front of an open oven. The flies were insufferable, drawn, no doubt, to the lumpy brown liquid that ran down the open gutter in the centre of the hard earth floor of the alley. The stench caught the back of Lock's throat until he was forced to breathe through his mouth. But this was just an open invite to the flies, so he closed it again and immediately wanted to gag.

'I recommend you keep a lighted cigarette between your lips at all times, sahib,' Singh said.

'I'd rather have one of those *kleinflammenwefers*.'

'Sahib?'

'A flamethrower. Like a water hose, but it sprays ignited petrol. The Germans have been using them against the French, poor bastards, outside of Verdun.'

Singh shook his turbaned head slowly. 'That is . . . inhuman, sahib.'

'That is modern warfare, Sid.' Lock patted the big Sikh on the arm, and sparked up a cigarette.

He puffed away energetically at first, creating a huge cloud of blue tobacco smoke around his hat-covered head, and grunted with pleasure. It worked. The flies seemed to move away from him to Singh. But, as he had already commented, his Indian friend didn't seem to be bothered by them. He didn't even seem to notice as the black pests buzzed around his youthful and chiselled face, settling on his forehead to feast on the beads of sweat that trickled from beneath his turban and down the edge of his large, straight nose to be lost in the neatly groomed mat of his beard.

'Disgusting,' Lock said.

Singh just grinned again, brown eyes shining brightly.

'You should be seeing your back, sahib.'

Lock glanced over his shoulder. His sweat-soaked shirt back was a mass of crawling flies.

'God damned—' He brushed his hand over his back, but it only served to disturb the insects briefly. 'I wish we could get off this street.'

Lock turned his attention back to the cafe opposite and continued to puff away on his cigarette. He was glad that he'd taken Sid's advice earlier, too, of leaving his tunic and tie behind and to just wear shirtsleeves. He even had a pair of shorts on for the first time since arriving in the Middle East, though they made him feel oddly naked and he had already made the decision to change back at the first opportunity.

The area was busy with off-duty officers, soldiers and the local populous, merchants, traders, and women carrying bundles of food and other goods. The market was close by and the central Post Telegraph Office was only a few hundred yards away around the corner, too. Runners, mostly uniformed sepoys, were hurrying to and fro, weaving in and out of the crowds, slips of paper clutched in their sweaty fists all depicting, no doubt, vital pieces of information purporting to the state of the hot water supply in Brigadier General such-and-such's quarters. Lock snorted to himself. He wanted a bath, but a cold one, an iced one.

Lock checked his watch, pulling the hot metal back plate away from his clammy wrist. Already the timepiece, the silver-cased François Borgel trench watch with the wide leather strap that Major Hall had given him prior to the advance on Barjisiyah Woods, had left a pink indentation as if it was trying to melt into his skin.

'He's been in there for a good quarter of an hour now, Sid. What the hell is he up to?'

'Perhaps, sahib, he is taking refreshment.'

'Bollocks, Sid. Since when has the sergeant major taken refreshment? He's too wound up to relax. No, he's up to something, I can smell it.'

Half an hour earlier, Lock and Singh were keeping a close tail on Underhill, having picked the sergeant major up as he left the barracks in the Sarraj district. They kept out of sight and followed him as he hurriedly made his way through the Hanna-Sheikh Bazaar, batting off eager vendors as if they were so many irritating flies.

The bazaar was a mass of clashing colours, smells and sounds. The creaks of wooden cartwheels melded with the shouts of alarm and of greetings to fellow traders and passing shoppers. Arab men, bent forward, carried huge sacks of produce on their backs, while the Arab women used rough-weaved baskets of reed balanced upon their heads.

Underhill skirted by a withered old Indian man holding out green coconuts fresh from the Karachi boat; and pushed aside an elderly Arab, who was standing beside a stack of caged, beady-eyed chickens, his sandalled feet only just visible above the carpet of white feather and potent faeces. The sergeant major slipped and cursed at the trader and his birds, and hurried on. It was obvious to Lock that Underhill had an appointment to keep, despite Singh's doubts, for no man would want to be walking so fast in this heat, and the sergeant major would never miss an opportunity to stand and berate a native.

'Sahib, he perhaps just has the Basra hop? Look at the way he clenches his buttocks,' Sid said, as they struggled to keep up.

Lock smiled, but he wasn't about to give up his theory. Underhill was a devious man and, no matter what Major Ross kept insisting, was untrustworthy and one of many who wished Lock ill.

Despite their working together under duress the previous month, when they both found themselves being chased out of Daurat while trying to track down the pipeline saboteur,[1] the men

1. See *Kingdom Lock*

had a history that went back to Lhasa in 1904. Lock could not, would not, forget or forgive what he'd seen Underhill do. The sergeant major was a bastard and knew that Lock had something on him that could utterly destroy his military standing. And the military was everything to Underhill.

However, Lock did have a nagging doubt, a faint voice whispering in the back of his mind, reminding him that Underhill was no idiot. Paying someone to gun him and Singh down in the streets – although Lock was convinced that he was the true target; Sid was just unlucky in that he happened to be standing right next to him when the would-be assassin struck – it just wasn't the sergeant major's style. The act wasn't beyond him, of course, but Lock knew that Underhill would rather do the deed himself. Lock still believed the sergeant major was up to something highly suspicious and that was enough for him to keep trailing him. He was determined to discover just what it was. Besides, he told himself, it was better than lying around in damned hospital. Despite the flies.

Lock grunted. If he was honest, this was actually fun. Of course, Underhill could be on White Tab business, as Ross had said he was, but there was no sign of the American girl that the sergeant major was supposed to be chaperoning.

They arrived at a crossroads. Lock watched as Underhill, standing staring across the street, removed his topi and mopped his brow with a handkerchief. Was that a signal? Lock followed the sergeant major's eyeline, scanning the faces sat in and walking by the cafe. His eyes shot back.

'Look, Sid, beside the awning support on the left, half in shadow. Is that . . . ?'

'Yes, sahib. I see. It is Bombegy.'

'Curiouser and curiouser, my friend.'

Lock couldn't be sure, but from where he was standing, the skinny little cook appeared to be making hand signals. Then the Indian bobbed his head and scuttled off to the right, where he was quickly swallowed up by the crowd.

'Shall I follow him, sahib?'

Lock put his hand up to stop Singh. 'No, Bombegy will keep. Let's stay with the sergeant major for now.'

Underhill checked his watch, then dodging a passing ox-drawn cart and the milling pedestrians, he trotted across the street and into the open front of the Café Baldia. Lock urged Singh to hurry and both of them dashed into the alleyway. It offered a good vantage point to spy on the cafe frontage where natives, Indian and British officers, and a few of the lower ranks, were sitting out on the pavement sipping lime juice or hot mint tea. Underhill had chosen an empty table just inside and was sat stiffly erect with his back to the wall. Lock could see the sergeant major's bristly whiskers twitching as if he was muttering to himself.

'You seem nervous, Ebenezer, old chap,' Lock said.

'Sahib?'

'Underhill. His Christian name is Ebenezer. Like Scrooge.'

Singh nodded his head. 'Charles Dickens. Very good, very fine storyteller.'

Lock kept his eyes on Underhill. The sergeant major placed his topi on the chair beside him and checked his watch again. A scrawny Arab shuffled up to him, wringing his hands obsequiously. Underhill said something and the Arab nodded and shuffled away again. But rather than wait for whatever beverage he had ordered,

Lock was surprised to see the sergeant major rise from the table and, not forgetting to take his topi with him, follow the scrawny Arab further into the cafe where he was quickly swallowed up by the gloom.

That was fifteen long minutes earlier.

'Right, Sid. Enough of this. I'm going in. You wait here in case he comes out from around back.'

Lock didn't wait for Singh's reply as he stepped out of the alleyway into the blinding, concussive sunlight, and made his way across the road to the cafe.

It was cooler under the large canvas awning that stretched across five or six tables and benches. No one gave Lock more than a cursory glance as he weaved his way towards the inside of the cafe, a stuffy, dark room buzzing with conversation and laughter. The scent of lime and mint was stronger in here, as was an underlying odour of stale sweat and cooked meat. Lock followed his nose and passed through the obligatory beaded curtain that hid the horrors of the cook's domain. He emerged into a filthy, dimly lit kitchen. Here, the scrawny Arab whom Lock had seen talking briefly with Underhill moments earlier, was now arguing loudly with an Indian man. He was crouched down spooning some lumpy mixture up off the greasy floor and back into a blackened cauldron. A second Indian was working away at the stove, engulfed in steam and the distinctive aroma of grilled fish. All three men were too focused on what they were doing to notice Lock as he deftly slipped across the kitchen and through a door on the far side.

Lock was standing alone in a cramped, dank corridor. A single grimy window was high up on the wall to the right, but it threw little light into the gloom. Lock fumbled in his pockets and fished out a match and scratched it against the rough stone wall. Cupping the flame, he could see that the corridor doubled as a storeroom and was stacked from floor to ceiling with tins, sacks of grain, coffee, packets of tea, baskets of dates and earthenware pots of olive oil. Quite a stockpile for a humble street cafe, Lock thought. He moved forward and something small and brown darted across the hard earth floor in front of him and disappeared amongst a stack of crab tins. The flame went out.

'You're not the only rat around, are you?' Lock said.

He struck another match. Lifting it higher, and moving on past the rows of produce, Lock eventually came to a dead end where a tatty, foul-smelling Persian rug hung limply down from an iron pole fixed to the wall. Lock pressed his palm against the surface of the rug and it gave until it came up against something solid. He drew the rug to one side, exposing a wooden door so riddled with woodworm that it was a wonder to him that it still stood. Light was coming through from the other side in a dozen places and Lock could also hear low voices in conversation. He let the rug fall back, shook out the match, then lifted the rug once more, stepped behind it, and let it fall back again. He was now hidden from view should anyone enter the storeroom from the kitchen.

The air was fetid in the small space between the rug and the brittle door and soon Lock felt the prickly itch of heat as sweat began to rise all over his body. He pressed his face to the rough, cool surface of the wood, feeling the flaking old paint scratch at his cheek, and peered in through a jagged slit to the room beyond.

Lock had a momentary and inexplicable flash of guilt at

this game of eavesdropping, then immediately dismissed it as a ludicrous response. Underhill was behaving suspiciously and as his superior officer and an officer in the White Tabs, he had a right, a duty, to find out what the sergeant major was up to.

Beyond the door, through the gap that wasn't as convenient as it could be, for Lock had to stoop and half-crouch to get a good view, pushing the brim of his hat up against his forehead, he could see a plain room furnished with a table and two chairs. There was natural light inside, and Lock guessed it would be from another grimy window cut high into the wall, similar to the one that illuminated the corridor-cum-storeroom behind him. Seated in one of the chairs, surrounded by a thick cloud of blue-grey tobacco smoke, was a fat, sweaty man who, when he wasn't puffing on the large cigar jammed between his thick, fleshy lips, was mopping at his face and neck with a red and white polka dot patterned handkerchief.

Lock didn't recognise the man, though his close-cropped, white-blond hair and his flushed complexion gave him away as a North European; Scandinavian, Dutch or, perhaps, German. He was dressed as a businessman, in a dark cotton suit with a shirt and tie. There was a felt trilby on the table beside an ashtray and a small black box. Opposite him sat Underhill, as stiff and as uncomfortable as he always looked when 'at ease'. He was saying something and nodding, but Lock couldn't make out the words. There was another object on the table between the two men, and Lock watched as the businessman gathered it up, put it carefully inside the black box, and closed the lid. Underhill handed the fat businessman a coin purse. In exchange, he was passed the black box. The sergeant major then got to his feet, put the black box in his side pocket and held out his hand. The fat businessman rose also, shook Underhill's hand, said something relating to Bingham-Smith, and both men laughed.

Lock slunk away from the door, throwing the rug back, and quickly made his way through the stacked goods back to the door to the kitchen. He hesitated, with his fingers on the handle, and glanced back to see a spill of light and a hand reaching out from behind the rug, about to pull it aside. Lock wrenched open the door and darted across the kitchen, bursting through the beaded curtain, colliding with the scrawny Arab and sending the tray of terracotta beakers that he was carrying flying. There was a shout of irate Farsi, but Lock just kept on going, squeezing by a fellow Australian, a bronzed lieutenant in the Flying Corps, who was about to tuck into a plate of what Lock had earlier seen being scraped up off of the kitchen floor.

'I wouldn't eat that, mate,' Lock said, as he rushed on through the cafe and back out into the dazzling daylight of the oppressive street. He sidestepped the pedestrian traffic and disappeared into the shadows of the alley opposite where Singh was still waiting. Drenched in sweat, his shirt glued to his back, Lock stood bent double, hands on his knees, wheezing and gulping in huge lungfuls of fetid air. His head was throbbing and stars were dancing before his blurred vision.

'Sahib?' Singh said, putting a huge palm on Lock's shoulder.

Lock waved the Indian's concern away, straightened up and groaned as he stretched his back. He nodded his head in the direction of the cafe.

Underhill had just stepped out from beneath the awning, followed closely by the fat businessman. The two men didn't bid one another farewell, but turned in opposite directions without a second glance.

'You . . . follow the fat man, Sid. I'll . . . take our dear . . . sergeant major,' Lock said.

Singh frowned down at his captain. 'Sahib, I think perhaps you should be back in the hospital.'

'Nonsense. I'm . . . just a little . . . out of practice. Close . . . close thing . . . The . . . they . . . nearly saw me.' Lock grinned up at Singh. 'I'm all right . . . Honestly . . . Now get after the fat man . . . Havildar.'

'Sahib.'

Singh reluctantly left Lock's side, and made his way west along the thoroughfare in the trail of the waddling businessman, whose trilby hat stood out like a beacon amongst so many turbans, topis and kufiyas.

Lock pulled his hat off, wiped his brow with his rolled-up shirtsleeve and gathered himself for a moment. He put his hat back on and stepped out of the alley and headed east, after Underhill.

The sergeant major was already quite a way ahead of him, weaving in and out of the throng of people, aggressively brushing off the inevitable offers of trinkets and wares that were shoved under his nose. He was easy enough to see, but Lock was struggling to keep pace, feeling weaker and more light-headed with every step. The sun was directly behind him now and its heat was punishing on his neck.

'Think, Kingdom. Where's the bastard going?' Lock muttered under his rasping breath. 'Back to barracks? To meet someone else? Ross perhaps?' He had to get a look at what was in that box. A million questions raced around his mind as he pressed on. Was the sergeant major up to no good? The fat man . . . Was he a German? One of Wassmuss's agents? If so, then was Underhill a spy? A traitor? The rat? And what about Bombegy? And what about Bingham-Smith? His name was mentioned in that room, too, he thought.

Lock stopped to rest. His head was swimming. He put his hand out to lean against a wall, and closed his eyes. He knew he should move on, he knew he should keep after Underhill, but all he wanted to do now was to sit and perhaps sleep for a while. Even the flies had stopped being a bother to him.

Lock groaned. Someone was kissing him. He could feel the wetness of . . . something? A tongue? Licking him, licking his face? Amy? There was a snuffling close to his ear, then the cold wetness again.

'Sahib? Sahib?'

Lock opened his eyes. He was surprised to find that he was no longer leaning against the wall, but was sat on the floor, legs stretched out before him. Singh's face loomed close.

'Was that you, Sid? Kissing my ear?'

'No, sahib. A dog.'

'A dog?'

'Yes, sahib. A puppy. It will not leave you.'

'Salt.'

'Sahib?'

'The salt in my sweat.'

'No. It will just not leave you. Look.'

Lock followed Singh's indication. Barely a foot away sat a mangy mongrel puppy, one ear perked up, the other flopped forward. Its head was slightly inclined and two brown eyes glinted back at him. It was panting, its pink tongue hanging down, covered in white spittle, its tail wagging ferociously in the dust.

'Hey there,' Lock said.

The puppy tensed, then shot forward. Singh pushed it back. It yapped playfully.

'Come along, sahib, let us get you to your feet.'

Singh took a hold of Lock under the arms and hauled him up again. He hooked his left arm around his shoulder and supported him by the waist.

'Come, sahib. Into this cafe. We need to get liquid inside of you.'

Lock mumbled something but didn't resist as Singh practically carried him off the street and into a pokey but cool cafe that was a few feet away. The owner, an elderly Arab with a face as lined as a railway junction, helped Singh to seat Lock down at a table, then quickly set about placing a terracotta jug of cool lime juice and then a pot of steaming Indian tea in front of them. He nodded and clucked and stood by, watching with watery eyes as Singh helped Lock drain four cups of juice before he felt able to sit back and relax.

'*Sokkar?*' the Arab proprietor said, as he placed a tray of sweet cakes on the table.

'*Shokran,*' Singh said. 'Eat, sahib.'

Lock shook his head. He wasn't hungry. But Singh picked up one of the sweet delicacies and tried to force it into Lock's mouth, like a parent feeding a petulant child.

'All right, all right, Sid. I can do it,' Lock said. He took the cake from Singh and began to eat.

* * *

69

'How long have we been here now, Sid?'

The shadows were longer on the street outside and the heat seemed less intense. Three flies circled and dodged in the air directly above the small collection of plates and cups on the table. Having polished off the cakes, Singh had ordered salted meat and date bread, as well as good strong Turkish coffee. Lock now felt energy returning to his body.

'Three hours, sahib. Maybe a little more.'

'Bugger. They'll be long gone. Why did you come after me?'

'I followed the fat man back towards the city, but he jumped into a taxi bellum and I could not keep up with him.'

'Pity.'

Singh bobbed his head. 'Not so, sahib. I overheard where he asked the taxi to take him: Heaven.'

'Heaven? Really? You are sure he said that?'

'Yes, sahib. Do you understand what he was meaning?'

Lock shook his head and frowned. 'No . . .' He picked up the last piece of salted beef, took a bite, then dropped his hand to below his seat. The pup snatched the morsel from his fingertips.

'Hey, gently,' Lock said, pulling his hand sharply away.

'A new recruit for Green Platoon, sahib?' Singh said.

'We need them.'

Singh nodded his head thoughtfully. It was clear to Lock that the big Sikh had something on his mind.

'Speak up, Sid.'

Singh looked up at Lock. 'Sahib, do you truly think that the sergeant major is a spy? I find this most very hard to believe.'

'Well, he works for Ross and the major *is* a spy. But whether Underhill is also working for the Germans, I just don't know. I don't trust or like the sergeant major, as you know. He's done some evil, terrible things. But a traitor?' Lock shook his head. 'I'm not so sure . . . But I am sure that he's up to something. And that fat man . . .'

'He reminded me of Lord Shears, sahib.'

'The fat man? In what way?'

'A similar suit of clothing, the same pattern of tie.'

Lock slammed his palm on the table top, causing the plates to jump and the pup under his feet to yelp in surprise.

'Good God, Sid, you're right! I'm such a bloody blind bugger. I knew there was something about the fat man. I bet you a bottle of arrak that he's an APOC man.'

'I do not drink, sahib,' Singh said.

'What? Oh, stop being so . . . pure,' Lock said, with a dismissive wave of his hand. 'So, Underhill and an Anglo-Persian oilman . . . I wonder . . . I did hear one thing that they said to each other in that room behind the cafe, "I am sure Assistant Provost Marshal Bingham-Smith will be delighted with the package".'

'But what does it mean, sahib?'

'It means we need to find Bingham-Smith. Underhill and that . . . slimeball together is more than enough grounds for suspicion, don't you agree?'

Singh bobbed his head slowly and scratched at his beard, but he didn't commit to an opinion.

'Tell me you don't think it was Wassmuss as well. Who shot at us.'

Singh hesitated. 'No, sahib. But I think perhaps one of his agents . . .' He trailed off. He didn't seem convinced himself now that he had said it out loud.

'See,' Lock said, 'even you don't really believe it. Why would Wassmuss risk coming back into enemy-occupied territory just to seek me out and assassinate me? To what end? Revenge? Wassmuss may be many things, but he's not stupid and he's not petty. At least, as far as I can imagine. He got his notebook back and if he did escape, he'd be well away by now, working on some scheme or other to continue with his plan of seizing the oilfields and ridding Mesopotamia and Persia of the British. How am I possibly important to him?'

'I think, sahib, that perhaps you not only underestimate Herr Wassmuss, but that you underestimate your own worth.'

'Shut up, Sid. That's an order.'

'Yes, sahib.'

Lock eyed the big Indian thoughtfully for a moment. He was pleased to see that Singh's uniform bore the chevrons of his promoted rank, and more so that Ross had not overridden his decision to promote the Sikh.

'Three stripes suit you.'

Lock turned his head and clicked his fingers to attract the attention of the proprietor.

The old Arab gave a nod of his head and slowly shuffled over towards them. Lock paid him generously for the food and for letting them rest and then, with the dog at their heels, he and Singh made their way back out to the narrow streets of Basra. The sun was low on the horizon now, and already the temperature and the flies were a thousand times more tolerable.

They carried on walking in silence, side by side, the puppy darting this way and that, sniffing at every corner, but more or less keeping up. Despite the time of day, the streets and the narrow

72

waterways were still busy with traffic and Lock began to slow his pace. He stopped and squinted into the setting sun.

Singh halted and turned to his friend. 'What is it now, sahib?'

'I'm getting slow, Sid. I've been too woolly-headed. I'm not thinking straight. The answer's there, in front of us.'

'Sahib?'

'Heaven, Sid, heaven. You said the fat man asked to be taken to "Heaven".'

'Yeeees?' Singh was frowning, clearly not following Lock's train of thought.

'Come on, Sid. Remember? Heaven. We were shot on its bloody doorstep. The brothel, Sid. *Cennet* or "Heaven".' Lock smiled up at his friend.

Singh showed sudden understanding, but then he shook his head, doubt clouding his face.

'I do not think that is very wise, sahib. You are still very weak.'

Lock was momentarily baffled by his friend's words. Then he laughed.

'Sid, you drongo! Not for that. Although, perhaps some leisure time with one of Heaven's angels of ill-repute would be a welcome tonic,' he grinned sheepishly. 'No, I'm talking about leads and coincidences.'

'I do not understand, sahib.'

'Think, Sid. The brothel where we were shot . . . Underhill is a chief suspect for the crime, as far as I'm concerned. Right?' Singh nodded. 'The fat man is a shifty APOC man with a German accent. Right?' Singh nodded again. 'Well, then?' Lock shrugged and opened his arms. 'More than a mere coincidence, don't you agree?'

Singh bobbed his head slowly in that infuriating way Indians did, neither making it clear to the observer whether it was a sign of agreement or a negative response.

'All right, sahib,' Singh said. 'Just a look-see.'

'Just a look-see, Sid,' Lock said. 'I promise.'

CHAPTER FIVE

By the time Lock and Singh and their four-legged companion arrived at the doors of Heaven, the sun had dipped below the horizon and the sky was now a golden blaze of red and orange. The shadows were long and there were fewer people about now. The call to prayer from the many mosques had helped clear the city of all but the non-believers, the British and Indian troops, on and off duty. Even the flies had disappeared.

Lock felt the hairs on the back of his arms rise as he stood where the shooter must have been standing barely three weeks previously, in the recess of a doorway opposite the main entrance to the brothel. There was nothing to see, no shell casings or cigarette ends or bloody palm prints, nothing left that Ross or the attractive Petty Officer Boxer wouldn't have seen or found. And why would there be? Still, he needed to be there all the same, despite the stale odour of cat piss radiating up from the dusty, hard-baked earth.

Singh was a silent presence at his side, even the pup was relatively quiet, content to sit and chew at his bootlaces.

Lock let his gaze slowly wash over the brothel facade. It looked as quiet and as unremarkable as the many other double-fronted Mesopotamian buildings. Only the flickering of the oil lamp hanging above the door gave any indication of what could possibly lie beyond the threshold, a threshold that Lock himself stepped over and nearly drowned in not so very long ago. He gave a little snort thinking he'd still be there now, if Singh, on orders from Ross, hadn't come and dragged him away. Yet, if Singh hadn't, then would he have been shot? Or would the assassin have sought him out in his room? He would have been an easier target, lying drunk and semi-conscious. He probably would have succeeded.

A bawdy shout snapped Lock from his thoughts. The door to the brothel was flung open, spilling golden light and a cacophony of sound into the dusk. The traditional twang of an oudist struggled for dominance over the raucous chatter beyond the threshold. There was clearly some kind of party going on inside. Then a completely intoxicated young lieutenant of His Britannic Majesty's army burst out. The officer stumbled once, then sprawled onto all fours and vomited violently across the dusty street. Two more officers stepped out of the brothel, jeering and laughing at the man being sick.

'Bah, blardy whimp, Jackers! S'only blardy seven o' clock. In the strit lick a gal. Haw, haw!' The officer who spoke belched loudly and put his hand to his mouth.

Lock didn't know the officer on all fours, nor the taller of the newcomers, the man slurring his upper-class education, who was also a lieutenant. But he did know the shorter man at his elbow, the

76

chubby one with the carrot-red hair, the one swaying unsteadily on his dumpy feet. It was the cowardly, bloated turd that went by the name of Gingell. And if Gingell was here then, by God, he knew his master, Bingham-Smith, would be, too. But more than anything, this was just too much of a coincidence for Lock. They'd come here to follow up on the fat man, which in turn was from tailing Underhill. And what do they find? Bingham-Bloody-Smith. Lock couldn't believe it. He glanced at Singh, knowing what he must do now. The fat man could wait.

'Here, don't let him follow.' Lock scooped up the dog and pushed him into Singh's arms.

'Sahib, no.'

But the Indian was unable to stop Lock, as he was too busy keeping a tight grip on the squirming dog. Lock strode quickly across the street, snatching off his slouch hat and folding it away in his pocket.

Gingell didn't even see Lock approach until it was too late. His chubby face drained of all colour and crumpled in recognition, as Lock, shoving the taller man aside, reached out and grabbed hold of the fat lieutenant's lapels.

'I say, steady on, ol'chap.'

Lock ignored the other officer and all but lifted Gingell across the threshold and back inside the brothel.

'Wh-wh-what . . . d-d-d'you . . . ? Wh-wh-what—'

Lock bared his teeth in a grimace of hate. 'Where is he, lard arse?'

But Lock wasn't really after a reply. Gingell couldn't even speak properly, being in such a state of nervous surprise, his green eyes bulging out of their sockets. He just kept blustering and spitting out random half-words, his fleshy, wet lips quivering like two landed fish.

Lock suddenly let go of Gingell's lapels.

Gingell stumbled backwards and fell heavily on his backside. He flinched, holding his short arms up for protection, as Lock stepped over him and into the familiar surrounds of the brothel's foyer.

Gone was its opulent beauty, its decadent style, its rich, sensual aromas that Lock recalled so vividly from when he had first entered into the brothel's warm embrace. Now all he could see was something akin to one of the more disturbing paintings by Hieronymus Bosch. The place was in bedlam and the noise was deafening. There was laughter, shouting, arguing, coupled with slurred conversations, as well as the playful and not so playful yelps from some of the women, and all of this competing with the continuous strain of music coming from an unseen musician playing the oud.

There were about twenty young officers scattered about the foyer. They wore mess dress uniforms, not the familiar scarlet jacket, but the open-fronted, warm-weather whites with lapels, over a stiff-fronted shirt, with studs, detachable collar and black tie. Their trousers were the high-waisted type in khaki green with a wide, paler *galon* stripe on the side, as well as stirrups buckled underneath dress boots. A cummerbund in Mendip regimental green was worn over the waistband. Normally it was a very smart appearance. However, Lock doubted any would pass muster now. All were in various states of intoxication, some worse than others. Hardly a man was fully clothed, there was even one with his breeches gathered around his ankles. He was slumped, passed out in a chair, his shirt, thankfully, covering his manhood.

The girls of the house, though experienced in dealing with all types of clients, appeared out of their depth here. Each one had a haunted look upon their face, eyes bright with . . . not fear, but something not far off. They were mostly naked, sat on laps, or were being pushed and pulled and prodded about, like toys belonging to a bunch of spoilt brats.

Then Lock spotted the proprietor, the portly Arab with the large mole on his left cheek. He was waving his sausage-fingered hands in the air and was moaning in his native tongue, as he clucked and darted about in a most distressed manner. He stopped short when he spotted Lock, mouth dropping open in surprise. Then he rushed over, golden aba billowing around him.

'Capateen Lock, you are not dead! Allah be praised,' he said, beaming and patting Lock's chest as if he couldn't believe his own eyes that he was real and not an apparition.

'Not yet, Jalal Al-din Bahar, not yet,' Lock said.

'Please, Capateen, please, in the name of the Prophet, please tell these . . . gentlemen to leave,' Jalal Al-din Bahar said. He was gripping Lock's hands now and squeezing them tight.

Lock pulled his hands free and wiped his now wet palms off on the back of a nearby semi-conscious subaltern. He then pushed the soldier aside.

'These, as you may have surmised, my dear Jalal, are not gentlemen,' Lock said, as he began to walk slowly through the foyer, scanning the room in search of Bingham-Smith. Jalal Al-din Bahar scuttled along at his heels.

The once plush interior was now a wreck; the wall hangings

were torn, seats were upturned and their cushions were strewn everywhere; some even had their horsehair stuffing exposed through what Lock surmised to be sabre cuts. The carpet in places squelched underfoot and was stained dark with damp patches and worse, and was littered with broken glass, empty bottles and items of clothing that ranged from a leather riding boot to a torn sari. There was even a topi with a sabre jammed in its crown. Potted plants were upturned, their roots and soil scattered everywhere, and the once heady aromas of spices had been replaced by the sharp tang of urine and vomit. Lock approached another young officer who had his back to the room. He was standing pissing up against a beautiful Persian wall hanging. Lock shoved the man hard in the back. His forehead smacked into the wall and he bounced back, collapsing, groaning, in a heap on the floor.

'*Effendi* Capateen, please, you must get these . . . officers to leave,' Jalal Al-bin Bahar said. 'They have ruined me! A whole night and a whole day they have done this and I cannot stand more . . . Look at my beautiful palace . . .'

The Arab gave a sob of despair as he watched a painfully young lieutenant with a fluffy, pencil-thin moustache, stagger and tumble forward, taking a large urn with him, as he crashed to the floor.

'I'm looking for one man in particular, probably the ringleader,' Lock said.

Jalal Al-din Bahar nodded his head vigorously. 'Beegham Smeeth. It is his . . . How is it said? "Stag"?' The Arab spoke the word as if it was a total mystery to him.

'That's the chap. Where is he?'

Jalal Al-din Bahar shuffled forward and beckoned Lock to follow. They picked their way through more detritus until they came to an arched alcove. Lock heard Bingham-Smith before he saw him, his pompous tone immediately recognisable even in its drunken state.

Beyond the alcove was an opulent annex, a large room of wooden panels and elaborate Persian tapestries, all earthy colours of browns, oranges and golds. The atmosphere in there was thick with cigar smoke, wine and sweat. Four lamps, one in each corner, shone a warm yellow light through the tobacco haze. Two of Jalal Al-bin Bahar's girls were standing erect against the far wall, jugs of wine clutched to their naked breasts. They were dressed only in flimsy golden loincloths. In the centre of the room was a large oak dining table, surrounded by eight high-backed, carved wooden armchairs. Each was occupied by a young officer. Drinks and lighted cigars were at their elbows and each man held a fan of playing cards in their hands. That was, all except for the man with his back to Lock. He was slumped forward, head on the table, snoring softly.

Bingham-Smith was at the head of the table, slouched with one leg over the armrest. He was dressed in his shirtsleeves, open to the navel. His bare chest was smooth and glistening with alcoholic sweat, a sheen that his pasty, thin face reflected. His blond hair was damp, glued to his clammy forehead, his eyes glazed and unfocused. But when Jalal Al-din Bahar stepped aside, and Bingham-Smith caught sight of Lock, his face changed. It flickered first with startled surprise, then immediately hardened and took on its familiar arrogant smugness.

'Lieutenant Lock,' he said, sitting upright and laying his hand of cards face down on the table, 'I don't recall inviting you to my lil' party.' He talked slowly and managed to keep his slurring to a minimum.

'Smith, how are you and your hyphen? Having fun?' Lock said.

There was a flicker of anger in Bingham-Smith's pale eyes, but the blond officer didn't bite, he just grinned and picked up his cards again. He frowned at his hand, then placed two kings and two sevens down on the table, face up. He picked up the smoking cigar from the ashtray at his elbow and puffed away, keeping his gaze away from Lock.

'You seemed surprised to see me just now,' Lock said.

Bingham-Smith snorted. 'Did I?' he said, rubbing the scar under his right eye absentmindedly.

It was the only mark left from his encounter a few months ago with Lock back on the RIMS *Lucknow* when he and Gingell had tried to jump Lock and had received a bottle in the face for their troubles. The irony was that the scar actually gave Bingham-Smith some character, gave some depth to his otherwise bland, aristocratic visage.

Lock's attention moved briefly to the card game and to Bingham-Smith's companions gathered around the table. They were all of a similar age, in their late teens or early twenties and all of similar breeding. He watched the officers take turns at cards, laying down pairs face up, then offering their hand face down to the person on their left. That player then selected a card and added it to their own hand, checked it, then after laying any pair they had face down, turned to their left and continued the routine. Only the men here seemed to be struggling to focus, often dropping cards or putting down pairs that weren't pairs at all. It was all rather comical, Lock thought, if it wasn't all so pathetic.

'Even I'm surprised at how bad a shot you are. All that grouse shooting when growing up on Daddy's estate, and one still can't kill a man at a few yards,' Lock said.

Bingham-Smith's eyes darted to Lock's momentarily and then he frowned. But whether it was from guilt, anger or confusion it was impossible to tell. The man was clearly very drunk and was finding it increasingly hard to focus on the card game and keep up his vain attempt at seeming to be in control. He moved his hand of cards closer to his nose, shook his head as if to clear it, then snatched up his glass of wine, knocked it back and thrust out his arm. The girl to his left stepped forward and filled the empty glass to the top. Bingham-Smith drained it a second time, then grabbed the girl by the wrist and yanked her towards him. She yelped in surprise, spilling wine from the jug all over Bingham-Smith's front.

'You stupid whore!' Bingham-Smith shoved the girl away hard, sending her tumbling backwards and sprawling to the floor. The jug she was holding smashed against the wall.

The two officers either side of Bingham-Smith laughed.

'Ha! Looks like the bint's the old maid,' said the officer with the head of tight curls.

'No, no, no, Hazza,' the other officer slurred, 'Bing's the one stuck with the old maid.'

Whether this was a reference to Amy Townshend or to the card game they were playing wasn't clear to Lock, but it certainly riled Bingham-Smith.

'Shut up!' the blond officer said, getting unsteadily to his feet.

His two companions just laughed louder.

'And for Christ's sake, will someone please shoot that bloody musician,' Bingham-Smith barked. 'I can't stand that incessant twanging! Bahar? Bahar?'

Lock saw Jalal Al-bin Bahar shirk back behind him, but Bingham-Smith's outburst just served to amuse his fellows all the more. Even the girl on the floor was smirking. The loud music carried on regardless in the background.

'Look at this!' Bingham-Smith said, pulling at his wine-soaked and stained shirt. 'You bitch, you stupid goddamn bitch!' He grabbed at the girl's long brown hair and clenched his other fist ready to strike her.

The girl screamed, and the men around the table cheered in unison.

Lock sprang forward, blocking Bingham-Smith's down-swinging fist. A jarring pain shot up his arm to his shoulder, but Lock just gritted his teeth, clenched his own fist, and punched Bingham-Smith in the face. There was a sickening crunch.

No other body part hurts the way the nose does. Lock knew this and it gave him an enormous sense of not just satisfaction, but release. All that pent-up frustration he had felt ever since discovering that Amy had chosen Bingham-Smith over him, the lies, the betrayals, the manipulation of her family. And then there was the shooting. He expected to be shot, to die, every day he was put in the field, but not from stepping out of a brothel in the middle of a British-held city, not then. He remembered the overwhelming sense of indignation he'd felt as he lay in the dirt of the street feeling his consciousness slip away. He knew it was unlikely to have been Bingham-Smith who shot him and Singh, he even knew it was unlikely to have been Underhill, but he didn't want to admit that to Ross let alone to himself. Besides, it felt so good, to smash this bastard in the face. Again.

Bingham-Smith staggered backwards, toppling over his chair.

But before Lock could inflict more punishment on his rival, he was wrestled down onto the tabletop. Cards, glasses, wine and money scattered everywhere, tinkling and crashing to the floor. Chairs scraped back and toppled over and one of the girls screamed again. Lock heard Jalal Al-bin Bahar yelp, and then he just concentrated on protecting himself, protecting his head wound. He felt blows to his stomach and arms and to his thighs, and his ears filled with shouts of outrage and drunken bravado. He kicked out, felt his boot connect with something soft and smacked his left fist into someone's face. His knuckles sang with pain, but it gave him a vital moment to roll to one side, up off the table and onto his feet again. Glass scrunched under the soles of his boots. A glancing blow stung his cheek and he dodged to the left, raised his right arm in defence and thrust upwards with his left fist, hammering the air from the gut of whichever officer happened to be in front of him. The man doubled up and Lock brought his knee up sharply to crack against the man's jaw.

Lock staggered back, breathing heavily, leaning against the alcove wall, wiping a slick of salty blood from his lip with the back of his hand. To his surprise he wasn't being ganged up on, as he had initially thought. It seemed that Bingham-Smith's party was a tinderbox ready to explode and that Lock making the first move, throwing the first punch, was all that the other officers needed to set them off. The fight had spilt out of the annex into the wider field of the foyer and those who could still stand were now brawling amongst themselves. The girls were taking the opportunity to scamper for cover and were being herded to safety by the huge whimpering form of Jalal Al-din Bahar. Glasses and chairs and plant pots and jugs and plates of both china and brass were being flung all over the place like so much shrapnel. The sound of ripping cloth, of splintering wood and body blows was swirling about Lock's head all underlined, much to his amusement, by the continuous melodic and unwavering accompaniment of the lone unseen oudist.

Lock began to laugh at the farce of it all.

Just at that moment a shrill whistle sounded and a group of provosts burst in the front door, all NCOs sporting SD caps with red tops and black cloth armbands bearing the letters 'MP' in red. They were wielding batons and had no hesitation about laying into the melee, clubbing the drunken officers and pulling them apart from one another. The lieutenant who had been sat at Bingham-Smith's table, the one referred to as 'Hazza', staggered up to Lock glaring, his fists raised.

'You bloody colonial runt,' he said, spittle flying over a cut, swollen lip. He threw a punch, but Lock easily deflected it.

Before Lock could hit back, three burly red caps stormed towards the alcove and pinned both he and Lieutenant 'Hazza' up against the wall.

'Get your hands orf me, Corporal! Do you know who I am? I am Lieutenant Harrington-Brown, your superior officer!' His voice was shrill and a vein throbbed at the side of his now very red temple.

The provost corporal didn't react at all and just held his baton hard against Harrington-Brown's throat.

'You men are all under arrest.'

Lock struggled to free himself from the tight grip of the two other red caps, but relaxed when he heard the familiar voice calling out the order. It was Major Ross.

There was a crash of a chair tumbling and Lock glanced over his shoulder to see Bingham-Smith, hand pressed to his bloodied nose, stumbling out of the annex.

'Major Ross, look! Look at what that thug of yours has done!' Bingham-Smith staggered, waving his hand about at the foyer as if it was all Lock's handiwork.

Ross stepped aside as two more red caps entered the alcove and seized Bingham-Smith by the upper arms.

'I protest! I protest! Major! I am the assistant provost marshal. You cannot arrest me! These are my bloody men!'

'Shut up, Bingham-Smith,' Ross said. 'Take him away.'

The two provosts dragged the struggling and fuming Bingham-Smith out. Ross turned to follow.

'Sir?' Lock said.

The major paused, but didn't turn around. 'Bring them,' he said, 'bring them all, including those upstairs.'

Lock and Harrington-Brown were manhandled away from the alcove and frogmarched through the remains of *Cennet*'s foyer and out of the front door.

Outside, the street was lit up from the headlights of two AEC Y-type 3-ton trucks, which were parked about ten yards from the entrance. The provosts were pushing and prodding the drunken officers up into the backs of the trucks, shouting at them to get a move on and to keep their traps shut. Lock could see a couple of dishevelled businessmen and a perplexed-looking general amongst the prisoners. They must have been upstairs, away from the party. An NCO red cap was talking to them and taking notes in a little pad. But there was no sign of the fat man. Perhaps he hadn't gone to the brothel after all? Perhaps Singh misheard?

Lock's focus turned to the deep recess opposite where he had last seen his Indian friend. There was a staff car parked there, a Vauxhall 25hp D-Type, with an Indian *naik* at the wheel. Its engine was running. Ross was standing next to it with his back to the brothel, talking with Singh. Between his feet sat the dog, ears pricked, fascinated by the goings-on.

'I could have used your help in there, Sid,' Lock called.

The dog barked with delight at recognising Lock's voice and darted over to him, too quick for Singh to stop. The dog pranced around Lock's legs, tail wagging and then suddenly it yelped in pain and backed away snarling. The provost corporal to Lock's right had kicked him away.

'Filthy mutt. Piss off!'

'Hey!' Lock said, and he shouldered the red cap corporal, sending him stumbling hard into the edge of the truck.

Lock felt a blow to his back and he crashed to his knees.

The first provost collected himself and raised his fist to strike Lock.

'Enough!'

Lock glanced up to see the American girl, the USNRF Yeoman 1st Class, Elizabeth Boxer, leaning against the first truck's fender, arms folded, a cigarette between her lips. She was even more alluring than the first time he had set eyes upon her a few weeks back at Command Headquarters. She wore the same smart navy-blue military uniform, the three chevrons on the arm of her tightly buttoned jacket showing her rank, the same ridiculous straw hat upon her head of raven hair, with a ribbon stating *U.S. Naval Reserve* around the crown in gold lettering.

'Miss Boxer.'

The girl stepped forward and indicated for the two provosts to pull Lock to his feet. '*Petty Officer* Boxer, Captain.'

Lock scoffed. He was in no mood for games. 'There are no women in the US forces. Who are you kidding?'

'What d'you know about it, buster?' she said.

Petty Officer Boxer stood a little over five feet tall, peering up at him from under the brim of her straw hat, a look of bemusement upon her soft, round face. She pulled the cigarette from her lips, exhaled and raised a dark, slim eyebrow.

'You look worse than you did in hospital.' Her distinctive, husky accent was that of Boston, where every 'a' is spoken long.

'You don't.'

'Huh. Well, what did you discover in there?' She jutted her chin to the building behind him.

'That aristocrats and alcohol don't mix.'

She tut-tutted and shook her head. 'The major told you I was investigating the shooting and all you've gone and done is screw things up for me.'

'How so, Elizabeth? It is Elizabeth, isn't it?'

She narrowed her dark brown eyes and Lock caught a momentary flash of annoyance. But she just gave a lopsided grin.

'All right, boys, put him in the back with the others.'

The red caps yanked Lock on towards the back of the truck.

'Was Sergeant Major Underhill's interview at the Café Baldia part of your investigation?' Lock said over his shoulder. But he was suddenly more interested in the familiar rotund figure who was at that moment being escorted out of the brothel.

The fat man was half-dressed, his shirt tails hanging out and his bright-red braces dangling down to his thighs. One chubby hand was clutching the waist of his trousers to keep them up, the other had a tight grip on his trilby. Lock saw Ross indicate to the staff car, and the provosts either side of the fat man bundled him into the back seat.

'Hey,' the American girl called, tossing her cigarette aside. The provosts stopped again and Lock turned back to face her.

She stood, legs slightly apart, backlit from the lamplight coming from the entrance to the brothel, the side of her face illuminated by the truck's headlamp.

'It's Betty. Only my Ma calls me "Elizabeth".'

Lock had time to throw her a smile before he was yanked away and shoved up into the truck with the rest of the prisoners.

CHAPTER SIX

Lock swore. Once again he found himself sat on the rough wooden bench of the familiar 6ft-by-6ft cell. The last time he had been here was, he guessed, barely a month previously, just prior to the Battle of Barjisiyah Woods. But he doubted he'd get a summons from the General Staff to free him this time.

Despite the rising temperatures of the days, the cell was still damp and stuffy. The barred window high up on the wall near to the cut-stone ceiling showed an inky black sky sprinkled with stars. There was no moon. The only illumination he had was from the weak yellow light coming through the open, narrow observation hatch in the cell door. Sounds of groaning, of vomiting and of loud snoring seeped through from the occupants of the other cells, all those nice young officers who had been arrested with him, who had been thrown in a cell to sleep it off and to await either a severe dressing-down or worse for their unruly behaviour at poor Jalal Al-din Bahar's house of ill-repute.

'Belt up!' came a shout from somewhere outside. It sounded to Lock like Bingham-Smith.

Rubbing his hand across his bristly chin, Lock fished a cigarette from his pocket. He struck a match and inhaled the sweet, strong tobacco deep into his lungs. He coughed, winced and put his hands to his ribs. They were tender to the touch. He spat onto the mud floor and was relieved to see no blood. He inhaled again, a shallow puff this time, and stared down at the floor watching his trail of saliva as it snaked its way between the seven cigarette butts, each one marking a further fifteen minutes in which he had been incarcerated.

'Bugger,' he muttered.

'Bugger, indeed.'

Lock snapped his head up. Someone was watching him through the observation hatch. They moved away. A harsh light spilled over Lock as the bare bulb dangling from the ceiling was switched on. Then a key turned, and the heavy door to the cell creaked open.

'Hello, sir,' Lock said.

Major Ross glared down at Lock, arms folded across his chest, his face dark with anger. He didn't step into the cell, but remained standing on the threshold, a slight twitch pulling at his left cheek. Lock hadn't seen the major look quite so angry before.

'I was bored of lying in bed.'

Ross just glared back.

'I thought I could help. With the investigation.'

Ross said nothing.

'God damn it, sir. It was me who got shot!'

Ross remained tight-lipped.

Lock sighed, threw his cigarette end to the floor and crushed it out with his boot.

'All right. I disobeyed you. But I had to follow my instincts, my suspicions.'

The major unfolded his arms and pulled his pipe from his pocket. But still he didn't say anything.

'About Underhill and Bingham-Smith,' Lock added.

'And just what did your suspicions tell you, laddie?' Ross said. He put his pipe in his mouth and struck a match against the door jamb repeatedly, without luck.

'That they were behind the shooting. My shooting.'

Ross scowled as he struck a second match, but that too failed to ignite.

Lock pulled himself to his feet and offered his matches to the major.

'You should get yourself a lighter.'

Ross grunted his thanks and tried again. This time he got a flame. His tobacco caught and he sucked and wheezed and puffed away until he was satisfied and surrounded by a cloud of smoke. As was his habit, the major then pocketed Lock's matches. He pulled the pipe from his mouth and squared up to Lock.

'I told you to leave Underhill alone. How could they both be behind the shooting? Answer me that. That faux aristocrat and the belligerent but, I might add, fiercely loyal sergeant major have nothing in common—'

'Their hatred of me.'

Ross hesitated. 'Do you really think you matter that much? Bingham-Smith is getting married to the Townshend girl, to Amy; Underhill is working for me, working hard. You are an irrelevance to them, a mild irritation at most.'

'Underhill and I have history, sir.'

Ross raised a questioning eyebrow.

'Lhasa. 1904.'

The major chewed on his pipe thoughtfully for a while. Lock couldn't be certain if Ross knew exactly what had happened between him and the sergeant major, but he must know about the atrocities committed by the British in Tibet, and Lock was sure that Ross could put two and two together and guess what Lock was getting at.

'Things happen in times of war, laddie. Stop being so naïve.'

Lock shook his head. 'We weren't at war, sir. And there is nothing that can excuse wh—'

'Shut up!' Ross took a step forward, jabbing his pipe into Lock's chest. 'That's an order. Or do you want to spend the rest of the war in this cell?'

Now it was Lock's turn to remain quiet.

Ross nodded. 'Yes. A good agent should have a fast brain and a slow mouth. You seem to be behaving in the exact opposite manner.' He paused, squinting at Lock's left eye and then his right. 'Perhaps that bullet did affect your brain, after all.'

Lock shook his head. He still had something to say.

'There's a rat in the White Tabs, according to Wassmuss's own notebook. Yes?' he said. 'Unless that's a double bluff to cause discontent, suspicion and paranoia amongst our own ranks. But if it is true, then just why do you think that the sergeant major is secretly meeting with foreign business dignitaries in the back rooms of cafes?'

Ross did an almost perfect job of keeping a straight face, but Lock spotted the merest hint of surprise.

'There was no sign of Bett . . . Pretty Officer Boxer either at this cafe, so I'm presuming Underhill's being there can't have been to do with the "investigation", as you so quaintly put it. Sir.'

'Who did he meet?'

'A fat man. In a suit. Spoke with a strong accent, possibly Dutch or German.'

'More,' Ross said, turning away from Lock. He began to pace the cell, tapping his pipe stem against his teeth. 'Go on, go on,' he waved irritably.

'I didn't get a clear look, sir,' Lock said, 'but I would say that he was in his fifties, very overweight, sweated profusely. He had tightly cropped blond-grey hair, a round, red face, fleshy, moist lips. He's a snappy dresser, a dark suit with a red and white spot—'

'Spotted handkerchief,' Ross interrupted. 'Kept in his front breast pocket.' He pointed to his own breast pocket. 'Smokes a cigar?'

'Do you know him, sir?'

The major nodded. 'Oh, yes. An old colleague of our dearly departed Lord Shears.'

'Another oilman?' Lock was inwardly pleased. He and Singh had already guessed as much.

'Yes, another APOC director. Not Dutch or German; Swiss. His name is Günther Grössburger.'

'Apt.'

'Very. And you didn't hear or see what they were talking about or doing?'

'Some negotiation. There was something on the table between them. Then the fat . . . Grössburger gathered it up, put it in a small black box and handed it to Underhill.'

'Handed?'

'Yes. I couldn't see it clearly, but whatever it was, it was small and Underhill put it in his pocket.'

'Money? Papers?'

'From the sergeant major?'

'Yes, of course from the sergeant major. What did he give Grössburger? Tell me you saw that much.' The major stopped pacing and raised an expectant eyebrow.

Lock shook his head. 'Nothing. He gave him nothing.'

'Damn.'

'Except a coin purse.'

'So he did give him something. He gave him money.'

'If that was what was in the purse. Yes, sir. But not papers. Unless it was folded into a tiny square.' Lock held up his hand with his thumb and forefinger squeezed close together as an illustration of the size.

'Don't get smart with me,' Ross glowered.

'No, sir. Sorry, sir. But do you believe me now? That the sergeant major is up to something?'

Ross fished the matches out of his pocket again and relit his pipe.

'And you didn't hear anything?'

'Only a name, sir.'

'A name?'

'Bingham-Smith.'

'Oh, for pit—'

'That's what I heard, sir. Something is going on and it's to do with both the assistant provost marshal and the sergeant major. And the German, Grössburger.'

'Swiss, Lock, he's Swiss.'

'If you say so, sir.'

'And there was no one else?'

'No, sir.' Lock decided to keep Bombegy's presence outside of the cafe from Ross for the time being. He would question his Indian cook himself later on.

Ross was scowling again, staring off into the middle distance. His face seemed troubled now.

'Did they see you?'

'Who?'

'Underhill and Grössburger,' Ross snapped.

'No.'

'Certain?'

Lock frowned, thinking. No, he was positive that he'd managed to get away from the cafe without causing too much of a disturbance. Hopefully his pale, sweating complexion and his haste, not to mention his warning comment about the cuisine to the Australian officer sat eating there, marked him out as just another case of food poisoning making a quick exit before his bowels did.

'Absolutely, sir. Why?'

Ross glared back at him. The colour around his neck was flushed, but he was keeping the pent-up fury at bay.

'Because, you idiot,' Ross said, through gritted teeth, 'Underhill is on a job and if you'd been seen by Grössburger, or the sergeant major, or confronted them, then you may well have blown weeks of hard work.'

Lock was taken aback. 'I don't—'

'Of course you don't understand, Lock. You weren't in the loop. You were in hospital recovering from an attempt on your life.

Christ, I wish that bullet had been more true.' Ross, his face the colour of beetroot now, such was his anger, glared up at Lock. 'Or you were *supposed* to be in hospital. I told you to stay put. I told you the investigation was well underway. I told—'

'Perhaps, if you had told me what was going on, what you were doing, sir, then may—'

'What!?' Ross said, spraying Lock with spittle. 'Let me remind you, Captain, that you,' he jabbed Lock's chest with his pipe for emphasis, 'work for me. You,' he jabbed Lock's chest again, 'take orders from me and you—'

He went to jab Lock's chest for a third time, but Lock was quicker, grabbing hold of the major's pipe.

'Will you please stop poking me with your bloody pipe.' It was a stupid thing to do.

The major wrenched the pipe from Lock's grip and pressed his face close.

'You,' Ross said, 'will do as you are told. Do you understand?'

Lock straightened up and stared the major right in the eye. He wasn't going to back down. Not yet. There were too many questions.

'It's too much of a coincidence, sir. The brothel, Grössburger, Underhill, Bingham-Smith . . . They're all linked somehow.'

Ross glared back at him but he didn't attempt to interrupt again.

'So,' Lock said, 'if Underhill is working for you and some lead ended up with the sergeant major holding a clandestine meeting with Grössburger, then what does it all mean?'

Lock hesitated, his thoughts suddenly turning to Bombegy. He cursed. No, not Bombegy? Surely not? Was he the lead?

The major scowled back at him, hesitant about adding something of his own.

'Was it just a coincidence that Grössburger was at the brothel when Bingham-Smith was?' Lock continued. 'Was your raid really to keep the peace? Or was it all an elaborate plan so you could legitimately arrest Grössburger without arousing suspicion from any of Wassmuss's other agents who may have been watching?'

Lock paused. His head was throbbing, but he was waiting for the major to either deny or to confirm what he had said thus far. But Ross wasn't saying anything. He was just standing there letting Lock's mind continue to try to unravel the mess.

'What about the two merchants and the general I saw being questioned by a red cap outside of the brothel? Are they here? In a cell? Or did you spirit them away, too?'

Still the major remained tight-lipped.

'You planned it, didn't you?' Lock said. 'The fight. One or more of those pals of Bingham-Smith's is a White Tab.'

There was a faint flicker of amusement on Ross's face, but the major was too shrewd to give much away, and was quick to suck and puff on his pipe again to hide any telltale expression.

Lock nodded slowly, realisation dawning.

'My turning up at the brothel was actually a bonus for you, an even better spark to ignite the fight.'

Now the major visibly relaxed. He shrugged.

'We spotted you and Singh approaching, so held back until you went inside. That's why Singh never came to your aid. I stopped him.'

'I see.' Lock was absent-mindedly rubbing the sore spot on his chest where the major had been poking him.

'Come, laddie, he'd be under arrest too if he had done. And I'd imagine there'd be a few more broken heads.' Ross chuckled at the thought.

'And Grössburger? What have you got out of him so far?'

Ross looked mildly surprised. 'How do you know we have him?'

'I saw him being bundled into that staff car that was parked opposite *Cennet*.'

Ross nodded. 'Of course you did. Well, nothing of particular interest. Yet. But he'll break. Underhill and Petty Officer Boxer are questioning him at this very moment. How about we pop along and see how they're doing?' He held his hand out towards the open cell door.

'*Petty Officer* Boxer!' Lock scoffed. 'Come off it, sir. I said the same to her; there are no women in the Services. Not ranked, anyway.'

Ross gave a wry smile and put his finger to his lips. 'A little experiment. But it's coming. As surely as votes for women is coming.'

Lock followed Ross along the corridor that was lined with metal doors all bearing faded tin numbers, and on up the worn stone steps he'd climbed before.

They emerged out into the empty antechamber and then into the vast echoing hall. As he was the last time Lock was here, the lone provost sergeant was still sat at the same desk writing in presumably the same ledger.

Lock headed for the main door, but Ross took his arm and steered him in the other direction, over towards a recess in the mud-brick wall. This, in turn, led to another dimly lit corridor, again lined with metal doors, four on either side. However, there were no numbers here, only letters. They walked to the far end where, leaning against the wall, stood a provost sentry.

He stood bolt upright on seeing Ross and Lock approach.

'At ease, Corporal,' Ross said.

The sentry gave a stiff nod, then turned and unlocked the door marked 'G'. Lock followed Ross inside.

Beyond the door, the cell was similar in layout to the one Lock had just left, only it was bigger, nearly three times the size. The walls and floor were of mud brick and hard earth, and again a single, barred window high up on the far side was the only source of ventilation and natural light. There were two items of furniture, a kitchen table pushed up against the right-hand wall and, in the centre of the cell, directly beneath a single electric bulb that hung limply from a rope flex, shining a sickly yellow light down, was a wooden kitchen chair. Here sat the fat man, the man Ross referred to as Grössburger, the man whom Lock had spied with Underhill in the Café Baldia, the man whom Lock had seen being bundled away from the brothel. He wasn't tied down, but the questioning he had been subjected to had clearly involved physical violence. His nose and lip were bleeding, his left eye was swollen, and there was a cut above his eyebrow. There was a dampness around his crotch and a pool of sharp-smelling liquid at his bare feet. He was still dressed the way he had been on leaving *Cennet*.

Standing over the fat man, sleeves rolled up past his elbows, and soaked in the sweat of exertion, was Underhill. He turned on hearing the door open, sneered at Lock, then straightened up and nodded to Ross.

'Sah.'

Lock caught a familiar smell of perfume cutting through the stench of fear and turned his head to see Betty Boxer, arms folded, a burning cigarette in her hand, standing inside, next to the door.

She looked, even in the weak, yellow light, pale and disturbed.

'I took you more for an equestrian than a pugilist,' Lock said.

Betty put her cigarette to her lips and glared back. But Lock could see her hand shaking. Was she here under duress?

'What the hell is this?' Lock said, turning back to Ross.

'This is war, laddie. The gloves are off when we deal with spies and terrorists. You think you can do better?' the major challenged.

Lock shook his head and walked over to the table that was pushed up against the wall. Spread out across its surface was a number of personal items: a pocket watch, a fountain pen, some coins, mostly Indian rupees, which wasn't surprising as they were now the official currency of Mesopotamia, having recently been introduced by the occupying British. There was also a money clip containing Swiss franken, English pounds and German papiermarks, the red and white polka dot handkerchief, a small leather-bound notebook and the small black box Lock had seen Grössburger hand to Underhill. It was open now and inside, resting on a black velvet cloth, was a pair of pearl earrings. They looked very expensive. Lock noted that there was no sign of the coin purse, however, that Underhill had given to Grössburger in exchange for the box.

Lock picked up the notebook and flicked through its pages. They were all blank. No, what was that? He fanned the pages again, slower this time, and stopped a third of the way through. One page had three words written down, in black ink, in neat, flowing script, three very familiar words:

Lieutenant Kingdom Lock

'Intriguing, don't you think?'

Lock glanced up. Ross was peering over his shoulder.

'So who is he really?' Lock said. He closed the notebook and put it back down on the table.

'Günther Peter Grössburger. Born 1861 in Basel. Swiss national, APOC director. But he's also a pearl smuggler, a German sympathiser, and a spy.'

'*Nein*,' Grössburger muttered. '*Ich bin kein Spion.*'

'Shut it, Fritz!' Underhill slapped the fat man across the jaw.

Lock saw Betty wince and turn her gaze away.

'Does she have to witness this?'

Betty glared back at him. 'I choose to be here, Captain.'

Lock frowned. He didn't understand the American girl at all. She made no sense; her presence here, in this cell, in this city, even in this war made no sense. What was she trying to prove? Another suffragette? To what ends? He looked back at the major, but he just gave an almost imperceptible shrug.

'Pearl smuggler?' Lock said, changing the subject.

Ross picked up the earrings and held them up. They were very beautiful and appeared to change colour as the major turned them slowly in the light.

'Captivating, aren't they? The pearls come from Bubiyan Island, at the mouth of the Shatt al-Arab. They are worth a fortune and are the favoured currency, we believe, and the main source of funding, for Wassmuss's network.'

'A fortune?'

Ross nodded. 'Sir Percy Cox estimated the pearl market for 1914 to be worth somewhere in the region of three million pounds. That's something like sixty-three million German marks.'

Lock gave a low whistle. 'So he's the paymaster?' he said, staring down at Grössburger.

'That's what the sergeant major has been trying to find out,' Ross said. 'But we aren't getting very far. We've searched his rooms at the Hotel Ezra. All there is, is that notebook containing the two names.'

The major picked the notebook up from the table and flicked through until he found the page he wanted. He held it up for Lock to see.

Marmaris

'That's a sleepy little fishing village on the Mediterranean coast of Turkey,' Lock said.

'It's also the name of a boat.'

'A boat?'

The major nodded. 'Yes, a Turkish steamer, in fact.'

'Where is it?'

'Up the Tigris, north of Qurna.'

Lock glanced at the fat man slumped in the chair. 'A rendezvous? A centre of operations?'

The major shrugged. 'Could be, laddie. I hadn't thought of that. A mobile command centre . . .' Ross said, stroking his moustache thoughtfully. 'Very good, Lock. I like it.'

Underhill snorted derisively.

Grössburger lifted his head slowly and turned to focus on the two officers staring down at him. His eyes found Lock, and he squinted as if to see better through fogged vision.

'*Was? Was haben Sie . . . gesagt?*' he gurgled weakly, as if he were trying to speak with a mouth full of water.

Underhill slapped Grössburger sharply across the jaw again.

'Stop talkin' that filth, Fritz!'

Lock stepped forward to intervene, but Ross held him back.

'Leave the sergeant major to do his work, laddie.'

'This is barbaric, sir.' Lock wrenched his arm away.

'Now, listen, Lock. This isn't a game. We need to crack Wassmuss's network, or thousands will die.'

'Thousands are dying every day in this goddamn war. Sir.'

Ross scowled back at Lock. 'You know exactly what I'm talking about.'

Grössburger made a rattling sound, cleared his throat, then spat to his side.

'Lock? You are Lock?' he said in heavily accented English, his voice barely a whisper.

Underhill slammed his fist into the fat man's belly. 'I said shut yer mouth.'

Grössburger doubled up gasping for air.

'All right, Sergeant Major, enough for now,' Ross said.

Underhill moved away from the prisoner, rubbing his knuckles. His eyes met Lock's, inviting him to challenge him, make some comment.

But Lock held his tongue. He took the notebook from Ross's grip and opened it up at the page with his name written on, and held it under Grössburger's bloodied nose.

'Why is this name here? Why is *my* name here?'

Grössburger groaned and shook his head. 'You are Lock? Lieutenant Kingdom Lock?' he said.

'Yes. But I am a captain now.'

Grössburger chuckled, or at least that's what Lock presumed he was doing. It could just as easily have been an involuntary spasm.

'So the British do reward murderers.'

'I'm a soldier, Herr Grössburger.'

The fat man shook his head again. '*Nein, Sie sind Auftragsmörder* . . . You are killer . . . a paid assassin.'

'All soldiers are killers, it goes with the job.'

'Pah! Your excuses are feeble. We know what you did, what you are.'

'We?'

'*Was?*'

'You said "we". That means you are part of something . . . bigger. A network? Wassmuss's network?'

Grössburger blinked up at Lock, but said nothing more.

Ross leant close to Lock and whispered, 'Very good, laddie.'

'Are you a smuggler?' Lock said, ignoring the major.

Grössburger snorted. 'Of course I am not. But I do deal in the pearls. There is a big market in this country with many soldiers wanting . . . How do you say? Trinkets? . . . *Ja*, trinkets for their sweethearts. What do you think they are?' He jerked his double chins at the table.

'The earrings?'

'*Ja*, the earrings. That . . . pig,' he flicked a limp wrist at Underhill, 'he contacted me through my source . . .'

'Source? Who?'

'The Indian cook.'

Lock glanced questioningly at Underhill, although he knew the answer.

'Bombegy. 'E means Bombegy,' the sergeant major said.

Lock's mind turned over momentarily, wondering just how deep his cook was involved in this mess. 'Carry on,' he said to Grössburger.

'The sergeant major wanted something expensive and delicate for a friend. I met with him and he purchased the earrings. That is all.'

'The sergeant major,' Ross said, stepping forward, 'was working at exposing the German spy network that is being funded with pearls. Pearls *you* supply.'

Grössburger shook his head. '*Nein, nein, nein.*'

'Then why,' Ross said, 'did you meet secretly in a cafe back room?'

'Thieves, Herr Major, they are everywhere.'

It was Ross's turn to give a shake of the head. 'No, no, no.'

Grössburger smiled thinly up at him. 'How ironic then, Herr Major, if what you say is true, that British money is funding your own destruction.'

The room fell silent.

'Did you arrange the attempt on my life?' Lock said, after a moment.

Grössburger turned his gaze back to Lock. His eyes were bloodshot and watery, but they burnt with arrogance. It was a look he had seen before, in Wassmuss. For a moment the hairs on the back of Lock's neck bristled. Was this man Wassmuss in another elaborate disguise? Impossible. No, his eyes, they were different. But still, it was a haunting thought that took a while to fade.

'Assassinate the assassin?' Grössburger said. 'No, Herr Lock. But there *is* a price on your head.'

'I beg your pardon?' Lock said.

Grössburger chuckled again. 'You, Lieutenant—'

'Captain.'

'*Ja, ja*, Capitan Kingdom Lock of the A.I.F. who, contrary to the Hague Convention of 1907, shot and killed in cold blood *Kaymakam* Süleyman Askerî Bey of the Ottoman Empire. There is a price on your head. An eye for an eye.'

Lock was stunned. He had no idea what the fat man was talking about.

'What? When? When was I supposed to have done this . . . murder?'

'Three weeks ago.'

Lock shook his head in disbelief.

'I presume the attempt on your life,' Grössburger said, 'was an act by one seeking the reward.'

'Who, who says I assassinated this . . . Süleyman Askerî?'

'The witness. *Binbaşi* Feyzi.'

'Never heard of him,' Lock said.

Grössburger shrugged.

'This is ridiculous.' Lock turned away from the Swiss. 'What does it mean, sir?' he said to Ross.

The major was pulling at his moustache, his brow furrowed, a puzzled look across his face as he studied Grössburger.

'Outside. All of you.'

Sergeant Major Underhill rolled down his shirtsleeves, rapped twice on the cell door and, when the sentry on the other side unlocked it, he pulled it open and waited for Betty to step out first. She caught Lock's eye on her way out, but Lock could read nothing in her expression. Did she think he was an assassin? Lock followed Underhill out, and the major came after.

'Corporal, keep an eye on our guest,' Ross said.

'Sir.' The provost sentry stepped into the cell.

'I demand to see the Swiss cons—' Grössburger shouted.

Ross cut the protest short by slamming the cell door shut.

'Well, that at least sheds some light on your shooting, laddie.'

Lock shook his head. He didn't believe it, he couldn't believe it. It made no sense.

'Did you kill him?' Ross said, as he began to lead the way back down the corridor.

'I've never even heard of Feyzi or Süleyman Askerî.'

Ross looked doubtful, and glanced at Betty and Underhill.

'Come on, sir,' Lock said. 'I've either been drunk or laid up in hospital since the Battle of Barjisiyah Woods. You all know that. How the hell can I have killed him? By magic?'

Ross nodded his head. 'I know, I know.' He gave a heavy sigh and passed a hand through his hair. 'Well, it must be Wassmuss up to his tricks again. A rat in the White Tabs, Bombegy working for the enemy, and now this. Oh, he's a proper little spider, our slippery German friend, isn't he? The more I think about it, more's the pity that your bullet missed him at the quay.'

'What about the fat man? He must know more than he's letting on,' Lock said, jerking his head back towards the cell door.

'I doubt we'll get anything else out of Grössburger,' Ross said. 'Perhaps we'll have better luck with Bombegy.'

'I can't believe Bombegy's involved, sir.'

'Up to 'is scrawny brown neck, sah, 'e is,' Underhill said, with a certain amount of glee.

The group paused as they came back out into the vast hall.

'All right, everybody, go get some rest,' Ross said. 'We'll assess the situation in the morning.'

'It is morning, sir,' Betty said. She smiled at Lock, then turned

109

and slipped her way past the lone provost sergeant still sat at the desk and on towards the main entrance.

Underhill stiffly saluted. 'Sahs,' he said, then marched after Betty, the clump of his hobnailed boots echoing loudly.

Lock walked with Ross in silence for a moment, his mind a mass of inexplicable questions and theories. He stopped short.

'And Bingham-Smith?'

'What about him?' Ross said.

'We should interrogate him, too, sir. He's hiding something. I can feel it.'

Ross shook his head. 'He's been released. They all have, those delightful young officer chums of his. Seems somebody paid off Jalal Al-bin Bahar rather handsomely and he's dropped all charges. Gracious of him, don't you think, considering?'

'Bugger,' Lock said. He so wanted to see Bingham-Smith sweat some more. But perhaps the major was right. Perhaps it was Wassmuss behind the attempt on his life. 'Do you think it was Grössburger?' he said. 'That organised the shooting?'

'Maybe.' Ross put his hand on Lock's shoulder and guided him on through the hall. 'However, if what Grössburger says is true, about a price being on your head, and I don't doubt it, my boy, I don't doubt it, then we need to get you out of the firing line. You were lucky, very lucky last time. But the next assassin's bullet might be true, and we can't have that now, can we?'

'Meaning?'

'Meaning that every Tom, Dick and Abdul with a bad debt or an insatiable greed will be looking to take a potshot at your golden goose of a bonnet. Therefore, I think it best we get you well away, and back to the front.'

'Back to the front? Where every Johnny will be taking a potshot at me. How in the hell is that going to help?' Lock said.

'Aye, the enemy will do that,' Ross said. 'But we need to get you out of Basra, until things quieten down, until we can get a clearer picture of this murder accusation. I'll get Betty onto it first thing.'

Lock grunted. A fat lot of good that was going to do, he thought.

'Look, sir. I'm part of your White Tab network. You recruited me to catch Wassmuss, to help smash his network and put a stop to the threat to the oilfields. How is removing me from the picture going to help? It makes no sense.'

'But, my dear Kingdom, it makes perfect sense. Who do you think the commanding officer at the Tigris front is? For the Ottoman Forces, I mean?'

Lock looked blankly back at the major.

'Why, a certain Major Feyzi, that's who.' He paused and rubbed at his moustache. 'That is, if our sources in the area are correct. Still, I can think of no one better than you to go and find out.'

CHAPTER SEVEN

Lock tried again, this time a little louder and a little harder.

He was on the landing outside Amy and Mary's apartment on the top floor of the house on the Street of Allah's Tears. He knew the girls still lived here as their surnames were staring back at him, written in pencil, from the card attached to the door. He was taking a risk coming here, but he had to see Amy before he headed off for Qurna, the new front about thirty miles north up the Tigris River. Singh and Lance Corporal Elsworth, the young sharpshooter Lock had adopted from the 104th shortly before the Battle of Barjisiyah Woods, and whom he had duly promoted for his sterling efforts and eagle eye, were waiting and keeping watch downstairs. Lock didn't need the escort, but Singh had insisted. He hoped the big Indian was being overcautious, but a part of him said that the sooner he left Basra the better. And not just for him, but for Amy, too.

He knocked again, just to be sure, and held the back of his hand up for a moment longer contemplating the half-moon white scar that ran from the knuckle at the foot of his index finger to the base of his thumb. Yes, Elsworth was a damned good shot, he smiled to himself, remembering how he had got the scar.

A burst of staccato chatter broke out from the floor below. Lock peered over the banister to see the Arab mother who lived in the apartment downstairs shouting at two children, boys of about seven or eight. Both, from what Lock could gather, had just returned from playing outside, and both were somehow soaked in muddy water. There was a waft of cooking meat as the woman ushered the children inside their home and slammed the door behind them. Lock could still hear her scolding voice as he smiled and turned back to Amy's door. The electric light went out.

Lock pressed the push-button switch on the wall, and again he was bathed in the dim yellow light of the naked bulb hanging down from the flyblown ceiling. There was a buzz and a faint rustle as a large moth was disturbed once more by the sudden luminescence. Lock raised his fist, and as he went to knock for a third time, the door sprang open.

Amy stood at the threshold, emerald eyes ablaze with anger.

'What?' she snapped.

She looked dishevelled, auburn hair all tangled and loose down to her shoulders, a robe pulled tightly about her small frame.

'Did I wake you?' Lock said. 'Sorry.'

They stood staring at one another for a moment listening to the muffled scolding of the woman downstairs.

The light in the hall clicked out again.

Amy opened the door to her apartment wider, and turned and

114

walked back inside. Lock followed her, closing the door softly behind him.

The apartment hadn't changed since he was last there. The square hallway was as cramped as before, with coats, hats and jackets hanging haphazardly on one side, whilst the other was wall-to-ceiling shelves crammed with books and neglected pot plants. In a tiled room opposite, through a door that was slightly ajar, Lock could see part of a tin bath. The second door off to the right led into the living quarters. The room was square like the hallway, crammed with furniture, more books and more choking pot plants. An elaborately carved screen separated the room in two, living quarters on one side with an old leather armchair and a rickety wardrobe, and sleeping on the other. Here was a large, unkempt, wooden bed that Amy and Mary shared. Despite being dominated by a large pair of French windows, which opened up onto a latticed-shuttered balcony overhanging the street, the room was stuffy, musty and damp. Clothes, shoes and old newspapers covered just about every surface that Lock's eye fell upon.

'Still as tidy as ever, I see,' Lock said, standing on the threshold.

His gaze moved left to the kitchen area. This was decorated with criss-crossed washing lines from which limp, drying clothes hung down over a table piled high with dirty dishes.

'Hard to find help, what with the servants all away at the front,' Lock added.

'What do you want, Kingdom?' Amy sighed. 'I've only just finished a twelve-hour shift.' She emerged from the bathroom behind him with a steaming kettle in her hand. 'I was about to take a bath.'

'Don't let me stop you,' Lock said, stepping aside to let her pass. 'I could scrub your back.'

Amy ignored him and moved over to the pot-bellied stove at the end of the kitchen area, placing the kettle on the hotplate.

'Would you like some tea? There's enough water here.'

Lock removed his hat and tossed it onto the armchair. 'No tea,' he said.

'Oh, yes, I forgot,' Amy said, rubbing her eyes.

'You look like you just got out of bed.'

'I did. I was asleep when you knocked. Repeatedly.'

'I thought you were having a bath?'

'I . . .' She glared back at him. 'What time is it?'

'Time we talked.'

'I have nothing to say.'

'Well, I have.'

Amy started to move away, but Lock reached out and grabbed her arm, pulling her close. He stared down into her eyes, captivated by the fire that burnt there defiantly.

'Why, Amy? Why are you being like this?'

She tried to shrug him off, but Lock held firm.

'Let me go you . . . *salaud!*'

Lock shook his head. 'Not until you tell me just what the hell has gotten into you.'

Amy turned her gaze away. '*Rien.*'

Lock gently pulled her face back again. There were tears welling up in her eyes now.

'Please, Amy. Talk to me.'

She looked back at him, eyes darting from one to the other. Her lips parted.

'*Je—*'

Lock pressed his mouth to hers and kissed her hard. She didn't struggle and as their tongues met she gave a little moan, but whether it was of pleasure or despair Lock neither knew nor cared. He pulled her body to him, holding her tighter, his desire rising. He could feel her body through the robe, knew she was naked underneath, could feel the crush of her breasts against his chest. His hands wandered down her back to the firm roundness of her behind.

Amy pulled sharply away and slapped Lock hard across the cheek, the crack of her palm stinging the air.

'*Non!*'

Lock was momentarily stunned. He put his hand to his stinging cheek and glared back at her, anger and annoyance welling up in his chest.

'We can't,' Amy said, voice husky, her breathing rapid. 'I'm getting married.'

'Bollocks.' Lock made to grab her, and she took a step back, raising her fist.

'*Arrêtez!*'

'Why? What the hell are you playing at now?'

'I'm . . . pregnant.'

Lock froze.

His vision seemed to swim before his eyes as his mind exploded with a hundred thoughts. What did she say? Pregnant? How? Fool! What do you mean how? Christ, was this the reason? The reason why she avoided him? Why she was so cruel and hard? Why she was so determined to marry Bingham-Smith? Because she was carrying the odious prick's child. No, it couldn't be.

And then everything fell into place. He knew, knew the truth. He felt his jaw go slack.

'It's mine, isn't it?' Lock's voice was very quiet, very calm.

Amy gave a little cry, her hands shooting up to her mouth, and turned away.

Lock pulled one of the hard wooden chairs out from under the table and slumped down heavily. He passed his hands over his tightly cropped hair and gave a mournful sigh.

Amy stood where she was not saying a word, just watching and waiting for Lock to speak. The sounds of the street wafted in on the light, hot breeze and along with it came the putrid smell of the stagnant creeks that flowed nearby. The woman below was still haranguing her children, but her voice was little more than a muffled drone now.

'Why, Amy? Why didn't you tell me?' Lock looked up at her accusingly.

She couldn't meet his gaze, keeping her eyes glued to the kettle steaming away on the stove top.

'How long have you known?'

Amy remained silent.

'Amy!' Lock smashed his fist down on the table.

She started and her eyes snapped angrily round.

'A month,' she said, her voice little more than a whisper.

Lock slowly shook his head. 'Does he know?'

'Who?'

'Who do you think? Bingham bloody Smith. Have you told him?'

Amy took a pace towards Lock. 'No,' she said. 'He can't, he mustn't. Please, Kingdom.'

'Please what?'

'Don't tell . . . anyone. You and *maman* . . .'

Lock smiled cruelly. 'I see. Well, that explains it.'

'Explains what?'

'Your mother. Why she gave me the sudden cold shoulder.'

'Try to understand, Kingdom. It is for the best.'

Lock shot to his feet, scraping the chair back noisily against the wooden floor. He marched over to the other side of the room to retrieve his hat. Amy followed and pulled at his sleeve.

'Wait, Kingdom . . . I . . .'

'What, what do you want, Amy?' Lock said, rounding on her. 'Really?'

Amy bit her lip, eyes searching his face. Then she stepped over to the bed, and reaching under the pillow, pulled out a small oblong package wrapped in brown paper and tied up with string.

'To give you this,' she said, holding out the gift.

Lock hesitated, then accepted the package, and glared back at her.

'Aren't you going to open it?'

'Not now.'

'It is a knife. I had it engraved.'

Lock stared back into her wide, emerald eyes. He so wanted to take her in his arms, to pull her over to the bed and to make love to her. He took a breath.

'Why?' he said.

'I wanted to give you something.'

'Why?' Lock repeated.

She scowled. 'To say thank you.'

'Is that all? "Thank you".' Lock slowly shook his head.

'What do *you* want from me, Kingdom?' she said, throwing his earlier accusatory question back at him.

'For you to be true to your heart, Amy. To be . . .'

Amy's eyes had hardened again, and there was a flame of anger deep within the dark pools of her pupils. '*Merde. Je ne peux pas être ce que je ne suis pas. Il suffit de laisser!* Leave!' she screamed, turning her back on him.

Lock sighed heavily and made his way over to the door. He paused, tempted to throw the gift back at her, but in a flash of stubbornness he decided against that and pocketed it instead.

'Did you ever love me?' he said, without turning to face her.

Amy gave a sob, but didn't say anything.

Lock's shoulders dropped. He needed to get away from her as quickly as possible. He needed to think, to decide what to do. Bugger it, of all the times.

'If you breathe a word to father, to Casper,' she called out, 'I shall deny it! I shall deny everything.' There was real venom in her voice.

At the threshold Lock turned back to look at her. Tears were rolling down her cheeks. She seemed so vulnerable and small now and his heart ached for her. He shook his head sadly.

'Why would you even ask that?' he said.

Amy thrust her chin up defiantly. There was fire in her eyes once more.

'If you do I shall never speak to you again.'

Lock pulled on his slouch hat, swore under his breath, and without another word, stormed out.

Slamming the door behind him, Lock stood still for a moment in the dark stairwell. The Arab woman downstairs was still chastising her children and Lock wanted to scream at her to shut the hell up. He closed his eyes and cursed bitterly. That had all gone so terribly wrong. He hadn't even told Amy about the price on his head, that he was leaving for Qurna, or that Wassmuss was probably still snooping around. He didn't believe it himself, but he wanted her to be on her guard, just in case. He thought about going back inside, about taking her in his arms forcibly, about making her see reason, to abandon her stubborn idea of marrying Bingham-Smith, about keeping bloody secrets.

'Bugger.'

The light flickered on and footsteps began to make their way up the stairs. Lock moved away from the door just as Mary turned the corner. Her smile was warm, her face slightly flushed with exertion.

'Captain Lock! I . . . Hello,' she said. 'Is Amy not in?'

'I was just leaving. Duty calls. Back to the front for me.'

Mary paused. 'Are you fit enough?' she scowled.

'According to Major Ross I am,' Lock said, then smiled. 'No, I'm fine. On the mend.'

Mary smiled back. 'I'm glad.' She moistened her lips.

They both stood there in awkward silence and the light clicked off. Mary slapped it on again.

'Keep an eye on her for me,' Lock said. He touched the brim of his hat and started to make his way downstairs.

'Be careful,' Mary called after him.

'Always,' he said over his shoulder.

CHAPTER EIGHT

'Always, indeed,' Lock scoffed to himself.

He was back at the front lines now, back where the Grim Reaper was waiting in the corner of the eye, scythe glistening in the harsh sunlight. An assassin's bullet was no different to a bullet fired by a Turk *Mehmetçik*. It meant the same thing after all, an end to Kingdom Lock. He took a deep, fetid breath from the still, stagnant air hanging heavy over the reed marsh in front of him, and found his thoughts constantly dragging him back to Amy.

Lock's anger at her had taken some time to dissipate. He had emerged from the girls' apartment building back into the stifling dusty heat of the Street of Allah's Tears where Singh, Elsworth and the dog were waiting for him. Singh had his nose buried, as it so often was when he had a moment alone, in his tatty copy of *Nitnem Gutka*, the Sikh prayer book, and Elsworth was playing another of his insufferable army tunes on his harmonica, tapping his foot along to the beat as if he didn't have a care in the world. The dog sprang up at Lock's approach, barked once and then bounced around his ankles excitedly. Singh handed Lock his haversack, shouldered his own, and from there the three men had set off in silence towards the quays at Ashar.

Singh knew Lock's moods well enough by now not to engage him in conversation; not so Elsworth. But the young marksman, bristling with pride at the chevron sewn on his sleeve, got the message soon enough when Lock glared blackly back at him in answer to an innocently put question regarding Miss Townshend's health.

'Sorry, sir,' Elsworth muttered. But he didn't keep quiet for long, and soon he was whistling and humming one of his tunes.

Lock sighed, catching Singh's eye. But he gave a brief shake of his head, indicating that he didn't want the big Indian to stop Elsworth from having his musical moment. Although, when the young sharpshooter began to sing the words to his tune, Lock regretted the decision.

Come on Tommy. Come on Jack,
We'll guard the home till you come back.
Come on Sandy. Come on Pat,
For you're true blue!
Down your tools and leave your benches,
Say goodbye to all the wenches.
Take your gun, and may God speed you,
For your King and Country need you.

'Enough,' Lock growled.

'Sir. Yes, sir,' Elsworth said, and fell into a hurt silence.

They walked on through the quiet streets, and when they were nearing the quay, Singh tugged gently at Lock's arm.

'We have company, sahib.'

Lock stopped and glanced back at the deserted street they had just walked through.

'I know, Sid. He's been following us since we left the Street of Allah's Tears.'

'Trouble, sahib?'

'I doubt it. He can't be more than eleven years old.'

'Sahib?'

'Didn't you see him, loitering in the shadows outside of Amy's apartment building? Young Mesop Arab lad.'

'A spy maybe, sir?' Elsworth said, dropping his haversack to the floor, and removing his rifle from his shoulder.

'Steady on, Alfred. We don't know that.' Lock scanned their immediate surroundings and indicated to a dank side alley that wound off to the left. 'Quick, in there. Come on, come on.' He clicked his fingers impatiently at the dog, and all four of them moved to the alley and shrank back into the shadows.

Lock kept his eye on the street, but there was still no movement.

'We seem to be spending many moments in alleyways, sahib.'

'Hush, Sid.'

There was nothing but the sound of their breathing and the beat of their hearts. Then the dog growled.

'Look, there!'

Halfway down the street there was a stack of wooden crates piled near to the latticed entrance of a storehouse. Peering up from behind the crates, Lock could see the small figure of a young native. The boy hesitated, then scampered across to the middle of the road, glancing from left to right. He came to a stop again, darted forward and stopped once more, spun round, then slumped down on the spot. He sat with his legs crossed, resting his chin on one hand, looking decidedly dejected at having lost his prey.

Lock smiled to himself and stepped out of the alley, followed by the others. All three stood watching the boy whose head was down now as he picked at the dirt of the road with his fingers. Lock glanced down at the dog and gave a soft click of his tongue. The dog darted off towards the boy and was almost upon him before the lad looked up at the sudden rush of feet. He jumped up, startled. The dog yapped noisily and bounced around him. The lad moved in a tight circle, hands raised up, eyes wide with unease and fixed on the animal.

'*You, what do you want here?*' Lock called in Arabic.

The lad's eyes shot over to Lock and the others and his face burst into a huge grin.

'Very tired horse, *as-sayed!*' the boy said in English and waved, the dog still yapping and springing up at his knees.

Lock frowned. Then he remembered having met the lad once before. It was when he had galloped back to Basra from Barjisiyah Woods to see Amy. The boy had looked after his mount for him.

'Very tired, *as-sayed*,' he said and beckoned the lad over.

The Arab boy sprinted to him, the dog scampering along at his heels. He pulled up grinning from ear to ear, looking from Lock to Singh to Elsworth and back to Lock again. He was perhaps a little older than ten, indicated by the downy hairs sprouting above his upper lip. He was dirty, rather smelly in a musty, dank kind of way, not unlike the alley they had just left, Lock thought, and was dressed in the common Mesopotamian clothing of a threadbare

126

waistcoat worn over an ankle-length thobe. The lad had no shoes on his feet. He was slight of frame, wiry, probably malnourished, but looked sprightly enough. He had broken, jagged nails and discoloured teeth, but his brown eyes sparkled with life as they peered out from beneath a thick matt of dark-brown hair.

'No horse, *as-sayed?*'

'No horse,' Lock said. He narrowed his eyes and looked sternly down at the lad. 'Are you a spy?'

The lad shook his head vigorously and threw out a smart salute. 'I am cook. Like father, like mother.'

'And where is like father, like mother?'

The lad's face dropped. 'Dead, *as-sayed*. Turk man beat and kill them for poison. But they did not poison, they—'

Lock held up his hand to stay the lad's staccato chatter. 'You speak good English.'

'Best bloody Engleesh, *as-sayed*,' he said saluting again.

'Stop saluting.' Lock gave a wry grin to Singh and Elsworth. 'What say you? New cook?'

Elsworth shrugged, but Singh didn't look too happy.

'I am not sure, sahib. Can we trust him?'

'Have a little faith, Sid.'

'It is up to you, sahib, but I am telling you now that Sergeant Major Underhill will be very purple about this. He is not liking the native Arab very much at all.'

Lock had noticed that colours were Sid's new way of describing the Sergeant Major's level of anger of late. Purple, naturally, being the highest.

'Sod Underhill, Sid,' he said.

'So you keep on saying, sahib.'

'Besides, since when has he liked anyone very much anyway?'

Lock turned back to the boy. 'Well, a cook's not much use without pots and pa—'

Before Lock could finish his sentence, the boy darted off back the way he had come and soon disappeared from sight.

Elsworth collected their haversacks from the alleyway and then the three men, with the dog sat at their feet, stood watching the empty street for a while.

Lock began to fidget, rubbing the fingers of his left hand. He sighed. 'Bug—'

'Listen, sahib.'

Lock strained his ears. Above the soft breeze and the gentle lapping of the nearby water against the quayside he could make out the slap of feet and a soft clump-clump not unlike the sound of someone plumping up a pillow. God damn it, there she was again, a picture of Amy flashing into his head, of her leaning over him, dressed in her nurse's uniform, helping him to sit up while she made his bed more comfortable. The dog began to growl and Lock shook the thought of his hospital bed away.

'Here he comes,' Elsworth said.

The young sharpshooter's keen eyesight had spotted movement at the far end of the street and it took Lock a moment to see the same. He squinted ahead and then saw the Arab lad running back towards them, a huge pack over his shoulders.

The dog gave a solitary bark and began to wag its tail.

The lad ran up to them, panting. 'Pots and pans, *as-sayed*,' he grinned.

Lock was impressed. The lad had a large canvas haversack bulging with equipment, but what was even more impressive wasn't the amount of pans and ladles and serving spoons dangling down, tied to the outside of the pack by rough twine, but the fact that each and every one was wrapped in a protective rag to dull any noise.

Lock looked to Singh, who nodded his approval.

'What's your name?'

'Jawad Saleem, *as-sayed*.'

'Well, I'm Captain Lock. This is Havildar Singh and Lance Corporal Elsworth. Welcome to the Mendip Light Infantry, Cook Jawad Saleem.'

'And dog, *as-sayed*?'

'And Dog,' Lock said.

The boy saluted again, and the group turned and continued on their way towards the quay and the waiting steamer that would be taking them upriver to Qurna.

The dockyard was as frenetically busy as always, with equipment and troops cramming every available space. A terrific cacophony of human cries, orders and chatter filled the air, all of which was occasionally drowned out by the sudden toot from one of the steamers lined up along the quay. Arab and Indian dockhands manning the crude wooden pulley cranes added their own colourful tones to the atmosphere as they loaded ammunition, guns and supplies aboard the various ships.

Lock weaved his way through the bedlam scanning the various steamers.

'Here, we are,' he said.

Their transport vessel, the *Mejidieh*, was a surprisingly airy tub, a shallow draught, 150ft long stern-wheeler river steamer of around 463grt tonnage. Despite being armed with two 18-pdr guns and crammed with sweaty, parched soldiers, the boat still had a romantic air about it that brought to Lock's mind the tales of Huckleberry Finn he'd so enjoyed reading as a boy.

As they approached the gangplank leading across to the lower deck of the steamer, a familiar figure rose up from a group of men sat on a pile of sandbags at the edge of the quayside.

'Sergeant Major,' Lock said. 'All here?'

Underhill gave a stiff nod. He had gathered together the remnants and new additions to the original Green platoon, those few men who had survived the Battle of Barjisiyah Woods. The three sepoys, the scrawny, eager and serious Ram Lal, the nervous Chopra and his bosom-buddy Toor, all jumped to their feet and saluted smartly, greeting Lock with enthusiastic smiles.

Lock had not seen the Indian boys since the march back to Basra after the battle, nearly a month earlier. He returned the salute. 'Good to see you, lads.'

'Sahib,' they said in unison.

Sat just behind them, his nose buried in one of his homemade jam-tin bombs, was stocky Sergeant Pritchard from Dorset. He had requested, and was granted, permission to join the Mendips, specifically to stay with Lock.

'Glad to see you got your stripes, Pritchard,' Lock said.

Pritchard gave his new captain a grin and a nonchalant salute with a finger to his forehead, then carefully began to pack away his deadly hobby in his haversack.

'Too many bloody NCOs in this unit,' Underhill mumbled, but loud enough for all to hear.

'Yes, but only one sergeant major,' Lock said. 'For now.'

'Huh. Well, I 'ope we get some more bloody lads when we get to Qurna, that's all,' Underhill said, with a shake of his head. 'Sah,' he added in his usual, belligerent way as an afterthought.

Lock grunted in agreement and turned back to the busy quayside. He gave a shrill whistle and moments later the mangy mongrel pup darted up to them.

'Great, a bloody mutt to stink up the place.'

'Just you show some respect, Sergeant Major, this is your new lieutenant.'

Underhill's face fell momentarily before he realised Lock was pulling his leg. 'Piss off!'

Lock smiled and the others began to laugh. The dog yapped and Lock bent down to rub its ears.

'Another straggler who won't let go,' Underhill sneered.

'He may come in handy, Sergeant Major.'

'If we run outa food, mebbe.'

Again the men laughed. They were in good spirits, obviously eager and looking forward to getting back to the war. Boredom, Lock had quickly realised, was a worse health hazard than a Turk or Arab bullet.

'And, talking of food . . . Where is he?' Lock said, straightening up and scanning the crowds. He raised his hand up. 'Jawad Saleem,' he called.

Underhill was still glaring down at the dog. 'All we need now is one of yer bloody Buddoo mate—'

He abruptly stopped when he spotted the young Arab boy pushing his way towards them, a huge pack of pots and pans upon his back.

Underhill turned and gave Lock a withering look. 'Tell me it ain't so.'

Lock shrugged. 'We need feeding. He can cook.'

'What is this?' Underhill spat, his face turning purple with barely controlled rage. 'You the bleedin' Pied Piper of 'Amlin? We ain't some fuckin' orphanage, sah.'

Jawad Saleem came up to them and threw out a smart salute, then pulled a dead chicken from his waistcoat and held it aloft.

'Very sorry, Captain *as-sayed*, made supply stop,' he grinned.

'Good lad, Sergeant Major Underhill here loves a chook dish.'

Jawad Saleem turned his grin on Underhill. 'I make good chicken dish for you, *as-sayed* Sergeant Major.'

Underhill's jaw began to grind. ''E'll slit our throats, first opportunity.'

His voice was shaking with anger, but the sergeant major knew he was fighting a losing battle, so he snatched up his haversack, and turned on his heels.

The others watched in mild amusement as the sergeant major made his way along the gangplank, shaking his head and muttering under his breath.

'Right,' Lock said. 'Follow our dearly beloved sergeant major. Make your way up to the roof deck and settle down. I'll be along in a while.'

Lock headed to the stern with the dog, its claws clip-clipping over the wooden deck, darting about around his heels. It wasn't as deserted at the rear of the steamer as Lock had hoped, but there was enough space along the guard rail overlooking the slats of the vast wooden stern wheel for him to be alone with his thoughts. Standing nearby were a couple of lanky sepoys from the 22nd Punjabis. They were having a heated debate in their native tongue that involved lots of gesticulating and banging of the guard rail.

132

But one icy glare from Lock was all it took for the two Indians to shuffle away, and before long Lock had the guard rail properly to himself.

When the steamer finally got underway, pulling out of Ashar to begin its five-hour journey northwards up the Shatt al-Arab to the furthest point of the British lines, the chugga-shoosh chugga-shoosh of the stern wheel turning in the water soon brought a hypnotic feel to the voyage. It would, under different circumstances, be a very sedentary way to travel, Lock imagined, letting his mind drift while watching the choppy wake fade off into the hazy distance.

The floods were more evident in the land they passed through now, and as far as the eye could see, the water stretched. It was broken up only by occasional oases of palm trees that were clustered together in little copses or belts. Here and there the flat-roofed, mud-brick Arab villages jutted up. They were built on the slightly higher ground and looked like islands adrift in a vast ocean of milky water. It was as insane a place to wage war as it had been between Basra and Shaiba. The land was totally submerged, which made it impossible for a proper mobile army to function. Even horses would find the going near-impossible. Their destination was only forty miles or so upriver, but against the current and under the stifling, thick and oppressive heat, even the *Mejidieh* seemed to struggle, panting and wheezing with the effort.

Lock stood, hands resting on the guard rail, and stared out at the choppy wake. Amy suddenly pushed her way into his thoughts. He frowned and patted his pockets, suddenly remembering her gift. Taking the package out, he tore off the string and the brown paper, tossing them to the wind. In his hand was a plain wooden

133

box, about twelve inches long by four inches wide and two inches deep. A miniature coffin? he thought with a wry smile. It had brass hinges and a brass clasp. He opened it up

Inside, resting on a deep-red velvet lining, was a beautifully crafted dagger of fine, polished steel, with a smooth carved handle in ivory. Lock lifted the knife out and ran his thumb lightly across the edge of the blade. It sliced into the skin of his thumb like a thumbnail pierces an overripe peach. He sucked the tiny cut and smiled, holding the blade up to let its edges catch in the sunlight.

'Beautiful,' he muttered. Then he peered a little closer. Engraved along the flat edge was the simple legend, *For Kingdom and Country*.

Lock smiled again and slowly shook his head.

'You couldn't even put your name. Silly, stupid, beautiful girl.'

He put the blade back in its box, put it away in his pocket, and fished out a pack of Woodbines. He selected a cigarette, struck a match against the pitted iron of the guard rail, and put the flame to the tip. As he exhaled slowly, the light breeze churned up from the stern wheel blew the smoke back into his face. His eyes smarted and he waved his hand in front of his nose to dissipate the fog cloud.

Fog cloud . . . Early morning mist . . . He frowned, remembering the fat Swiss oilman's words in the prison cell back in Basra.

'Who, who says I assassinated this . . . Süleyman Askerî?' Lock had demanded.

Grössburger had blinked back at him and replied, 'The witness. *Binbaşi* Feyzi.'

'Jesus,' Lock said. 'I remember you now.'

He grinned to himself as he recalled standing on the west bank of the Shatt al-Arab near to the unmanned southern gate of Basra, listening for Wassmuss's invasion party and how he had suddenly caught sight, through the early morning mist hanging over the water, of a lone bellum loaded with a Turk raiding party. And standing at its bow, a Turk officer in a white summer uniform. Lock had called out to him in Turkish, had asked if he was Herr Wassmuss, and the Turk officer had replied, '*No, I am Erkan Feyzi of the Imperial Ottoman Army.*' But the voice was unmistakable, and Lock knew that the officer was Wassmuss in disguise.

'You shifty bastard,' Lock said softly. 'Well, all right then, if you want to play it that way, then so be it.'

A blast from the steamer's horn made the dog start and begin to yap. Lock turned his head upriver. It appeared as if they were nearing their destination at last. He took a final drag on his cigarette, tossed the remainder over the side, then turned away from the guard rail to go in search of his platoon.

CHAPTER NINE

Qurna was a town of some 5,000 inhabitants, situated on the left bank of the Tigris. It was some forty-five miles north-west of Basra, at the end of the Shatt al-Arab, sited at the junction of the Tigris and the former channel of the Euphrates. The British had made camp here on one of the narrow spits of dry land. It was late afternoon now, but the sun was still unbearably hot and, as the *Mejidieh* rounded the bend of the Shatt and headed towards the docks, Lock found himself staring out at a most unusual spectacle, that of what appeared to be a whole brigade practising manoeuvres in boats.

'Crikey, sir, it's just like Cowes week.'

Elsworth, along with Singh, Underhill and the rest of Green Platoon, had joined Lock at the guard rail on the port side of the roof deck, and the young sharpshooter wasn't alone at being agog at the strange scene before him.

Lock had never been to the Isle of Wight, but he knew of it, and Elsworth was certainly right in that the amount and range of vessels certainly did make the gathering look like some regatta.

'Townshend's Regatta,' Lock muttered.

'Sahib?' Singh said.

'Oh, nothing, Sid. Quite a sight, isn't it?'

The big Indian bobbed his head in agreement.

'Only I don't think this is for pleasure,' Lock said.

'I very much am doubting it, sahib.'

They all fell back into a kind of captivated silence, along with most of the troops aboard the steamer, and watched the various companies getting to grips with their amphibious activities. Lock was familiar with the vessel that was most prolific amongst this floating army, the native bellum. They were the flat-bottomed, gondola-like boats that were generally poled along, rather like punting on the Thames. The bellum was narrow, around three-foot wide and twenty-foot long, with a small platform at each end. But they were sturdy, well-balanced and could carry ten men and their kit and ammunition. There were also kalaks in use, another traditional vessel of Mesopotamia, but one that was generally used for downstream transportation. They were rafts of timber supported on inflated goatskins. But, despite being able to carry loads of up to thirty-five tons, and Lock could see a number with mounted guns on board, one bullet striking the goatskin and the whole lot would become unstable and more than likely topple its load into the Tigris.

Lock's attention was distracted from the floating spectacle by a sudden acrid waft of burning metal. Over to the far side of the docks, in an atmosphere of arc lights, sparks and molten solder, he could make out the engineers and sappers working hard at what appeared to be modifying and adding armour of some kind to the river craft. Most of the bellums were being fitted or already had attached, he now noticed, steel plates to protect them from enemy rifle fire. Obviously the sheet metal was in short supply, though, because Lock could also see that many of the boats had armour improvised from mats and dried dates. He shook his head. How the hell that would protect from shrapnel and bullets he couldn't imagine, remembering what it was like back in Barjisiyah Woods when the Turk machine guns opened fire on them and the trees all around were shredded into so many thousands of matchsticks.

'Bloody fools,' Lock said.

His eye wandered up the quay to the naval flotilla. There were three armed launches there, the *Shaitan*, the *Lewis Pelly*, and the *Miner*, all basically small tugboats with armoured shields, as well as two naval horse-boats, both carrying 4.7 guns, a paddle steamer, the RIM *Lawrence*, with a 4-4-inch gun, three sloops, the HMS *Clio*, the HMS *Odin* and the familiar HMS *Espiegle*. Lock had spent time aboard that vessel when Major Ross had managed to secure passage on her when they were racing from Mohammerah to Basra ahead of Wassmuss's invasion force. It gave Lock a warm feeling to know that its captain, the red-whiskered Hayes-Sadler, would be providing invaluable naval support to this ragtag armada. There were also two more steamers already docked, the *Blosse Lynch* and the imaginatively named *P.1*. They were similar to the *Mejidieh*, and would, no doubt, be acting as troop transports.

The *Mejidieh* began to slow, and Lock spotted a familiar figure standing alone on a horseshoe inlet down at the point of land where the Shatt flowed into the Euphrates. As the steamer continued to chug towards the docks, Lock watched the figure until it was lost from sight. The *Mejidieh* slowed, drifting closer and closer towards land. Shouts came up from the quayside, tie ropes were thrown out, and the steamer moved into its designated berth before coming to a complete stop. There was more calling and shouting from below as the steamer's mooring ropes were secured, then the gangplank grumbled and creaked as it was slowly lowered. A great toot exploded from the ship's whistle signalling their arrival.

'All right, lads, let's go say hello to our new home,' Lock said, shouldering his haversack. He pushed his way through the throng of troops towards the gangplank, and joined the file slowly disembarking.

The docks were noisy, smelly and uncomfortable to be in such was the stifling heat, the clatter of diesel engines, the shout of dockhands and NCOs and the miasma of flies. Already Lock could feel his shirt sticking to him like a second skin. The heat radiating up from the dusty, hard baked earth underfoot was suffocating and the flies were insufferable. No matter how many times he waved them off, another cloud quickly descended, trying to get into his eyes, his mouth, his nose. Lock led the men southwards in the direction of the horseshoe inlet where he had spied the familiar figure standing by the water's edge.

On they marched, passing boats of all sizes and forms, strung together along the quayside, until they came to a rickety wooden pier. This was crammed with crates, and at its far end a wooden hoist was busy unloading more supplies from a shallow barge docked below.

Lock glanced across the water to the eastern bank. It was lined with mud-brick and wooden constructed stores above which ran a string of telegraph wires. He followed their line that ran unbroken and all the way northwards, upriver, disappearing into the hazy distance. Lock wasn't surprised at them being here, for he knew well enough the time, money and effort that the Ottoman Empire had spent on a vast communication network. After all, he was involved in its very construction for a number of years prior to the war. He had been working as a civil engineer for the *Société Ottomane des Téléphones* before Major Ross came along and recruited him into British Intelligence's White Tabs unit. He was just surprised that the lines hadn't been cut down or blown up by now.

Lock looked towards the south and could see the docks were coming to an end. He waved his hand irritably in front of his face again, and wiped the sweat from his eyes.

'This way,' he called over his shoulder. Singh, Underhill and the others followed his lead as he picked his way across a scrubby wasteland at the end of which was a number of bellums lined up in dry dock. They came to the bank. This ran down to the small horseshoe inlet that looked out across the waters to where the three rivers met.

Major Ross was standing at the water's edge observing, through a pair of binoculars, the training session out on the river. Lock could see, as he got closer, that the troops nearest to the major out on the water were in fact part of the Mendip Light Infantry. They were all practising in bellums and gufas in the deeper waters of the Euphrates to the south-west of the main town, at a point where a large creek headed back up north. Lock recalled from his map that it led to the tiny settlement of Nikarat.

'Well, we've found the rest of our regiment,' Lock said.

'Jesus, would you look at these fanti idiots,' Underhill smirked, dropping his haversack, and standing, arms folded, with a huge grin across his face.

The rest of the platoon gathered around and stood watching the training exercise unfold, a murmur of amused conversation quickly bouncing around between them.

'Wait here. I'll go talk to the major,' Lock said, and made his way down the muddy bank.

Ross glanced up as Lock came alongside and gave him a pained grimace.

'That bad?' Lock said.

'Bloody awful, laddie. You'd think they'd never seen a boat before. Didn't any of them take a sweetheart out for a row on a pleasure lake?'

Lock couldn't argue with the major. Everywhere his eye fell, the men of the Mendips were poling and rowing and paddling in the most haphazard, uncoordinated way, while red-faced NCOs standing thigh-deep in the water looked on in exasperated frustration.

'Don't stir it like it's a bowl of bloody soup!' shouted one sergeant to his hapless platoon aboard one of the bellums.

'You there! Stop laughing! Stop, I say!'

Lock recognised that voice. It was Bingham-Smith and he looked as red-faced and as exasperated as the rest of the junior officers. He was a little away from the main body of men, just inside the mouth of the creek, trying to direct a team in the art of mastering the gufa.

The gufa was a vessel totally different to the bellum in every way. It resembled a flattened ball of woven reeds covered with pitch, and there was a hole of varying sizes from five to ten feet across at the top in which passengers and freight were put. To propel the thing along one had to paddle, first on one side, and then on the other, rather like steering a canoe. Two or three experienced men can make a good old progress with it, as Lock had seen for himself back in Basra, watching the local Arabs ferrying everything from wooden crates to sacks of grain and even live, bleating sheep across the Shatt al-Arab. However, a novice – and the major was right, for every man here seemed to have not the faintest idea of how to treat a vessel on water – could do little more than make the thing spin around on its own axis. Not only did this make the occupants dizzy, but it also invariably led to frustration then exasperation, which turned then into fits of giggles and then, more often than not, uncontrollable laughter. Matters and progress were naturally made worse by the watching, cheering and goading off-duty Tommies and sepoys that were lining the banks of the rivers.

If Lock didn't know that death and the enemy were only a few miles further north, he would be led to believe that this gathering of men was all part of some elaborate water festival. It was as ridiculous as it was hilarious and pathetic.

'I'd ask you not to laugh, laddie,' Ross said. 'This is serious. These men need to master these tubs. And quickly.'

'Don't slap the water!' Bingham-Smith screamed shrilly.

Suddenly there was a terrific whine as a bullet ricocheted off of the armour-plated bellum nearest to the creek's edge. There was a pause as everyone nearby seemed to freeze. There followed the distinctive crack of a rifle shot and the muddy ground at Ross's feet spat up splattering his boots with dirty water.

'Sniper!' Lock shouted, as he grabbed Ross and flung himself and the major to the ground.

Pandemonium broke out as the watching troops scattered and the NCOs screamed at their men to take cover.

'Jildi! Jildi!'

'Toot sweet, lads!'

'Iggry! Iggry!'

The men in the boats threw themselves into the water.

A third shot cracked and whined overhead.

'Where's it coming from?' Ross said, wiping mud from his face, eyes darting about left and right. He remained lying flat.

'Somewhere behind us, up the creek,' Lock said. He turned on his side and shouted up the bank. 'Elsworth, can you see anything?'

'Not from here, sir,' the young sharpshooter called back. 'Too many trees for cover. But the shots came from the western bank.'

Lock's men had taken cover behind a number of bellums that were up out of the water, in the process of having the armour plating attached.

A stillness had fallen across the water now, with all the troops involved in the amphibious exercise deathly silent, heads down, peering out from their various hiding places for any sign of movement in the undergrowth further up the creek.

'Sir, crawl slowly down into the water. Better cover,' Lock said, and he began to worm his way into the river, belly down. The major followed close behind.

'How many do you think, Lock?' Ross said, scooping mud from the lenses of his binoculars before pressing them to his eyes.

Only their heads were visible above the surface now, but Lock knew that they were still horribly exposed.

'Two, maybe more.'

'Pity we're not practising with live ammunition in those field guns,' Ross said, jutting his chin in the direction of the heavy artillery mounted on the kalak rafts.

'Hang on!' Lock said. 'What the hell . . . ? Pass me your glasses, sir.'

He was keeping an eye on the western bank of the creek and had been distracted by movement in the water on the opposite side. Ross handed Lock the binoculars. Lock adjusted the focus until he could clearly see Bingham-Smith wading out into the water and scrambling into the gufa he'd been trying to train his men to use. There were now six of them crouched down in the boat. There was a tremendous amount of splashing as the vessel began to rotate and the men started to paddle towards the snipers' side of the creek.

Bingham-Smith's distinctive accent carried on the warm breeze as he shouted, 'Faster! Faster!'

'Jesus, what an idiot!' Lock muttered.

The gufa bobbed along, then suddenly began to spin like a top. Lock could see the men inside desperately trying to steady the boat and stop its rotation. Bingham-Smith was gesticulating wildly, but before long the gufa was caught in the current and began to bob back the way it had come and then bounce back down the eastern bank towards the mouth of the river.

'No, no! The other way!' Bingham-Smith screamed.

A glint of light on the western bank caught Lock's eye. He could see a rifle barrel protruding from the reeds near to the water's edge. But the sniper didn't open fire.

'Is that laughter?' Ross said.

Lock strained his ears and grinned. 'I believe it is.'

'What the hell are Bingham-Smith and his men playing at?'

'It's not them laughing, sir. It's the snipers.'

'Really?' Ross said. Lock handed him back the binoculars.

The major dared to raise his head up a little out of the water to try and get a better view.

'You bloody idiots!' Bingham-Smith was shouting, 'Look what you've done!'

Evidently one of his team had kicked a hole in the bottom of the gufa for it was now listing to one side as it rapidly took on water. The laughter from the snipers carried further on the breeze and Lock could now make out the odd word of Turkish.

'Marsh Arabs?' Ross asked.

Lock shook his head. 'Turks.'

The occupants of the gufa made a clumsy attempt at abandoning their vessel, and then the whole thing tipped onto the side and sank within seconds. The men began to swim towards the eastern bank and haul themselves up out of the water.

Lock saw the Turk snipers, two men wearing distinctive kabalaks, the unique form of Ottoman military headgear that resembled the British topi, emerge from the undergrowth. Their laughter was clearly audible now and, with huge grins across their faces, they let off a couple of shots. But their bullets went harmlessly over Bingham-Smith and his men's heads. The Turks clearly had no intention of hitting anyone.

Lock was up out of the water now. He glanced over towards the bellum where Elsworth was sheltering. The young sharpshooter was kneeling, his rifle aimed at the snipers, finger on the trigger, ready for the order to fire. He opened his left eye and looked to Lock for a signal. Lock gave a gentle shake of his head and watched as Elsworth raised his aim a fraction. He fired a shot that showered the two Turks with debris from the palm tree above them. Both men quickly darted back into the undergrowth. Their laughter was slow to fade away as they made their retreat.

Ross pulled himself to his feet and brushed his soaked uniform down.

'See. A laughing stock. Even Johnny's too amused to pick us off.'

'They don't have to, sir, with idiots like Bingham-Smith in command. Look.'

Ross followed Lock's gaze back over to the eastern bank where the last of Bingham-Smith's men was scrambling out of the water and up the muddy bank. Out in the water of the creek was the stricken gufa. But there was also a body, half-submerged nearby, floating on the surface.

Ross peered through his binoculars at the scene, then lowered them again.

'Damn,' he said. He cupped his hands together. 'Bingham-Smith, what the hell happened?'

Bingham-Smith passed his hands through his sodden hair and shook the water away. He glanced out to the stricken gufa, then over to Ross.

'Wasn't shot, sir,' he shouted back. 'Drowned. Got his boot caught—'

'Right-o. Bad luck, Captain. Retrieve the body and report back to camp,' Ross called.

'Bad luck?' Lock said, raising a questioning eyebrow at Ross.

'Don't start, laddie.'

'How long have we got to get this . . . shambles right, sir?' Lock said.

Ross pulled his pipe from his pocket and frowned down into the bowl. He tipped it over and a small amount of muddy water dribbled out.

'General Townshend wants to start at 5 a.m. on the 31st.'

Lock puffed out his cheeks. 'Tomorrow?' He shook his head. These men just weren't ready.

Ross was in tune with Lock's thoughts. 'Oh, most of them are ready, I assure you. Townshend's had his division in training in bellums since the beginning of the month. It's only Godwinson's Mendips, as you can see, that are . . .'

'Useless?' Lock said.

'Raw,' Ross smiled thinly. 'Mostly fresh recruits, that's the problem.'

They began to walk back up the bank towards Lock's waiting platoon, their soaked uniforms already steaming as they dried off in the searing afternoon heat.

'And just where is our esteemed commanding officer? I don't see him here, offering moral support to his troops.'

'Godwinson? Oh, he's somewhere about,' Ross said with an airy wave of his pipe, 'keeping out of the heat. Probably on the *Espiegle* taking in the view.'

'Huh. Well, at least Hayes-Sadler won't be too obliging towards the fool,' Lock said.

Ross shook his head. 'Sadly Hayes-Sadler's no longer captain of the *Espiegle*. He's returned to his ship the HMS *Ocean* and taken her to the Dardanelles. Pity. But his replacement, Captain Nunn, is a good man. You'll like him.'

'Yes, but will he like me?'

Ross gave Lock a withering look. 'But, as I was saying . . . The rest of the troops are ready. Some 126 men per battalion have been trained in using the bellum, and as many above that number as time has allowed, of course.'

'Of course.'

'We've got sixteen boats per company, some thirty-two trained men being necessary for the task of handling the vessels, and a good few more in case of casualties and such.'

They reached the top of the bank, and Lock nodded towards the bellums parked there.

'This armour is intriguing,' he said, running his hand over the rough, thick plates attached to the front and sides of the boats.

'Well, each battalion has a quarter of its boats armoured in this way.'

'What about guns? Heavy artillery?'

'We've mounted machine guns on specially constructed rafts, as are the guns of the 30th Mountain Battery.'

'Quite the armada. Do you think it'll work?'

Ross shrugged. 'I haven't the faintest idea, laddie. I thought Townshend was a Napoleon enthusiast, not a student of the Duke of Medina Sidonia. But, well, I think you need to see the task before us. I'd value your opinion.'

'Very well, sir, I'm listening.'

'No, not here, not in front of this rabble,' Ross said, peering into his tobacco pouch. 'Balls, absolutely sodden. Got any pipe tobacco on you, Lock?'

'No, sir. It'll dry out soon enough if you lay it flat in the sun.'

Ross grunted. 'I suppose so, but I have more in my quarters. Get your men settled at camp and then come along to the observation tower at the northern perimeter. I'll join you shortly.'

'There's something else, isn't there?'

'Whatever makes you say that?'

'Come on, sir, I'm not stupid.'

Ross frowned back at Lock for a moment. He leant a little

closer and lowered his voice. 'There's news about the investigation.'

'Wassmuss?'

Ross leant away and stared back at Lock. There was a touch of surprise in his face, but it quickly vanished. 'At the observation tower. Dismissed, Captain.'

Lock sighed. Bloody secretive bugger, he thought. 'Very well, sir. Come on, lads,' he said, turning to Underhill and the others, 'let's go find our bivouac.'

Lock gave the major a casual salute, then taking his haversack back from Singh, turned on his heels and trudged back northwards with his men in tow.

As they made their way back past the dockyards and into the town, joining a road that was busy with ASC lorries trundling by in choking clouds of dust, Lock's mind was whirring. What news did the major have?

'Christ and bugger,' he muttered. Where was that German bastard? Was he behind the shootings or not? He was beginning to doubt it himself. No, the German had a larger plan. He wanted to see Lock humiliated. Like he himself felt Lock had done to him. But then why . . . ?

Lock pulled up and after a moment Singh and Elsworth halted and turned back to wait for him, puzzled. The dog turned and sat down, wagging its tail in the dust. The rest of the platoon carried on.

'What is it, sir?' Elsworth asked.

'Hush,' Singh said, holding his large, rough palm up to silence the young sharpshooter. His brown eyes were fixed to Lock's profile. Lock was scowling, staring down at the ground.

After what seemed like a long minute, the dog gave a slight

whimper and Lock looked up, noticed his two companions were waiting at his side.

'He's a crafty bastard, isn't he?'

'Sahib?'

'Very crafty. All right. I need to head for the observation tower to take a look at our situation.'

Lock stepped out in front of an approaching lorry and held up his hand. The 40hp Wolseley 6-tonner rattled and squealed to a halt. It loomed above Lock, its engine grumbling like an angry beast, and the metal of its bodywork ticking under the hot sun. Lock rummaged in his haversack and pulled out a leather lens case. He handed the pack to Elsworth, and then clambered up into the open cab. He nodded affably to the sweating ASC corporal sat at the wheel, then turned and leant down to say one last thing to Singh and Elsworth.

'You two catch up with the others and get Jawad to rustle up some food. I'll be along as soon as I can. Take the dog.' The pooch barked at the mention of its name. 'Stay, boy,' Lock said, then sat back and waved for the driver to carry on. With a crunch of gears the lorry jerked forward. Lock could hear the dog yapping and glancing over his shoulder, he could see the mutt chasing after the lorry, with Elsworth trying to catch him. The lorry picked up speed, passed by Underhill, Pritchard and the others, and soon there was nothing for Lock to see behind him but a cloud of dust.

CHAPTER TEN

Just north of Qurna, situated in a cluster of date palms, an observation tower had been constructed that offered a magnificent view of the Turk positions astride the Tigris. The tower was a rickety thing constructed of wooden scaffolding and reminded Lock of a lighthouse on sands, not unlike the ones he'd seen at Burnham-on-Sea in Somerset. It was about a hundred feet high and looked out across the top of the trees it had been built amongst for protection. There were three officers already on the observation platform when Lock made the climb up the narrow wooden ladder to the summit. He recognised one as Lieutenant 'Hazza' Harrington-Brown, the obnoxious drunken friend of Bingham-Smith that he'd last seen at the brothel in Basra. Hazza caught his eye, then abruptly turned back to his whispered conversation with his fellow officers.

Lock caught snatches of their talk, the odd hostile word carried on the light breeze and whirled around him like taunting spirits. It seemed the rumours of his being accused of murdering that Turkish commander had spread like wildfire and, as was the way with men, they were quick to judge and quick to believe the false accusation. He wasn't liked by the officer class anyway, Lock was well aware of that, and this just fed the fires of hatred. He heard the words 'court martial' and glanced across at the officers. All three were looking over in his direction now, all with an expression of disapproving disgust clearly written upon their faces. Lock mouthed a curse back at them, then turned his attention back to the vista laid out before him.

'Bugger you, Wassmuss. It's not going to work,' he muttered to himself. 'I'm going to find you and I'm going to drag you back and make you tell the truth.'

But there was still a nagging doubt pricking at his mind. Lock squeezed his eyes tightly shut, trying to clear his thoughts. His head wound was throbbing. 'Snap out of it, Kingdom!' he said.

Lock opened up the lens case and pulled out a used pair of Carl Zeiss DF model 8 x 26 binoculars that he had picked up the previous day in the bazaar at Basra. He lifted the glasses to his eyes, adjusted the focus, and began to study his environment closer.

From such an elevated position it was easy to see just how the floods had overwhelmed the banks of the river. One of the officers on the other side of the platform said that the view brought to mind the Lake District in England, another of Lake Superior in America. Lock disagreed. To him the floodwaters gave the landscape the air of Erçek and Van, two tranquil lakes he knew well from his time in Turkey. But this vista was anything but tranquil. Looking north over the canopy of trees, Lock's eye followed the river Tigris as it snaked, bloated and milky brown, to the horizon and beyond. To where the enemy lay in wait.

To his immediate left, on the west bank, was a raised portion of land dotted with palms. This was where some of the heavy artillery under Lieutenant Colonel Grier's command, boasting four 5-inch howitzers, two 4-inch guns and two 5-inch guns, were placed. Beyond this, the sand and trees thinned out until they met and were engulfed by a vast area of unfordable swamps and marshes. Even from where he was standing, Lock could taste its sickly-sweet stench as it caught the back of his throat.

Dotted about this great, putrid sea were a number of small yellow sand islands, and these were the redoubts occupied by the Turks, named already by the British commanders as Shrapnel Hill, Gun Hill, Norfolk Hill and One Tower Hill. Beyond these formidable obstacles was the settlement of Alloa, the two brick kilns of Jala and the town of Bahran running along the horizon. From where Lock was standing, they looked like a half-moon of sandhills rising out of the water with some houses denoting a village and what looked to be gun embrasures in a redoubt or two.

Even from this distance, it was easy to make out other redoubts there and see the enemy moving about, such was the clarity of light. Lock pulled the binoculars away for a moment to give his eyes a rest. His stomach growled and his mind turned to food. He was hungry and worse, he had a raging thirst on. Hopefully Jawad Saleem had Bombegy's skill at brewing coffee so that it didn't just taste of hot mud.

Lock glanced over his shoulder towards the ladder. Still no sign of Major Ross. He turned his attention back to the vista.

There was a trail of smoke on the horizon rising lazily into the heavy atmosphere. Lock put the binoculars back to his face, and after adjusting the focus, he studied the two Turkish ships anchored across the river, the steamer *Marmaris* and the gunboat *Mosul*. They would have to be removed if progress was to be swift. He wondered whether the *Marmaris* was the command ship, the rendezvous for Wassmuss's spies. It was a long way away.

Lock could see a number of other masts beyond the two enemy vessels, but they looked to be little more than dhows. Probably anchored at Maziblah where the Turks were known to have heavy gun emplacements, he thought. Further east on the right bank of the river, Lock could see Rotah camp and two others, and then closest to the British lines was the final speck of land named One Tree Hill, appropriate as it was little more than an island with a hill and one solitary gnarled tree, and not a palm tree at that. Running from that Turk position right to the foot of where Lock was standing was more flooded plain. A simple boat bridge connected the two banks.

It looked to be an impossible task, to push the Turks out. There was no way to march towards the enemy and there was no way to outflank them either. It appeared to be a stalemate and Lock wondered just what General Townshend had in mind. He knew the planned attack involved bellums, but he couldn't quite fathom the method beyond the madness.

A meeting had been called for six o'clock that evening involving all the company commanders, including Lock, and he wondered if that was to be his punishment. He lowered the binoculars and checked his watch. Five-thirty. He gave a wry half-smile to himself, what he meant by punishment was 'reward', for the success at Barjisiyah Woods: promotion in rank and in standing within the Mendip Light Infantry. Was he now to have more than just a platoon to look out for? A whole company amounting to some seventy-five men under his wing? As Singh had predicted? He knew Ross would push for this, perhaps Townshend as well. But he couldn't imagine for a moment that his immediate commander, Lieutenant Colonel Godwinson, would agree to such a travesty without substantial pressure, perhaps even a little blackmail or double-dealing, from behind the scenes. After all, Godwinson was all but disgraced for his vast incompetence after sending his half of an entire regiment to their almost complete doom at Shaiba, and against direct orders, too.

If the 1st Battalion of the Mendip Light Infantry hadn't been back in England, and earmarked for France, the colonel probably would've sacrificed them as well. With the death of so many men at Shaiba, the Mendips had practically been rebuilt, for the second time in less than six months, too, the colonel having lost them all in the battle for Qurna back in November the previous year. But Godwinson had somehow not only managed to secure his regiment's future, recruiting new men from India, Egypt and even England, but he had also secured a full colonelship. Friends in very high places, Lock snorted with a shake of his head.

The structure of the Mendips had changed, too, with a number of other promotions. Major Janion, the former commander of C-Company, was now Lieutenant Colonel of the entire 2nd Battalion. B-Company was under the wing of a Major Reginald Isles-Buck and a Captain Sharp, both men Lock had never met or heard of before but whom he took to be, naturally, cut from the same arrogant cloth as the rest of the officer class. A-Company was under the command of Janion's former second, Captain Carver, newly promoted to major. And as for C-Company itself . . . Well, Lock still hadn't had confirmation, but Ross had told him it was his. However, Lock had learnt very quickly that until he was told so from the horse's mouth, the horse in this case being Godwinson, he didn't believe anything. Not that it would really matter, as Lock was still his own boss with his own platoon to use for those special White Tab assignments. However, if he was to be given command of an entire company then perhaps it was a turning point in the attitude of his fellow officers towards him.

Lock felt a brief flicker of happiness wash over him. Then he shook his head. 'Don't be a naïve fool, Kingdom.'

He lifted the binoculars back up again and scanned the vista from left to right, slower this time. How in the hell were they going to push past this lot? he thought. The 2nd Mendip Light Infantry overall was a small force, albeit now at full strength again and ready to be thrown back into action. But . . . Lock scoffed. Thrown to the wolves, more like. Still, he was glad of the problem, at least it would take his mind off Amy.

'Bugger,' he said under his breath. There she was again. No matter what, she always rose to the surface when least expected.

Was she really going to go through with the pretence and let Bingham-Smith think the child was his? Lock knew it wouldn't be the first time in history that a woman had hidden a past liaison behind a marriage and given the impression that the child was her husband's. It would be presumed, no doubt, that it was a product of their lustful and passionate consummation on their wedding night. Lock swore foully. Why the hell was he torturing himself like this? But what if the child . . . had his eyes, had heterochromia? There could be no denying who the real father was then. And there would be no way of hiding the fact. Ever. From anyone. Yes, his heterochromia was from a childhood 'accident', but the defect could be hereditary, couldn't it? He sighed, a wave of sadness flowing over him. The girl was heading for a world of trouble. He'd have to try to talk to her again. Calmly this time, but he knew he had to make her see sense.

'What do you think?'

'That she's a bloody fool.'

'I beg your pardon?'

Lock glanced to his right. Ross had climbed up to the observation tower platform and was now at his side. The major was a little out of breath, but that didn't stop him from beginning his usual routine of filling his pipe.

'The bloke who ordered this attack,' Lock said, lying.

'Come, laddie, it's a challenge, I grant you, but not an impossible one,' Ross said.

'A frontal attack? With no flank support? Suicide.'

Ross nodded. 'Maybe. But you'll get us through.'

'Me?'

'Of course,' Ross beamed, lighting his pipe and gazing out at the enemy positions.

'And what exactly is the objective here, if I may ask. Sir.'

Ross glanced over at the three officers to their right, then took a step closer to Lock and lowered his voice.

'Sir John has told Townshend to drive the enemy from his present positions between the Pear Drop Bend, that's north of Bahran, and Qurna and capture his guns.'

'Yes? Is that all?'

'But also,' Ross continued, 'to push him upriver and occupy Amara, without stopping.'

Lock fell into silence, contemplating the task ahead. The major was right, of course, it wasn't impossible, but it could be a bloodbath, depending on the strength and attitude of the Turks.

'What exactly are we up against?'

Ross, using his pipe as an indicator, turned to face the scene stretching out below them. 'Right, well, the main line of Turkish resistance is Bahran, what, six miles away?

Lock grunted. He'd guessed the distance at near enough the same.

'The Rotah and Maziblah positions are just about visible, but in front of them we have a curtain of redoubts. Norfolk Hill is about 4,000 yards from us, beyond which is One Tower Hill and Two Gun Hill. Nearest to us, opposite Norfolk Hill, rising on that spit of sand, which is actually the east bank of the Tigris, is One Tree Hill. All are supported by the artillery we know to be a further 5,000 yards away at Bahran. Add to this that that position is being supported by the artillery fire from Rotah and Maziblah.'

Lock nodded sagely. This knowledge still didn't help. It still seemed like a thankless task and one that was going to be getting in the way. He was just itching to set off and pick up Wassmuss's trail again.

'I know who Feyzi is,' he said.

But the major wasn't finished with his rundown of the Turk positions yet.

'Then, of course, there's Sakricha, that's a further 4,500 yards from Maziblah. However, before our main force can even begin to attack, there's the matter of the mines. They're strewn across the Tigris channel north of the boom at Fort Snipe down there,' Ross indicated at the raised position below them, to the left, where the heavy artillery was based. 'Our most northerly point of the Qurna defences.'

'Did you hear what I said, sir?'

Ross fixed him with his hazel eyes. 'According to the intelligence I've gathered,' he continued unperturbed, 'the Turkish force comprises a small division of some six battalions, ten guns and around six hundred Mujahidin. Then there's the other name written down in Grössburger's notebook, *Marmaris*. Is it the ship out there?' he said with a jerk of his chin over to the smoke trails on the horizon. 'Maybe. Is it their command ship? Possibly. Then there's the river gunboat *Mosul*, not to mention our dear friends, the Marsh Arabs. There's over a thousand of the blighters installed in the marshes and thick reeds on the west flank of Norfolk Hill and Gun Hill.'

Lock sighed and moved his binoculars to that part of the landscape. The major wasn't going to engage in any other conversation for the time being until he had gone through what lay before them.

'Yes, I can see movement down there, all right,' Lock said. 'If our military advances against the Turk positions, they'll counter-attack or delay any flanking movement we make from the west.' He paused, thinking, adjusting the focus. 'How many guns did you say the Turks have?'

'Two a piece on Gun Hill and on One Tower Hill, as well as at Rotah. Plus four at Bahran.'

'Jesus, sir. That's a bloody strong position they've got.'

'Aye, it is, and all this water doesn't help, either,' Ross said. 'The floods are a good two feet above the level of our camp. I know. I've been out there. Still, the Turks are no better off. In fact, they are spread out and in a worse state really, cut off from one another on those four sand islands, particularly the solitary outpost of One

Tree Hill on the east bank. That's what we will take first. Although it's technically behind enemy lines. Norfolk Hill is closer to our positions, on the west bank. However, if we can take the east bank we will have at least some flanking capability.'

'How deep is the water, do we know?'

'Mostly little more than three feet, but the trouble is the irrigation canals. We've no idea where they are until we hit them, and they can be some twenty feet deep.'

Lock nodded and continued to scan the water.

'There's very little cover, except the reeds, which at least mark the edges of the river itself, or presumably do. But they can't be more than five feet high. No good unless you've got a company of circus midgets at your disposal.'

Ross snorted. 'Not even a Welsh detachment, I'm afraid.'

'Well, that rules out any surprise approach. In daylight.'

'Yes. Townshend's fretting about that and the fact that everything you see rules out any outflanking movement, too.'

'So what the hell are we going to do?' Lock said, lowering his binoculars.

Ross waved his hand in a slow sweeping gesture in front of him.

Lock blinked back at him. 'You are joking? A frontal attack across this lake? Madness.'

'Perhaps, but that's the plan. That little gathering of floating vessels isn't just for a colonial re-enactment of the Henley Regatta to appease the homesick aristocracy. No, Townshend's Regatta is to be our latest weapon in modern warfare.'

Lock snorted. He had called it the very same thing upon arrival.

'That's what the men have christened the little armada down by the quay,' Ross said. 'Townshend's plan will be costly,

162

but he believes it's the best and only way to get the job done.'

'And?'

'Like you guessed, a full frontal attack, but methodically undertaken in successive phases.'

'As in siege warfare.'

The major nodded. 'That's the idea.'

'Do you know, sir,' Lock said, taking his pack of cigarettes and a book of matches from his pocket, 'if I had the position of whoever the Turkish general is out there . . .' He paused, selecting a cigarette from the packet and striking a match, '. . . I'd be rubbing my hands with glee at the bloody defeat I was about to inflict on the damn fool British.' He drew in a lungful of tobacco and exhaled slowly. 'All he has to do is stand firm.'

'Not very helpful, Kingdom,' Ross said after a while.

'No, sir, but it's the truth. And you know it.'

The major puffed away on his pipe, contemplating Lock's words of warning.

'Do you know, laddie, that Shaiba was a pretty damned important battle. I believe it could prove to be a turning point in the war, in the Mesopotamia theatre, that is.'

'How so, sir? The Turks seem pretty solid to me. You and I both know they are a damned better and more competent fighter than our bloody idiot generals give them credit for.'

'Yes, undeniably, but it's their allies, the Arabs, you see. They sense a change. Like a storm on the wind. A number of the Shi'a mujtahids are beginning to distance themselves from their Ottoman overlords and that, of course, will put an end to our German friend's jihad campaign.'

'Wassmuss?' Lock shook his head. 'He isn't going to give up so

163

easily, sir. I know him, he'll never concede defeat. Not until I put a bullet between his eyes.'

Ross nodded his head in agreement and puffed on his pipe some more. 'Yes, but what can he do if the tribes won't play ball? There was an open revolt last month in Najaf and my sources tell of unrest brewing in Karbala. That's only fifty miles south of Baghdad. Once it starts it'll spread like wildfire, and then Wassmuss's plans are finished.'

'He's still very strong in Persia, sir. The whole country is so fractured, what with the Russians pressing from the north and the British barely keeping a lid on things in the south. The centre of the country is a free-for-all.' Lock drew on his cigarette again and shook his head once more. 'No, sir, the only way Wassmuss's plans are finished is when the bastard's dead.'

'Maybe so, laddie, maybe so.'

'I know so, sir. He's out there somewhere, I can smell him, and I aim to get him before he gets to Amy, before he gets to me.'

'The girl is in no danger, Kingdom, not whilst you're away from her. This is the safest place for you to be, for her sake.'

Lock pushed himself away from the rail and turned to face the major. 'You know something, don't you?'

Ross kept his lips tightly wrapped around the stem of his pipe as his gaze wandered about over the Turk positions on the distant horizon.

'Don't I have a right to know?'

'You're a soldier. You have a right to obey orders and a right to die. Nothing more.'

'Excuse me, sir, but you're talking bollocks.'

Ross couldn't help but break into a lopsided grin. 'Well, I

have to keep up appearances, don't I, laddie? Still . . .'

Lock gave a sigh of resignation. 'What do you want me to do?'

Ross beamed back, and patted down his pockets. 'Here, what do you make of this?' From his side pocket he pulled out what looked at first like a stubby stick and handed it to Lock.

Lock turned the object over in his hand. It was a bound piece of metal cable, rusted and pitted. 'Ordinary telegraph cable.'

'Like that?' Ross said, indicating to the telegraph poles and the wires strung between them that ran the length of the east bank opposite.

'Yes. Why?'

'Well, this came from down there not up there,' Ross said pointing down to the murky, fast-flowing waters of the Tigris.

'Very well. That would explain the rust.'

Ross nodded. 'Yes, but this was taken from one of the mines a sapper detail pulled out of the river a few days ago.'

'Tangled?'

Ross shook his head. 'Connected to.'

Lock frowned and studied the cable a little closer. There was nothing out of the ordinary about it that he could see.

'I have a feeling that they are all connected in this way, Kingdom. The mines. And if that's the case then it corroborates one of my intelligence reports.'

'Which is?' Lock was getting a little impatient now. He wished the major would just get to the point so he could get down from this damned platform and go and get some coffee and food in his belly.

'That the whole network of mines that we know litters the Tigris are connected to an electronic switch that—'

165

'That can be set off by one man. Jesus.' Lock's attention returned to the north and his eyes focused on the Turk redoubts that were scattered all the way up to the horizon and beyond. 'It could be anywhere along their lines.'

This was bad news, bad news indeed.

'I know. That's what worries me. If the attack goes ahead . . . *When* the attack goes ahead, no matter how many mines we clear or sweep away, the whole network could still be set off automatically, and then that's the end of that. Townshend's entire force will be blown from here to India.'

'So what's your plan, sir?'

Ross scratched the side of his head with the stem of his pipe, then looked Lock directly in the eye.

'It'll be risky.'

'When isn't it?'

'Quite. Still, there's a hell of a lot of enemy troops out there, not to mention the Marsh Arabs in the surrounding countryside just waiting to snipe at us.'

'I have an idea about the Marsh Arabs.'

'Oh?' Ross raised an eyebrow. But Lock wasn't prepared to elaborate for now, so the major continued to lay out his plan. 'It was before your time, but there was a group of farmers during the Boer War who were highly adept at making quick raids and reconnaissance behind enemy lines. They were very effective, very skilled, and very successful. We did capture and kill one such unit and the only survivor was held under interrogation in one of our concentration camps. When I visited, he told me that he was a *Kommando*.'

'I've never heard of them, sir.'

166

'No, well, we didn't really advertise any Boer successes . . . Politics, propaganda and all that . . . Still, why I'm telling you this is because I want you to be like one of these units now and head upriver to find and disable that electronic switch. As soon as you do, send up a flare, and the assault will begin. The Turks will be confused enough with flares and rifle fire coming from behind their own lines.'

'How so?'

'Well, there'll be just your platoon,' Ross held up his hand to stop Lock butting in. 'Just a moment. There will be you and your platoon, no explosives, no side arms, just rifles, so that the Turks in the redoubts will at first think they are being raided again by some disgruntled Marsh Arabs.'

Lock nodded slowly. 'That could work . . . But you said "platoon". What of my company?'

Ross pursed his lips and shuffled on his feet. 'Ah. Yes. About your company . . .'

'There is no company is there?'

Ross shook his head. 'Sorry, laddie. I tried, believe you me. It was yours but then the rumours . . . You know, of you supposedly having murdered this Turkish officer and of an impending court martial . . . Your promotion has been suspended for the time being, as a company commander, I mean. It took all my power to keep you in this regiment as it was, and with your platoon, not to mention your rank, although Godwinson tried. But as you are technically in the AIF he was powerless to do anything about that. Mind you, I'm sure he's written to the Australian High Command. We'll have to wait and see on that one. But there was no way he was going to let you have command of one of his companies. I'm sorry, but that's how it is. For now. We'll get it sorted, don't you worry.'

'It's all right, sir, I didn't really believe it would happen, anyway,' Lock said. 'I take it you've already had the meeting. For the commanders, that is?'

Ross nodded.

Lock turned back to face out towards the enemy positions. He was about to ask another question and then he stopped, frowning. There was something more that the major wasn't telling him.

'What else?'

'Um . . . How shall I put it . . . ?' Ross hesitated, then shrugged. 'Carver's been promoted, as you know, so C-Company does have a new commander . . .'

'Yes?' Lock had a bad feeling that he wasn't going to like what the major was about to tell him.

'It's Bingham-Smith.'

Lock was momentarily stunned. And then he let out a single mocking laugh, shaking his head. 'You have got to be kidding.'

'I wish I was. But nepotism is rife in this army of ours, as if you didn't know that already.'

'I thought the little shit was an assistant provost marshal? A base-wallah, safely tucked up in the barracks back at Basra.'

'Not a glamorous enough position for the future husband of Amy Townshend, it seems.'

Lock felt a sudden surge of angry betrayal. 'General Townshend's behind this, isn't he?'

Ross shook his head. 'I think it is probably more likely to be pressure from Lady Townshend. Sorry, laddie. Anyway, did you really think Godwinson would let a nephew of his not have the chance at proving his bravery on the front lines? He'd have Bingham-Smith as his second in command if he could. Can you imagine? The whole thing's a joke. Assistant provost marshals are supposed to be combat-experienced, not the other way around. Godwinson's already trying to push for Bingham-Smith's rank to be that of major, that's the army equivalent to assistant provost marshal. I'm afraid I put a stop to that little farce. Had a quiet word in General Townshend's ear.'

'That's good of you.'

'Oh, come, come. You didn't want the responsibility of a company, did you? Not really? All that paperwork? Having to act upon Godwinson's battle directives? This way you can remain independent, to go about as you please, to have the freedom—'

'To do your bidding,' Lock interrupted. 'Don't try and bullshit a bullshitter, Major. I'm not stupid. I'm more use to you as . . . this *Kommando* than as a company commander having to lead seventy-five or so men into battle.'

Ross smiled wryly. 'Well, perhaps. But I am right, aren't I?'

'And the *Marmaris*?'

'One thing at a time, laddie.'

Lock wasn't happy. He was angry and frustrated and . . . He sighed. The major *was* right. He didn't want the responsibility, but he did want the respect. All right. He was back to where he started. So what? He'd said it before and he'd say it again, he would prove his worth in his own way. Sod the lot of them.

'And my rank?'

'You're still a captain. For now.'

Lock scoffed again. 'How long have I got?'

Ross frowned. 'Got? Oh, yes, your mission . . . Good,

169

good . . . Glad you came round. Not that I didn't think you would. Well, Townshend wants to set off at dawn. The bombardment of the Turkish redoubts will start at 5 a.m. and then the advance is scheduled for an hour later. He's worried that if we sit and wait here any longer, we'll lose more men to heatstroke and sunstroke than we will to enemy bullets.'

The major gave a heavy sigh and stared off towards the horizon.

Lock knew Ross was troubled by events to come, more so than normal, and he was aware just how many fronts the little Scot was fighting on.

'Don't worry, sir. What you have said in the past is right, about my proving my worth in the field. If I can pull this little task off, then perhaps those officers keen to see me fall will think again. I know they'll never accept me as one of their own, but if I can earn their respect, even grudgingly, that's a start.'

Ross gave Lock a warm smile.

'Aye, laddie, that's the spirit. Now, tell me,' he said taking Lock by the elbow and steering him back over towards the ladders to begin their descent down from the platform, 'what it is you propose about the troublesome natives in the marsh?'

CHAPTER ELEVEN

Night had fallen swiftly and with it came total darkness. The heat hadn't let up, so baked was the earth, but the burning sun and the threat of sunstroke at least wouldn't trouble the men for a few hours. Even the flies had gone. They were replaced by clouds of mosquitoes. Then, around 2 a.m. the moon rose and a pale, silvery light spread out across the surrounding floods like a glistening white fire.

Lock had arranged for the local sheikh of the nearby Marsh Arabs to meet with him at the sight of an old ford, just north of the boat bridge where the marsh and the sand dunes ran down to the water. The ford was used by the Marsh Arabs to cross their livestock over the Tigris during the dry season, when the river was less treacherous and flooded. Right now, the dark waters were flowing by at a terrific speed.

Above the roaring, inky blackness, Lock, jacketless with his sleeves rolled up, was deep in conversation with a gesticulating Arab. He was a tall, painfully thin man, barefoot, dressed in a long, ragged shirt open at the chest, which revealed the dark-brown skin taut over his ribcage. On top of lank, greasy black hair he wore a loosely wound kufiya headcloth. A worn, black cloak was draped over his left shoulder. He carried no visible weapon, not even a knife.

'*My dear Ahmad. Shokran, shokran. You are a good friend and you have done me a great a service*,' Lock said in Arabic, careful to emphasise that the Arab had been helping him personally and not the British in general. '*Please take this as a symbol of my gratitude. Go in peace. Maa as-salaamah.*'

The Marsh Arab took the bag of coin from Lock's hand, bowed his head graciously and gave the gesture of farewell. He then turned and scuttled off back up the bank. When he got to the summit there were two officers standing there. Lock couldn't be sure but he thought he recognised the figure on the right as Bingham-Smith. The Arab nearly bumped into them, dodged sideways and disappeared over the summit. The two officers were watching him go when there came a shout from over their shoulders.

''Ere, 'ere, mind yer backs, sahs!'

Sergeant Major Underhill's gruff voice was unmistakable and Lock allowed himself a wry smile as he watched the two officers jump out of the way. Underhill and five sepoys from Green Platoon mounted the summit, carrying a bellum between them. They stumbled, skidded and slid down the muddy bank until they reached the water's edge where Lock was standing. They lowered the boat down.

'Good lads. Take a breather,' Underhill said, wiping the sweat of exertion from his brow with his rolled-up sleeve. The sepoys slumped down where they stood, glad for a respite.

'This armour plating looks cumbersome, Sergeant Major,' Lock said, looking over the bellum. It was the same familiar vessel, but modified by the engineers, and Lock wasn't impressed with the so-called improvements. 'I saw the engineers attaching these plates when we arrived, but on closer inspection . . . they just won't do.'

''Ow so, sah?'

'It's not just open water, is it, all around us, but reed marsh of varying denseness. Are you not forgetting what we crawled through on the east bank of the Shatt al-Arab outside of Basra? When we discovered Wassmuss's little armada?'

Underhill was rubbing his chin and casting his eye over the armour. The plating projected over both gunwales for several feet and dropped to water level.

'They're really going to hamper our progress if we end up in the reeds, and I think it highly likely that we will do, seeing as they offer us the only cover,' Lock said.

'So what yer sayin'? It's gonna takes us bloody ages to remove this lot,' Underhill said, irritation already building in his voice.

Lock shook his head. 'I agree, but I have a better idea. Go fetch another.'

'Another?'

'Bellum, Sergeant Major, bellum.'

'But—'

'Do it,' Lock snapped, turning away. Conversation over. He stepped down to the water's edge and pulled out his pack of cigarettes.

Underhill stood rooted to the spot for a moment in exasperated silence. 'Right you lazy black bastards,' he said, 'you 'eard the man, up and fetch another bloody barge.'

He tramped off back up the muddy bank muttering under his breath as he went. The five sepoys groaned, but pulled themselves to their feet and made after the sergeant major.

'I say, Lock . . . Can I have a word?'

Lock glanced over his shoulder, cigarette dangling from his lips, match at the ready. Major Carver and Bingham-Smith were picking their way down the bank towards him. Both officers were wearing the summer British Service caps with the inbuilt sunshade that could be lowered to cover the back of the neck. Carver approached, but Bingham-Smith held back. Lock had last seen Carver over a month ago in the officers' mess tent at the army encampment outside of Mohammerah in Persia.

'Sir,' Lock said, nodding, putting the lighted match to his cigarette. Then he looked to Bingham-Smith. 'Recovered from your little swim, Smith?' he called.

Bingham-Smith turned his head away and made a show of studying the bellum that Underhill and the sepoys had deposited nearby.

'That filthy Arab fellow . . .' Carver said in his distinctively impeccable diction, '. . . Did I see you give him money?'

'Sir.' Lock inhaled deeply.

Carver narrowed his hazel eyes and his thin mouth curled up. 'Look here, Lock . . . I don't think—'

'No, sir, I imagine you don't,' Lock said, slowly letting a cloud of tobacco smoke escape from his mouth.

'I beg your pardon, Captain?' Carver said, the pencil moustache twitching above his top lip as a look of indignation clouded his youthful face.

'White Tab business. Sir.'

Carver glanced over to Bingham-Smith as if looking for moral support.

'Lock, you—' Bingham-Smith said.

'It's *Captain* Lock, Assistant Provost Marshal.'

Bingham-Smith snapped his jaw shut, and scowled.

'Well, Captain, I am your superior officer,' Carver interjected, 'and I insist *you* tell me what the hell is going on here. You are in my company and under my command.' He stepped forward a pace and pulled Lock's arm to make him turn to face him.

Lock looked down at Carver's hand resting on his forearm and then slowly raised his eyes to meet Carver's.

The young major swallowed and let go. He cleared his throat, shifted uneasily on his feet and his eyes fell, as so many men's eyes had done before him, to the bullet hole just above the left breast pocket in Lock's tunic.

Lock pondered on whether to keep up his aloof manner, but inside he was smiling. He just couldn't stop himself from being obnoxious to these kind of men, these officers with their holier-than-thou attitude, the way they spoke to their so-called inferiors, their general manner in dealing with the lower ranks. It stank and it left a nasty taste in Lock's mouth, a taste he wanted to hack up and spit right back in to their smug faces. He took a last, long drag on his cigarette and let out a sigh, tossing the end away into the water. He wished Ross was here to field these inevitable questions. But the major was with General Townshend and the other senior commanders briefing them on

Lock's forthcoming *Kommando* raid. Lock removed his slouch hat and passed a hand through his sandy hair. It was beginning to grow thick again, though he could still feel the raised wound where the bullet had passed, a constant reminder of just how close he had come to shuffling off this mortal coil. He beamed back at Carver.

'Major. Sir,' Lock said calmly. 'I may be in your company, which is under your overall command, but my men and I are not. I hold a commission in the Australian Infantry Force. Note the flashes on my uniform. My subsequent' – he paused here, searching for the right word – 'attachment to the Mendip Light Infantry was arranged by General Townshend himself. I operate outside of the normal chain of command. I'm sorry, but that is a fact. If you have any complaints you will have to take them up with Major Ross, who, I'm sure, will pass on your worries to the general. Now, I don't want you to think me rude,' Lock smiled, to which Carver gave a snort of disbelief, 'so I will let you know the gist of my mission.'

Carver glanced over to Bingham-Smith, then back to Lock again. He scowled. 'Well?' he snapped, clearly growing increasingly frustrated with Lock's roundabout way of coming to the point.

'I have been directed to clear the mines ahead of the main attack,' Lock said. 'That "filthy Arab", as you so eloquently put it, has just been helping me to do just that.'

Carver frowned. 'I don't understand, Lock. Surely *they* were the ones who planted the damned things in the fir—'

Lock shook his head. 'The Turks trust them about as much as you do. Sir. Ahmad and his tribe live by the river. They live off the river. They *are* the river. They see everything, they know everything, and it stands to reason that they watched their Turk overlords lay the mines in the first place. Therefore I offered a reward of four hundred rupees for each and every mine my good friend and his fellows discovered.'

Carver glanced over to Bingham-Smith once again, who gave the merest of shrugs. The two officers, it would seem, couldn't argue with the logic.

'Granted they won't have found them all,' Lock continued, 'as the German engineers – Yes, I got that little bit of information from our Arab friend, too – the German engineers have littered the river with mines. But it's a start. The effect has also been marvellous in stopping the Arabs sniping at us, too. Hundreds of them since dusk have spent their time hunting for the mines. Did you not see the activity on the river this evening?'

Carver shook his head. 'I've been training with my me—'

'Of course you have. Sir.' Lock's focus shifted to over Carver's shoulder. 'Ah, you'll have to excuse me now, my platoon is back. Time is of the essence.'

Lock stepped away from Carver. Underhill and the sepoys were making their way down the bank once more, lumbering a second armoured bellum between them. Following close behind were Singh, Pritchard, Elsworth and the rest of Green Platoon. They were all carrying rifles, equipment and supplies. Bingham-Smith skipped out of their way as the boat was lowered down near to the first one. Jawad Saleem came running over the rise, a large metal tea urn strapped to his back, and with the dog bounding around his feet.

'Right,' Lock said, 'I want the two boats side by side, attached for stability, then reverse the armour plates so that they don't project below the level of the gunwales. Got it?'

Underhill nodded. 'Aye, that should work. At least we'll still 'ave protection from any rifle fire.'

'Well, Sergeant Major, I'm hoping we won't run into any.' Lock glanced over his shoulder to check he was out of earshot of Carver and Bingham-Smith, then lowered his voice. 'It's a *Kommando* raid, not a full-on attack.'

Underhill gave a grunt of acknowledgment and set about organising the sepoys to their task, barking orders left and right. Lock noted that the sergeant major appeared to be in his element again and even pondered if he could finally trust the man. Then he shook his head softly.

'Don't get too complacent, Kingdom,' he said to himself. 'Not where Underhill is concerned.'

Lock stood and watched as the sepoys eagerly set about tackling the armoured plating, glad to have something to do at last, no doubt. Pritchard and Elsworth were checking each and every rifle, while Singh and the other sepoys took up tools and began to remove the armour plating from the first bellum.

Earlier, Lock had gathered the men together to brief them on their mission. Standing away from the sea of white canvas tents that were nestled beneath a canopy of date palms at the water's edge, Lock surveyed his platoon all sat around him in a semicircle, giving each man a moments full attention, etching their features in his mind. He had a number of new recruits now that brought his platoon not just back up to size, but almost to the minimum regulation quota of twenty-five. It was under that, of course, but seventeen men would be enough for his needs. The new men were all Indian sepoys, all Sikhs, which suited Lock fine. They were hard workers and disciplined soldiers, so Singh assured him. But the big Indian was delighted with them, and that was good enough for Lock.

Of his original group, Lock had promoted Chopra, Toor and Ram Lal to lance naik, with Elsworth also being given the equivalent rank of lance corporal. Pritchard was a sergeant and Singh was of the same rank but under the Indian title of havildar. Though still a sergeant major, Lock had gained a rare mumble of gratitude from Underhill when he presented him with his promotion to regimental sergeant major, an appointment that was even signed off by Godwinson, much to Lock's surprise. Not that it would have mattered if he hadn't anyway, for Townshend had given his full blessing already. Undoubtedly Ross had a hand in persuading the colonel to accept, but clearly had caught him on a good day.

Lock had no junior officer and that suited him fine, because he would be splitting the platoon into squads and then sections at some point, and each section would have a leader, an experienced man. Age didn't matter, they were all young, except for himself and the senior NCOs; combat time was what counted here. With Bombegy behind bars back in Basra, Jawad made up their numbers as the newly appointed cook, to nineteen, including Lock himself, and thus far the lad seemed to be coping. At least no one had the Mesop trot yet, anyhow. Besides, Jawad and the dog had bonded and that was a blessing, for Lock really didn't want to find the hound following him into a battle zone. He had enough to worry about with keeping his men alive without being distracted by a four-legged friend. And so Jawad would stay safely behind the lines with the animal for company.

Lock fished out a cigarette, lit it, and nodded his head in satisfaction as he exhaled. He stood smoking a while, watching and listening to the men chatter amongst themselves. He had a platoon again. He just hoped he could keep them alive this time. Lock glanced at his watch, then tossed the spent cigarette aside, and pulled a folded sheet of paper from his side pocket. Using his new knife, he pinned the paper to the nearest tree. It was a map of the area.

'All right you lot,' Lock said. 'Listen up, and listen up good.'

Hush fell over the men and Lock waited until all eyes were on him.

'We have a task set us by our dearly beloved Major Ross,' Lock said with a wry smile. 'One in which he probably hopes I won't come back from.'

There were a number of knowing chuckles from amongst the men, plus a few concerned glances from the new sepoys. But Lock didn't let this worry him, they would all be up to speed soon enough once out in the field.

'However,' Lock continued, 'we do get to be the first to push through enemy lines. Now,' he said, pointing at the relevant sections of the map, 'it seems our German friends have been encouraging their Ottoman allies to litter the Tigris with mines. While most of them will be cleared up to the bridge of boats, the rest of the river north of Fort Snipe is inaccessible, seeing as Johnny has redoubts on both banks. But, although there will be minesweepers leading the attack, there is a rumour that Johnny has gone and connected all the mines together via a telegraph wire and that he can set the whole bloody lot off with the throw of an electric switch.'

The men began to mutter excitedly to one another.

'Shut it!' Underhill bellowed, to instant effect.

'Our first objective is here,' Lock said, pointing to the map once more, 'One Tree Hill, on the east bank. Once this is taken, a squad will be left to guard any prisoners, while the rest of us move on upriver in search of the switch. As soon as the switch is located,' Lock continued, 'we disable it and then send up a flare signal. This will be the trigger to start the main assault by our forces on the Turkish positions. We will then drop back and await Lieutenant Colonel Blois Johnson's 22nd Punjabis to arrive, then we too will join up with the main thrust. Hopefully we'll be in Amara by this time tomorrow. Questions?'

It was an unusual thing for an officer to ask his men if they had any input or queries. The new recruits looked taken aback, but the others were used to Lock's style of leadership. He would rather any worries or gripes were aired now than later, particularly from Underhill. He set his gaze on the sergeant major, but Underhill just stared blankly back.

Pritchard raised his hand. 'Do we know how well fortified One Tree Hill is, sir?'

'A garrison, Sergeant, consisting of no more than twenty Arab irregulars.'

'And what if this . . . switch is at One Tree'ill?' Underhill said.

'Then, Sergeant Major, we shan't have to risk our bloody necks going further behind Turkish lines on a damned fool treasure hunt.'

Underhill grunted, but seemed satisfied that caution was an option.

Lock scanned the men and his eyes rested on Singh.

'Sid? You look troubled.'

Singh looked up and bobbed his head. 'Not troubled, sahib, merely struck by a thought.'

'Which is?'

'Will the Turks not hear our gunfire when we attack One Tree Hill? It will raise the alarm, this is for certain.'

Lock indicated to the map. 'Norfolk Hill is here, two miles to the south-east, and One Tower Hill – here – is on the opposite bank, about a mile away. So even if a sentry or lookout at one of these redoubts happens to be looking in the direction of One Tree Hill rather than at the British lines, he may only catch a muzzle flash. The plan is to overcome One Tree Hill in relative silence. However, if we are overheard, then I am hoping to give the impression that it is a Marsh Arab raid, nothing more.'

Underhill shook his head, but was careful not to voice the exasperation that Lock could see written across his face in front of the new recruits.

'Trust me, Sergeant Major,' Lock said, 'it *will* work.'

Underhill turned his scoff into a cough, and put his clenched fist to his mouth.

The sepoys began to mutter again and Lock quickly snapped them out of it by clapping his hands.

'Enough.'

The men quietened down once more and Lock waited until he had their full attention.

'This is war, lads, and we are soldiers. This is our duty and this is our mission' – he tapped the map with his finger – 'whether you think it stupid, suicidal or just plain impossible. But together we can, and we will, succeed. I will be with you all the way, at the front, the first into any building, the first into any firefight. The RSM and Havildar Singh will be at your side, Sergeant Pritchard and Lance Corporal Elsworth will have your backs.'

Lock let the words sink in for a moment, then gave a quick, winning smile.

'Besides, I'm not impressed with Qurna. It's supposed to be the site of the Garden of Eden, but as far as I can see, it's just a collection of filthy lanes and mud and reed hovels, with a few brick houses, barracks and a Customs House thrown in. And I'll be damned if I can find any bloody apple trees here. Just sodding dates.'

There was a ripple of laughter, added to a few words and nods of agreement.

'But,' Lock continued, 'I hear that the Turks have fruitful orchards in Amara and I'd like to see those for myself. Anything to get away from these goddamned floods. And Amara's that way,' he indicated over his shoulder, 'through the Turkish lines. So are you ready to lead the way out of this mosquito-infested biblical hellhole?

'Sahib!' came the uniform cry.

'Good, then let's get to work.'

. . . To work. The clang of metal on metal brought Lock back to the moment and his eyes refocused on the men battling at changing the configuration of the armour plating on the bellums. His gaze fell on Jawad and the dog. They were a little away from the work detail, playing with each other, the gurgling, steaming urn resting on the bank beside them. He would have to make sure that the lad didn't try and follow them on the mission.

Underhill arched his back and swore. 'Oi, Abdul, let's be havin' some char. 'Op to it, you little runt.'

Jawad jumped to his feet, grabbed the urn and hoisted it up onto his back. He jangled across to the boats. The men downed tools and gathered round the Arab lad as he began to pour hot, steamy tea into tin mugs and pass them out.

'Captain Lock?' a clipped voice called.

Lock turned and was surprised to see that Carver and Bingham-Smith were still down by the water's edge. He didn't say anything, but instead hunted out his pack of Moguls. He struck a match against the rough worn part of his Sam Browne belt, and cupping the flame, lit a cigarette. He blew out a long, slow trail of blue smoke and waited for Carver to say his piece.

'I note,' Carver said after an awkward pause, 'that you have no lieutenant. Since your promotion to . . . er . . . captain, that is.'

'Sergeant Major Underhill and Havildar Singh are more than capable of fulfilling those duties,' Lock said, guessing what was coming next.

Only Lock's guess was way off. Carver wasn't about to land him with some spotty aristo subaltern. No, he was about to be a damned sight more vindictive.

Carver shook his head. ''Fraid not, old chap. Orders. You may be White Tab and all that, but you're still in the Mendips, and the chain of command must be upheld. I'm now in command of A-Company, naturally . . .'

'Naturally,' Lock said.

Carver glared back, then continued. 'Which leaves a vacancy at the top of C-Company.'

'Yes . . .' Lock said with an element of hesitation and dread.

'Bingham-Smith here—'

'Is to be my lieutenant? Very well, if you in—'

Carver was shaking his head again and his thin mouth had curled up into a smug grin.

'No, no, Captain, quite wrong, I'm afraid,' he said. 'Harrington-Brown is to be your lieutenant, Bingham-Smith here, *Acting Major* Bingham-Smith I should say, is your new company commander.'

It took all of Lock's willpower to keep his face blank, to keep his hands from scrunching up into hard fists, but inside he was raging. He knew of this already, of course, as Ross had broken the news, but he still felt as if he had been punched in the guts, and his head was swimming. He took a long pull on his cigarette, holding the smoke in until it stung his lungs.

'Two hyphens for the price of one. How very decent of you. Sir,' Lock mumbled, as he exhaled.

'Eh? What's that Lock?' Carver said.

'I said, "acting *major*?",' Lock lied.

Bingham-Smith was standing a few paces away, beside the water, face half in shadow. But even from where Lock was, he could see the arrogant smirk on Bingham-Smith's lips. Lock ran his eyes over Bingham-Smith's uniform. He hadn't noticed before, but the young faux aristocrat was no longer dressed as an assistant provost marshal, but in the khaki of the regular army. He wasn't wearing a tunic with shoulder insignia, either, but one with the older style cuff insignia. However, it still only had the two rings of braid and three stars indicating a captain.

Bingham-Smith caught Lock's puzzled expression and self-consciously folded his arms behind his back.

'My . . . er . . . my promotion isn't . . . you know, official yet,' he said. 'But it will be. In time for my engagement party, Lock.'

'Like uncle, like nephew,' Lock said.

'What do you mean by that?' Bingham-Smith said, stepping over to him.

'Your uncle, Godwinson, a lieutenant colonel who likes to pretend he's a full colonel. And now you, his nephew, an assistant provost marshal who is, somehow, now a captain. But a captain who is pretending to be a major.'

There was a flash of anger in Bingham-Smith's eyes and he took a futher step towards Lock, fist half-raised. But he stopped himself from reacting fully, the memory of their last encounter in the brothel still smarting. He forced a thin smile and dropped his hand again.

'Maybe so, Lock. However, I will remind you that assistant provost marshal is of equal rank to major. So, technically, I do not need a promotion. I am a major already, to all intents and purposes. Just some tedious paperwork to be sorted out. But at least I am made to be an officer. It's in the breeding, you know. Ever since I was head boy at Trent College—'

Lock sighed heavily. 'Spare me the personal history lesson, Smith.'

'That joke's wearing a little thin, old chap,' Bingham-Smith said.

'It's not a joke. Smith.'

'Enough, gentlemen,' Carver said, raising his hand between the two men. 'It is, as Bingham-Smith says, Lock, a matter of formalities.'

'So he's actually a captain?' Lock wasn't ready to let the matter rest just yet.

'Er . . . yes. But—'

'Then as senior captain, this is my command.'

Carver went silent. He was blustering, trying to find an intelligent response, but couldn't quite work out the words. 'Look here, Lock, I—'

'Until his promotion comes through,' Lock added. He knew he wasn't going to win this argument.

Carver stared back at him, eyes narrowed. 'Very well. But as the *pending* company commander I insist that he accompany you—'

'On this mission? Are you serious?'

'Deadly.'

'It will be,' Lock said, giving Bingham-Smith a withering look. 'However, I will remind you, sir, that this is a White Tab mission. It's not a place for—'

'Godwinson's direct orders,' Carver interrupted.

Lock shook his head in disbelief. The stupidity and arrogance of these officers was astounding. They'd get them all killed. He glanced back to Bingham-Smith. His face was half in shadow, but Lock could still see the smirk on his lips. He turned his gaze back to Carver.

'All right,' Lock said, 'but he's not up to speed with the way we do things in my platoon, so for now Bingham-Smith will work under my sergeant major's guidance.' His tone made it quite clear that it wasn't a debatable suggestion.

Carver glanced at Bingham-Smith, who narrowed his eyes suspiciously, but then gave a curt nod. 'Agreed,' he said.

'One last thing,' Lock said.

'Yes . . . ?' Carver said with trepidation.

'*My* mission, *my* command.'

Carver put his hands behind his back and slowly raised himself up on his toes and then back down again, making a show of considering Lock's demand.

'Very well, Captain,' he said. 'Your mission, your command. But Bingham-Smith goes along. As an observer.'

'You leave me with little choice, Major.'

'Jolly good,' Carver said, with an audible sigh of relief. 'I'll send Harrington-Brown down to you. Bings,' he nodded to Bingham-Smith. Then he turned on his heels and made his way back up the muddy bank as quickly as he could should Lock try to complain any further.

Lock watched the major go with contempt, cursed aloud and leant to one side and spat to the ground.

'You really are the most vile man.'

'Piss off, Smith.'

Bingham-Smith chuckled and moved a little closer to Lock. 'There you go,' he said. 'Such breeding. It is little wonder that Amy chose me.'

Lock glared back at Bingham-Smith's obnoxious face. His left eye was puffy and half-closed, and although his nose was swollen, it didn't look broken. For now, Lock thought wryly.

'She didn't choose you, though. Did she? Her parents did.'

Bingham-Smith smiled thinly. 'The bloodline must remain pure, old chap.'

'What the hell is that supposed to mean?' Lock was using all his will power to keep his voice calm, to stop himself from grabbing hold of Bingham-Smith and pitching him head first into the Tigris. He clenched his jaw.

'The future, Lock,' Bingham-Smith said, with an airy wave of his hand. 'Heirs and all that.'

'You mean you and Amy.'

'Why, of course, Lock. Amy and I shall breed, breed fine, strong babies. We shall provide England with future dignitaries, prime ministers, upstanding pillars of society.'

'Like your good self?'

Bingham-Smith ignored Lock's sarcasm. 'It's more than just a marriage of two people, don't you know? It's the union of two distinguished families, a forging of houses, a duty to God, a duty to King and country.'

'For King and country? My god, you really do believe that crap, don't you?'

Bingham-Smith turned his body to face Lock, and put his hands behind his back in a very relaxed pose. He was smiling and shaking his head softly as if addressing an irksome child.

'Whereas you, my dear fellow, are all for Kingdom and country, aren't you?' He snorted at his own joke.

Lock's hand went to his belt, and he touched the hilt of the knife Amy had given him. He smiled to himself. If only Bingham-Smith knew what was inscribed there.

'When our child is born, Lock, it will be one of the proudest moments of my life,' Bingham-Smith said. 'Provided she bears me a son. Amy seems to be under the impression that it will be a girl.'

Lock shot Bingham-Smith a dark look.

But Bingham-Smith misread his reaction and chuckled again. 'Oh, dear chap, you didn't know, did you? Oh, capital, capital.'

Lock kept a straight face. He so wanted to tell the odious prick what he knew to be the truth, but Amy's pleas of secrecy made him bite his tongue. Lock cleared his throat. 'When?' he said. 'When is she due?'

Bingham-Smith stretched his shoulders back. 'Christmas.'

Lock put his hand to his face and rubbed the bristle on his chin. Eight months.

'Perhaps you are just a little . . . concerned. About your future, I mean.'

Again Lock was puzzled by what Bingham-Smith was getting at.

'I hear rumours that a court martial is on the cards.' Bingham-Smith could barely suppress his glee at the prospect.

'Do you now? For your uncle's incompetence at Shaiba?'

Bingham-Smith's face hardened. 'You are the incompetent one, Lock. Nothing more than a killer.' His hand went subconsciously up to his bruised face and he narrowed his eyes, leaning forward a little. 'You are little more than a filthy street brawler, a murdering brute and I shall, of course, offer my services to the prosecution.'

Lock jerked forward as if to attack.

Bingham-Smith flinched and stepped back involuntarily. But Lock was faking and was smiling cruelly back. Bingham-Smith straightened up, collecting himself, pulling his tunic into shape. Then, clearing his throat, he jutted his chin out and looked down his long nose, grey eyes cold with contempt.

'I'm not afraid of you, Lock.'

'You should be, Smith. It will be dangerous out there, more dangerous than anything you've ever even imagined. And you'll be close, close to me all of the time. In the dark. I could easily slit your throat and no one would see. I'm a murderer, remember? What have I to lose?'

Bingham-Smith opened his mouth to reply, but stopped short. He smiled ruefully back at Lock. 'The more you open your filthy mouth, the more you dig your own grave.'

'I'm good at that, Smith. All right, if you insist on being part of Green Platoon then you best get on up the bank and join the men,' Lock said, with a watery smile. 'We all get our hands dirty in this platoon, no matter what our rank.'

'I don't follow.'

'Go and help the lads turn those armour plates.'

Bingham-Smith's gaze followed Lock's over to where the sweating, cursing group were busy working on the two armoured bellums. He had a look of bewildered disgust across his face.

'But that's . . . coolie work, something the damned sepoys do . . .'

'Then go back to the officers' mess and take tea with Carver.' Lock tossed his cigarette end into the water, turned his back on Bingham-Smith and trudged over to his men. He scooped up a crowbar and started hacking away at one of the bellums alongside Singh and Ram Lal. Both Indian's were shirtless, their torsos already grimy and glistening with sweat.

Out of the corner of his eye, Lock could see Bingham-Smith standing looking up at them, mouth agape. Then, walking tall and erect, chin held high, he made his way over to the second bellum where Underhill was working, muttered a curse, and snatched up a hammer. He began to pound feebly away at one of the plates.

'Not there, sah, you bloody idiot,' the sergeant major yelled at him. 'There!'

Lock began to chuckle to himself.

'You will soon have Sahib Bing Ham Smith in shape, sahib.'

'Maybe, Sid. But keep an eye on him, will you?'

'You do not trust him, sahib?'

'You know the answer to that, Sid,' Lock said, giving his Indian friend a knowing glance.

Singh bobbed his head in understanding and returned to the iron plate he was wrestling with.

'By the way, Sid, did you get them?'

Singh straightened up, winced, and wiped the sweat from his face. 'Yes, sahib.'

'Those ribs troubling you, Sid?'

Singh shook his head. 'I am fine, sahib.'

The Indian put his mallet down and, with Lock at his side, walked over to the rotting rickety fence that ran partly along the crest of the bank. There was a pile of equipment at the foot of one of the fence posts and Singh knelt down and began to rummage in one of the haversacks. He pulled out two folded dark-blue cloths and passed them to Lock.

'Good work, Sid.' Lock folded one of the cloths tighter and smaller still, then stuffed it in his jacket pocket that was hanging on another of the fence posts. 'You keep the other.'

'What, if I may ask, sahib, are they for?' Singh said, putting the other cloth back in his haversack and taking out a water canteen.

'Just a little insurance, Sid. Just a little insurance.'

Singh bobbed his head, but whether in understanding or confusion he didn't let on. He unscrewed his canteen, put the end to his mouth, took a long swig, and passed it to Lock.

'Water?' Lock said.

'Always, sahib,' Singh smiled.

Lock took the canteen, removed his slouch hat, and threw back his head dousing himself in water. He swigged a mouthful and spat it out, then took a long drink. He brushed his hand over his wet head, handed the canteen back to Sid, and slapped the slouch hat back on. 'Disgusting stuff, Sid.'

'Very, sahib. Back to work?'

'No rest for the wicked, Sid,' Lock smiled, patting his friend on the shoulder.

CHAPTER TWELVE

Two hours before dawn, with a pale moonlight reflecting off the dark waters of the Tigris, Lock and his platoon sat in their two conjoined and armoured bellums on the east bank. They were ready to set off towards One Tree Hill, the isolated Turk redoubt some four miles upriver and two miles within enemy lines. Behind them, ready to advance on Lock's signal when he had located the electric switch, were the 22nd Punjabis and the rest of C-Company from the Mendips Light Infantry. They would begin their assault once One Tree Hill was captured, and once firing had opened up upon Norfolk Hill two miles to the south-west on the opposite bank. This would force the Turks held up there to turn their position and, in doing so, expose them to attack from the waiting Company of Ox and Bucks Light Infantry and A- and B-Companies from the Mendips.

Lock glanced back down the line of waiting boats and could

just make out the figures sitting motionless, helmets and puggarees silhouetted against the pale, moonlit sky. Now and again came the faint sound of half-whispered orders or the hollow knock of a bamboo pole against a boat, or the slap of skin against skin as yet another mosquito met a crushing end. Beyond the bellums sat the armed launches the *Shaitan* and the *Lewis Pelly*. Both were waiting at the point where the bridge of boats had been opened, and had a heavy chain strung between them to sweep up any mines that had been missed. And behind these two vessels, was the familiar shape of HMS *Espiegle* itself, ready to begin its glide slowly upstream, to keep pace with the main flotilla. Townshend had decided to make the *Espiegle* his flagship for the battle to come, and although Lock couldn't see the general, he knew he and Ross would be watching events unfold from the foretop, watching as Lock set off on his predawn *Kommando* raid.

'We're all marines now, laddie,' Ross had quipped, before leaving Lock to his preparations.

Now Lock was ready. He turned back to face north, adjusted his position in the bellum, the crack of his knees making him suck his breath in between his teeth.

Townshend had set the start of the artillery bombardment for 5 a.m. Lock had until then to get the job done. He gave the order to set off and the tandem bellums glided away from the rest of the flotilla.

'Steady, lads,' he said softly, 'steady.'

The boat made good progress and Lock gave his men a cursory glance. They were all crouched low, but eager and alert. Bingham-Smith cut a rather comical figure, though, eyes darting left to right, crouched low and clutching his SMLE as if it were an umbrella, with an Arab kufiya head cloth on his head. All the men wore these, even the sepoys over their turbans, just in case their silhouettes should give them away as being obviously British. The regulation topis were stored under the raised platform at the stern.

'I thought you'd be used to a rifle, Smith, what with all that pheasant shooting you presumably get up to back in England,' Lock said.

'I'm not a bloody gamekeeper, Lock,' Bingham-Smith said nervously.

'No, fox hunting's more your thing, I'd wager.'

Bingham-Smith flashed his eyes in Lock's direction. 'That's right, Lock, I'm a gentleman, and gentlemen—'

'Fall on their arses all too often,' Lock said.

'You are an intolerable blaggard, Lock. Intoler—'

'If you want to get off, Smith, be my guest. You can swim back to Uncle.'

Bingham-Smith sniffed but didn't reply, and Lock, grinning, turned his attention back to the landscape ahead of them.

The going had been steady and easy while they kept to the inky black, fast-flowing waters of the Tigris. But it wasn't long before they had to veer off to the east across the flood and into the reeds, and then the going became tougher. More than once they all had to climb out of the boats and physically push the bellums along, as the water was so shallow and the reeds so thick that they obstructed the poles. Men slipped, tripped and splashed their way forward, but only once did one of them disappear from sight completely, having walked into a ditch or some other unforeseen depth. That man was Bingham-Smith and his sudden vanishing and immediate gasping return, soaked to the skin, cursing in his clipped accent, the kufiya down over his eyes, caused much amusement amongst the sepoys.

'Put a sock in it, sah!' Underhill hissed. 'And stop larkin' about.'

'Stop larking about? What do you blood—'

'Quiet!' Lock said, holding up a hand.

The platoon came to a dead stop, each man holding his breath. They stayed like that for what seemed like an age, Lock straining to pick out anything above the creak of the reeds in the light breeze and the slap and slosh of the water around his waist. But there was nothing to hear other than the buzz of the insufferable insects and the beating of his heart in his ears. He waved the men on, and before long the reeds thinned out again and they all climbed back inside the bellums.

On they poled, each man alert to the impending danger around them. The water evened out and the reeds fell away. Lock was fully aware that this was the moment of acute danger, for if any enemy lookout should be concentrating in their direction then they couldn't fail to spot the dark mass of their bellum illuminated on the shimmering floodwater.

The dark silhouette of One Tree Hill loomed large as the bellums approached its eastern shore. The sandy hill with its lone tree on the western edge was hidden from view here, but Lock could, in the soft, pale light of the predawn, make out the block structure of the khan used as the first Turkish redoubt nearest to the British lines.

Lock tried to keep his breathing as quiet as possible even though he knew no enemy would hear him. But as they got nearer and nearer to the shore, he felt his body tense, half-expecting a sudden pattering of gunfire to spit out at them from the dark, and to see muzzle flashes light up the sky. But nothing came, nothing stirred in the eerie stillness. The armoured bellums ground to a halt again as their flat bottoms this time scraped against the shallows of the shore.

'Scramble lads,' Lock hissed.

Men from both boats leapt out into the water, which was now little higher than their ankles. They split off up the shore in four sections. Skirting round to the north, Underhill led Toor and two of the new sepoys, with Bingham-Smith keeping close by, while Harrington-Brown with Chopra and two more of the sepoys, moved further west. Sergeant Pritchard and Ram Lal, with another two of the new sepoys, circled the shoreline to the south. Lock, with Singh and new recruits, Addul Tarin and Karamjeet Singh, at his heels, headed straight for the khan's eastern perimeter. Elsworth, with his keen eye and scoped rifle at the ready, waited with the last two sepoys at the bellums.

Lock and his squad moved quietly, but swiftly, through the scrub that dotted the sandy ground, until they came to the rough-hewn, mud-brick wall of the building. Singh and the two sepoys fell in behind him. They all held their breath, ears pricked to the moonlit landscape around them and to the silent dark building at their backs. There was a closed, solid wooden door cut in the wall and, above it and to the left at about head height, an elongated horizontal embrasure or loophole. It would offer those inside a protected view and firing position to the south. There was no sign or sound of human activity from within the khan.

Lock tightened the grip on the Lee-Enfield rifle. It made him feel strangely exposed, though he was happy to feel the weight of his trusted Beholla in the holster at his hip. He also had the dagger Amy had given him, which was lighter and less constricting than the bayonet he usually carried. Singh had his ever-reliable kirpan sword drawn, gripped in his huge palm, a rifle strung across his shoulders, and the two sepoys carried their regulation SMLEs.

There came a fall of loose rocks off to their right, and all four men instinctively ducked down, staring off into the moonlit predawn, weapons poised. From the shadows a low whistle sounded twice, paused, then came again. Lock returned the tune, and Pritchard quickly approached.

'Nothing down by the shore, sir,' the sergeant whispered, falling in at Lock's side. 'Just a rickety jetty and a couple of gufas moored. I spotted two more mines in the shallows, too. Looks like they're connected by wires. They head off westwards into the deeper water of the river. I left Ram Lal and the two sepoys there on watch.'

Lock nodded. Pritchard had been sensible not to leave the raw recruits alone should their nerves get the better of them. Ram Lal was an astute and good soldier and could be trusted to keep his head.

'Sahib.' Singh touched Lock's arm and indicated to their left.

Underhill and Bingham-Smith were returning.

'All quiet on the west and north sides, sah,' Underhill whispered. 'Sentry sat on a jetty facin' the river. That's where the main entrance is. 'E was dozin', but 'e ain't no more.'

'Will he be missed?'

Underhill shook his head. 'Nah, left 'im slouched in the same position. Just ain't breathin' no more. Toor's keepin' watch with the new lads should anyone come out.'

'What about the lieutenant?'

'Passed 'im on my way back 'ere. The north wall is quiet, just an embrasure like this,' he said, jerking his head at the wall above them. 'No sign of movement, though. 'E's dug in, in the scrub.'

'The south wall has no door, just two embrasures,' Pritchard added.

'Then it would appear we're lucky and the majority of this post are still inside,' Lock said. 'I'm guessing this is a simple two-roomed khan. The stable doors are where the animals are sheltered, and this side is the living quarters. All right, fall back to the scrub and take cover. Pritchard, you wait with me.'

The men all moved back silently, and spread out amongst the low scrub grass. They lowered themselves down, flat on their bellies, and waited. The growing dawn light was shortening the shadows now, and though the moon was still out its glare was fading.

Lock knelt down with Pritchard, huddled close to the wall. He pulled out his cigarettes, lit one and puffed away until he had a good burning end, careful to keep the smoke away from the embrasure above him.

'You got it?' Lock said, pulling the cigarette from his mouth.

'Here, sir,' Pritchard said, pulling out one of his home-made grenades, a jam-tin bomb, from his haversack.

'No, Sergeant, the honour is yours.'

Lock held out the cigarette to Pritchard.

The sergeant grinned and held the fuse to the ember stub. It sparked instantly and he began to count down softly, 'Five, four, three, two . . .'

He tossed the jam tin through the embrasure and ducked away.

Lock held his head between his hands and felt his heart skip a beat. There was a second's delay followed by a shout of alarm from inside, cut short by a muffled explosion. Lock could feel the shockwave beneath his feet. The door to their right was blown out of its frame with a great splintering of wood, and a cloud of smoke and debris was pushed out of the embrasure above them.

Lock held up his hand, telling his men to hold fast. Five pairs of eyes glistened back at him from the gloom, sparkling with anticipation. There came a muffled cry from within the khan, then a white flag was thrust out of the embrasure.

'*Min fadlak, min fadlak,*' pleaded desperate voices from inside.

'I think they're in no mood for a scrap,' Lock said to Pritchard, getting to his feet but keeping his back to the wall. He turned his head towards the open doorway and shouted out in Arabic, '*Come out! Hands raised!*'

There was a moment of stillness, then the remains of the battered door were pushed fully open and a second white flag was thrust out and frantically waved about.

'*Min fadlak . . .*'

A stream of bleary-eyed, coughing, dust-coated Arab irregulars stumbled out, hands raised, some supporting wounded, groaning comrades.

Lock signalled for his men to approach, and with their rifles raised, they herded the Arab soldiers away from the khan.

'Check them over for weapons, Sergeant Pritchard,' Lock said.

Pritchard took charge and he and a couple of the sepoys began to push and pull the shocked prisoners into an orderly line.

'*Where's your officer?*' Lock demanded in Arabic. But he was only met by blank stares.

'All right, Pritchard, you and the two sepoys keep guard here,' Lock said, handing the sergeant his rifle. 'Look after this will you?

Sergeant Major, take our illustrious Captain Bingham-Smith with you and circle back to the north and west, check the positions. Sid, follow me.'

Bingham-Smith was about to protest, but Lock had turned away.

Lock paused at the side of the doorway, Beholla held up, his back to the wall. Singh was at his shoulder.

'Ready, Sid?' Lock said.

'Sahib.'

Lock hesitated, then wafting the smoke from his face, dodged inside.

Once Lock had stepped over the threshold, he was met by a grisly sight. Pritchard's jam-tin bomb had done untold damage and it was hard to recognise anything in the small room such was the devastating effect of the explosive in so confined a space. Everything was black and scorched. The walls were pitted with shrapnel, and twisted bits of furniture and body parts littered the hard-earth floor. The acrid smell of burnt metal and scorched flesh caught Lock's throat and he grimaced. The bomb had landed in the sleeping quarters and had taken out most of the small garrison.

There was an open doorway at the far end of the room that led further into the khan. Lock beckoned for Singh to keep close, and they both edged towards the doorway, carefully picking their way through the smouldering debris and cadavers. Lock raised his hand and both he and Singh paused, ears pricked for any sound of life coming from beyond the doorway.

'*Come out with your hands held high*,' Lock called in Arabic.

Wood scraped against stone, as if someone had knocked a chair. Then it was silent again.

'*Surrender or die,*' Lock said in Arabic.

The silence was broken by a patter of running feet. A heavy wooden door was shaken vigorously. Someone was trying to make a run for it out of the main entrance. A muffled rifle shot came from outside and there was a screech of surprise followed by a heavy thud. Panicked whispering gave way to hushed silence once more.

Lock glanced about him, then reached down and picked up a chair leg. He tossed it through the open doorway. A pistol shot rang out, the bullet smacking into the mud wall opposite.

Lock dropped to his knees, poked his Beholla round the corner, and fired wildly and blindly into the darkened room.

'*Min fadlak, min fadlak!*' came the familiar response. '*We surrender, we surrender!*'

'*Throw out your weapons,*' Lock growled.

Two Mauser rifles and a pistol clattered out of the darkness. Singh scooped them up.

'*Come out, hands above your heads,*' Lock said.

There was a scuffle of furniture and boot leather, then three men, two Arab irregulars and a clean-shaven young Ottoman officer, shuffled bleary-eyed out of the room. The officer was a slim, rather trim man with one arm hanging limply at his side, a wound bleeding from just below his shoulder. His sharp eyes widened in surprise when he saw Lock and Singh.

'*Breetaanee?*' He looked almost relieved.

Singh shoved the trio towards the door, and marched them outside to join their comrades.

Lock remained inside the khan. He poked his head around the corner where the three soldiers had been making a stand. The second room was empty but for a dead Arab irregular slumped beside the barn doors.

'All clear,' Lock shouted for the benefit of his men outside. His call was met by a shrill whistle. Lock holstered his Beholla and picked his way back through the khan to join Singh and the others on the eastern side. Harrington-Brown appeared from the northern perimeter and walked over to where Bingham-Smith and Underhill were standing. The two officers stepped away from the sergeant major and began a hushed conversation, throwing glances Lock's way every now and again. Lock was about to shout over to them when Pritchard approached.

'No weapons, sir,' the sergeant said. 'Though I don't think they've much fight in them.'

'I'm guessing they're just happy we weren't a Marsh Arab raiding party, after all,' Lock said. 'What's the count?'

'None for us, sir. For them . . . Eleven dead, nine survivors. One with a serious wound. It appears this garrison had just twenty men.'

Lock scanned the prisoners. Eight Arabs and just the one officer. They looked a sorry sight, dishevelled, blank-eyed, despondent, all sat in a small group with two sepoys watching over them. The Ottoman soldiers were all wearing the Arab kufiya head cloths, and standard Turkish infantry uniforms but with bottle-green patches on their collars. Many of them didn't have any boots, but feet bound simply with cloth. Lock's gaze fell on the Turkish officer. He was bareheaded and wore a brown-grey field uniform similar to that of his men, but with a full bottle-green collar and plain gold epaulettes stating his rank as a *mülazimi sani*, a second lieutenant.

'Was there a machine gun in the khan, Sid?' Lock said over his shoulder. The big Indian was crouched down checking over the weapons the Ottomans had surrendered.

'Not that I noticed, sahib,' Singh said, getting to his feet.

'This lot are part of a machine gun detachment, according to their uniform facings.' Lock rubbed his chin and scanned the prisoners. '*Mülazimi Sani*,' he said in Turkish.

The young officer looked up with nervous eyes, and Lock beckoned him over.

The Turk scrambled to his feet. '*Yes, effendim?*'

'*How is your arm?*'

The officer was clearly taken aback by the question and his eyes fell on the bullet hole above Lock's left breast. He frowned slightly, then looked up into Lock's eyes, first at the left one, then at the right. He quickly collected himself and gave a thin smile.

'*I . . . it . . . it is but a graze, effendim Yüzbaşi.*'

'*I need your help, Mülazimi Sani.*'

The Turk nodded. '*If I can, effendim.*'

'*I'm looking for the electric switch . . . for the mines.*'

It was a long shot, Lock knew, but one worth taking. Their luck had held out so far, but the more time that passed, the more likelihood of their discovery, particularly as dawn was rapidly approaching.

The Turk shook his head. '*I do not know . . . Wait, effendim . . . perhaps . . . There is an older officer, a miralay, I think. He is stationed at . . .*' His brow furrowed in thought.

'*Hold on,*' Lock said as he pulled the map out of his pocket. He unfolded it and showed it to the Turk officer, pointing at One Tree Hill. '*This is where we are now . . .*'

The Turk scanned the map and pointed to One Tower Hill,

the redoubt directly across the Tigris on the west bank. Lock nodded. It made sense. This was situated at a natural bend in the river and was two miles further north from Norfolk Hill, the redoubt closest to the British line. If the Ottomans saw that the British were advancing, then there was more than enough time for them to get word to the officer controlling the mines, and for them to be detonated before the attack got anywhere near them.

'There? One Tower Hill?'

The Turk shook his head. '*No, effendim. The little island beyond.*'

Lock looked closer at the map. There was another sand island marked to the north-west of One Tower Hill.

'Is there a building there? Defences?'

The Turk shrugged. '*I have never been there, effendim, or seen it. I just know that this . . . elderly miralay is stationed there.*'

Lock scratched his stubbly chin. He judged it to be about two miles from where they were now to the little sand island. He stared off to the east. It wouldn't be long before sunrise.

'*All right, Mülazimi Sani, thank you. Return to your men. If you cooperate then you will be treated well, I give you my word.*'

The Turk saluted Lock. '*Then you shall have my word also, Yüzbaşi.*'

Lock nodded and the young officer started to head back to his men.

'Mülazimi Sani?'

'Effendim?'

'One last thing. Do you know if there is a Binbaşi Feyzi among the officers? Stationed in one of the other redoubts, perhaps?'

The Turk rubbed his lip for a moment, and shook his head.

'*It is not a name I am familiar with. But there are many officers, effendim. Particularly on the steamer Marmaris.*'

'*What about German officers? Herr Wassmuss?*'

Again the young Turk shook his head. '*I do not know, effendim.*'

'*All right, never mind. You can return to your men.*'

The young Turk gave a quick nod and went to sit back down with his soldiers.

Lock called Underhill over, and Bingham-Smith and Harrington-Brown, not to be left out, followed. Lock opened up his map again and tapped the small sand island the Turk officer had just pointed out.

'It's highly probable that our target is on this little island, here.'

'Christ, that's bloody close to that Abdul redoubt,' Underhill said. 'It's one of the bigger ones, ain't it?'

'One Tower Hill. Yes, I know, Sergeant Major, that's why I'm going to go on alone, with a smaller team.'

Underhill shook his head. 'Too risky, sah. You'll get spottid' an' the 'ole place'll get blown to kingdom come.'

Bingham-Smith gave a snort of laughter here, but no one else shared in his humour.

Lock shook his head and smiled.

'Such faith, Sergeant Major, that's what I love about you. Look, I want you and the lieutenant to take charge of this garrison here. Post lookouts on all corners of this redoubt, and try to keep low. Hold until the 22nd arrive. Keep a watch on the prisoners, too. But unless they look like starting any trouble, and I doubt that, treat them well.'

Harrington-Brown grunted. 'Huh, can't trust the bloody Buddoos. We should shoot the blighters just to be on—'

'Their officer gave me his word, Lieutenant,' Lock said. 'You'll have no trouble.'

'I have to say I agree with Harrington-Brown,' Bingham-Smith said.

'I said, you will have no trouble.'

Underhill snorted. 'You an' yer bloody Johnny mates. It'll get you an' the rest of us killed one day.'

'But not today, Sergeant Major,' Lock grinned. 'Now, Pritchard . . .'

'Sir?'

'I want you to return to the bellums. Separate them again, then take one back to our lines. If you hug the east bank you should avoid getting snagged in the reeds. Use your electric torch to signal your approach, otherwise you may buy it from a friendly.'

Pritchard nodded his understanding.

'When you get back,' Lock continued, 'tell them what's happening, where I'm heading and for them to hold the artillery bombardment until they see my flare. Take the two sepoys down there with you and send Elsworth back up to me. Oh, and get that kufiya off. Topis and turbans only. Just in case.'

Pritchard threw a quick salute then trotted off down to the shoreline.

'I think I should go with him, Lock,' Bingham-Smith said.

Lock shook his head and smiled thinly. 'No, my dear Casper, you're coming with me.'

'Good God, you are quite mad, aren't you? Reckless and mad. The sergeant major's right, you'll kill us all!'

'You wanted to observe, Smith, so you can come and observe.'

'I . . .' Bingham-Smith started to protest but thought the better of it.

Lock knew he wouldn't say too much more in front of Harrington-Brown for the risk of looking like a coward in front of his peer.

'And just how do we get there, Lock?' Bingham-Smith said. 'You and I can't manage a bellum alone.'

'We're taking one of the gufas that Pritchard found tied to the jetty on the south shore. Besides, Elsworth is coming with us to help row.'

As if on cue, the young sharpshooter came trotting over. Lock gave him a nod.

'Ready for another little boat trip, Alfred?'

'Sir,' Elsworth said with an eager smile.

'Sid, you help the sergeant major and I'll see you soon.'

'Very good, sahib. Here, you will be needing this I am thinking,' Singh said, as he tossed a rifle in Lock's direction.

Lock caught the rifle and hitched it over his shoulder. 'Yes, must try and keep up our ruse of being Marsh Arabs. Right, come along then, Smith, Alfred, we need to get a move on,' Lock said, as he headed off in the direction of the southern jetty and the moored gufas.

CHAPTER THIRTEEN

'I must . . . protest, Lock . . . just why . . . in the hell . . . isn't the lance . . . corporal . . . being an . . . oarsman?' Bingham-Smith hissed between puffs and pants, working his arms in a steady 'C' stroke as he paddled away.

'Because . . . Smith . . . young Elsworth . . . is a far . . . better shot . . . with far . . . better eyesight . . . than you . . . or I . . . put together,' Lock whispered in between strokes. He was sat shoulder to shoulder with Bingham-Smith, working his paddle in the same way. 'He is more . . . value where . . . he is . . . at the aft . . . using his . . . senses . . . to guide us . . . through the Turk . . . lines.'

'I'm a damned . . . good shot . . . too . . . you know?' Bingham-Smith replied petulantly.

'I'm sure . . . you are . . . but right . . . now . . . you're a damned . . . good paddler . . . So shut up . . . and concentrate . . . We're drifting . . . too much . . . to the left.'

'All right . . . all right,' Bingham-Smith mumbled, and he quickened his stroke to match Lock's.

They were making rapid progress and, having battled the currents to cross the Tigris, were now approaching the larger Turk redoubt of One Tower Hill over the floods.

Lock checked his watch. It was a little after a quarter-to-five. Time enough. He just hoped Pritchard would get word to the British lines in time to delay the bombardment. He looked down at his feet to check that the Very pistol he had taken from Ram Lal was still there. It was.

The sky was lighter still and the redoubt was a dark silhouette just to their right. It was another large sand island rising to higher ground in a similar way to One Tree Hill, only with a large tower, which loomed above them like a sleeping giant, instead of a simple khan as its main building. The tower had been built in four stages superimposed, with indications of a winding ascent from one storey to the other and crowned with a chapel. It stood alone, with just a single-storey building off to the side, and both were constructed in traditional mud brick. And, just like One Tree Hill, there was no sign of life.

Once they had paddled by, Elsworth hissed over his shoulder, 'Sir, up ahead, about 500 yards away . . .'

Lock craned his neck to look above Elsworth's shadowy form. He could make out a tiny island with some sort of object in its centre, a sloping roof of some kind with a dark bulk underneath.

'All right . . . gentle strokes now . . . slowly and . . . quietly,' Lock whispered.

There was an extraordinary stillness all around them as they paddled on across the flood. Lock glanced up. High overhead he

212

could see a flock of pelicans, their white plumage tinged pink with the coming golden dawn. They seemed to be drifting on the air like blossom blown from the trees and Lock was suddenly, momentarily reminded of his rooms back in Karachi, of the trees he could see from his balcony. His eyes fell to the landscape now bathed in the orange glow of sunrise. Far to the north he could make out more of the Turkish redoubts, Shrapnel Hill and Gun Hill and the village of Alloa. It was going to be a brilliant, crystal-clear day. He held his breath. They were moving further and further into enemy territory. He glanced behind him again at the now distant One Tree Hill and at that moment the sun shot up above the level horizon. The magic colours of the dawn landscape faded from the sky and the reed marsh and the flooded land all around turned to a harsh metallic blue, sprayed with vivid green.

'Shit . . . Paddle fast!' Lock hissed. 'Elsworth . . . get ready.'

Lock knew that unless Pritchard had managed to get an audience with Townshend, very soon the general would more than likely order his artillery to open fire. Lock could now see that the tiny island they were making for was little more than twenty yards square. Plonked in the middle of it was a table and chair shaded by a huge tasselled parasol. Sat dozing in the chair, legs stretched out before him, hands folded across a large rising and falling belly, was a man in a dark uniform. His capped head was drooped forward, chin resting on his chest, and his snoring was clearly audible above the splash of the gufa's oars.

Lock strained his eyes. There was something hanging down from the table and running off into the water. 'Oh, bugger,' he said. It was a vast rope of wiring, the same wiring that connected the mines on their approach to One Tree Hill.

Lock dropped his oar and went to draw his knife, but the sheath was empty. His mind tumbled for a second. When had he last had it? On the shore at Qurna? Had he dropped it when taking the redoubt?

'Elsworth, your bayonet!' he hissed.

The young sharpshooter slapped his blade into Lock's outstretched palm without question, and Lock vaulted over the side. He was only a few yards out and the floodwater was but a foot deep. He waded forward, legs driving through the water as if it were thick mud, and soon his thighs began to ache with the effort. The dozing man in the dark uniform gave a snort and time seemed to slow as Lock watched him laboriously raise his head. Lock threw himself at the wires just as the man became aware of what was happening. His pale eyes widened in shock and he jerked forward, stretching his hand out desperately for the instrument panel on the table next to him.

As the gufa slammed aground, Elsworth leapt over the gunwale, rifle raised.

'Don't!' he shouted.

The man sprung back in his chair with such force, thrusting his stubby hands into the air, that his cap flew off his round head.

Lock seized the rope of wires running down from the back of the instrument panel and, with a slash of the bayonet, severed their connection. He let out a long sigh of relief and looked up. The man in the dark uniform was staring back at him through hooded, watery eyes.

He was an elderly officer, somewhere in his sixties, short and stocky with bushy eyebrows, bald on top with straight gunmetal grey hair around the sides of his head. He had a large, bulbous nose that twitched nervously like a frightened rabbit's above a magnificent walrus moustache. He was a naval officer and his dark-blue uniform bore the three rings and loop of the rank of *liva amiral*, commander, on his sleeves. So not a *miralay*, a colonel, as the young Turk officer on One Tree Hill had said.

'*Good morning, Liva Amiral,*' Lock said in Turkish, giving a wolfish grin as he stood tall. He pulled the now soaking kufiya from his head and dropped it to the sand with a wet slap.

The *liva amiral* thrust his hands even higher in the air, eyes darting over Lock's face and uniform.

'Now, let's have a litt—'

Lock was cut short by four booms in the distance.

Either Pritchard didn't get there in time or Townshend's impatience had gotten the better of him and he had ordered the howitzer battery to open fire.

The attack had begun.

'But we haven't sent the bloody signal!' shrieked Bingham-Smith from the gufa. He was staring south, at the distant smoke of the forty-gun artillery bombardment as they began to unleash hell upon the Turkish redoubts.

Soon, the air was full of the ominous whistle of hundreds of falling shells. And then came the shuddering thump and spasm as they impacted all around.

Lock checked his watch. It was 5 a.m. on the dot. 'The punctuality of the British,' he scoffed. 'God help us all.' He waved the naval officer to his feet. '*Hands down, Liva Amiral. You'll be coming with us.*'

'Here, sir,' Elsworth scooped up the naval officer's peakless cap

215

and handed it to him. The elderly Turk took the offering, nodded his appreciation, and turned and saluted Lock.

'*Liva Amiral Hulusi Özel, at your service, Yüzbaşi.*'

A string of shells landed one after the other not 200 yards to their left as they faced south, throwing up dark columns of mud and water. The artillery were quickly finding their range and were getting ever closer to hitting the nearby redoubt of One Tower Hill.

Elsworth, used to Lock's calmness under fire, turned his attention to the distant shore of One Tower Hill, rifle at the ready should any sentry suddenly spot them and decide to take a potshot.

The *liva amiral* seemed totally unconcerned by the artillery fire, but Bingham-Smith was flinching and pacing the gufa, as much as its constant rocking would allow him to.

'We m . . . must leave!' he stuttered, looking exasperatedly on at Lock's seeming indifference to their increasingly hazardous position.

'*Well, Liva Amiral Özel Bey,*' Lock said, returning the Turk's salute and ignoring Bingham-Smith, '*just what have we here?*'

Lock was staring down at the table. On it rested a simple electric keyboard, not dissimilar to a telephone operator's keyboard, with a number of switches, sockets and plugs. A great string of wiring snaked out from the back of the keyboard forming one larger rope that had run down and out into the water, until Lock had cut it. Next to the keyboard was a string-bound cardboard folder, thick with papers, and a drawstring cloth bag. Lock picked up the bag and opened it. He stared in at the contents, then raised his eyes. The *liva amiral* was watching him intently.

Lock studied the elderly Turk's face for a moment.

'*Do you know a Binbaşi Feyzi?*'

The Turk shook his head.

'*A Herr Wassmuss?*'

Again the Turk shook his head.

'Look here, Lock, we need to get the hell off of this bloody island,' Bingham-Smith said shrilly. 'We must take this . . . this prisoner to the *Espiegle* immed—'

'Shut up, Smith.'

'*But Yüzbaşi,*' the elderly Turk interrupted, '*there is a German officer . . .*'

'*Where?*'

'*I believe,*' the *liva amiral* turned and pointed towards the village a little further north, '*there . . . at Alloa.*'

'*You are certain?*'

The Turk shrugged. '*Nothing is certain any more, Yüzbaşi.*'

'*And the pearls?*' Lock shook the cloth bag in his hand, making the contents rattle like a child's stash of prize marbles.

The Turk licked his lips, staring at the bag in Lock's hand. '*I . . . I am a collector . . .*'

'*Bullshit. Pearls are currency . . . the currency of spies.*'

The Turk gave a non-committal shrug. '*I know nothing of spies. I only know we do not get paid very often. I was paid in pearls. The pearls you now have.*'

'*Paid?*'

'*To man this station . . . to be ready with that,*' the *liva amiral* flicked his chin at the switchboard on the table.

'*What about duty?*'

The Turk chuckled. '*Germans buy duty.*'

Lock scoffed, closed the bag again and pocketed it. He picked up the bulky cardboard file, opened it up and flicked through the papers.

'*And these?*'

The *liva amiral* shrugged. '*I was given them to look after.*'

'*Look after? Why?*'

Again the *liva amiral* shrugged again. '*I am too old a man to question why, Yüzbaşi.*'

'*Who gave them to you to look after?*'

The *liva amiral's* eyes drifted to a point over Lock's shoulder and seemed to glaze over as if lost in thought.

'*Liva Amiral?*'

The elderly Turk lifted his gaze back to Lock. '*The German officer. I do not know his name. On the Marmaris. He . . . he was the one who gave me the pearls. For my trouble. But it is no trouble to look after a cardboard file.*'

'*And you didn't find his . . . "request" at all strange?*'

'*Why should I, Yüzbaşi? War is strange.*'

Lock scoffed, closed the file up again, and returned his attention to the other objects on the tabletop. There was a telescope, a large artillery-type parabellum pistol in its holster, a tin mug and a leather-bound book. Lock picked up the book and read the spine. It said, *Şair Evlenmesi*. Lock was familiar with it. It was a one-act comedy regarded as the first modern Turkish play. He opened it up at the marked page and smiled.

'*I saw a production of this at a theatre in Constantinople, back in the spring of '14. I like İbrahim Şinasi's humour,*' Lock said, closing the book with a snap, and holding it out to the naval officer.

'*I was learning it for a performance I was to put on for my men,*' the *liva amiral* said, taking the book from Lock with a short nod of thanks.

'*Well, you will probably still be able to in the future. Here.*' Lock handed the telescope to the officer, but kept hold of the pistol, stuffing it in his pocket. He put the cardboard folder under his arm, and scooped up the electric switchboard. '*If you would be so kind . . .*' he said, jutting his chin in the direction of the gufa.

The *liva amiral* nodded, and stepped towards the boat

Lock quickly scanned the island. There was nothing else other than the parasol to keep the sun off and a small stove with a kettle on top. The smell of coffee had been making Lock's stomach growl since the moment he'd scrambled out of the gufa, but this wasn't the moment to stop and take refreshment.

'Time to leave,' he said to Elsworth, glancing up at the horizon to the south. 'Here, keep these safe, will you.' He handed Elsworth the cardboard folder, and the young sharpshooter stuffed them into his haversack.

'Shall I signal?' said Bingham-Smith. He was still staring off nervously towards the British lines, his voice was wavering with barely controlled panic.

'No need,' Lock said.

'Wh . . . what?'

Bingham-Smith turned, wide-eyed. He was holding the Very pistol in his shaking hand.

Lock shoved the *liva amiral* aside and threw himself in the opposite direction at the exact moment that the Very pistol went off in Bingham-Smith's hand. The flare shot out passing so close to Lock's face that he felt the burn of its trail hot on his cheek. It slammed into the table, exploding in a shower of sparks and smoke. Elsworth scrambled up and helped the stunned *liva amiral* to his feet again, handing him his cap and telescope. The Turk still had a tight grip of his book. Lock raised his head and glared blackly back at Bingham-Smith, who was stood, gawping at his handiwork.

Lock looked back at the table. It was a charred mess of scorched wood, the parasol was on fire and the chair had a large, round, blackened hole where its back used to be.

'I assure you, Lock,' Bingham-Smith said, 'my w . . . word as a gentleman, it was an accident. It just went off in my . . . my hand.'

Lock pulled himself to his feet and dusted himself down. Whether or not Bingham-Smith had fired the Very pistol intentionally didn't matter now, they needed to get away from the little sand island and join up with the main assault as quickly as possible. He glanced over at One Tower Hill. The redoubt was taking a terrific pounding from the British artillery, and Lock didn't want to hang around for a stray shell to obliterate their little island. He picked up the electric keyboard, walked over to the burning parasol, and tossed the keyboard into the flames.

'In the boat everyone, quickly,' he said, turning back.

Elsworth steadied the gufa as the *liva amiral*, still clinging to his telescope and book, climbed awkwardly in. Then he helped Lock push off, before they both scrambled on board. Lock snatched up a paddle and thrust the other one into Bingham-Smith's hand, and they both began to row like crazy. The *liva amiral* sat down at the back, and Elsworth moved to take up his position at the front of the boat, rifle at the ready.

As they moved away from the little sand island, Lock watched the bombs fall on and around One Tower Hill. Why were the Turks not returning fire? he thought.

'I'm truly . . . mortified . . . Lock,' Bingham-Smith said. 'I know we . . . have our . . . differences . . . but I . . . would never . . . you know?'

Lock gave Bingham-Smith a withering look. 'Forget it . . . just paddle . . . There's a rain . . . of shells . . . heading . . . our way . . . that will do . . . a lot more . . . damage . . . than your . . . inept . . . signalling.'

A shell dropped not ten feet away from them, spraying the gufa with muddy water.

Bingham-Smith flinched, pulling his oar up out of the water. 'Christ, Lock. We're done for!'

'Just . . . paddle . . . Smith,' Lock said.

Elsworth started to whistle one of his many tunes and then the young sharpshooter began to softly sing,

Hush! Here comes a whizz-bang.
Hush! Here comes a whizz-bang,
Now you soldiers, get down those stairs,
Down in your dug-outs and say your prayers—

'Oh, do shut up . . . Lance Corporal!' Bingham-Smith snapped over his shoulder.

Elsworth stopped singing.

'Leave him . . . alone,' growled Lock, 'and . . . row.'

Another shell whined down and exploded even closer than the last, spraying them all with more muddy water, then Elsworth returned to his song,

Hush! Here comes a whizz-bang,
And it's making straight for you:
And you'll see all the wonders of No-Man's Land
If a whizz-bang—

He suddenly slapped his hand nosily against the gunwale of the gufa. Bingham-Smith flinched again, but kept paddling.

'—*hits you.*'

'Very good, Alfred,' Lock said. 'Now shut up . . . and keep your . . . eyes peeled.'

'Yes, sir,' Elsworth said.

'Where the . . . bloody hell . . . are we . . . going, Lock . . . ? This is . . . madness!' Bingham-Smith said.

'We need . . . to scoot around . . . to the south . . . west . . . try and avoid . . . the artillery . . . fire . . . and the main . . . thrust . . . of the attack,' Lock said. 'We should . . . meet up . . . with the Ox . . . and Bucks . . . as they . . . head for . . . One Tower . . . Hill . . . providing . . . they've overwhelmed . . . Norfolk Hill.'

'If that's Norfolk Hill on the horizon there, sir,' Elsworth said, 'then I'd say it won't be long. It's taking a hell of a pounding.'

Lock craned his neck around. He could see the same. There was black smoke trails and clouds of debris rising up into the clear morning sky from the redoubt that was nearest to the British lines.

All around them, the air was angry with the rumbling booms of shell impacts, and Lock just hoped that they could get through unscathed. At least any mines they had missed, not to mention those further up the Tigris, couldn't be detonated remotely. That was a huge relief, despite the fact that he nearly didn't make it to the electric keyboard in time.

'I was lucky . . . that you were . . . asleep . . . old man,' Lock said. He spoke in English to the *liva amiral*, not knowing or caring if the elderly Turk officer could understand him or not.

Liva Amiral Özel blinked back at Lock and then gave a shrug. 'I am old man, Capteen,' he replied in broken English. 'I sleep more than wake. War is very . . . How say you? Tired?'

'Tiresome.' Lock grinned as he continued paddling. 'Tiresome . . . is a perfect . . . description . . . *Liva Amiral*.'

There was a huge explosion off to their left and everyone instinctively ducked down again as they were showered with more water and debris. Lock looked up to see that the tower of One Tower Hill had disappeared in a billowing cloud of black smoke and fire. Suddenly, the noise above their heads increased to a terrific, continual roar, as if thousands of shells were hurtling through the air all at once.

'They'll have to rename that redoubt soon,' Lock shouted to Bingham-Smith with a smile, putting his oar back into the water ready to start paddling again. 'Won't be any tower left.'

'My God, Lock,' Bingham-Smith bleated, 'what the blazes is there to joke about? If the 17th don't recognise us as friendlies then . . . What if they open fire on us? We'll be cut to pieces!' Bingham-Smith was rapidly losing whatever dignity he had, and was nearing blind panic.

'Calm yourself, Captain,' Lock snapped. 'Show some self-respect. You're an officer in His Majesty's Britannic Army. What will our guest think?' he said, indicating with a subtle jerk of his chin to the elderly Turk.

'Damned that blasted tinpot admiral!' Bingham-Smith spat. 'What about that?' He pointed a wavering finger to the south-east where a dark mass was creeping ever closer over the water.

'*Liva Amiral*,' Lock said to the elderly Turk, '*may I?*' He held his hand out.

The Turk looked momentarily dumbfounded, then his face lit

up in understanding. '*With pleasure, Yüzbaşi.*' He passed Lock the telescope.

Lock gave a nod of thanks. 'My binoculars are in my haversack,' he said to Bingham-Smith, 'and that's with Sid, somewhere . . .' He unfolded the 'scope, twisted round, and stared long and hard at the horizon to the south-east.

'What a sight,' he breathed. Up ahead, as far as the magnified eye could see, hundreds of bellums were powering towards them. 'Extraordinary.'

'What is? What is it, Lock?' Bingham-Smith bleated.

Lock lowered the 'scope and passed it to his fraught companion. 'See for yourself.'

Bingham-Smith struggled to focus the telescope, mumbling a complaint, and then he sucked in his breath and fell silent for a moment.

'Oh . . . my . . . Lord,' he gasped. 'We're heading right for them, Lock! We need to take evasive action! Signal them! Something . . .'

'We will be all right as long as you do as I say,' Lock said calmly. 'Firstly, kufiyas off, regulation headgear on.' He had already pulled his slouch hat from inside his jacket and was moulding it back into shape.

Elsworth snatched off his kufiya, tossed it away into the water, and put on his topi.

'What about the Buddoos, though, Lock?' Bingham-Smith said, fumbling with his own topi.

'Hopefully we won't run into them,' Lock said. He reached inside of his jacket as he spoke, and pulled out the blue folded cloth Singh had given him when they were working on the bellums back at Qurna.

'They're mostly installed in the marshes and thick reeds on the west flank of Gun Hill.'

'But what about between here and Norfolk Hill?' Bingham-Smith said, staring off into the reed marshes.

'We'll stick to the deeper water, the less dense patches of reeds. But now that the shelling is well and truly underway, I doubt the Marsh Arabs are even there anymore.'

'How can you be sure of that?'

Lock shrugged. 'We won't know for certain until we get closer.'

'We won't know for certain!?' Bingham-Smith gasped.

'Just keep your head down and your voice to a whisper,' Lock said. 'Alfred, hand me that pole down by your feet there.'

Elsworth reached down and felt around in the briney slosh that was swilling about in the bottom of the gufa. He pulled out a long wooden pole, which was usually used to push the gufa out of thick reeds and off of sandbanks, and passed it to Lock.

'Now,' Lock said, 'let's hope the 17th have good eyesight.'

He began to unfold the blue cloth to reveal that it was, in fact, made up of three colours: red, white and blue. He threaded the pole through the eyelets that ran along one edge of the cloth, then raised it up.

'*Liva Amiral, if you would be so kind?*' Lock said, holding the pole out for the elderly Turk to take.

The *liva amiral* squinted up at the unfurled cloth and gave a shrug. He took a firm grip of the pole, resting it between his knees, then raised it up in the air and wrapped his arms around it to keep it steady.

Bingham-Smith gave a huge sigh of relief and smiled. 'I

have to say it. It galls me so, but . . . bravo, Lock, bravo.'

'Now, paddle, Smith,' Lock said, 'paddle.'

The British Union flag opened up and began to billow and flap above the *liva amiral's* head as it caught in the light, warm breeze.

CHAPTER FOURTEEN

'You there!' came a shout from the armoured bellum at the head of the small flotilla that was rapidly moving north from Norfolk Hill. 'Are you Captain Lock?'

'That's right. You the Oxfords?' Lock called back across the water, through his cupped hands.

'At your service,' came the reply.

Lock could now see a tall British officer standing at the bow of the lead bellum. There were about thirty manned bellums spread out behind him, but his was the only one flying a red flag.

Townshend in his memorandum issued to all senior officers had given each attack group a coloured flag as identification. Brigadier General Dobbie's advanced guard group, consisting of the 17th Infantry Brigade, were allocated red flags, No.1 Group, the 16th Infantry Brigade under Brigadier General Delamain, flew green flags, while No.2 Group in general reserve had yellow flags.

No.3 Group, the artillery under Brigadier General Smith, were allocated blue flags.

Lock had voiced his dismay to Ross about the use of red flags, far too similar to the Ottoman flag. But the decision had been made.

Bugger that, Lock had thought. There was no way he was going to rush back towards his own troops, following his *Kommando* raid, from behind enemy lines flying a red flag! His own side would open fire on him. Hence the reason he'd insisted on Singh finding him a Union flag. There'd be no mistaking that for an enemy standard.

'Are the Mendips with you?' Lock called, the gufa getting ever closer, Elsworth now sharing the paddling with Bingham-Smith. Lock was standing at the head of the boat.

'Bringing up the rear. Chap called Carver has a company, I believe.'

The two vessels bumped to a halt next to one another, and the British officer gave a warm smile as he held his hand out to Lock.

'Captain Brooke. Major Ross said we may bump into you.'

'How very astute of him,' Lock said.

'Pleasure to meet you, Lock. Damned good show at Barjisiyah Woods.'

Lock shook the youthful captain's firm grip.

'Saw your flare, Lock. Then my sniper spotted your flag. Little confused by the Johnny general holding it sat in the stern. But, well . . . here you are,' Brooke said, eying the elderly Turk naval officer sat with the Union flagpole still held tightly in his hands.

Lock nodded. 'Well, Captain, that was the idea.'

'I'm Captain Bingham-Smith, commanding officer of C-Company in the Mendips,' Bingham-Smith said, thrusting his paw rudely out in between Lock and Brooke.

Brooke took the offered hand and gave it a brief shake. 'Two captains make for an unhappy ship, do they not?' he said with a raised eyebrow.

'You wouldn't believe,' Lock said.

'So, what's the situation?' Brooke said, indicating to One Tower Hill and beyond.

'The redoubts are taking a pounding, as you can see, but don't seem to be retaliating,' Lock said. 'We took One Tree Hill over on the east bank easily enough. Just a small garrison of twenty Arab irregulars and a young Turk officer. There was some minor resistance, but we haven't suffered a single casualty.' Lock removed his slouch hat and rubbed his head. 'So far it's been the strangest attack I've ever been involved in. This chap,' Lock waved his hat at the elderly Turk officer, 'was all alone on a tiny sand island just to the west of One Tower Hill. He was manning an electric switch that should have set the mines off.'

'Mines?'

Lock nodded and put his hat back on. 'Whole string of them from Qurna to God knows where. I'd already removed a number of them, but the switch was the worry. I cut the wires. Mind you, they looked so corroded from having been in the water that I doubt they would have worked anyway.'

'Good Lord,' Brooke gasped, 'I had no idea.' The Oxfords captain looked momentarily stunned as he turned his gaze back the way he had come.

'I think, Captain,' Lock said, 'that the majority of the mines are in the deeper waters of the Tigris itself. But it can't do any harm to warn your lookouts.'

Brooke gave a nod of agreement. He removed his topi and passed a hand through his sweat-damp mop of fine brown hair. 'Marsh Arabs?'

Lock shook his head. 'Not a sign. But I'm not surprised with all the shelling.'

'Well, as soon as we reached Norfolk Hill,' Brooke said, 'the general's spotters would have told the artillery to switch their firepower to One Tower Hill. Now,' he checked his watch, 'we've already signalled our success, so the artillery will start concentrating its fire on Gun Hill and Shrapnel Hill. Are you joining us?'

Lock gave a wry smile. 'Well, we don't have any prior engagements.'

'Good,' Brooke said, 'then let's get this show on the road.' He twisted round and waved his hand forward, then gave Lock a quick salute.

The bellums wavered, then slowly gathered speed again as they moved off.

'Should we not wait for Major Carver, Lock?' Bingham-Smith said.

'No we should not. The war will be over by the time he gets here,' Lock said. 'We follow Captain Brooke. Besides, my platoon is liaising on the east shore and I want to keep moving forward.'

'But I really feel that we should be escorting our prisoner here to the command ship wher—'

'No, Smith. We'll wait for the *Espiegle* to come to us rather than try to weave our way back against the advance. Now get paddling.'

As the sun rose, the advance of bellums powered on. The three

RN sloops, the *Espiegle*, the *Odin* and the *Clio*, were close by now, keeping pace with the main flotilla, their guns continuously pounding in order to keep the Turkish redoubts silent. Lock knew Townshend, Ross and Godwinson were on board the *Espiegle*, and he knew that he couldn't let Bingham-Smith delay him or insist on transferring the *liva amiral* to the command ship. He had to keep moving forward, whatever happened; he had to keep chasing Feyzi, he had to keep chasing Wassmuss.

The forward advance of the Oxfords sped on, with Lock only two boats behind Captain Brooke's lead vessel.

'Look, sir.' Elsworth said, jerking his head to his left. 'It's our . . . lot.'

Lock was happy to see that a bellum flying a Union flag was rapidly approaching from the east. Singh had used the flag in the same way as Lock had, as a clear indicator of whose side they were on, and now the rest of Green Platoon were on their way.

'I see them, Alfred.'

A whistle blew and Lock's attention was drawn back to the shore of One Tower Hill. Up ahead Brooke was waving his arm, signalling the advance.

'Come on, boys,' the captain shouted, 'off we go!'

The lead bellums slammed into the shore and the men sprang out, rushing towards the buildings on One Tower Hill, their bayonets glistening in the dawn sunlight. All around the troops sprang out of their bellums as one by one the boats ran ashore. The men splashed through the last few inches of floodwater until they hit the sandy beach. A shrill whistle blasted from the right, and Lock could see Green Platoon's bellum judder aground just a few feet away. The men of Green Platoon, with Underhill and

Harrington-Brown at their head, stormed ashore. Singh and one of the sepoys splashed over to Lock and helped drag the more cumbersome gufa up out of the water.

'It is good to see you, sahib,' the big Indian beamed.

'You, too, Sid. Put your man on guard with this chap, would you?'

Lock unholstered his Beholla and turned to the elderly Turk naval officer. '*I'd kindly ask you to stay put, Liva Amiral*,' he smiled. '*Wouldn't want you getting shot now, would we?*'

The elderly Turk nodded his head in agreement and sat rooted to the raised platform at the rear of the gufa, clinging dearly to the Union flag on its pole, knuckles white with the force of his grip.

'Good,' Lock said. He turned about and leapt over the edge and into the shallows, with Elsworth at his heels.

'Any trouble at One Tree Hill, Sid?'

'None, sahib. The 22nd came quick sharp and began to shoot their machine guns at Norfolk Hill. We then saw a signal flare and guessed that you had found the electrical switch.'

Lock nodded. 'Something like that.'

He glanced over his shoulder to see that Bingham-Smith was still in the gufa.

'Shift your overprivileged arse!'

Bingham-Smith was fumbling with his rifle as he tried to climb out of the gufa. He slipped and landed on his hands and knees, dropping the rifle in the water. He fished it out, cursed, and stumbled on after Lock, Singh and Elsworth.

Lock laughed and ran up the sandy shore, troops running to his left and right all stooped, rifles at the ready. There was very little cover, just a scattering of stumpy reeds and scrub grass leading all the way up to the redoubt wall. Over to the eastern edge of the island, Lock could see a small mud-brick hut, exposed and alone, with a wooden jetty jutting out, similar to the layout at One Tree Hill. But the redoubt up ahead was an ominous mud-brick mound some two storeys high. There was a track that weaved its way round the western side, and there was a carved stepped footpath leading directly up from the hut. Lock could make out two more buildings on top of the mound, as well as the Ottoman flag standing tall and proud, flapping in the warm breeze.

Singh was running alongside Lock now, his kirpan sword drawn, his face fixed in a grimace of concentration. Or pain. Lock knew that his Indian friend was suffering with the wound to his ribs.

'Better than lying in hospital, Sid?'

Singh's eyes momentarily darted to Lock. 'Better, sahib.'

A volley of rifle fire suddenly spat forth from the top of the redoubt and the men instinctively ducked down. Bullets zipped and fizzed about their ears like angry hornets, thumping into the ground and kicking up the sand at their feet. Then Captain Brooke, urging his troops on at the head of the company, was hit. He was thrown back off his feet and disappeared from sight.

'On, men, on!' Lock bellowed, immediately taking over should the attack falter. But they were good men with good NCOs amongst them, and not one soldier hesitated. Lock's battle cry was taken up, and the Company of Oxfords swarmed up the path like an army of ants, following the track up into the redoubt.

Elsworth knelt down, rifle levelled, the butt jammed hard into his shoulder. He began to fire calmly, with deadly precision, at the enemy manning the walls above them. Bingham-Smith, skin grey with fear, was stumbling on behind, his rifle held out in front of him awkwardly.

'Use it, Smith, use it!' Lock shouted, grabbing the young officer by the shoulder and shoving him on.

Bingham-Smith pushed his ill-fitting topi up out of his eyes, raised his rifle, and let off a wild shot.

Lock urged the troops coming up behind him forward, turned to run with them, then paused. Captain Brooke was lying at his feet, arms flung out to his side, legs twisted at an odd angle. He looked like a broken doll. His half-open eyes were glazed and still, and there was a small hole in his forehead.

Lock ran on, raising his Beholla, firing up to his left at the high point of the redoubt. He saw two bullets strike and splinter the top of the brick wall, a third hit home, snatching a Turk back and out of sight. Lock's gaze fell on Bingham-Smith's back. It was tempting. He licked his lips, gripped his Beholla tighter, but he kept moving.

All of a sudden the shooting from above stopped. Lock had reached the foot of the stone steps. He moved to one side and crouched low, looking back down the length of the beach. The last of the men were running up, and Lock indicated for them to move both to the left and right, to take cover at the foot of the redoubt wall. There were surprisingly few casualties, much to his relief, and a blessed absence of the plaintive calls for mothers, gods or sergeants from the wounded men. Movement in the corner of his left made Lock turn. Underhill was scrambling towards him.

'What's 'appenin', sah?' the sergeant major said, breathlessly, his face red from exertion.

Lock leant out cautiously, and peered up the stone steps. 'I'd say it was over, Sergeant Major.'

At the top of the flight of steps, Lock could see a British NCO. He was waving his arm from side to side.

'All clear,' the sergeant shouted down.

Lock got to his feet and slowly the rest of the men around him followed suit. Elsworth lowered his rifle, but kept scanning the walls above, ever watchful and untrusting. Lock fished out his Woodbines and lit one. He turned to Underhill.

'Casualties? Ours, I mean?'

'None, sah. Not even a scratch.'

'Good,' Lock said, exhaling a trail of tobacco.

'Lieutenant's missin', though.'

'Harrington-Brown?' Lock said, his cigarette dancing between his lips as he checked the bullet clip of his Beholla. Satisfied, he slammed it back home again. 'Well, see if you can find him, Sergeant Major, there's a good chap.'

Underhill shouldered his rifle and gave a curt nod.

'Then prepare the men,' Lock added. 'We're heading north.'

Underhill turned back. 'Sah? We not joinin' the *Espiegle* and the rest of the regatta?'

'Not yet, Sergeant Major.'

'Look, sahib,' Singh interrupted, pointing to the track.

Marching down, two abreast, their heads dropped and their hands held up, were a number of Turkish troops. They were all dishevelled, disarmed and despondent. Lock studied their faces for a moment searching for the familiar looks of Wassmuss, then his eye was drawn up the track to the flagpole at the top of the tower. It was bare now, but as he watched, the British flag was hoisted high. A cheer rose up.

'Where the hell is Bingham-Smith?' Lock said, looking about him.

Elsworth pointed off to the right, down the beach. 'There, sir.'

Bingham-Smith was hobbling slowly towards them.

'Where's your bloody rifle, Captain?' Lock said. He kept his face as hard and as straight as he could, but he was smiling inside. Bingham-Smith looked like he'd had a torrid time. He'd lost his topi, his face was blackened and streaked with sweat, and his tunic was torn all the way down the left sleeve.

'Bloody thing exploded in my hand, Lock! I knew I should not have listened to you and left my Webley behind,' Bingham-Smith croaked.

'Are you injured?'

Bingham-Smith shook his head. 'I think not.'

'Pity,' Lock said. 'Well, you best arm yourself again, and sharpish. Take a dead man's gun. Second thoughts, here.' He holstered his Beholla, and pulled the *liva amiral's* cumbersome Parabellum pistol from his pocket and handed it to Bingham-Smith.

'But this is a bloody Johnny gun.'

'A gun is a gun, Smith,' Lock said, glancing back towards the Turkish prisoners. Could Wassmuss be here? he thought, in the guise of *Binbaşi* Feyzi, amongst these captured men?

Lock turned his back on Bingham-Smith and walked over to the prisoners who were being corralled on the western shore by a sergeant from the Oxfords.

'Sergeant?' Lock said.

The NCO, a short wiry man with a sour face and dark, humourless eyes, didn't take his attention from his prisoners as he acknowledged Lock. 'Sir?'

'Any senior officers? Here or above?'

'There's an artillery colonel or some such.'

'Where?'

The sergeant jerked his head. 'Back up top. He's explaining the layout to your lieutenant.'

'My lieutenant?'

'Yes, sir,' the sergeant said, turned his dark eyes on Lock. 'You're the Mendips aren't you?'

Lock nodded.

'Then he's yours. Some double-barrelled toff type.'

Lock glanced back over towards his own men. He could see Bingham-Smith standing beside Elsworth. Then he realised. The sergeant had said 'lieutenant'. It must be Harrington-Brown. How in the hell had he gotten so far ahead?

'What does he look like?' Lock said.

The NCO narrowed his eyes for a second. 'Sir?'

'The Turk officer, Sergeant. Describe him for me. Young? Old?'

'Oh, he's old, sir, older than my grandfather,' the sergeant said. 'Old, bald and fat, with one of those moustaches, waxed and pointing up.' He mimed the description, waving his fingers under his nose.

Lock nodded. Wassmuss's disguises were good, but he knew that this artillery officer wouldn't be him. Besides, he reasoned Wassmuss would be somewhere a little more secure than a redoubt under threat of invasion. One of the steamers, perhaps?

'Thank you, Sergeant. Carry on.'

'Sir.'

Lock left the sergeant to guard the prisoners, and walked back over to where Singh, Elsworth and Bingham-Smith were standing along with the rest of Green Platoon.

'Right, lads, back to the boats. This isn't over yet.'

'What do you mean, Lock?' Bingham-Smith said. 'We won, didn't we?'

'No, Smith, we haven't won. Not yet. This is just the beginning.' Lock glanced at his watch. It was a little after 10 a.m. He raised his eyes back up to Bingham-Smith's face.

It would appear that Bingham-Smith had found himself a new cap, a captain's cap. Lock thought that only one captain had been wearing a cap, and that captain was now dead. And although he knew it to be irrational, Lock felt a sudden surge of anger that Bingham-Smith had taken Brooke's cap for his own. Lock rubbed his chin irritably and tried to calm himself.

'What now, then?' Bingham-Smith said, clearly mistaking Lock's silence as hesitation.

'North. Towards Amara.'

'But we need to get the prisoner, that *liva amiral*, to the *Espiegle*,' blustered Bingham-Smith, indicating down the beach to where the gufa and the elderly Turk naval officer were.

Lock shook his head. 'First things first.'

'And what in God's name does that mean?'

'It means, I'm the captain of this mission, and the miss—'

'Your mission, Lock,' Bingham-Smith sniffed, 'was to disable that electric switch. That prisoner is invaluable, and you should—'

Lock took a step forward.

Bingham-Smith instinctively flinched, then straightened up, holding his ground.

Lock flashed a smile. 'I see, Smith. Desperate to get off the front line. Very well, you take him, then. But you need to get him to the *Shaitan* or the *Lewis Pelly* and fast. He'll be able to help spot the mines, or at least guide our ships through.'

Bingham-Smith scoffed. 'And why on earth would he do that, Lock? He's the bloody enemy.'

'He'll do that, Smith, because like you he's an officer, but unlike you he's also a gentleman and a man of his word. Besides, he'll do it because I've told him that if he doesn't, I'll slice off his eyelids and then tie him to the bow of the lead ship so he'll be the first to go should it hit one of his mines.'

Bingham-Smith stared back at Lock in mild surprise. 'Isn't that a tad . . . barbaric, even for you?'

'This isn't a game of cricket, Smith, in case you hadn't noticed.' Lock had finally come round to Major Ross's thinking. This was war and sometimes brutality was necessary.

'But just where are the *Shaitan* and the *Lewis Pelly*? It will take us an age to catch the mine ships in the damned bathtub you've got us using. And I've had enough of bloody paddling.' Bingham-Smith nodded over Lock's shoulder. 'No, I think I shall take the *liva amiral* there.'

Lock turned around. The floodwater and the Tigris beyond was full of bellums now, British troops all powering on towards the next Turkish position. And keeping pace with them was the *Espiegle*. There was a crack and a boom, and the *Espiegle*'s guns began to spit more death and destruction upon Alloa and Gun Hill, the next Turkish positions just north of Birbeck Creek that ran westwards.

'It will be a damned sight quicker, Lock. They can then take the *liva amiral* by launch to the . . . er . . . *Shaitan*.'

Lock narrowed his eyes and studied the progress of the flotilla. Bingham-Smith was right, a launch from the *Espiegle* would get the Turk officer to the lead ship far quicker than rowing the gufa ever would.

'Very well,' Lock said. 'But I'm sending Elsworth with you and a couple of sepoys. They can help paddle. You'd be circling around all week if you went alone.'

Bingham-Smith stared back at Lock in silence, his mouth a tight, thin line. Lock beckoned Elsworth over. The young sharpshooter had been standing a discreet distance away with Singh and Underhill.

'Yes, sir?' Elsworth said.

'Get back to the gufa. Take two sepoys with you to paddle, and escort our Turkish friend to the *Espiegle*. Then take him and that cardboard folder I gave you straight to Major Ross. He'll know what to do.'

'Yes, sir,' Elsworth snapped a sharp salute and turned about.

'Oh, and Alfred . . .'

'Sir?'

'Don't take any shit off anyone. Straight to the major, you hear?'

Elsworth grinned and saluted sharply. 'Sir. Yes, sir.'

'No, Lock,' Bingham-Smith said, 'we will report straight to my un . . . to Colonel Godwinson. He's our commanding officer—'

'*Your* commanding officer.'

'He's a senior officer in—'

'He's a senior moron, Smith.'

'I'd ask you to stop insulting my uncle, Lock.'

'Why? He does nothing but insult me.'

'That's different. You're . . .' Bingham-Smith cleared his throat and fell silent.

Lock glared blackly back at him, clenching and unclenching his fists.

Bingham-Smith's eyes fell to Lock's hands, then flicked back up to his face. 'Er . . . very well, Lock,' he swallowed. 'Officers together, and all that . . . I'll report to . . . Major Ross as you . . . suggest.'

Lock gave a slow nod, but didn't take his eyes off Bingham-Smith's for a second. He knew he was lying.

'Right then,' Bingham-Smith said, 'lead the way, Lance Corporal.' He hesitated, then gave a stiff nod to Lock in return, and headed after Elsworth, back down to the shoreline.

Lock was standing, binoculars in hand, up at the highest point of One Tower Hill, on the baking flat roof of the tower itself. It was difficult to breathe up there such was the concussive heat being thrown up from the surface. Sweat was already pouring down Lock's face, stinging his eyes and making his neck smart. He removed his slouch hat, wiped his brow with his sleeve. He unfastened his canteen, and swilled his mouth with tepid water. He spat it out, then raised the binoculars to his eyes again.

On Townshend's Regatta went, steadily encroaching the Turkish ribbon of defence. Gun Hill, Shrapnel Hill and the village of Alloa were receiving a merciless pounding from the British artillery, both from land and sea. The 4.7 guns of the flotilla had a devastating effect on the Turkish resistance and morale. There were white flags appearing everywhere Lock turned his gaze, from all along the banks of the Tigris to the redoubts themselves, and long before any British or Indian troops even got close. The 22nd Punjabis had joined the main thrust, moving across from One Tree Hill on the east. The distant thump of artillery to Lock's left made him turn his attention to the redoubt of Shrapnel Hill, the furthest Turkish defence to the west. He could make out the report of gunfire coming from the Turks' position and watched as the

103rd Mahrattas pushed on up through the thick reeds. But just as the first of the British bellums landed, the white flags appeared and Lock watched as dozens of Turks emerged from the buildings, their hands and weapons held high as they quickly surrendered.

Directly opposite, Gun Hill was now silent. Lock scanned across until his eyes rested on Alloa. It was a tiny settlement just a mile to the north-east, sitting on the banks of the Tigris. Again there was no sign of life down there, just more white flags fluttering in the wind from various embrasures in the south-facing walls. If he and his platoon left now, Lock thought, they would get there long before the *Espiegle* and the rest of the flotilla. Admittedly, there was more reed marsh to negotiate either side of Birbeck Creek before they hit the southern shore of Alloa, but there was a small channel that Lock could see and he estimated that it would just allow his two boats to move up in single file. The flotilla, in the meantime, would have to follow the bend of the river, the reed marsh being too impenetrable for so many of them to take a short cut.

Lock lowered the binoculars and stood gazing out into the mirage.

'Where are you?' he muttered, his thoughts turning to Wassmuss. He checked his watch. Time to get going.

He stepped over to the eastern edge of the tower. Below he could make out his platoon at work by the water's edge, loading up their equipment in the bellum and the gufa, all under the watchful eye of Sergeant Major Underhill.

Lock made his way down the open stairs to the dank lower levels, and emerged out onto the main courtyard of the tower. It was busy with conversation and activity as British and Indian troops checked through the stockpiles of ammunition and food supplies that had been captured from the Turks. As Lock glanced to his left, he spotted the familiar figure of Harrington-Brown. He was standing in the shadow of a stack of grain sacks, engaged in an animated conversation with an Indian *naik*.

'Lieutenant?' Lock called.

Harrington-Brown disengaged from the Indian and walked briskly up to Lock and saluted. His face was grimy and there was a cut across his left cheek.

'Sir?'

'Where have you been?'

'Got separated in the push up the beach, sir. Found myself in the thick of the throng bursting into the redoubt,' he said, pointing to a breach in the redoubt wall. 'Over there.'

'And?'

'Nothing, sir. Light resistance with some ancient artillery officer in command. Seems it's either old men or young boys in charge of hapless Arab irregulars left to defend the line. Poor resistance, really.'

Lock studied Harrington-Brown's face. He didn't trust this man. He hadn't since the first time he'd met him.

'Yes, it would appear so. All right, Lieutenant. Go and give Sergeant Major Underhill a hand loading up the boats. We're moving on to Alloa.'

'Very well, sir.' Harrington-Brown gave a quick nod of his head and trotted off.

Lock lit himself a cigarette and watched the lieutenant go. He thought he saw Harrington-Brown glance briefly in the direction of the Indian *naik*, but he couldn't be certain. The Indian *naik* caught Lock's eye and quickly went about his business of counting off the grain sacks. Lock drew in a deep lungful of tobacco and sighed. Everywhere, it would seem, there was some conspiracy going on.

'It's enough to make a man paranoid,' Lock said to himself, and scoffed.

Lock made after Harrington-Brown, picking his way through the troops and the debris and abandoned Turkish equipment, down towards the shore. As he hit the scrubby sand, a voice called out to his left.

'Sahib! Sahib!'

Singh was scrambling down the sand towards him.

'What is it, Sid?'

'You had best come. Trouble with Bing Ham Smith, sahib.'

'Oh, for fu—' Lock tossed his cigarette aside and trotted up the bank with Singh at his side.

When they crossed back over to the southern beach, Lock could see that most of the Oxfords had set off again to join the main flotilla of bellums. Only the gufa was still there, tied to the shore.

Bingham-Smith had the Parabellum pistol raised and Elsworth was standing, ankle-deep in the water, between the officer and the *liva amiral*. The elderly Turk naval officer was sat, stony-faced, in the back of the gufa, still clinging on to the Union flagpole. Two of the new sepoys were standing a little further up the bank, watching with wide, worried eyes.

To Lock it appeared that Elsworth was trying to stop Bingham-Smith from shooting the *liva amiral*.

'I'll have you court-martialed for this, Lance Corporal,' Bingham-Smith barked. 'Now, I shan't ask again, move!'

'What the bloody hell is going on, Alfred?' Lock said.

Elsworth had his hand held up facing Bingham-Smith, as if he was a policeman holding up traffic. 'The *liva amiral* refuses to budge, sir. Just keeps saying "*hayir*", which I'm guessing is "no".'

'But just paddle off!' Lock said in exasperation.

'Can't, sir. He keeps whacking me with that bloody flagpole.'

'Oh, for Christ's sake,' Lock said, knocking Bingham-Smith's pistol upwards. The gun went off and Lock shoved the aristocrat away. He pushed past Elsworth, jumped into the gufa, and stormed towards the elderly Turk. He ducked as the naval officer swung the flagpole at his head, grabbed hold of it, and shoved the Turk forcefully back.

'*What is the meaning of this?*' Lock bellowed in Turkish, spittle flying as he glared down at the elderly officer.

The *liva amiral* blinked myopically up at Lock and shrugged. '*I am your prisoner, Yüzbaşi, I will not go anywhere unless I am escorted by you.*'

'*I'm not your bloody batman, sir,*' Lock fumed.

The elderly Turk merely tutted and turned his gaze out to the Tigris.

Lock's shoulders dropped. 'Fine,' he sighed. 'Bingham-Smith, Elsworth, we'll take the old goat with us to Alloa. *Liva Amiral Bey*,' Lock said, switching back to Turkish and holding his hand out, '*please step out of the boat. You're coming with us.*'

'That's not on, Lock,' Bingham-Smith fumed. 'I already told you that I am returning to the *Espiegle*. With the prisoner.'

Lock flicked his chin out towards the main flotilla on the river. 'And so you shall, Smith. But she's well ahead of us now.'

'Then we must catch her, Lock. We must catch her.'

'In this thing?' Lock said pointing to the gufa. 'Look, Smith, the *Espiegle*'s due to halt at Alloa anyway and has to follow the bend of the river. So we will rendezvous with her there.' He turned away from Bingham-Smith and climbed out of the gufa. 'Sid, Alfred and . . .' He paused, glancing at the two sepoys. The Indians stepped forward apace, and snapped smart salutes.

'Sepoy Addul Tarin, sahib.'

'Sepoy Karamjeet Singh, sahib.'

Lock nodded. 'Good lads. Right, dump your gear in the gufa and help Havildar Singh and Lance Corporal Elsworth drag it out of the water and over to the north-west beach.'

The two sepoys readily did as they were ordered, while Lock lent a hand to the elderly Turk, helping him to climb back out of the gufa and on to dry land. The *liva amiral* still kept a tight grip of the Union flag.

Lock eyed the flag with amusement. '*Liva Amiral, you can let go of the flag now, if you wish.*'

The elderly Turk turned his watery gaze on Lock. '*Oh, no, Yüzbaşi. It is insurance.*'

Lock smiled and held his hand out, directing the Turk naval officer to walk on ahead. He then waited for the sepoys, Singh and Elsworth to trot by with the gufa held up between them, and then he turned to face Bingham-Smith.

'I was beginning to get more and more suspicious, Smith.'

'Of what?' Bingham-Smith narrowed his eyes.

'Of you.'

'What the devil do you mean?'

'As to why you are so keen to abandon the chase.'

'Preposterous!' Bingham-Smith spat.

'Is it? But then I realised that you're not suspicious at all.'

'Precisely,' Bingham-Smith nodded in agreement.

'You're just a coward.'

Bingham-Smith's mouth went slack.

'I . . .' he spluttered, but Lock had already turned on his heels.

'You coming, Smith? Or are you going to try and swim after Uncle Goddy?' Lock called back over his shoulder.

Bingham-Smith muttered a curse, then scooping up the Parabellum pistol from the sand, he followed the others up the beach.

CHAPTER FIFTEEN

Already the heat was so terrific that it was hard to concentrate properly. The temperature must have been well into the high nineties and Lock found it energy sapping just watching the sepoys struggle to move the bellum and the two gufas through the thick reeds. Salt-sweat stains were already creating intricate circular patterns on the backs of their khaki tunics, but the Indian lads kept at it. Progress was slow, and the men had begun to appear drowsy under the effort. The insects buzzing and biting around them were relentless, as was the merciless furnace of the sun overhead. The only break in the monotony was Underhill's hoarse voice barking out 'wake up, darkie!' whenever a sepoys' head bobbed forward. And even Elsworth hadn't the energy to sing one of his insufferable tunes.

Lock had split Green Platoon into three squads ready to attack the village. In the gufa with Lock, sat working the paddles, were the two sepoys, Addul Tarin and Karamjeet Singh. Elsworth, as before, was at the bow, scoped rifle at the ready, Singh was sat just behind the young sharpshooter, while Lock himself was sat towards the rear with the *liva amiral* at the very back. The old Turk officer had nodded off and was snoring softly now. He still held the Union flag and pole between his crossed arms, but it was now lying flat across the gunwales.

In the second gufa was Harrington-Brown, with Chopra and Ram Lal and two of the new sepoys at the paddles. Taking point was the bellum, with Bingham-Smith out at the very bow. Lock could see the pompous arse's shoulders hunched forward, his head low as it jerked from left to right like a nervous chicken. Behind him sat Toor, then four of the new sepoys manning the oars, while Underhill was at the stern manning the guiding pole.

Everyone was crouched as low as they comfortably could be, in silence. The only sound they made above their harsh breathing was the repetitive lifting and plunging of the poles and oars in the water and the occasional smack of a hand against the bite of incessant mosquitoes. The water splashed and sloshed about them, with the reeds rustling gently as the boats squeezed by. Way over to the east, Lock could hear the continuous distant thump of shellfire, and the crack of rifle shots mixed with the occasional rat-tat-tat of machine gun fire. But up ahead, Alloa appeared silent and deserted.

Lock removed his slouch hat and wiped the dripping sweat from his brow. His wound had begun to itch like crazy and it took all of his willpower not to scratch at it. He slapped his neck and cursed under his breath. He checked his watch for the umpteenth time. It was now well past midday. Squinting forward into the hazy mirage, he hoped there wouldn't be any surprises waiting for them at the village, and that he could at least let the men rest up for a bit in the shade of the buildings.

So far they had been fortunate; not one casualty or injury to a member of his platoon. He still didn't know if Pritchard and the two sepoys had made it safely back to Qurna. But he trusted that they had, and that they would now be with the main thrust of the attack. Lock knew that this good fortune couldn't last, but, by God, he was going to savour it while it did. Yet, doubt was nagging at the back of his mind. Yes, he was eager to push on after Wassmuss, but did he have the right to risk his men's lives for, if he was honest, what was rapidly becoming a personal vendetta? He mentally shrugged. No, he was being hard on himself. Wassmuss *was* the enemy, his network vast and destructive, and by bringing the German down, the threat would be at an end. Wouldn't it?

Lock pinched the bridge of his nose. Fatigue and the heat was making his head swim. He could use a rest himself, just thirty minutes of blissful sleep. And a drink. Christ, he could use a proper drink. He licked his dry lips, but didn't reach for his water canteen. That was not the kind of drink he wanted, anyway, no matter how parched he was. He swallowed dryly and grimaced. Best to wait until they hit the shore and knew what lay ahead.

They were to beach and spread out to the east and west, encircling the redoubt as they did on One Tree Hill. Lock's squad would go in through the centre. This time, however, he was acutely aware that they didn't have the cover of darkness, albeit, a darkness illuminated by the full moon. And despite the number of white flags flapping in the heavy hot breeze, Lock wasn't going to be complacent. The men were on high alert, bayonets were fixed, and although the atmosphere was draining, Lock knew they were ready to storm the redoubt.

He wiped his brow again and fixed his slouch hat back on his head. The reeds were beginning to thin out and the village of Alloa was drawing ever closer.

'Be wary, lads,' Lock called when the boats finally passed through the reed marsh and out on to open water. All three vessels spread out, with Underhill and Bingham-Smith's on the left and Harrington-Brown's on the right, furthest east and closest to the wide expanse of the Tigris.

Alloa was little more than a collection of dilapidated reed and mud huts, mostly roofless and most with little more than half a wall left standing. But it was still a perfectly adequate spot for a concealed machine gun nest, or for a sniper to lie in wait. So, everyone instinctively ducked down as low as they could during that last hundred yards of flood. The boats were making slow progress to cover the distance, but then Lock felt the bottom of the gufa he was in begin to catch against objects beneath the surface of the water.

'Over the side, boys!' Lock called, and followed his words up and out of the gufa.

Everyone plunged ashore. Lock ran, crouched low, Beholla drawn. He made it to the first piece of suitable cover, a low wall behind which stood a row of fishing poles, broken and twisted like an abandoned child's climbing frame, and paused.

Each moment that passed, Lock expected gunfire to spit forth its indiscriminatory fury. But the crumbling walls of the village outskirts offered nothing but a great, yawning silence. Lock glanced to his left, catching the eye of Underhill. Lock held up his hand, fingers splayed, and mouthed 'five minutes.' Underhill nodded his understanding, then scooted off with his squad in tow. Bingham-Smith hesitated, staring directly at Lock. Then, stooped so low that he was practically running bent double, and with one hand clutching onto his officer's peaked cap should it fall off, and the other gripping tightly to the Parabellum pistol, he stumbled after Underhill.

Lock turned to his right and again held his hand up and mouthed 'five minutes' to Harrington-Brown. The lieutenant gave a curt nod, then he too led his squad off, picking their way cautiously towards the eastern side of the redoubt.

Lock turned his attention to the main building of the redoubt that loomed directly ahead of him. It was an imposing wall at least three storeys high. There was a large set of barn doors in the centre, one of which was blown off from its hinges. There were no windows, only two embrasures, one either side of the doors, cut high enough for a man to stand behind with a rifle poised. Only there was no rifle barrel or heavy gun turret poking out, just a solitary white cloth flapping limply from the right-hand embrasure.

'It looks as if Johnny has left this place to its fate, sahib,' Singh said from close to Lock's side.

'Yes, but be wary of snipers, Sid. All right, I'll go in first.'

Lock scrambled up and vaulting over the low wall, zigzagged through the fishing poles and made a dash for the barn doors. His heart was in his mouth as he skipped over the scabby, debris-strewn ground, but it was only a matter of seconds before he reached the gaping black doorway. He thumped his back into the wall to one side and stood still, catching his breath, ears peeled for any sound of movement inside. He signaled for Singh to follow.

The big Indian leapt over the low wall, and made a darting, weaving run. He stood with his back to the redoubt wall on the opposite side of the doorway and gave Lock a brief nod. Singh then gave a low whistle and Sepoys Addul Tarin and Karamjeet Singh scampered over to join him.

A fall of rocks made Lock snap his head back to the low wall behind the fishing poles. He caught sight of the Union flag hanging limply. Elsworth's face peered over the wall and Lock held his hand up indicating for him to wait there. The young sharpshooter nodded his understanding and ducked back down. The *liva amiral*'s face appeared briefly, but was quickly dragged away again.

'Jesus, why didn't I just shoot that stubborn old goat in the first place?' Lock muttered.

He turned back to the doorway and checked his watch. Thirty seconds to go before the five minutes he'd indicated to both Harrington-Brown and Underhill had passed. But there had been no gunshots, so no one had run into any resistance.

'So far, so good,' Lock said to Singh. He unbuttoned his breast pocket and pulled out the silver trench whistle Major Hall had given him at Shaiba. Placing it between his lips he watched the second hand on his watch tick home, then blew three short, sharp blasts.

Lock burst through the door with Singh and the two sepoys close behind. At the same instant, he was aware of Underhill's and Harrington-Brown's squads rushing in from the left and from the right, their guns at the ready.

Lock held up his hand and stopped dead in his tracks. Underhill and Harrington-Brown did the same.

Inside, the place was knocked to pieces. It was a vast open shell, nothing but four walls with embrasures on each side, and open doorways. Most of the roof was missing, with many bare and charred joists visible above. It was as if they were standing inside the ribcage of some great prehistoric skeleton. Daylight streamed down through the broken ceiling making intricate patterns with the shadows of the joints and the dust particles that floated and danced in the air. The walls were as pockmarked on the inside as they were on the outside, with bullet and shell holes. A rickety wooden staircase ran up the left-hand wall and disappeared through an open access to the roof.

There were no bodies visible, but in the middle of the building, sat next to a silent Krupp field gun, his head held in his hands, was a dishevelled Turkish artillery officer. He hadn't even looked up when Lock and the others had burst in.

Lock indicated for his men to stand down and holstered his Beholla.

'Sergeant Major . . . Lieutenant . . . Sid . . .' he said, 'secure the perimeters of the building and place a man at each and every corner.'

The trio quickly set about organising the sepoys under their charge to place themselves at the embrasures and crouched near to the open doorways, ready to defend against any sudden attack.

Lock walked over to the Turk officer and stopped in front of him.

'*Yüzbaşi?*' Lock said softly.

The Turk didn't stir.

'*Yüzbaşi?*' Lock snapped, clicking his fingers in front of the Turk's nose.

The young artillery officer started, and lifted his grimy and tear-streaked face, looking around bleary-eyed. He eventually settled his bloodshot gaze on the bullet hole in Lock's left breast pocket and frowned.

'*Where are your men, Yüzbaşi?*' Lock said.

The young artillery officer's eyes focused on Lock's face momentarily, and then they drifted away again, peering in confusion past Lock's shoulder. Lock turned to see that the elderly Turk naval officer had wandered into the redoubt and was standing looking about in bewilderment, the Union flag still in his grip. Elsworth was a pace behind him, rifle cradled across his belly, scanning the rubble of the ruined interior.

'Elsworth,' Lock barked, 'take that bloody flag off of him, and get up to the roof and raise it before our sodding artillery starts shelling this place again.'

Lock thought it unlikely that there would be further bombardments, but it wouldn't do any harm to take preventative measures.

'Sir,' Elsworth snapped a smart salute, and went to take the flag.

But the Turk naval officer stubbornly refused to let it go.

'*Liva Amiral Bey, it is vitally important that you relinquish the flag and take a seat,*' Lock said.

The *liva amiral* blinked over to Lock, then back to Elsworth. He nodded and let the young sharpshooter take the flag from him. The *liva amiral* looked about his immediate surroundings. Spotting an upturned chair, he shuffled over to it, straightened it up, and pulling a handkerchief from his pocket, began to dust the seat down. Satisfied, he slumped down, opened up his book, and began to read.

'Quick sharp, Alfred,' Lock called.

'Sir. Yes, sir.' Elsworth dropped his haversack by the foot of the stairs, shouldered his rifle, and with the flag and rod in his hand, bounded up to the roof.

Lock turned back to the young artillery officer. '*Your men?*' he repeated.

The Turk shook his head slowly. '*My men?*' he croaked. '*Fled, the entire garrison . . . gone.*' He dropped his head and began to silently sob in shame.

'Sergeant Major?' Lock called over to the far side of the redoubt.

Underhill was standing at one of the embrasures facing north. He turned his head to glance back at Lock. 'Sah?'

'Organise a sweep of the buildings to the west and north. If it's clear, post sentries, then report back here.'

'Sah.' Underhill said. He barked a few orders at his squad and then they quickly made their way outside.

'Lieutenant,' Lock said, turning to Harrington-Brown, who was over by the embrasure looking out towards the Tigris, 'you do the same to the east and north. Again, if it's clear, post sentries and return to me here.'

Harrington-Brown hesitated momentarily, his eyes remaining fixed on the Turk artillery officer.

'Problem, Lieutenant?' Lock said.

'No, nothing. Sir,' Harrington-Brown said. He snapped a quick salute and set off back out of the building.

Lock watched him go thoughtfully as Singh came up to him. Lock glanced up at his big Indian friend.

'Sid, you best post lookouts along the southern shore.'

'Sahib.' Singh saluted smartly and moved away. He briefly spoke in Punjabi to Sepoys Addul Tarin and Karamjeet Singh, who were sat near to the barn doors. All three went back out of the main entrance, just as Bingham-Smith was coming in. He strode over to Lock and gave the weeping Turk artillery man a scathing look.

257

'What a pathetic sight,' he sneered. 'Do any of these Johnny fellows know how to fight?'

Lock sighed. 'Still here, Smith?'

'You told me to observe, Lock. And that is what I am doing, observing the Turk to be no match for the might of the British army. I shall inform my uncle of the very same as soon as I see him.'

Lock shook his head slowly. 'Yes, you go on thinking that, underestimating them at your peril.'

'I've seen nothing to say otherwise,' sniffed Bingham-Smith. 'An old man wondering about in a daze clutching the Union flag like he's leading the church parade for the Boy Scouts, and a crying child distraught that his friends have run off and left him all alone. Is that it, I ask? Is that all they have to offer? Pah, this war will be over by—'

'Christmas?' Lock said. 'They said that *last* Christmas.'

'I don't care what you say, Lock. Uncle and General Townshend will be delighted with the news.'

'Your uncle may be a 24-carat fool, Smith, but the general will scoff at your assessment.'

Bingham-Smith straightened his tunic and sniffed. 'To coin one of your less vulgar expressions, Lock, "bugger off".'

'*Touché*, Smith. *Touché.*'

Lock turned his attention back to the artillery officer. He placed a hand on the Turk's shoulder and said softly, '*Yüzbaşi, I need to know about the German. Herr Wassmuss. Or perhaps there is a Binbaşi Feyzi here?*'

The artillery officer sniffed and looked up at Lock. He wiped his face and forced a strained smile.

'*German? Yes, he was here until . . .*' He paused, frowning, '*. . . until the shelling started. I cannot be certain.*'

Lock felt his wound itch in anticipation. '*Can you describe him?*'

The artillery officer seemed to go off into a trance again, eyes looking past Lock's shoulder.

'*Yüzbaşi?*'

But the officer just shook his head. '*I . . .*'

He dropped his chin and started to sob again.

Lock glanced over his shoulder to the eastern doorway. It yawned back at him.

'Captain Lock, sir.' It was Elsworth. He was calling down from the roof.

Lock craned his neck to see the young sharpshooter's head and shoulders peering through a hole in the ceiling.

'What is it, Alfred?'

'You'd better come and see for yourself, sir.'

'Bugger it,' Lock said under his breath.

'Smith, can I trust you not to shoot these two if I leave you alone?'

Bingham-Smith's lip curled up. 'I think not, Lock. I shall be accompanying you up to the roof . . . to observe.'

At that moment the fall of footsteps made both men turn to the eastern doorway. It was Harrington-Brown. He was alone.

'Lieutenant?' Lock said.

Harrington-Brown removed his topi, scratched at the tightly cropped curly hair underneath, and gave a nod to Bingham-Smith. 'Reporting back. Captain.'

'I'm the captain in charge here, Lieutenant. Don't you forget that,' Lock said.

Harrington-Brown gave an almost undetectable sniff of contempt and looked to Lock.

'Well?'

'All men stationed as you ordered. And . . . er . . .' he glanced at Bingham-Smith again and the two men shared a barely disguised smirk, 'there's nothing to report. No sign of the enemy. Just a load of abandoned equipment. Rifles, helmets, packs, that sort of thing. There's an empty medical station, too. Plenty of supplies, and empty beds. With linen. D'you know that I even found a kitchen with food on the boil. It's as if the bloody Johnnies have just vanished into thin air.' He clicked his fingers for effect and said, 'Poof! Just like that,' then grinned. But the smile never reached his eyes.

'Well,' Lock said, 'as you are here, I want you to keep an eye on these two officers.'

Harrington-Brown looked from the naval officer to the artillery officer.

'Very well, Captain.'

Lock nodded. 'If you're coming, Smith, come,' he said, picking his way through the rubble and over to the staircase.

Up on the roof, over in a corner on the eastern side, lay a Turkish soldier. Only he wasn't any ordinary soldier from what Lock could see. His face, hands and arms were painted green and he was wearing a green uniform, not khaki, but a green the colour of the reeds in the surrounding marsh and of the leaves of the nearby date palms. He was a sniper. And apart from a bandage wrapped around his head, the sniper appeared uninjured. But his eyes told a different story. They stared back up at Lock, Elsworth and Bingham-Smith, searching their faces vainly for pity. But Lock felt no pity for this Turkish sniper.

'Weapon?' Lock said.

'None, sir. Not even a penknife.'

'Strange. He's clearly from a gun-nest hidden in a tree judging by his camouflage. But how in the hell did he come to be up on this roof?'

Lock scanned the area. The nearest foliage to them was a cluster of date palms that ran along the western bank of the Tigris, just to the east of the roof. But those trees were a good 500 yards away.

'Well, whatever the answer, he's of no threat to us now,' Lock said. 'Go fetch a stretcher from that medical station Lieutenant Harrington-Brown found and have one of the sepoys help you get him back downstairs.'

'Why not just put the fellow out of his misery, Lock?' Bingham-Smith said.

Elsworth hesitated.

'Because, Smith,' Lock said, 'we're not barbarians—'

'I beg to differ. In the case of certain individuals.'

Lock ignored the jibe. 'We'll make him comfortable downstairs, out of the sun, and leave him for our M. O.s from the hospital ships to deal with. They're following the regatta, picking up and patching up as many of the wounded as they can.'

'Bloody waste of time. I'd say he's a goner. Look at the back of his head.'

Lock leant in closer. He hadn't noticed initially, but from where Bingham-Smith had been standing it was hard to miss. The back of the Turk's bandage was dark with blood. Already blowflies were crawling over the sticky mess.

'Give him some water, Alfred, and stay with him,' Lock said.

'It won't be long. Make him as comfortable as you can.'

Elsworth nodded. He shouldered his rifle and unhooked his water canteen from his Sam Browne belt. He knelt down beside the Turk sniper and uncorking the canteen, held it up to the Turk's mouth.

'Easy, easy, Johnny,' Elsworth said. The Turk gulped the water down thirstily.

Lock made his way back to the staircase, with Bingham-Smith at his heels.

'You're soft, Lock. Soft and sentimental. Which, I must say, I find rather amusing,' Bingham-Smith smirked.

Lock wondered if Bingham-Smith would break his neck if he shoved him down the stairs. He sighed and peered down through the shell-damaged roof into the vast, debris-strewn room below. He suddenly pulled up. The *liva amiral* was still in his chair but had dozed off with his book resting on his belly, and in front of the dormant Krupp field gun sat the young artillery officer. Only he wasn't alone. Harrington-Brown was standing over him, finger out, pointing and prodding. If Lock were a betting man, he'd say that the lieutenant was haranguing the Turkish captain. Momentarily losing sight of the pair as he passed through the ceiling to descend the stairs, Lock emerged back on the ground floor only to find the room as he had left it earlier, with both Turk officers sat alone. Harrington-Brown was once again over by the threshold of the eastern doorway.

The *liva amiral* was snoring softly, his belly rising and falling like a great bellows, while the young artillery officer sat staring ahead. Only he looked scared now, rather than distraught, all the colour having drained from his face.

'*Yüzbaşi*,' Lock said, striding over to the young Turk officer. '*Is there a mobile base of operations hereabouts? Perhaps on one of the Turk steamers?*'

The artillery officer's eyes snapped to Lock's, then flicked over to where Harrington-Brown was standing, before returning to meet Lock's gaze. He shook his head.

From up on the roof the soft, plaintive notes of Elsworth's mouth organ drifted down as the young sharpshooter started playing a gentle, sentimental tune. Then his voice began to softly sing,

Rolling home,
Rolling home,
Rolling home,
Rolling home,
By the light of the silvery moo-oo-oon!
Happy is the day
When you draw your buckshee pay
And you're rolling, rolling, rolling, rolling home.

'*Come, Yüzbaşi, I know about the boats. We have good intelligence,*' Lock said. '*I just don't know which one.*'

Again the young Turk officer's eyes were drawn like magnets in the direction of Harrington-Brown. Lock deliberately took a step to the right, blocking the lieutenant from view.

'*Is it the Mosul, Yüzbaşi?*'

The artillery officer looked blankly back up at Lock.

'*Or the Marmaris?*'

The Turk officer's chestnut brown eyes widened momentarily, then he averted his gaze altogether.

Lock had his answer. He turned away from the young officer and, ignoring the watching Harrington-Brown, walked over to where Elsworth had left his haversack at the foot of the stairs. He pulled out the cardboard folder of papers the *liva amiral* had with him on the tiny sand island, and strode out of the main entrance and into the hazy sunshine.

Lock leant heavily against the baking wall, pulled off his slouch hat and wiped his brow. He fished out his Woodbines and sat down. So there was a German here, he thought, striking a match against the rough brick wall behind him. The *liva amiral* had said that he was given the file to look after by the German officer from the *Marmaris*, and now this young artillery officer was talking of a German officer. But was it Wassmuss? Lock put the lit match to the cigarette between his lips and frowned. Most of the Turkish divisions had German officers 'advising', but Lock had a gut feeling that this one was Wassmuss. It had to be. Hadn't it? He exhaled and cursed.

'I should have shot you dead the first time I saw you,' Lock said to himself. 'Well, I won't hesitate next time.'

Lock smoked in silence, trying to empty his mind. His eyes were heavy, but he resisted the urge to doze. What he needed was a good cup of coffee. He shuffled himself into a more comfortable position and unfastened the string-bound cardboard folder.

There must be something within these pages, Lock thought, something that you want me to see? Is that it? Are you toying with me, Herr Wassmuss? I wonder . . .

Lock slowly picked through the papers. There were pages and pages of tedious quartermaster lists, details of equipment, food stuffs, arms, as well as sentry rotas and memos relating to water ration quotas. He came to a circuit diagram of the mine network.

'Now this would have been useful before I'd disconnected the switch,' Lock smiled to himself, 'but at least it will help to locate them further should the *liva amiral* prove untrustworthy.'

A thought suddenly struck him. He didn't want to take the risk of Bingham-Smith seeing this document. It would just give him the perfect justification for taking the *liva amiral* with him back to the *Espiegle* as he'd wanted to do in the first place. That would scupper Lock's plan of getting to the *Shaitan* and the *Lewis Pelly*, and so away from Godwinson and Townshend's grasp.

'I think not,' Lock muttered, folding the document up and stuffing it in his inside pocket.

The next document he came to was a map of the various redoubts along the Tigris. Interesting, but again obsolete now, for the British had already passed through and taken control of the majority of the Turkish defences. Then Lock froze, his cigarette held in his fingertips, halfway towards his mouth. The paper he had just turned to was at first glance nothing more than another list. There were German, Turkish, Arabic, Russian, British and even a couple of Indian names typed there, and next to each one was a monetary value in German marks and the name of a city or town. Lock presumed this was where the person on the list was located. But as he read down, his eyes suddenly came to a halt at a familiar name.

The Ottoman Pearl (Natural) Fisheries Corporation,
Cape Al-Qayd,
Bubiyan Island,
Mesopotamia.

February 1915.

Payments (M) for the quarterly period up to and including
January 1915:

Name	Amount	Location
Assadi	10,000M	Fao
Bicherakov	50,000M	Kermanshah
Bratov	25,000M	Kasvin
v.Brauchitsch	100,000M	Constantinople
Chatar	40,000M	Karachi
Dukhonin	10,000M	Ispahan
Grössburger	100,000M	Basra
Godwinson	100,000M	Basra
Halder	50,000M	Baghdad
Hamid	125,000M	Mohammerah
Henry	30,000M	Karachi
Isham	50,000M	Cairo
Kasravi	30,000M	Ahwaz
Meskoob	25,000M	Daurat
Omurtak	75,000M	Constantinople
Reghubir	30,000M	Karachi

| Total: | 850,000M | |

Signed: G

There it was again, that initial 'G', the same initial that had
signed the order for Wassmuss to attack Basra from the Persian side

of the border. But more than that was the fact that the document made reference to Godwinson. Colonel Godwinson? Of the Mendips? Was it one and the same? And if so, then what did it mean?

Lock scratched his head and took a deep drag on his cigarette. His brain hurt. It was swimming with questions, but void of any answers. He looked down at the list again, and again his eye rested on the one name that shouldn't be there: Godwinson.

Was he on the German payroll? Impossible! Or was it? How was the colonel actually funding his private regiment? Perhaps the fool didn't even realise it was German money he was getting from . . . an innocent pearl venture? The rich were involved in all sorts of deals to do with stocks and shares. Oil, gold, pearls . . . It could be perfectly innocent. But then why was his name on this list, a list that looked to Lock suspiciously like a list of agents or paymasters.

'Christ, what a mess,' Lock muttered, scrunching up the paper and leaning his head back against the wall and closing his eyes.

But why was this list in the possession of the *liva amiral* in the first place? Was this some kind of game? Was this Wassmuss mocking him? Playing with him? Mocking the British? But to what ends?

'Bugger,' he muttered aloud.

A footfall broke Lock from his thoughts, and he opened his eyes to see Singh trotting towards him, returning from the shore.

'Well?' Lock said, unscrunching and flattening out the list. He folded it up and put it away in his pocket. He then closed the cardboard folder and pulled himself to his feet.

'The lookouts are posted, sahib. There is not a thing else to report. All very quiet and empty. Johnny did leave quick sharpish. Much much equipment and the usual food left on the stove. It seems they are always cooking, sahib, does it not?'

Lock smiled up at his friend. 'Yes, Harrington-Brown said he found much the same thing. Still, more for us. Any coffee?'

Singh nodded. 'I will bring the pot up to you, sahib. We also found many rifles and one boat abandoned further up the shore.'

Lock drew on his cigarette thoughtfully for a moment.

'All right, Sid. Thanks.'

'What is next, may I ask, sahib? Do we wait for the *Espiegle* to transfer our prisoners ?'

Lock shook his head, and pulled himself to his feet. 'No, Sid. I'm going on. Wassmuss is not far. I can feel him.'

Singh frowned back at his friend, a look of worry written across his face.

Lock smiled. 'Don't worry so, Sid. I'm not being reckless. Besides, I'm still taking the old Turk to one of the launches at the head of the regatta, to put him to work mine spotting. That's the priority.'

'Very good, sahib. I shall accompany you.'

'Thanks, Sid.'

'And the others?'

'We'll take Lieutenant Harrington-Brown, Elsworth and three of the sepoys, in the bellum not the bloody gufa. The sergeant major can stay here until relieved and follow on. Hopefully Sergeant Pritchard and the others will catch up, too.'

'And Bing Ham Smith, sahib?'

'He can stay here with Underhill and wait for his uncle to arrive. I've had enough of his comp—'

'Again, Lock, I most certainly am not doing that,' Bingham-Smith said, stepping out of the redoubt, a look of arrogant smugness written across his face.

Lock glared back at him. 'You're not coming with me, Smith, not anymore.'

Bingham-Smith sniffed and jutted his chin out. 'I shall do as I please, Lock.'

Lock was sorely tempted to swing for him. God, he thought, I really, really should. He clenched his fist and felt a soft jolt as Singh made a poor attempt at pretending to stumble into him.

'Begging your pardon, sahib.'

Lock shot Singh a black look, then realising what his friend had done, he calmed himself. He turned back to Bingham-Smith, then was momentarily distracted.

'Listen,' Lock said, holding up his hand.

'What?' Bingham-Smith said. 'I hear nothing.'

'Elsworth.'

'Sahib?'

'He's stopped singing,' Lock said.

'Bloody good job, too,' Bingham-Smith said. 'One less prisoner to deal with.'

'Get lost, will you, Smith.'

Bingham-Smith straightened his tunic and adjusted his cap, squinting into the sun. 'You needn't worry, Lock. I have no desire to accompany you any further. I've seen quite enough. I will be returning to the *Espiegle* to make my report.'

'Report?' Lock said, suspiciously.

'Oh, yes,' Bingham-Smith said, turning his smug gaze to Lock. 'Remember, I've been . . . observing you and, as far as I can tell, your mission is over. You disabled the electronic switch, yet you have insisted we all keep moving, with important prisoners in tow.' He paused and smirked. 'Why, Lock? Is it this ghost chase Amy keeps harping on about? This German fellow everyone presumes is dead, except for you?'

'You heard what the artillery officer said in there,' Lock said, jutting his chin towards the redoubt.

'I don't speak Turkish, Lock,' Bingham-Smith said. 'So, as far as I'm concerned, you are just telling us what you want us to believe, that this German is alive and just over the next horizon.' He shook his head mockingly. 'Pathetic.'

'He isn't dead,' Lock insisted.

'So you keep saying, Lock. But how in the hell do you actually know?'

'I just do, that's all.'

Bingham-Smith shook his head again.

'You wouldn't understand.'

'I understand perfectly that you are reckless, selfish and obsessed. Dangerously so. I also understand that by keeping the . . . the ghost of this German fellow . . .'

'Wassmuss. His name is Wassmuss.'

'By keeping the ghost of this Wassmuss chappy alive, you think that you can keep his threat to Amy alive.'

'The threat isn't a fantasy, Smith. She's in danger—'

'Pah! Of course it is, for the more you insist he's out there, the more you hope Amy will need you, will be scared. But do you know something, Lock?' Bingham-Smith said. 'It's me that she comes to for comfort. It's my arms around her when she needs reassuring.'

It was Lock's turn to shake his head mockingly. 'Now you're the one making things up. Amy isn't that kind of girl. You'd know that if you really knew her.'

Bingham-Smith let out a snort of laughter. 'Of course she bloody is, Lock. They all are. Gals, I mean. Needy, delicate creatures, looking for protection from chaps like me. Amy's no different, you deluded fool.'

Lock felt his heckles rise again. He turned away before he did anything he'd later regret and then stopped dead. Regret? What the hell was he thinking? He spun round, fist ready to strike. Singh stepped forward to intervene once again.

'My, my, Lock, we are touchy today,' Bingham-Smith smirked. Then his eyes dropped to the folder under Lock's arm. 'And I think I should be taking that, don't you?' He held out his hand for the document files. 'I'll see that Major Ross gets them.'

'I don't think so, Smith.'

'Come, come, Lock. What if something happens to you and the files are lost? Do you know what's in them? What strategic information they contain?'

'I have had a read,' Lock said.

'And?'

Look hesitated. He didn't want to entrust the documents to this man, but what choice did he have? 'They need to get to Ross as quickly as possible,' he said.

'Very well,' Bingham-Smith sighed, 'then give them to Singh here or that lance corporal, and send them along with me.'

Lock shook his head. 'I need Singh and Elsworth with me.'

'Then you have little choice,' Bingham-Smith said, his hand still held out expectantly.

Look glared back at Bingham-Smith's smug face. Bastard, he thought.

'Or you could bring them yourself?'

Lock shook his head and held out the cardboard folder. 'Straight to Major Ross, you hear?'

'But of course, old chap,' Bingham-Smith said, taking the folder, and turning on his heels without another word.

'Damn you, Smith,' Lock muttered after him.

'So you keep saying,' Bingham-Smith called back over his shoulder. 'And I'm taking two of the sepoys to row me back to the *Espiegle*. D'you hear me, Lock?' He strode on down towards the shore like a strutting peacock, chin held high.

Lock threw a foul curse after him, then turned back to the redoubt.

'Come on, Sid. Let's get after those launches.'

CHAPTER SIXTEEN

You don't often meet people you take an instant liking to, Lock thought. An instant disliking for, yes, but the man he was standing next to on the deck of the *Shaitan* was the exception to that all familiar rule. His name was Mark Singleton, a Royal Navy lieutenant, and commander of the small flat-bottomed launch-tug that, along with its sister ship, the *Lewis Pelly*, was forging ahead of the main body of Townshend's flotilla. They had been clearing mines and obstructions as they travelled further up the main channel of the Tigris, penetrating deeper and deeper into enemy territory. Only now, the chain linking the two vessels had been disconnected. The *Shaitan* now had an elderly Turk naval officer standing at its bow, a brass telescope occasionally lifting to his eye, as he helped point out the location of the mines he'd spent months previously laying down. Lieutenant Singleton was both delighted and bewildered as to why the Turk prisoner was so amiable, but

Lock explained to him that the *liva amiral* felt it was his duty as a captive to assist.

Having left Sergeant Major Underhill in charge of Green Platoon back at Alloa until relieved once more, Lock had set off in the bellum. Along with the *liva amiral*, Lock had Singh, Harrington-Brown, Elsworth, Ram Lal and Sepoys Addul Tarin and Karamjeet Singh for company. They rowed on up the Tigris, passing the settlements of Jala, Halla and Bahran, now all flying white flags, eventually catching up with the *Shaitan* and the *Lewis Pelly* at the mouth of Rotah Creek. The two launch-tugs had been delayed there, having found the way obstructed by a sunken lighter. Luckily only half of the channel was blocked, but the other half was strewn with mines. Already the crews from both tugs were in the fast-flowing water up to their chests, cutting away with hatchets at the cables linking the mines.

Lock had hailed the officer he could see directing operations from the deck of the *Shaitan*, and had been invited aboard.

The launch was a small vessel, some 65ft long with a 12ft beam, and now with Lock and his men aboard, it was rather cramped. There was a central funnel and wheelhouse and a large wooden deck. Fortunately, the deck was covered by a large canvas awning, which stretched from bow to stern, with only the afterdeck exposed to the elements. She was armed with a single bow-mounted 1-3pdr gun, that boasted an 8ft barrel and which could fire off twenty rounds per minute. A Union Jack flew proudly from the mast at her stern.

Her commander, Lieutenant Singleton, was a clean-cut man in his early twenties, well-built, with light-brown hair, a square, rather bright face with wide-set chestnut-brown eyes and a mouth that smiled easily. When he spoke his voice was calm and surprisingly tinged with a subtle Portsmouth accent that replaced any 'ow' sound with 'ay'. He welcomed Lock and his men aboard with a salute and a firm handshake, as well as a puzzled but bemused expression upon seeing Elsworth help the *liva amiral* clamber up from the bellum. Lock explained who the Turk officer was, and then why he needed to get upriver as quickly as possible.

'Well, Lock, I can tell you, I've seen no sign of the Turk ships, not in a physical sense,' Singleton said with an air of mystery. Then he smiled at Lock's reaction. 'Sorry, what I mean to say is we've seen their smoke, but when we round a bend in the river, there's nothing. They're always just out of sight. I'd say they're fleeing pretty sharpish.'

Lock nodded. 'It certainly looks that way, Lieutenant. Resistance has been pretty light and, as I'm sure you've seen, there are white flags everywhere.'

Once the crews in the water called out that the cables were clear, Singleton invited the *liva amiral* to go and stand at the bow and point out the mines to his midshipman. Lock translated, and with a click of his heels and a bow, the Turk officer set about his task with diligence. In less than a quarter of an hour, they were underway.

Lock glanced back to see that the *Lewis Pelly*, though keeping pace, was tending to drift over to the opposite side of the river. Risky, Lock thought, particularly as they weren't certain how heavily mined this section of the Tigris was. The *liva amiral* was keeping a constant watch from the bow, shouting a warning in broken English now and then, to which the coxswain would swing the wheel, steering the launch to the left or right as needs be. But there was always a chance . . .

A huge blast made everyone rush to the port side. Astern, the *Lewis Pelly* was just passing under a shower of muddy water, having narrowly missed a mine. Fortunately, it looked as if no damage was done. But it was a close thing.

'Our wake luckily pushed the mine into the bank,' Singleton said. 'It must have exploded just as the *Lewis Pelly* drew level.' He turned his head and scowled at the *liva amiral*. 'Are you sure about this fellow, Captain? I only have a crew of eight. But I intend to still have a crew of eight by journey's end.'

The *liva amiral* shrugged at Lock apologetically. '*I cannot be one hundred per cent accurate, Yüzbaşi. There are many mines. But I would advise that the boat behind stays directly astern and stops drifting to our port side,*' he said, before turning back to face the direction of travel, pressing his telescope to his eye once more.

'I'd let your fellow commander on the *Lewis Pelly* know that he should stay in our wake,' Lock said.

Singleton gave a small smile. 'Yes. I guess it was his own fault. Let's just hope it doesn't happen again, though.'

The journey continued without further incident, but progress was slow. The *Shaitan* would normally be a fast vessel, but now, against a strong headwind and current, she could barely make four or five knots an hour. The river was full of mudbanks and the narrowing channel wound to and fro in such an unexpected manner that one of Singleton's men had to constantly sound to help gauge where to steer the ship. There was no way, Lock thought, that they would be able to travel after dark.

As the sun began to drop down towards the west, the heat just grew and grew. Lock felt his spirits wilt. He sat down beside the hot metal of the *Shaitan*'s gun, and pulled off his slouch hat. There was some breeze created by the movement of the boat, but the rushing waters of the Tigris did little to placate the raging thirst he felt. He rubbed his rough palm over his face and winced. His lips were cracked and sore again. He swallowed dryly. His stomach grumbled.

Elsworth remained at the bow with the *liva amiral* and the *Shaitan*'s midshipman, while Singh and the sepoys Addul Tarrin and Karamjeet Singh sat dozing nearby. Ram Lal was somewhere towards the stern and Harrington-Brown was standing portside staring off at the distant landscape. There wasn't a blade of vegetation to look at, but there were a large number of birds, mostly sandpipers, egrets and cranes, picking through the mudflats.

Lock yawned and rubbed his eyes. He watched the launch's crew shuffle about the deck performing the various tasks necessary for the smooth running of their ship, but from what Lock could see, with minimal effort. Still, he didn't – he couldn't – blame them. It was too hot to exert oneself. Besides, Singleton didn't seem to notice.

The Royal Navy lieutenant was standing in the open wheelhouse, scanning the river ahead with an intense concentration etched across his smooth features. Clearly, after the incident with the *Lewis Pelly*, he didn't trust the *liva amiral* not to run them straight into another floating mine. Perhaps Singleton was right not to trust him.

Lock twisted round, but the *liva amiral* was still there, studying the Tigris through his telescope.

Lock turned back with a yawn. Singh stirred and caught his

eye. The Indian smiled, pulled himself to his feet and wandered over to Lock's side.

'May I, sahib?' Singh said, asking permission to sit down next to Lock.

'Don't be daft, Sid,' Lock said, shifting over slightly.

Singh sat himself down and wiped his brow. 'How are you feeling, sahib?'

'I'm fine, Sid. My head wound itches like crazy, but apart from that and a continuous raging thirst, I'm all right,' Lock smiled. 'How's the ribs?'

Singh bobbed his head. 'They do not trouble me at all, sahib.'

The two men fell silent. Lock felt his mind wandering, a combination of the gentle throb of the *Shaitan*'s engines, the gentle pitch and heave of the water around them, and the intense heat.

Lock scoffed to himself.

'What is it, sahib?' Singh said.

'Oh . . . what? Nothing, Sid. Sorry, I drifted off for a moment. The heat . . . I was just thinking how quickly it took me to lose a full-strength platoon.'

'But, sahib, you have not lost any of the men to death.'

'True, Sid, true. But we are seven now and at dawn we were twenty.'

'Sahib, that is the nature of this very strange battle, if one may call it a battle. Men are being separated or left to guard redoubts or . . . deserting us like that Bing Ham Smith. If I may be saying so, sahib.'

'You may, Sid.'

'So what I am meaning, sahib, that when this is over it will be seventy men or more that you are having.'

Lock gave his Indian friend a sideways glance. 'A company? Ha! I doubt that very much, Sid.'

'Why not, sahib? You are bloody fine officer.'

'Thanks, Sid, but I cannot imagine Colonel Godwinson agreeing to that. Can you? Besides, they still want to court-martial me for this bloody assassination nonsense.'

Singh bobbed his head again. 'That is rubbish, and well you are knowing it, sahib.'

'I know, Sid. But the colonel and Bingham-Smith have got it in for me. Christ knows what that slimy bastard is saying now back on the *Espiegle* with his "report".'

Singh bobbed his head. 'Maybe the colonel will not be around to disagree . . .'

Lock grinned. 'Maybe, Sid. There's always hope he finds himself in the way of a Turk or Arab bullet.'

'Or a British one, sahib,' Singh whispered.

'Havildar Singh!' Lock said in mock surprise, then pressed his head back against the hot metal base of the gun. He squinted across at the sun and a trickle of sweat ran into his eye. He winced, wiped it clear and tried to focus on the sky again.

Lock turned his head to the right, facing east. There was something high up, moving slowly towards them. He wondered if it was a bird of prey at first, but the object was moving too true. He frowned and cocked his ear slightly. There was something else, something above the noise of the chugging of the *Shaitan*'s engines; a distant rattling buzz, not unlike a child blowing an intermittent raspberry. Lock sat forward and put his hand up to shield his eyes and stared long and hard at the dark object in the sky.

'Do you see that, Sid?' Lock said, getting to his feet. He pulled his slouch hat on and by now most of the crew had heard the same noise and were looking over to the eastern horizon, pointing at the object that was moving parallel to them.

'I see it, sahib . . .'

'Well, I'll be . . .' Lock said and turned his smile on Singh.

'It is an aeroplane, sahib. Where has it come from?' Singh was shading his eyes, too, and peering hard up at the sky.

'Don't you remember, Sid? Back in Shaiba? Those AFC boys we saw lugging fuel barrels?'

'AFC?' It was Singleton. He had stepped out of the wheelhouse and was now standing next to Lock and Singh, a pair of binoculars in his hands.

'Australian Flying Corps, Lieutenant.'

'I didn't know that there were any aircraft in this part of the world.'

'Just three, hence their name: the Australian Half-Flight,' Lock said.

'I see,' Singleton said, putting the binoculars to his eyes. 'Well,' he said after a moment, 'it looks as if this one is heading our way.'

The aeroplane was now clearly visible to the naked eye as it banked slowly and moved towards them. The beat of its engine grew louder and within minutes Lock could make out the blue, white and red stripes on its double tail fins and the shape of the pilot and his observer in the centralised, open-air nacelle. This aeroplane was different from the ones Lock was familiar with from his time in China in that, though it was still a two-seater biplane with a wood frame covered in tight canvas, this was a pusher aircraft, so called because the engine was located in front of the rear-facing propeller in the rear of the nacelle. The slab-sided nacelle had a rounded front end topped by a small windscreen, and was sat suspended within a network of struts connecting the upper and lower wings. The pilot and the observer sat well forward of the wings, making it ideal for spotting and, Lock guessed, bombing. The large registration '20' was daubed in white numerals just below the observer's seating position.

The windscreen caught the sun and flashed brilliantly as the aeroplane putted overhead. The observer waved down to them, then dropped something that fell onto the afterdeck with a clang. One of the seamen scooped the object up and handed it to Singleton. It was a metal canister.

The aeroplane backfired as it climbed again, hacking and spluttering its way back downriver towards Qurna. Lock's eye followed the plane as it swooped and banked down once more. There was another ship that had just rounded the corner of the river some 500 yards behind. It was the *Espiegle*. The aeroplane appeared to drop another object to them, then swooped and coughed its way up again and continued on its way south.

Bugger, Lock thought. Townshend was bound to hail the *Shaitan* to hold now that they had caught up with them.

Singleton unscrewed the canister and removed a folded paper from inside.

'Well, this confirms my suspicions, Lock,' Singleton said, as he read the note. 'Listen. "Enemy in full flight northward".'

Lock nodded, but he didn't smile. The *Espiegle* was right upon them and Wassmuss was slipping away. He squinted after the rapidly receding aeroplane. If only he could get in it and fly back on up the Tigris, catch and somehow stop the *Marmaris*. One of Pritchard's jam-tin bombs dropped from the cockpit would be all that he'd need. But Pritchard wasn't here, and the aeroplane was heading in the opposite direction.

'Captain,' Singleton said, 'I propose full steam ahead, as full as the bends and twists in this damned river will allow, that is.'

Lock turned to Singleton and smiled. 'Are you sure, Lieutenant? I don't want to jeopardise your command.'

'Balls, Lock,' Singleton smiled wryly. 'I'm as keen to end this as you. We delay any further and the Turk will just regroup and hold.' He jutted his chin downriver. 'Besides, the *Espiegle* and her sister ships won't be able to travel much further, I think. The river was some 270 yards across at Qurna. It's getting narrower all the time, down to under a hundred already. Those sloops are going to become increasingly encumbered with navigating.' He turned his gaze upriver and pointed. 'According to my map, Ezra's Tomb is just around this next bend and I'll hazard a guess that they'll have to halt there. If we hang back, the general will undoubtedly hail us to hold too.' He raised a questioning eyebrow.

'Well,' Lock smiled sheepishly back, 'we can't have that, can we?'

Singleton nodded. 'Jolly good. Right, hang tight. Coxswain?' he shouted, marching back to the wheelhouse. 'Full-speed ahead.'

The *Shaitan* steamed on, with the *Lewis Pelly* still keeping pace behind, and with the *Espiegle* and the rest of Townshend's Regatta following on some distance back.

The river current was quickening and in its convolutions round the bends, the tug jerked violently to either side. Singleton barked orders to his men, and between much cursing and physical strain they began to use poles to force the ship away from the muddy reed-choked banks. The coxswain wrestled with the wheel in his fight not to let the vessel slam into the mudbanks. All Lock and his men could do was watch and hold on tight as the *Shaitan* slid to either side of the banks seemingly out of control, then suddenly the launch swung back and straightened out again. Lock looked back to see the *Lewis Pelly* struggle in the same way, but then it too passed through and chugged on after them. How the larger sloops would cope with such a tight and powerful bend, Lock couldn't imagine, but no vessel looked to be slowing and soon he saw the *Espiegle* nose its way around the corner.

The river straightened out again and the launch-tugs chugged onwards, with the sloops racing after them. However, the river was narrowing at an alarming rate. Still there was no sign of the Turk steamers. But Lock, for the first time, felt a twinge of hope in his gut that they would catch them after all when finally he spotted their distant smoke.

The day moved on. The *liva amiral* was relieved of his task and escorted to the stern of the boat by Ram Lal. The elderly Turk settled himself down and spent his time either studying his play or dozing. There was no sign of any enemy troops or any Marsh Arabs on the banks both to the east and west, and there was little to do but watch the heat haze dance and shimmer on the horizon. When Ezra's Tomb came into sight, the sun had begun to sink towards the horizon.

On the western bank, nestling in a clump of date palms, an oasis sat on an otherwise open stretch of river, was a collection of buildings. Behind a battlemented wall, there was a domed mosque and what appeared to be a courtyard. The tops of a number of trees were just visible inside. There was also a string of telegraph poles running into the distance. Some of the outer buildings were in ruins, but the dome and yellow walls of the courtyard, decorated in bands and splashes with simple but beautiful glazed bricks of dark green, looked to be intact. The dome itself was made with perfect curves, coloured in a blend of every shade from sea-green, to lilac and mauve and blue, to a deep iridescent purple. It positively took Lock's breath away as they slowly chugged past, and such was the complete evaporation of enemy resistance, he, along with his men and the crew of the *Shaitan*, could stand and drink in the ancient beauty of Ezra's Tomb with time to spare. And as Lock watched, the red glowing orb of the sun dipped lower on the horizon to the west, and suddenly the whole tomb changed colour again, becoming a mirror to the pinking sky above them, to the swaying green tops of the nearby palms, and to the darkening tawny flood of the river below that sloshed and slapped right up to the very walls of the buildings.

'A magnificent sight, is it not, Captain?' Singleton said.

'Beautiful, Lieutenant,' Lock whispered.

'I'm just glad the shells from the *Espiegle*'s guns missed it,' Singleton said.

Lock nodded in agreement, and his gaze followed the line of the river and the smoke trails up ahead. 'How long before we have to stop?'

'It will be dark in half-an-hour or so, then we can't risk carrying on. Not until moonrise, anyhow. But we're gaining on them.'

As they passed the tomb, the land beyond flattened out considerably. The river still snaked on ahead like a serpent, but it was becoming increasingly hard to judge where the deeper channel of the Tigris ended and the shallow flood plains began. Singleton was shouting instructions from the wheelhouse to his midshipman and the crew, all of whom were leaning over the gunwales with sounding lines. The coxswain, in a mist of sweat and curses, had to throw the wheel to the left and to the right, constantly correcting the *Shaitan*'s direction to avoid running aground.

'Sid,' Lock called to Singh, 'have you got my pack?'

'Here, sir.'

Lock rummaged in his haversack and pulled out his binoculars. The rear of the enemy shipping was now clear to see.

At that moment Townshend must have spotted the very same, for suddenly the air was angry with the passing of screaming shells as the *Espiegle*'s 4.7 guns opened fire on the fleeing Turks. Lock watched as water fountains from shell impacts erupted into the air all around the Turk boats. It was only a matter of time now, surely. Lock's palms felt damp with anticipation, and he lowered the binoculars and pulled out his cigarettes. A smoke would help calm his excitement. But he couldn't help but smile to himself.

'I'm coming, you bastard,' he muttered staring ahead.

As darkness rapidly gathered around them like an enveloping cloak, the *Shaitan* pushed on, moving on up into the Narrows, the stretch of river between Ezra's Tomb and Qala Salih.

'Up ahead, sir,' came a cry from Elsworth at the bow.

Lock turned and stared ahead into the gloom. 'I see them,' he said, unholstering his Beholla.

Just up ahead was a mahaila, a Turkish barge, jammed on the muddy bank at the edge of a vast reed marsh.

'Action stations!' Singleton shouted, and there followed a great commotion as his sailors armed themselves with rifles and stood at the ready. Two gunners positioned themselves at the launch's 1-3pdr gun, and Lock indicated for his men to take up defensives positions with the *Shaitan*'s crew.

Singleton came up alongside Lock at the bow, a Webley gripped in his hand.

'Must have been cut adrift from one of the steamers,' he said. 'Slowing them down, I'd wager.'

Two powerful torches shot their beams out into the growing gloom, and as the *Shaitan* came alongside the barge, dozens of haunted faces squinted back at them. The barge was full of Turkish *Mehmetçiks* who to a man raised their hands in surrender.

'*Please, effendim, save us,*' came many a plaintive cry.

'Sid,' Lock called, 'take a couple of men and gather any weapons they have, and throw them into the water.'

'We'll have to anchor here, Lock,' Singleton said, 'and wait for the moon to rise. It's just too dangerous to carry on in the dark.'

'Very well, Lieutenant. I don't think we'll have any trouble with this lot,' Lock said, indicating to the Turkish soldiers.

'Good,' Singleton said. 'The *Espiegle* and the other sloops will have to be doing the same. And don't worry, the Turks up ahead won't be able to continue on, either.'

He signalled to the coxswain for the engines to be cut, and as soon as they were, a great cacophony of human voices could be heard crying out from further away in the gloom.

'Searchlight,' Singleton ordered, and at once a great beam cut through the dark. It wavered about the reed marsh, then came to a halt.

'Good Lord,' Singleton said.

Lock could see two more Turkish lighters packed with troops only a few yards off, and beyond them, just visible in the beam of light, was a half-sunken steamer, listing on its side.

'*Who are you?*' Lock called out in Turkish.

'*We surrender, effendim!*' came a cry from the dark.

'*What vessel are you?*'

'*The Bulbul, effendim. We were hit below the waterline. There are many Arabs creeping about in the marsh. Please help us.*'

'Sounds desperate,' Singleton said.

'They are. They say the surrounding marsh is teaming with hostile Arabs. Can you blast a few rounds into the distance? Scare them off if they are skulking about still?'

Singleton nodded and indicated to his gunners. 'Four shells. Two hundred yards. When you're ready.'

The gunners wheeled about, raised the turret and let off four rounds in quick succession. They fizzed off into the night and exploded in a mass of mud and water a good distance beyond the stricken *Bulbul*.

A great hush fell over the Turkish soldiers, and then, like a gathering cloud of insects, a general murmur of excitement filled the air.

'I don't think we'll have any trouble for a while. From these poor souls, or any Marsh Arabs.'

'Let's hope you are right, Lock. I feel rather exposed out here. This is a damned lot of men. And it's only one of their steamers. How many more barges full of troops are being towed by the other boats?'

'Don't worry, Lieutenant. The Turks can't have any idea how many there are of us coming up behind them. I think they're in a real panic. So, let's keep them guessing.'

Singleton didn't look too confident. 'Very well, Lock. But we'll have to go on alone as soon as the moon rises. I can't leave this many prisoners behind us without a guard. The *Lewis Pelly* will have to stay behind.'

'Agreed,' Lock said.

'And I think it best that we say goodbye to our Ottoman guest also.'

'Yes, I was thinking the same. *Liva Amiral?*' Lock called.

The elderly Turk officer shuffled out of the gloom clutching his book to his chest.

'*It is time for you to leave us.*'

The *liva amiral* blinked back at Lock, a look of suspicion clouding his face.

'*It is too dangerous for you to continue on upriver with us, so I'm having you escorted over to the Lewis Pelly. You will be well looked after, Liva Amiral, I promise you.*'

The *liva amiral* glanced back at the dark silhouette of the other launch, then nodded. '*I do not like it, Yüzbaşi, but I understand. I shall however refuse to talk until your return.*'

'*As you wish, Liva Amiral,*' Lock said. 'Harrington-Brown?'

The lieutenant came up to Lock.

'Sir?'

'Escort the *liva amiral* to the *Lewis Pelly*. We're going on without him.'

'You'll find a dinghy tied to the stern, Lieutenant,' Singleton said.

Harrington-Brown gave a stiff nod and then held his hand out politely for the elderly Turk officer to lead the way back towards the stern.

The next few hours passed peacefully considering the situation that Lock and his men and the crew of the *Shaitan* found themselves in. It was a still and stiflingly hot night, and as Lock sat alone on the deck, back against the gunwale, too wired to sleep, he wondered just how long the marsh would last. The occasional footfall broke the monotony as a sentry paced to and fro, and at one point Lock thought he heard the splash of an oar. But peering out into the darkness he could see nothing. He remained there at the gunwale listening intently, but he could pick nothing out other than the chorus of snores coming from prisoners and crew alike.

He settled back down on the deck, and suddenly found his thoughts turning to Amy. Perhaps the real reason for his desperation to keep moving, to keep chasing, was that it distracted him from thinking about her. And now, as he had to sit in the dark, up she popped again. Why was his mind so cruel? He sighed. Being sat on this boat deck just conjured up happier memories of when he and Amy would meet secretly, nightly, on the poop deck of the RIMS *Lucknow*. If only he could return to then, standing with her, embracing her under the stars as the ship pitched and heaved over the Indian Ocean.

Bugger, this had to stop. He'd lose his mind before long, and he couldn't afford to do that, to take his eye off the ball.

'Bugger you, Amy,' he whispered to himself. But he didn't mean it, he could never mean it. His feelings for her were stronger than anything he'd felt before, stronger than his love for Mei Ling. He knew that now.

Lock let out a soft moan of despair, and put his head in his hands. 'If I could just get you out of my bloody head. Damn you, girl, damn and bloody bugger.'

The sentry passed close by. 'You all right, sir?' a voice whispered from the dark.

Lock stared up at the shadow looming over him. 'Yes,' he said hoarsely, 'just a bad dream.'

'Well, try to keep it down, sir,' the sentry said, and moved away again.

'Bugger off!' Lock muttered after him. He shifted his tender buttocks, stretched, and felt his spine crack. He leant back and rubbed his stiff neck. Looking up through the gap between the gunwale and the canvas roof awning, he began to search the sky, and set his mind to finding as many constellations and planets he could in an effort to blank out Amy. He sighed and swore after what could have only been five minutes. It just wasn't working.

CHAPTER SEVENTEEN

A little before 2 a.m., the moon rose. Lock checked his watch and calculated that they had been stationary for just over five hours now. He just hoped that the *Marmaris* hadn't been able to navigate any further upriver than they had. He pulled himself to his feet, sucked in his teeth as his left knee cracked loudly, and stretched his aching, stiff limbs. His backside was numb.

Lock moved to the bow and peered ahead. It was as bright as day now, with the near full moon throwing a silvery light across the landscape that spread like a white fire. He was just wondering how long before the *Espiegle* came up to them when the heavens exploded.

The *Shaitan*'s crew scrambled to their feet and each man peered from under the awning back down the length of the Tigris. Behind them the *Espiegle*, the *Clio* and the *Odin* seemed to be moving up fast, their guns spitting roaring hate towards the Turkish vessels that were so easy to see now across the flat flood plain to the west. Great dark plumes of water exploded into the air as shells fell around the enemy ships.

Lock felt the deck shudder under his feet as the *Shaitan*'s engines fired up with a great cough of smoke and a bone-shaking jolt. The launch began to move forward once more, and Lock felt his spirits rise. They were so close, now. He turned back to the bow and stood, peering ahead into the steely light, his hand resting on the barrel of the 3-pdr that still radiated heat from a day in the sun and its brief call to action at dusk.

They rounded a bend, and the river widened again, opening up to nearly 200 yards in places. Lock leant forward, suddenly alert, feeling the skin on the back of his neck tingle with tentative hope. They were rapidly gaining on the ship at the rear of the Turkish retreat. His hand gripped tighter on the gunwale, and he clenched his teeth. God, they were nearly upon her.

'Come on, come on,' Lock muttered, impatience threatening to overwhelm him, as the ship ahead of them once again disappeared from sight as it rounded another bend in the river.

The shelling from the *Espiegle* continued to rain overhead, and the *Shaitan* chugged on. It came to the bend in the river and then swung far to the left and then seemed to stall, bounce and finally emerge back on the straight. Lock was suddenly met by a landscape bathed in an eerie, flickering glow. The ship they had been pursuing had run aground. She was lilting to one side and on fire. Her entire stern was nothing but a mangled mess of burning metal, spewing out a cloud of thick, toxic smoke. Near to her was a lighter with a number of soldiers aboard. They all had their hands thrust high in the air in surrender.

'Heave to!' Singleton shouted from the wheelhouse.

Lock pushed forward at the bow and cupped his hands around his mouth.

'*Are you the Marmaris?*' he called in Turkish.

'*Yes, effendim. Marmaris,*' came a reply from the lighter.

Lock turned back and called down the length of the launch, 'Harrington-Brown, Sid, on the double!'

Singh was quick to arrive, with Elsworth and Ram Lal at his heels.

'Sahib?' Singh said.

'Where the hell's the lieutenant?'

'He escorted the Turkish officer to the *Lewis Pelly*, sahib.'

'And he's still not back?'

Singh bobbed his head. 'I think that he may have missed our very sudden departure, sahib.'

'The bloody useless bastard,' Lock fumed, 'he's got the dinghy. He's more incompetent than Bingham-Smith. And that's quite an achievement.'

'He also took with him Sepoys Addul Tarin and Karamjeet Singh, sahib.'

Lock swore. 'Can't these bloody aristos do their own rowing?'

'It would seem not, sahib.'

Lock glanced over his shoulder at the burning wreck of the Turkish steamer.

'Well then, I have little choice. I'll have to swim over. It's too dangerous for Singleton to move the launch any closer, their magazine could go off at any moment judging by the way that fire's burning.'

'But, sahib . . .'

'No "buts", Sid,' Lock said. 'If the *Marmaris* is the Ottoman

293

command ship, as that artillery officer hinted, then what better place to find evidence of not only the Turks' plans, but hopefully of Wassmuss's spy network too? Anything that could help clear my name. Hell, the man himself may still be aboard. As himself or as *Binbaşi* Feyzi. Either way, Sid, I've got to get across and find out.'

Singh rubbed his beard thoughtfully. 'Yes . . .'

'I know it's a long shot, but what choice do I have? It's a strong possibility that I'm right, Sid. I mean, what better place to have an HQ than on a ship that can make a speedy retreat?' Lock paused, and pulled Singh a little closer. 'I'm running out of options, Sid. Godwinson and Bingham-Smith aren't far behind us now.' He glanced back down the river as if to check that the *Espiegle* wasn't already upon them. 'I doubt the general or even Ross can help me anymore.'

'The major will not let those horses' arses influence what he knows to be the truth, sahib.'

Lock shook his head. 'The only way I'm going to clear my name, Sid, is by catching Wassmuss myself and dragging him before General Townshend.'

Singh looked down at his friend, his brow creased with worry.

'I cannot let you go alone, sahib. It is too dangerous. Let me and Ram Lal accompany you. We do not know if the Turks have armed men still aboard. We can watch your back.'

The big Indian's brown eyes moved to the burning vessel, his pupils alive with the reflection of the flickering flames.

'That's just the point, Sid. It *is* too dangerous. I will not let you or anyone else risk themselves for me. I go alone. That's an order. I need Elsworth to cover me from here, and I need you and Ram Lal to go over to that lighter,' Lock said, pointing to the stricken barge full of pleading Turk soldiers, 'and search the faces of each man. Take an electric torch. Wassmuss may be able to disguise himself, but he can't disguise his piercing blue eyes. Remember that.' He began removing his jacket, his cross straps and his Sam Browne belt. 'And I wouldn't put it past the slimy toad to try to hide amongst the normal soldiers and then slip away when everything has calmed down a little. So, anyone with blue eyes, separate them and tie them up until I get back.'

Lock went to draw his knife and cursed. Bugger, he'd forgotten. He'd lost it somewhere in Qurna.

'Alfred, give me your bayonet again, will you?' he said.

The young sharpshooter unclipped his scabbard from his Sam Browne belt and handed it to Lock.

'Here you go, sir.'

'Thanks,' Lock said, and stuffed the blade in his waistband. He sat down and began to pull off his boots and socks.

Pulling the magazine from his Beholla, Lock checked it was full, before stuffing it in the inside band of his hat. He then put the main body of the handgun inside one of the socks, tied the second sock to the open end of the first, and finally tied the whole thing around his neck, so it dangled down on his bare chest like a crude necklace. He put the slouch hat back on his head, held his hand out, and Singh helped to haul him back to his feet.

'Thanks, Sid. As long as I keep my hat dry, I should be able to use my gun.'

Singh nodded. 'Very smart, sahib, but I am hoping you will not have to.'

Stuffing one boot inside the other, Lock then used his jacket as a kind of sling resting the boots inside, then wrapped the whole thing around his waist.

'All right, Sid, over I go.'

'Captain Lock, Captain Lock . . .' Singleton called, hurrying forward. He grabbed Lock's arm just as he was about to swing his legs up and over the gunwale.

'What is it, Lieutenant?' Lock said, turning back to face the Royal Navy commander.

'The *Espiegle* . . . and the *Clio* and the *Odin* . . . all three have run aground, and have signalled for us to hold.'

'Very well, Lieutenant. You do that. I'm afraid, though, that I'll be leaving you now. Need to go see if there's a German spy in that steamer over there,' Lock grinned, and nodded his head towards the stricken *Marmaris*.

Singleton's eyes widened in surprise. 'You can't, Lock. She could blow at any minute! If that fire reaches the ma—'

'I know, Lieutenant. Please, don't trouble yourself,' Lock smiled reassuringly, 'I won't be long. Could I borrow one of your torches?'

Singleton hesitated, then clicked his fingers at one of his crew members. 'Torch, Healy.'

The sailor rushed off to the wheelhouse, and came back with a torch.

Singleton handed it to Lock.

'Much obliged,' Lock said, securing the torch to the top of his slouch hat with one of his cross straps tied under his chin. 'Better than a miner's helmet,' he said.

Singleton was shaking his head. 'This is a very bad idea, Captain Lock.'

'My whole life is a very bad idea, Lieutenant.'

And with that Lock hauled himself up and over the gunwale, and disappeared over the side.

Singleton stepped forward and peered down into the inky-black Tigris. 'Lock, you damned fool, come back!'

Lock grinned sheepishly up at Singleton, but continued to lower himself down into the water. He was surprised to find the water to be as tepid as a day-old bath, and just as musty. Holding onto the guide rope strung around the hull of the *Shaitan*, feeling the rough fibres cutting into his hands, Lock paused to assess the strength of the current. It was strong and pulled hungrily at his breeches. Fortunately, though, it was flowing in the direction of the *Marmaris*. He glanced back up to see Singleton, Elsworth, Singh and Ram Lal all still peering down at him, then, careful to keep his head above water, he let go of the guide rope. The current whipped Lock about like a piece of driftwood, but he soon had his momentum under control and was able to guide himself in the right direction by kicking fiercely to his left. Using breaststroke, he began to move closer to the *Marmaris*.

As Lock neared the stricken steamer, the water around him became slick with diesel oil and strewn with debris. Lock tried to keep his mouth above water, but every third stroke he'd taste oil, and would retch.

'Jesus,' he spluttered, spitting oily water from his mouth. At least it kept his mind from worrying about the possibility of the fire igniting the oil around him.

From the starboard side, the *Marmaris* close up was badly damaged and looked as if she had taken a hell of a beating, all 500 tons of her was listless, dying, drowning and burning. Lock made a mental note to congratulate the *Espiegle*'s gunners on their marksmanship. If he ever got back alive that is, he smiled grimly to himself as an afterthought. He was now just ten feet away.

What the hell are you doing now, Kingdom? Swimming out to a burning ship in the vague hope that Wassmuss is still on board? That he'll be dressed as *Binbaşi* Feyzi, lying wounded, forgotten somehow by his comrades when they abandoned ship, with evidence on how he'd set you up clutched in his hand? Lock scoffed at his own foolishness.

But there was a chance, he reminded himself. Those papers he'd taken off the *liva amiral*, the pearls, the fact that this could be the command ship for the Tigris area, the fact that a German was directing operations according to the captured Ottoman officers he'd questioned on his journey to this point.

Lock reached the hull of the *Marmaris* and stretched up, grabbing hold of a twisted length of cable that was dangling down from the guard rail running along the upper deck. Lock tested that it would hold his weight. Satisfied, he pulled and heaved himself up out of the water. He hung there for a moment, glancing over his shoulder, back at the silhouette of the *Shaitan*, wondering if Elsworth was keeping a close eye on him through his riflescope. He gave a nod just in case. Then he turned, took a deep breath, and began to climb. His clothes were soaked and clung to him, restricting his movements, as the weight of his jacket sling pulled at his neck. The torch tied to his head was a ton weight pressing down on his skull. But he forced his aching limbs upwards.

A dull rumble made him check his ascent and he hung there, listening and feeling the boat shudder under him. He wiped the slime of oil and sweat that had run into his left eye with his shoulder, and blinked along the length of the ship, past the twisted broken 9-pdr guns that were sticking up at odd angles like gnarled branches on a fallen tree, to the very stern. It was nothing but a broken, twisted mass of iron and wood, like a toy that had been crushed under the foot of a petulant child. Thick smoke was still billowing out of a huge charred hole in the hull just above the waterline. Lock twisted his head to look up the length of the boat towards the bow. There was less damage here, but then he wasn't really concentrating on the state of the *Marmaris* anymore. He felt a sudden wave of apprehension. Bobbing about in the current, tied to a length of rope running down from the bow of the *Marmaris*, was a dinghy.

Lock hesitated, his mind running through the significance of that tiny boat. Then he continued his climb. He paused at the main deck. The ship was listing on its port side at an angle of no more than twenty degrees, and Lock guessed that it would roll and tip no further. The far side of the deck, though submerged under cloudy water, was well and truly wedged against the muddy bank. Lock could see reeds sticking up through the gaps in the rails on that side of the ship. He looked up. Not far to go now. If the design was similar to the British river gunboats, then the captain's stateroom would be just behind the pilot house. And that was on the upper deck. He continued his ascent.

With the sweat pouring off him, the breath rasping in his chest, his muscles screaming in complaint, Lock finally hauled himself up and over the gunwale, and onto the forward upper deck. Above him was a mounted 1-pdr gun, limp and obsolete, its turret splintered. Aft from that was the pilot house. Its glass viewing windows were all shattered. Lock peered inside. There was nothing to see but an empty seat and the wheel. He turned away and leant against the bulkhead outside, catching his breath for a moment, his bare chest heaving, eyes and ears sharp to any sign of life. For now, he was alone.

Lock unfastened the strap around his chin and eased the torch off his slouch hat. With his palm over the lens, he switched it on and then off again to check it still worked. He crouched down and began to untie his sodden jacket from around his neck, and removed his boots. He untied the socks and pulled out the Beholla, placing everything on the wooden deck in front of him. He felt for the bayonet that he'd stuffed in his waistband. It was gone. Bugger, must have been snatched away by the current. Idiot.

Lock discarded the socks and, after wringing the water out as best he could, pulled his damp jacket on. He poured the excess water out of his boots and worked his feet into them, cursing at their pinching, damp, cloying tightness. Taking the Beholla, he tipped it barrel down to let any excess water drain out. He then opened the breech and blew as hard as he could. He retrieved the magazine from within his hatband, and slammed it home. He adjusted his slouch hat, the only dry item of clothing he had on, then pulled himself to his feet.

Looking left to right, Lock strained to hear any sound above the water lapping against the hull and the distant crack and pop of the fire burning to astern. Satisfied, he began to ease his way along the greasy gangway aft on the starboard side.

About five feet along the bulkhead was the door to the captain's stateroom. It was wide open. Lock hesitated, his back pressed against the metal of the bulkhead, Beholla raised and ready. He waited. All was silent. He stole a glance inside. The room appeared to have been ransacked. Lock clicked the torch on and stepped cautiously inside.

Shining the light around the room, the beam picked out random items of clothing scattered over the floor: a pair of socks, a left boot, a pair of longjohns, one half of a leather gaiter. Books, stacked haphazardly, still lined the railed shelves, but the desk against the wall was bare, its drawers open and cleared. The bunk still had bedding on, unkempt, as if its occupant had been woken suddenly from his slumber, perhaps when the *Marmaris* was hit, Lock thought. There was a carafe and a glass, smashed, at the side of the bunk, the Persian rug on the deck stained dark with whatever liquid had been inside.

Lock scanned the cabin further, shining the torch into each and every corner. There were a number of loose-leaf papers littering the floor, but on closer inspection he dismissed them. They were nothing more than memorandums relating to ship's duties, menus, stores and alike. Not too dissimilar to what had been in the cardboard folder he'd found with the *liva amiral*. The stateroom disappointingly offered nothing significant. Lock switched the torch off, stepped back out onto the gangway, and continued aft.

The rest of the upper deck, from the edge of the captain's stateroom to the open section aft that housed a second 1-pdr gun, was covered by a canvas awning. It was ripped and torn and hung loosely down from its wooden frame in a number of places. Lock moved underneath, and stooping under a torn piece of canvas, passed between the funnel and the stairwell, and made his way to the port side where the radio room backed onto the captain's stateroom. However, this too proved to be empty. If there had been any codebooks they were gone.

Lock stared at the telegraph set and its cold, lifeless wires. He cursed. This was taking too long. He shone the beam onto his wristwatch. He'd been on board for fifteen minutes now and was no further on than he had been when stood on the deck of the *Shaitan*. He crossed back to the stairwell and peered down into its gaping mouth. There was a tangled mass of cabling and wires running all the way down from the telegraph mast that had collapsed and come crashing down through the canvas roof. But the way down looked passable. Just. He could see part of the main deck below, illuminated by the flickering flames, but the hold further below still looked to be nothing more than a deep black hole of trouble. He bit his lip and scratched at his stubbly chin. He flexed the grip on his Beholla and began to pick his way down the stairs.

Lock stopped at the first level, the main deck, which was again open to the elements. This would house an office and the galley, with a large section amidships being the enclosed upper section of the engine and boiler rooms. Unlike the upper deck, here the gangways were lined with strips of cocoa matting to try and give something of a footing.

Lock made his way forward for no other reason than it was away from the flames. The bulkhead of the section up ahead was riddled with bullet and shrapnel holes the size of fists. Lock could hear the familiar drip-drip of a faulty faucet coming from the other side and smell mouldy damp. There were three doors, one of which had a sign written in Turkish, *Tuvalet*. These were the bathrooms.

Lock pressed on, passing between two hatchways that he knew would lead to the magazines below the hull. He halted once he reached the open forecastle deck at the bow. Here there was a second flight of stairs leading down into the hull. It smelt of brine, oil and sweat. The crew's quarters. He turned the torch on and followed the beam down into the bowels of the ship.

The temperature was higher down here, and Lock's wet

uniform was already beginning to steam. As he descended the stairs, he listened for any sounds of human activity, but there was still nothing to hear but the click and creak of shifting metal, the distant crackle of fire and a muffled throb of engines on the water. The British flotilla was near to hand. He really was running out of time.

As Lock's boot came off the bottom step and hit the metal deck of the hold, the entire ship shuddered. He grabbed out for the stair rail with his gun hand to steady himself. The Beholla knocked against the metal of the rail sending an echoing clang all the way to the upper deck. Lock cursed at his clumsiness and remained still, his head cocked slightly to one side. He could make out a dull but distinct thud thud thud of running footsteps. Then they abruptly stopped.

'Wha—'

Lock felt his mouth go slack, as a huge explosion appeared to bend the air about him. A shockwave knocked the feet from under him and he slammed to the deck. Pain screamed across his temple. Then he felt nothing.

Lock didn't know if he'd been out for a minute or an hour when he opened his eyes. He took a moment to collect himself, mentally running a hand down his body. Nothing was broken, nothing sprained. He was lucky. His face was wet and his left eye stung. There was a metallic taste on his tongue and his bottom lip felt swollen. He was aware that he was lying on his front, his head pointing to one side. The floor beneath him felt hot and his nostrils were full of cordite. He blinked and tried to clear his blurred vision. He still had a tight grip on the torch and its beam was shining directly under the bunk opposite. He could see a pair of boots, an old newspaper and the barrel of a gun. It was pointing directly at him. He blinked again. No one was holding the gun; he could see that now. He groaned softly and tried to will the fuzz away from his stunned brain. Where was he? He shifted his eyes to the far left where he could just make out the foot of the stairs and a number of other bunks around him, all screwed to the deck.

Yes, he remembered now. He was in the crew's quarters. In the hold. On the *Marmaris*. But what else? The ship had run aground and was listing. And she was on fire.

The explosion!

The aft magazine in the hold must have gone up. Lock forced his neck up and to the side. It was like trying to lift a cannonball. Thick smoke was clinging to the ceiling and billowing up the stairwell.

'Move, Kingdom,' Lock muttered, and he pushed his hands against the slick metal deck and forced himself up onto all fours.

He grunted, and fighting off a wave of nausea, wiped his eye and looked at his palm. Blood. He tentatively felt his head. There was a fresh gash just above his ear. Not too deep. He felt a little higher. Thankfully his old wound was all right. He sucked in his teeth and sat upright.

'I really must start wearing a topi,' he muttered.

Spotting his slouch hat, Lock scooped it up and pulled it on. Where was his gun? He scanned the area and then moved across to the bunk opposite, remembering the barrel he had seen when he was lying on the floor. Feeling underneath, he pulled out the Beholla. He checked it over. It was undamaged.

The footsteps.

Lock spun round. Someone else was on the *Marmaris* with him.

The dinghy. Yes, of course. That was the slosh of water he thought he'd heard in the early hours before the moon came up. It was the dinghy passing by in the dark, the careless splash of its paddle.

'Shit, Kingdom, you're being slow.'

Lock grabbed hold of the bunk frame and pulled himself to his feet. He stood unsteadily for a moment, then leant forward and vomited. Gasping, he ran the back of his hand across his mouth and wiped it on the blanket hanging down from the upper bunk nearest to him.

Thud thud thud.

Lock flashed the torch in the direction of the stairs. Someone was up on the main deck. Lock switched off the torch and stuffed it in his jacket pocket. Cautiously, taking one step at a time, trying to keep his head out of the rising smoke, he began to ascend the stairs. He paused at each step, straining to hear anything above the burning and creaking ship. The smoke thickened when he was just at the top and, stifling a cough, he popped his head up through the top of the stairwell, quickly stealing a glance left and right, before ducking back down again. The ship appeared as deserted as before.

Holding his breath, Lock paused and waited for a waft of thick smoke to flow past him, then using it as cover, sprang up and rolled to one side. His eyes were stinging and streaming from the effects of the smoke, and his lungs were burning, but he just ignored it, stifling the cough he wanted to choke out, and peered about searching for any sign of life.

There was nothing but stillness.

Lock pulled himself to his feet, but remained crouched low, Beholla in his right hand levelled at his hip, his left hand out straight, stiff like a chopping blade. He circled slowly, backing up towards the bow. He darted a quick look over the side. The dinghy was still there, tied as before, bobbing in the current. He gave a wolfish smile, felt along the gunwale until he came to the knot of coarse rope. Keeping an eye on the stairwell and the gangways, he untied the rope and felt it pull from his hand immediately as the current whipped the now untethered dinghy away. He glanced out to the river just to make sure. The dinghy had already drifted out some twenty feet.

'Right,' Lock said with a certain amount of venom, turning back towards amidships, 'let's see where you are, my German friend . . .'

By now the fire at the stern, or what was left of the stern, was raging ferociously, making the shadows cast by the flames and the moonlight dance and dodge across the deck. Lock skirted the open stairwell that was still oozing smoke up from the hull, and began to make his way down the gangway that ran along the port side of the bathrooms. Here was in dark shadow, and the deck was submerged under a few inches of water and mud. It was slimy underfoot.

Lock edged forward, his back to the bulkhead, gun held up, ears straining for the slightest sound from within one of the closed bathrooms or just up ahead, round the corner by the central stairwell. His mouth was as dry as dust and when he swallowed, he winced. His throat felt like it was passing razor blades. The gash above his ear was stinging like mad, made worse by the sweat seeping in from his hatband and his damp hair. But at least the pain kept him alert.

At the edge of the bulkhead he paused, heart thumping in his ears. The bulkhead wall behind him ticked and popped like an erratic clock as the heat from the blaze started to expand the metal of the ship's very frame. Lock inched his eye around the corner. Across the small, open gangway beyond the stairwell was the ship's office and the galley. Further amidships was the enclosed section of the boiler and engine rooms. Beyond that nothing. Nothing but twisted, hot, broken metal. The propellers, the aft quarters, the sick bay, the dispensary and the rear guns were all gone. Destroyed. Lock could see the door to the office was open. A light was flashing intermittently from the inside.

In two quick strides, he moved across the open gangway, and sprang across the office threshold, his finger poised on the trigger of the Beholla.

Inside was a desk, with papers scattered across its surface, and a lamp hanging off the edge, upside down, by its flex. The lamp was flickering on and off at random intervals creating dancing shadows on the empty shelves that lined the surrounding walls. On the floor a chair lay on its side. And next to it, sprawled on his front, face turned to one side, was an officer. His arms were spread above the head, legs angled as if frozen in the act of running. There was a knife sticking in the back of the officer's neck, just above the shoulder blades. Blood had already spread from the wound staining his white tunic dark red.

Lock's heart skipped a beat. Could it be?

'Wassmuss?' he said aloud. But he knew it wasn't the moment he spoke the name.

Lock's mind tumbled. The body, the whole scene, looked strangely familiar. He stepped a little closer and stopped, spun round to the open door, pistol raised. Nothing. He turned his attention back to the dead body.

The officer was wearing a well-tailored uniform of the German navy. Lock crouched down, grabbing the lamp and holding it closer to the body to get a better look at the face. The officer's dark eyes were staring blankly back. Lock so wanted it to be Wassmuss. But it wasn't. This man had dark green eyes. He was clean-shaven and his salt-and-pepper hair was receding. Even though the body was still warm to the touch, the colour had already drained from the lean face, and the skin had taken on that waxy pallor of the dead.

Lock's eyes moved to the knife sticking out of the man's back. He hesitated, his hand hovering over the hilt. Then he pulled the blade out. Wiping it off on the dead man's uniform, he bent the flat edge in the lamplight and mouthed the inscription engraved along the flat edge, '*For Kingdom and Country*.'

Thud thud thud.

Lock sprang up. The footsteps were closer this time. He moved swiftly to the doorway and paused at the threshold. He glanced back at the dead body. Then he remembered, remembered where he had seen this before. It was almost the exact same scene as when he and Ross had discovered Lord Shears, stabbed, dead amongst the debris of a frantic search, on board the *Espiegle* when they were travelling from Mohammerah to Basra.[2] That was Wassmuss's handiwork then, surely this was his handiwork now?

Thud thud thud.

That was just outside. As Lock turned, something flashed by the opening of the door. Lock fired at the same instant, the roar of

2. See *Kingdom Lock*

his shot echoing around the office. From outside, there was a cry and a stumble, followed by a heavy fall.

Lock darted out of the office and turned, gun levelled, to see a dark smear of blood against the bathroom bulkhead opposite. He ran forward. There was a blur of movement in the corner of his eye, and a sudden jarring pain as a boot smashed into his wrist. The Beholla span out of his grip and skidded away across the greasy deck. Lock dropped the knife and grabbed the attacking foot, and yanked it hard. A man was jolted out from around the corner, and Lock punched him in the face. He felt a sting as his assailant's front teeth cracked and cut into his knuckles. The man gave a muffled cry, swung his own fist, and caught Lock with a glancing, but painful blow just above his left ear, catching the fresh wound.

Lock staggered back, and his assailant scrambled forward across the deck making a grab for the knife. But Lock was quicker. He kicked out and his foot met the assailant's stooping head, sending him crashing back against the stairs. Lock rushed forward. The assailant was still, slumped up against the stairs, his back to Lock, a hand gripping the rail above him. His left shoulder was a mass of blood where Lock's bullet had struck home when he had darted past the open office doorway.

Lock grabbed the man by the scruff of the neck, left fist clenched and ready to strike again, and twisted him round to face him.

Harrington-Brown, mouth swollen and bleeding, was gasping and wheezing as he stared back up at Lock, a flame of hatred burning deep within his narrowed eyes. Then his face changed and took on a look of hurtful innocence.

'Lock,' he spluttered. 'What the deuce? Thought you ... thought you were a bloody Johnny out to get me.'

Lock kept his fist high and ready.

Harrington-Brown winced and lifted his hand to his injured shoulder. 'You bloody shot me, old man,' he said weakly. His head began to sway and his eyes flickered as if he were about to pass out.

'Hey,' Lock said, slapping Harrington-Brown hard across the cheek. 'What the hell are you doing here?'

Harrington-Brown put his hand to his cheek, a stunned expression in his eyes. 'Steady . . . steady on. I feel damned faint . . . I . . .' His head lolled forward again.

Lock grabbed him with both hands and gave him a shake. 'Hey?'

Harrington-Brown sprang up and gave Lock a mighty shove, sending him staggering back off balance. Lock scrambled to one side, scooping up his knife, and turned just as Harrington-Brown pulled a Webley from his holster and fired. The bullet impacted on the gunwale just above Lock's right shoulder. Lock threw his blade. It fizzed through the air and slammed into Harrington-Brown's chest with a hollow thock. The lieutenant staggered back a pace startled, dropped the Webley from his grip, and crashed down on his backside as his legs gave way. He sat, eyes wide, opened his mouth to say something, then his chin fell forward just inches above the hilt of the knife, and he was still.

Lock sat blinking back at Harrington-Brown's body. 'Holy . . . bloody . . . shit,' he gasped, catching his breath.

He pulled himself to his feet, picked up the Beholla and pushed it in his waistband. He scooped up his slouch hat and walked over to Harrington-Brown. He prodded the lieutenant's wounded shoulder checking that he was actually dead. He didn't move. Lock crouched down beside him. There was a trickle of blood running out of the dead lieutenant's mouth, dripping down onto his tunic.

'Who the bloody buggering hell are you, Hazza? A man after the bounty on my head? I can't believe that.'

Lock began to rifle through the dead officer's pockets. The first thing he found was a packet of Pall Mall's and a Ronson 'wonderlite' strike lighter. Lock sat back, crossed his legs, and lit himself a cigarette.

'Jesus, I need this,' he sighed.

He had another couple of pleasurable draws on the cigarette, then scowled back at the dead British officer.

'All right, Hazza, let's see what else you've got.'

Lock, cigarette dangling from his lips, one eye squinting against the stream of smoke, began to empty the rest of Harrington-Brown's pockets out onto the deck.

A ball of string, a few dates, a folded red-spotted handkerchief. There was something inside it. Lock carefully unfolded it to reveal six translucent pearls.

'Now what are you doing with these, Lieutenant?' Lock muttered, searching Harrington-Brown's face for some clue.

The final thing he pulled from the dead lieutenant's pockets was a picture postcard. It was the kind of thing that would be thrust under your nose in the bazaar back at Basra, usually by some shifty-looking Arab with a twinkle in his eye and a phlegmatic chuckle of, 'Bint, bint. Two rupees, two rupees.'

This picture card, although in very soft focus, was better than the usual standard, but wasn't the most erotic thing Lock had seen. The naked girl had a nice figure, he thought appreciatively, though the display of fruit on the table next to her added nothing to the scene. They weren't even apples. They looked more like oranges.

On the flip side was a list of eight names written in pencil, laid out in two columns of four.

Braut	*Bräutigam*
Gen. Townshend	Col. Godwinson
Maj. Ross	Ast. Provt. Mar. Bingham-Smith
Cpt. Brooke	Cpt. Carver
Jem. Pahal	Ris. Shah

It was an old list because the second name under the *Bräutigam* column was Bingham-Smith's, but he still had the title 'Ast. Provt. Mar.'. Lock recognised two other names there, Col. Godwinson and Cpt. Carver (again under his previous rank). The fourth name was an Indian cavalry officer called Shah. The *Braut* column had Gen. Townshend, Maj. Ross, Cpt. Brooke and Jem. Pahal. Could that be the late Captain Brooke who had died only hours earlier? Lock pondered. And was that the Pahal who had helped Lock storm the Turk trenches at Barjisiyah Woods?

Lock reread the names for a third time and shook his head. *Braut* and *Bräutigam*? Something to do with Amy and Bingham-Smith's impending wedding? Seating arrangements? Teams of some sort? For Bridge? But why no women? Lock couldn't make head nor tail out of it. He turned the card back and studied the picture once more. The girl looked strangely familiar.

Lock gave a wry smile and said, 'You're coming with me, *chérie*.'

He pocketed the picture card along with the pack of cigarettes and the lighter, and the handkerchief containing the pearls.

Lock cocked his head. For the first time since he'd boarded the *Marmaris*, above the noise of the clanking and creaking of the ship's bulkheads expanding in the heat, he could hear the distant shout of men. He got to his feet and walked over to the gunwale. Out on the river, he could see that more and more of the British flotilla had caught up with the *Shaitan*. He could make out the dark silhouette of the familiar *Espiegle*, further south along the river, where it had run aground as Lieutenant Singleton had said. It would appear that the command sloop had been abandoned and that Townshend and whomever senior officers he deemed worthy were continuing on upriver in a smaller vessel, the *Comet*. Lock could see Captain Nunn's pennant, bright in the moonlight, flapping from the gunboat's mast.

A sudden shout and the scraping and banging of wood against metal came from the direction of the bow. Soldiers were coming aboard the stricken Turk steamer. Lock was running out of time. He moved back to Harrington-Brown. Clearly the lieutenant had been searching for something. But what? Was he the one who had killed the German officer? And the running footsteps? And the explosions? Was that the fire reaching the magazines or a deliberate act? Was Harrington-Brown, in fact, trying to destroy evidence? Was there something else still on board? Someone else? But why? Lock cursed. His head hurt. So many questions left unanswered.

He stared down at the slumped dead body of the young British officer and wished his throw hadn't been so true.

'Bugger,' he said, and stopped forward to pull his knife from Harrington-Brown's chest.

'Just hold it right there!'

Lock instinctively ducked down as a bullet smacked into the bulkhead above his head. He dived away. Glancing back, he could see four silhouettes, three distinctive with their topi helmets,

313

moving quickly up the foredeck towards him. The voice that had shouted out the warning he recognised as Bingham-Smith. Lock's eyes darted to Harrington-Brown's body and the knife that was still sticking out of his chest, his knife, engraved with a personal message and with his name. Lock swore but it was too late to go and retrieve it. He turned and ran to the port side, vaulted up over the gunwale, and slipped down into the dark, reed-choked water. Silt and mud swirled about him as he sank down. He quickly drew the Beholla out of his belt and held it up, but luckily the river only came up to his waist. He pulled himself closer in to the hull, melting into the dark shadow cast from the moonlight up above, and clung on to the side of the ship, pausing, ears peeled and alert. From up above he could hear snatches of whispered conversation, a barked order, and then a loud exclamation.

'That's Hazza. The bastard has killed Hazza!'

Lock slowly waded forward, feeling the mud suck and pull at his boots with every heavy step, until he eventually passed round the front of the stricken steamer. The water became deeper and tied to the bow was another dinghy. Lock presumed it was Bingham-Smith's. He held back in the shadows. Sitting at the rudder, silhouetted by the moon, was an Indian Sikh, the shape of his turban distinctive against the pale sky. Only this wasn't any ordinary sepoy, this was a figure whom Lock instantly recognised.

'Sid!' Lock hissed, giving a quick wave.

The silhouette turned sharply, glanced back up at the towering hulk of the *Marmaris*, then beckoned to Lock.

'Quickly, quickly, sahib,' Singh called back softly.

'Here, Sid. Catch!'

Lock tossed his Beholla to Singh who caught it like a cricket ball just level to his left shoulder. Lock pushed himself away from the hull and swam the few feet towards the dinghy.

Singh held out a huge paw and Lock grasped it firmly. The Indian practically yanked Lock up out of the water and dropped him into the dinghy. Singh released the tie-rope and with an oar pushed away from the *Marmaris* and out into the river. Soon the current grabbed ahold of them and with Singh pulling at the oars with graceful power, they were whisked rapidly away.

Lock kept low, chest heaving, as he caught his breath, and watched the *Marmaris*. But no one appeared at the bow. He turned, grabbed hold of the rudder and grinned up at Singh.

'Thanks, Sid,' Lock said.

Singh bobbed his head. 'I was thinking . . . that you may be needing . . . a quick exit, sahib . . . when Bing Ham Smith . . . appeared at the *Shaitan* . . . with a purple face . . . that would make . . . the sergeant major . . . most jealous.'

'Appeared?' Lock said.

'Yes, sahib . . . The *Espiegle* was soon . . . running aground . . . so General Townshend . . . Major Ross . . . and that horse's arse . . . Colonel Godwinson . . . and that other . . . horse's arse . . . if you will forgive . . . my rudeness, sahib . . . Bing Ham Smith . . . transferred along . . . with Captain Dunn . . . to the gunboat . . . *Comet*.'

Lock laughed. 'Yes, I saw Dunn's pennant on the *Comet* and guessed as much. But you tell it how it is, Sid. Horses' arses, one and all.'

'Yes, sahib . . . But there was much . . . arguing when . . . the officer sahibs . . . pulled up . . . alongside the *Shaitan* . . . and came aboard.'

'Arguing?'

'About you, sahib . . . Trouble . . . bad, bad trouble . . . sahib . . . Not good . . . Talk of . . . disobeying orders . . . of assaulting . . . a superior officer . . . of desertion . . . of this bloody rubbish . . . assassination and . . . court martial . . . business, sahib.'

Lock nodded his head sagely. Suddenly he didn't feel so elated. 'So nothing new, then,' he sighed.

'There was no . . . blue eyes on . . . the barges either . . . at all, sahib . . . Only brown . . . and green . . . and frightened . . . ones.'

'I didn't think there would be, Sid, but thanks anyway.'

'And nobody seemed . . . to know the name . . . *Binbaşi* Feyzi . . . either, sahib . . . Or of . . . Wassmuss.'

Lock turned his head and looked blankly at the passing bank. 'Bugger.'

'Yes. Bloody . . . bugger, sahib,' Singh said.

'More than you think, Sid. I've just added murder to that list.'

'Sahib?'

'Lieutenant Harrington-Brown,' Lock said, nodding over his shoulder at the receding bulk of the *Marmaris*. 'I just stuck my knife in his chest. Trouble is, I didn't have time to retrieve it before Bingham-Smith arrived on the scene.'

'I do not . . . understand . . . sahib.'

'It's engraved. The knife. With my name, Sid. A gift from Amy. Pretty damning evidence.'

Singh shook his head and stopped rowing for a moment. 'No, sahib, I do not understand. You say you killed the lieutenant sahib?'

'In self-defence, Sid, I assure you. Bastard tried to kill me first.'

'Oh,' Singh said, looking dubious.

'I was expecting, hoping, that Wassmuss as himself . . . or in the guise of *Binbaşi* Feyzi . . . or something . . . would be on that ship,

Sid. Some evidence to help clear me of this ridiculous accusation. Only I didn't find him,' he sighed. 'I found a dead German, all right. He had my knife in him, too, would you believe.'

'Sahib?'

Lock waved the question away. 'Never mind. He wasn't Wassmuss. But the place had been ransacked and I think someone, which turned out to be Harrington-Brown, was trying to rig the ship's magazines to explode. You know, to destroy the entire vessel.'

Singh was bobbing his head, but his face was a picture of confusion.

Lock smiled. 'I think Harrington-Brown worked for Ross, Sid, for the White Tabs. Only he was the rat, too. The one we've suspected was working within our organisation helping the Germans. A double-agent. Hell, he could have been German as well, for all I know. The major will be able to find out. If I can ever get to him without being arrested first.'

'I think, sahib, that the major sahib is well aware that you are in deep deep trouble. He was the one who signalled for me to slip away. I took him to be meaning that I get you out of there.'

'But where to?'

'The *Shaitan*, sahib. We are to rendezvous upriver where the reed marsh ends.'

'How far?'

'Perhaps two miles.'

'Well, let's hope the *Comet* doesn't catch us up.' Lock glanced over his shoulder again, but could see nothing coming up behind them.

'Do you think, sahib,' Singh said, 'that this Wassmuss could be in Amara?'

Lock turned back to face his friend again. 'Perhaps, Sid. But I'm beginning to think that he was never here in the first place. Nasiriyeh is where I was supposed to have killed this Turkish general, so why would Wassmuss, or Feyzi, not be there? Ross said he had intelligence that Feyzi was one of the commanders on the Tigris front, but I'm beginning to think that he's been playing me, Sid.' Lock shrugged. 'Either that, or perhaps it was false information supplied by Harrington-Brown, to throw me off the scent and get me into more trouble. I just don't know what to think anymore.'

Singh took up the oars again and started to row once more, pulling their dinghy smoothly and rhythmically on upriver and away from the burning *Marmaris* and the wrath of Bingham-Smith and Godwinson.

Lock shook his head. 'Shit, Sid. I can't get arrested again. I must get to Ross before anyone else.'

Singh bobbed his head and smiled. 'Do not worry . . . sahib . . . The major sahib . . . is on the *Shaitan* . . . also . . . He did not return . . . to the *Comet*.'

Lock let out a sigh of relief. 'All right then, Sid. The *Shaitan* it is.'

He leant back and then remembered the pack of Pall Mall's he'd taken from Harrington-Brown. He put his hand in his pocket and swore, pulling a soggy mess of tobacco leaves and paper and card out of his pocket. He cursed and tossed them into the river, turning his gaze to the passing landscape again, flat, empty and reed-choked.

The moon was still high and bright as they glided on towards another turn in the Tigris. Rounding the bend, Lock could see up ahead in the next reach of the river, pushed right against the western bank, another marooned vessel. As they got closer, Lock could see it was the Turkish steamer *Mosul*. Strung out behind her in a ragged row, all at odd angles like a discarded toy, was a lighter and seven mahailas packed with soldiers. They were crying and moaning against what must be a suffocating crush. The steamer was signalling downriver towards the British and Lock glanced over his shoulder to see a distant light flashing back. The *Comet* perhaps?

The thought that he should search this vessel crossed Lock's mind, but he quickly dismissed it as a foolish idea. He knew Wassmuss wasn't here now and he didn't have time to delay, not with Bingham-Smith somewhere close behind. Getting to Ross was the priority now.

Singh rowed quietly past the *Mosul*, and Lock watched as the haunted faces of so many Turk *Mehmetçiks* stared back at them, all as white as ghosts in the moonlight.

'That lot should slow the general and his entourage down for a while,' Lock said. 'All right, Sid, hand me an oar and let's try and catch up with the *Shaitan* as quick as possible.'

CHAPTER EIGHTEEN

Two hours later, just as the first streaks of dawn were beginning to break up the steel-grey sky, Lock was sat behind the wheelhouse of the *Shaitan* having his latest head wound cleaned and stitched. He sucked his teeth against the stinging pain as the young sailor designated with the task of being the gunboat's M. O. worked away diligently with a hot needle and thread.

Major Ross was standing nearby watching, arms folded, unlit pipe jammed between his lips, a deep scowl etched on his forehead. Lock's eyes kept being drawn to the major's face, but neither man said anything, as they waited for the M. O. to finish.

'There you are, sir. Nasty gash, but it'll heal in time. Try to keep it dry.'

Lock nodded. 'Thank you . . . ?'

'Ralph, sir, Able Seaman Ralph Amos.' He gave a quick smile, and began to pack away his medical kit.

'You done this before, Ralph?' Lock said, tentatively touching the tender and jagged scar above his ear.

'Mmm, hmmm, yes, sir. I was practising to be a vet before the war.'

'A vet?'

'That's right, sir. Well, if that'll be all?'

'Have you a cigarette? Mine got a little . . . damp.'

Able Seaman Amos pulled out a packet of Capstan Navy Cut and offered them to Lock.

Lock took one of the cigarettes. Amos struck a match and Lock leant towards the flame and inhaled deeply.

'Much obliged,' Lock said, with a sigh of tobacco smoke.

Able Seaman Amos gave a quick salute and left the two officers alone.

Lock pulled himself to his feet. 'Good to see you, sir.'

Ross took his pipe out of his mouth and stuffed it in his pocket. 'I'm sure it is, laddie, rather than the colonel.' He shook his head. 'Good God, Lock, what in the hell were you thinking?'

'Sir?' Lock frowned, a little mystified as to why the major was being so short with him.

Ross glanced into the wheelhouse and at the backs of the two naval men standing there, the coxswain and Lieutenant Singleton. Ross took Lock's elbow and guided him out of earshot, towards the stern. He lowered his voice.

'You know very well what I mean, running around with an important prisoner behind enemy lines, risking him getting shot while you join the attack on the redoubts. You should have brought him to me straight away.'

Lock pulled up. 'I wasn't going to jeopardise my mission by stopping and escorting the *liva amiral* back to the *Espiegle*. I was

322

behaving like a *Kommando*, sir, as you instructed. And it worked.'

'And how do you come to that conclusion?'

'I disabled the electric switch to the mines, capturing a senior enemy officer along the way. As well as some important documents and other . . . evidence.'

'Documents?'

'Yes, sir.'

'You have them now?'

'No. I gave them to Bingham-Smith to pass on to you.'

Ross shook his head. 'I received no such thing.'

'Bastard,' Lock said, taking a thoughtful puff on his cigarette. 'Still, it was mostly rubbish, dull administrative papers, memos and stores lists, quartermaster stuff. A few maps of the redoubts, as well as a detailed circuit diagram of the mines. I kept hold of that. And, more importantly, I kept hold of this. Here.' Lock pulled a damp, folded piece of paper from within his hatband and handed it to the major.

Ross opened up the document carefully and read through it.

'Do you recognise any names, sir?'

Ross shook his head. Then he nodded. 'Yes, a few.'

'How about . . . ?' Lock leant over and tapped Godwinson's name.

Ross pursed his lips. 'I see it, laddie. I see it.'

'And the signature at the bottom, sir. 'G'. Remember the telegram Aziz Azoo intercepted?[3] About the raid on Basra? That was also signed 'G'.'

Ross nodded. 'Yes, I thought then that it could refer to Lieutenant Colonel von der Goltz, the vice-president of the War Council under Enver Pasha.'

3. See *Kingdom Lock*

'And you don't now?'

Ross stroked his moustache, but didn't commit to an answer.

'What's going on, sir?' Lock pressed.

'I really don't know, laddie. Tell me,' Ross said, looking up from the paper, 'why didn't you have the prisoner transferred to the *Espiegle*?'

'The *liva amiral*? Because he was of more use being on the *Shaitan*, sir. Helping to spot the mines and so let us keep pace with the retreating Turks.'

'That's not the only reason, though, is it?'

Lock avoided the major's glare, and stared off at the passing landscape.

'Lock?'

'Wassmuss,' Lock said after a moment.

'Wassmuss?' Ross repeated.

Lock nodded. 'Or *Binbaşi* Feyzi. They are one and the same, sir. The *liva amiral* informed me that a German was running operations, so I followed up on that, followed the clues.'

Ross sniffed and gave a faint shake of his head.

'Am I or am I not a White Tab agent?' Lock said, a hint of anger building in his voice.

'Yes,' Ross said.

'Then, sir, as a White Tab agent, I acted on the evidence I found that suggested Wassmuss was nearby, or at least that a member of his spy network was.'

'What about this other evidence you mentioned?' Ross said.

Lock took a final drag on his cigarette, then dropped the stub to the deck and crushed it out with his boot. He pulled out the red-spotted handkerchief and the postcard he had taken from

Harrington-Brown. He handed the postcard to Ross and carefully opened the handkerchief up in his palm to reveal the six translucent pearls.

'I discovered these on the *Marmaris*. The *liva amiral* also had a bag of pearls in his possession. But he said they were payment. For military duties. One thing is for certain, though, these pearls seem to be in the possession of a great many senior officers along the Tigris.'

'Well, these are in the possession of most of our men along the Tigris, laddie,' Ross said, looking down at the postcard of the naked girl.

'The other side, sir.'

Ross turned the postcard over and squinted.

'The writing's a little faded, been in the water. But it's still legible. Just,' Lock said.

Ross was frowning again as he read through the list of names.

'I think *Braut* and *Bräutigam* are German for—'

'Bride and groom,' Ross nodded. 'Yes, I know, Lock. But what does it . . .' He trailed off, frowning, tapping the card against his teeth as his eyes glazed over, deep in thought.

'A kill list? Your name's on there. As is the general's.'

'Bride and groom,' Ross repeated with a shake of his head. 'I don't . . .'

'Amy and Casper?' Lock said. 'It would fit with the general and Colonel Godwinson being on the list.'

'But they are all men, Lock. There's no women's names.'

'There is that, sir, yes.'

'Where did it come from?'

'I can't be certain, but I think from the German officer I found dead on the *Marmaris*.'

325

'Can't be certain?'

'Well, the card and the pearls wrapped in the handkerchief weren't actually on the German officer when I found him.'

'I don't understand, Lock,' Ross said, scowling as Lock put the handkerchief in the major's palm.

'They were on Harrington-Brown.'

'How did he explain them?'

'He didn't.'

'Why not?'

'Because I didn't have the chance to ask him.'

Ross gave Lock a cold, hard stare. 'Why?' he said slowly.

'I killed him.'

'Jesus Christ!' Ross blurted out, glancing back at the wheelhouse and pulling Lock further away. 'You did *what*? Why?' he hissed.

'Self-defence.'

'Balls!'

Lock shook his head. 'The rat, sir.'

'The rat? What rat? Christ, what ar—'

'The rat in the White Tabs, sir. It was Harrington-Brown.'

Ross stared back at Lock in stunned silence. 'My God . . . But that would mean—'

'That would mean,' Lock said, 'that Wassmuss has been one step ahead of us all the time. Sir.'

Ross shook his head and stared down at the items in his hands, at the pearls and the postcard. He quickly put them in his pockets and fished out his pipe again and tobacco pouch. He began his ritualistic filling of the pipe, his hands working automatically. He patted his pockets for a match.

'Oh, here, sir,' Lock said. He pulled out the Ronson 'wonderlite' strike lighter he'd taken from Harrington-Brown's body, and offered it to Ross.

'What's this?' Ross said, with a questioning frown.

'Now you won't have to keep borrowing my bloody matches. Sir.'

Ross snorted. He opened up the lighter and struck a flame, cupped it against the breeze and puffed his pipe to life. 'Hmm, much obliged,' he mumbled.

'Harrington-Brown is a White Tab, isn't he?' Lock said.

Ross nodded absent-mindedly as he continued to puff away.

'I have a theory, sir. It's a little . . . fanti, a little wild, but . . .'

'Go on,' Ross puffed.

'That Wassmuss is more than just one man.'

'How so?' Ross frowned, refocusing on Lock's face.

'Could it be that he isn't a "he" at all, but a group, like the White Tabs?' Lock said. 'A group given a man's name to add an air of mystery.'

The major pulled his pipe from his mouth. 'I'm listening.'

'It would explain how "he" seems to be in more than one place at a time,' Lock added. 'First "he's" just ahead of us on the Tigris outside of Amara. Then "he's" supposedly held up in Nasiriyeh.'

Ross nodded. 'My God, laddie. But that's brilliant. I don't know why it never occurred to me. I mean, all the evidence points to such a . . . "fanti" theory, as you put it. Before I left Basra, I heard tell that Wassmuss, "he", was believed to have been leading a raid in Russian Persia. It would explain quite a lot. Perhaps even your shooting. After all, espionage is also about misinformation and misdirection. Sowing the seeds of doubt is just as powerful a weapon as planting a bomb or inciting jihad.'

'It would also explain the ridiculous legend of Wassmuss's mastery of disguise. One minute a fat businessman, the next a wiry Persian camel dealer, the next a stocky chauffeur to the APOC.'

Ross nodded in agreement.

'Or a British lieutenant in the White Tabs,' Lock added.

Ross frowned back at Lock.

'Harrington-Brown.'

Ross shook his head. 'Small fry. No, Wassmuss has his spies and agents throughout Persia, as we know, and thus far Grössburger is the only other European involved.' The major cursed under his breath. 'If only I hadn't lost that notebook. It'll all be in there, I just know it.'

'So Bombegy is innocent?'

Ross shrugged. 'He's involved somehow, Lock. I'm sorry to say, but it's true.' He paused, tapping the stem of his pipe against his teeth. 'We know Wassmuss has a contact in Constantinople, a Liman von Sanders. But that's all we know, his name. And a fat lot of good that is at the moment. We're a long way from the Turkish capital.' The major paused again, then pointed his pipe at Lock. 'And I have heard the name Brugmann bandied about.'

'But we have no proof, sir,' Lock said. 'It's all just theory.' He sighed. 'I need to find Feyzi, our blue-eyed boy who we thought was the actual Wassmuss. Then we'll know.'

Ross muttered something else under his breath that Lock didn't quite catch, and then the major's eyes took on a far away stare, lost in thoughtful silence once more.

Lock glanced about him. The crew of the *Shaitan* were busy going about their duties, and Lock was pleased to see that along with the major, Elsworth and Ram Lal were still on board too.

Singh was standing at the stern keeping a discreet distance from him and the major, but watching them with a look of troubled concern across his brow.

Lock gave his Indian friend a reassuring nod and Singh returned the gesture, but looked none the happier. Lock knew that Singh was convinced that he was in deep trouble, trouble that he would struggle to get out of.

'Trust me,' Lock mouthed.

'Did anyone else see?' Ross said after a while.

'See?'

'You kill Harrington-Brown.'

Lock shook his head. 'No, I was alone.'

'Good.'

'But . . .'

'But?'

'My knife was still sticking out of his chest when Bingham-Smith and a few Tommies boarded the *Marmaris*.'

'So?'

'I didn't have time to retrieve it.'

'Well, it's of no consequence, the knife could bel—'

Ross stopped short, noting the look on Lock's face. His eyes widened.

'Oh, laddie, tell me you—'

''Fraid so, sir. It's damnable evidence. The knife is personally engraved. From Amy.'

'Brilliant,' Ross fumed. 'You're supposed to be trying to prove your innocence about being a murderer, not leaving more evidence to the contrary. How in hell's name am I going to keep you from a court martial now?'

The major swore bitterly and jammed his pipe back in his mouth, scraping his teeth noisily. 'Well, we'll just have to make up some story. Tell them your knife was stolen.'

'It was.'

'Was?'

'Stolen, sir.'

Ross grunted.

'Tell me something, sir,' Lock said, 'you suspected Harrington-Brown all along, didn't you?'

'Whatever do you mean?'

'He works for you, yes? Is a White Tab, yes?'

'Yes.'

'Hence why he was at the brothel in Basra. Not as one of Casper's pals, but in the hope that he would make contact with Grössburger and perhaps expose himself. If you'll forgive the pun. But I'm right, aren't I? I imagine my turning up really did put a spanner in the works.'

Ross was silent, but Lock knew that he had guessed right.

'So even if the accusation sticks, about Harrington-Brown, I mean, then . . .' Lock shrugged, '. . . I've disposed of a traitor.'

Ross frowned and was about to add something when a cry came from the other end of the boat.

'Sahibs! Sahibs! I think that you best be seeing this.' It was Singh and he was beckoning them over to the starboard side of the gunboat, pointing over to the eastern bank.

'Now what?' grumbled Ross, as he followed Lock over to where Singh was standing.

There was a buzz of excitement amongst the ship's crew now, for all along the shore stood hundreds of Arabs. They had emerged from their mud huts that lined the banks of the river and were now waving white flags and uttering shrill cries of welcome. Women held young children up and men clutched their rifles by the barrels and were pumping them up and down in the air, cheering '*Salaam, salaam*', over and over.

'What is going on?' Lock said, scanning the seemingly joyous faces of the local populous.

'Ah,' Ross said, 'I may have had a little hand in this. Didn't expect it to work so beautifully, though.'

'Sir?' Lock said.

'Yesterday evening, I let slip to a local sheikh who hailed us from the bank, that some 15,000 British troops were rapidly "marching" upriver. I told the fellow to keep it under his hat. Which, of course, I knew damned well that he wouldn't do,' Ross said with a wry smile, gesturing to the waving, cheering mob. 'Obviously the sheikh spread the word. All hail the victors, yes?'

'And Amara, sir? Do you think . . . ?'

'Let's hope so. But it's a big place, some 10,000 inhabitants with caravan routes leading off to Kut Al Amara and the Persian passes. There's a heavy Turk presence in that town.'

Most of the figures on the bank were dressed in ragged black abas, and many of the women, Lock noted, as well as the girls, were carrying baskets of eggs. One even had a live chicken held by its legs. The boys, on the other hand, and there were dozens of them, all mostly naked, turned Catherine wheels, and shouted and waved in delight.

'*Baksheesh, baksheesh*,' one little girl shouted, as she ran down to the bank, clutching her basket of eggs. She was about twelve and skipped about coyly, showing off her gaudy cotton wrappings held together by a scarlet sash. Lock was instantly reminded of Aziz Azoo's daughter, Fairuza.

One of the *Shaitan*'s seamen gave a pleading glance to Singleton. The commander gave a nod of approval in return.

'If you're quick. Amos, do the honours.'

'Here, lads. Iggry, iggry!' Able Seaman Amos said, holding out his hands. 'Rupees. Come on, cough up!'

He collected a fair amount of coins from his crew mates, tied them up in a rag, and attached it to the end of a boathook. He thrust the boathook out to the bank. The girl snatched the bundle off the end, hooked the basket of eggs in its place, and whooped in delight when she opened up the rag to see how much money she'd made.

The crew cheered as Amos drew in the eggs, and they all grabbed at them greedily, eating them raw. One of the seamen handed an egg each to Lock and Ross.

Lock cracked his open on the gunwale and threw the contents into his mouth.

'God, that's good,' he grinned at Ross. 'If only we had some bacon.'

The girl didn't leave, though, and she kept screaming and shouting across as she ran along the bank trying to keep pace with them.

'What's up with her?' one of the seamen said, through a mouthful of raw egg.

'Dunno, mate. Perhaps we short-changed her?' Amos said.

'The basket,' Lock said.

'Eh, sir?' Amos said, glancing over to Lock.

'The basket. She wants it back.'

'Oh, right you are, sir,' Amos said. 'Here, lass,' he shouted, tossing the basket towards the girl.

It landed with a plop in the water at the edge of the bank, and the girl dived in to fish it out. She held it aloft as if it was some prize trophy, her face beaming with delight, and whooped in thanks.

As the *Shaitan* steamed on by, leaving the cheering Arabs behind, Lock could see, with the rising sun, that the landscape had changed tremendously. Gone was the stiflingly damp and cloying stinking marsh, and now, all around them, as far as the eye could see, was a vast, desolate plain covered in a low scrub. It was as flat and as green as a billiard table. The atmosphere had changed, too. It was still oven-hot, even at such an early hour, but the air felt much drier. For the first time in days Lock didn't feel as if his clothes were sticking to his skin. Above the *Shaitan*'s engines, Lock could even hear the odd bird call welcoming the new day.

'Major Ross, sir?'

Lock and Ross turned to see Lieutenant Singleton standing behind them, a pair of binoculars in his hands.

'Lieutenant?' Ross said.

'We're just about ten miles out of Amara now, sir. How shall we proceed?'

Ross glanced at Lock, then turned his gaze astern, staring back down the river. Lock could see the smoke plumes of the rest of Townshend's Regatta, the *Comet*, no doubt, at its head.

'I think, Lieutenant,' Ross said, 'judging by the white flags we've just seen, that news of our arrival has already reached Amara. I'm guessing that we'll find a similar welcome there. I say we push on.'

333

'And the *Comet*, sir?'

'Don't worry, Lieutenant, the general and I have already discussed the various scenarios along with your Captain Nunn. They'll be steaming up behind us soon enough.'

Singleton nodded. 'Very good, sir.'

Just then the distant rumble of an approaching aeroplane broke in over the chug of the *Shaitan*'s engines. Lock peered up out of the canvas roof, shading his eyes against the dawn sun.

'There, sahib,' Singh said, pointing to the north-east.

'I see him, Sid. Looks like our friend from the other day.'

'One of the Mesopotamian Half-Flight,' Ross said.

'Australian Half-Flight, sir,' Lock corrected.

Ross shook his head. 'New title, laddie.'

Lock scoffed. 'Of course. Can't be crediting colonials, can we?'

'Now, now, Lock. We're all in this war together.'

England first, Britain second, everyone else can piss right off, Lock thought, turning his gaze back to the approaching aeroplane.

The beat of its engine grew louder and Lock could soon make out the familiar blue, white and red stripes on its double tail fins and the shape of the pilot and his observer in the nacelle. It caught the sun and flashed brilliantly as it banked, spluttered and swooped and putted overhead. As he had before, the observer dropped a message canister. Only his aim was a little off this morning. It bounced off of the canvas roof and splashed into the river. But one of the seamen was ready with a fishing net on a rod. He scooped it up and hurried it over to Singleton.

Ross and Lock gathered round as the Royal Navy lieutenant unscrewed the canister lid and removed a piece of paper from the inside.

'Good news, Major,' Singleton said. 'Amara is in panic. Troops are fleeing north, a group are stranded to the south, being attacked by Arabs.'

Lock watched as the aeroplane spluttered and spat its way on downriver towards the *Comet*.

'Right then, Lieutenant,' Ross said. 'Amara, full steam ahead.'

Singleton gave Ross a smart salute and a beaming smile, and then he turned and barked orders at his crew.

The *Shaitan* shuddered and quickly picked up speed, pitching and heaving against the shifting current of the Tigris, as it steamed on towards Amara.

CHAPTER NINETEEN

As the sun rose higher into the brilliant deep blue of the cloudless sky, and the dry heat of the morning increased in temperature, the *Shaitan* entered the long straight of the river just below Amara. Up ahead, Lock could see movement on a bridge of boats that joined the east to the west banks.

'Have you—' Lock started to say.

Singh handed Lock his haversack with a grin.

Taking out the binoculars, Lock fixed them to his eyes, and adjusted the focus.

A column of Turkish troops were hurrying across and scrambling aboard a barge that was itself attached to a large steamer lying along the bank.

'Guns, fire a warning shot!' Singleton hollered to the seamen manning the *Shaitan*'s forward 3-pdr gun.

The 8ft barrel craned upwards and then, with a terrific cough,

337

sent a shell fizzing over the bridge of boats. It exploded with a great boom and a shower of water only about twenty feet from the steamer's port bow.

Lock watched through his binoculars as the Turks still crossing the bridge began to panic, pushing and shoving their way towards the barge. The steamer was already pulling away from the bank. The tie rope attached to the barge went taut and jerked violently, then seemed to snap. The barge crashed back into the bank and the troops on board began to scramble out of it again and run ashore. The steamer didn't stop, ploughing right through the bridge of boats, and charging on upriver and away from the *Shaitan*.

'Fire!' Singleton shouted, and again the 3-pdr sent a shell screaming off towards the Turks.

'Head straight for that gap, Carrington!' Singleton said.

'Aye, sir,' the coxswain replied, as he twisted the wheel about.

The *Shaitan* powered forward and had soon caught up with the stricken barge. Turk soldiers were fleeing in all directions, not one standing their ground and taking aim at the British boat. The *Shaitan* weaved easily through the gap in the smashed bridge of boats, debris and a number of dead soldiers bobbing about in its wake. The river then abruptly bent to the west and the Royal Navy gunboat bounced and skidded round the curve.

The river was about 150 yards wide now, and on the left bank Amara opened up before them. It was a large town of low, mud-brick buildings stretching along the eastern foreshore and opposite they passed a narrow fringe of date palms dotted with palatial riverside residences of two storeys, with open balconies, and jetties. Behind these were a few fields, and then open desert.

As they moved closer and closer to the town, everywhere Lock's eye fell he could see troops hurriedly retreating in confusion. There were dust clouds to the north, and just 500 yards distant from where he was standing at the bow, over on the west bank, he estimated there to be well over 1,000 troops moving off, but in a more orderly fashion.

'Jesus, I hope the *Comet* does catch up with us soon, after all,' Ross said. 'We'll need the men.'

But, to Lock's astonishment, still not one shot was fired at them, nor one company, one platoon or even one soldier turned to face them, nor made a stand to protect their town.

The *Shaitan* came to a quay that stretched away for about a mile, and on the river front was a long row of continental-looking houses with verandas and balconies, simple block-built offices, stores with latticed frontages, a three-storey hospital and what appeared to be rows and rows of army billets, judging by the stacks of rifles and equipment set out in their yards.

'There,' Ross said, pointing to the east bank. A large group had gathered on the river front, and were standing and waving outside of an imposing four-storey office-like building that had the Ottoman flag hanging limply from its roof.

Lock adjusted the focus on his binoculars.

'They look to be officials of some kind, sir,' he said. 'There are a few men in suits and quite a number of Turkish officers. No Germans, that I can see.'

'All right, Lieutenant,' Ross called back over his shoulder to Singleton, 'let's make for that Customs House over there.'

The *Shaitan* slowed and turned and began to drift towards the bank. The launch's crew and Lock's men kept their weapons trained on the waiting crowd. The *Shaitan* softly bumped into the quayside and the crew were quick to tie her off.

Lock, Ross and Singleton stepped ashore, along with Singh and Ram Lal who both kept their rifles held low across their midriffs. On the quayside, there were some thirty to forty officers with ranks ranging from *mülazimi sani*, second lieutenant, to *binbaşi*, major, standing in an ordered, silent group, along with a senior commander, a civilian dignitary and four *miralays*, colonels.

Lock slowly scanned the faces of the officers, searching vainly for that familiar pair of blue eyes. But he knew in his gut that Wassmuss wasn't amongst them.

The civilian dignitary stepped forward, clicked his heels, and bowed his head stiffly.

He was a tall, wiry man in his fifties, with a neat, long beard and small round glasses that hid an astute, peaceful face. He wore a dark business suit, a high-collared shirt and tie, and a lambskin kalpak hat on his head. He held out a ceremonial sword resting on the palms of his upturned hands. He shuffled on his feet nervously and cleared his throat. When he spoke, his voice was hoarse and weak, as if he'd been shouting for hours on end,

'*I am Vali Aziz Bey, the Governor of Amara, and I hereby surrender our town.*'

Lock translated for Ross.

The major stepped forward, saluted, and graciously accepted the sword with a stiff nod of his head.

'On behalf of His Britannic Majesty King George, I humbly accept your surrender. You and your men will be treated with dignity and respect.'

Again Lock translated. The governor gave a quick smile, a wave of relief washing across his face. He began to wring his hands now they were free of the sword, as if he were washing them in invisible water, washing them clean of his responsibility for this Mesopotamian town.

'*You, sir. What is your name?*' Lock suddenly asked the senior commander, the man standing just to the right of the governor.

'*Halim Bey, Yüzbaşi. Miralay Halim Bey,*' the senior commander said with an air of arrogance, as if Lock should be awed by the name.

Miralay Halim was a heavy-set man, jowly with small and dark fierce eyes, and his face was dominated by a stiff, upturned moustache. Like the rest of the military officers behind him, he was wearing khaki service dress, a kabalak military hat and leather riding boots. Lock had already marked him down as dangerous and his arrogant response confirmed the same.

'*Well, my dear Miralay,*' Lock said, '*do you see that man?*' He indicated over to Elsworth, who was standing at the bow of the *Shaitan* with his rifle pointing directly at the Turkish officer.

The *miralay* nodded. '*Yes, I am not blind.*'

'*Good,*' Lock smiled insincerely. '*Well, he has orders to shoot you between the eyes if there is so much as a cross word from any of your men. Understand?*'

The *miralay's* face dropped and his eyes darted from Lock to Elsworth's rifle. He swallowed. '*I . . . I understand. You will have no trouble, Yüzbaşi Bey.*'

'*Good,*' Lock said. He turned his back on the *miralay* and beamed at Ross. 'All yours, sir.'

'Lieutenant,' Ross said to Singleton, 'have a couple of your men take that flag down and run up our Union Jack.' He jerked a thumb towards the roof of the Customs House.

Singleton smiled. 'With pleasure, Major.' He turned and clicked his fingers at the two seamen standing beside the open gangway to the *Shaitan*. 'Bates, Amos . . . You heard the major. Go grab the spare Jack from the locker and get that gaudy red pirate flag down. On the double.'

'Aye, sir.'

Amos darted back onto the *Shaitan*, and returning with a folded Union Jack in his hands, he and Bates hurried into the Customs House to make their way up to the roof.

Ross leant forward and hissed in Lock's ear, 'Do you know who that fellow was you threatened?'

'Threatened? What makes you think I threatened him?' Lock said innocently.

'Come, laddie, I don't need to speak the language to know the tone. Besides, the look on his face told me plenty.'

'Whoa! Whoa, there!' came a shout.

Two of the *Shaitan*'s crew were nervously pointing their rifles at a rapidly approaching Arab infantry cyclist.

'Hold your fire,' Singleton ordered, and his men lowered their rifles.

The cyclist gave a tinkle of his bell and a wave of his hand as he wobbled down to the quayside. He skidded to a halt in front of Ross and gave the major a smart salute, immediately spewing forth a rapid stream of Arabic, pointing and gesticulating back up the street he had just ridden down.

Ross turned to Lock and Singleton.

'Seems there's a whole battalion of Turkish *pompiers* at the main barracks ready to surrender.'

'*Pompiers?*' Singleton asked.

'Fire Brigade.'

'Firemen? Wanting to surrender?' Singleton said, looking bewildered.

'Don't let the name fool you, Lieutenant; the Fire Brigade Regiment are the crack troops of the Ottoman Empire,' Ross said. 'Well, Lock, would you do the honours? I'm staying here to await Townshend's imminent arrival. Need to get this governor chap to organise supplies for our men. Fifteen thousand mouths to feed, remember?' he beamed, having raised his voice on mentioning the amount of British troops that were soon to be expected. He, as did Lock, knew damned well that some of the Turkish officers amongst the little gathering on the quayside would have a good knowledge of English.

'Besides,' Ross added with a wink, 'can't wait to see Godwinson's face when he hears you took the surrender of a crack regiment of Turkish troops.'

'Very good, sir,' Lock said. 'Sid . . . Ram Lal . . . come with me.' He turned to the Arab cyclist.

The man was wearing a grubby white uniform and the traditional Arab kufiya headcloth with an 'aqal camel hair ring around his head. And, despite having a bandolier full of shells wrapped around his waist, Lock could see that he was unarmed.

'*Right my friend,*' Lock said in Arabic, '*lead the way.*'

The Arab's dark face cracked into a jagged-toothed smile. He wheeled his bicycle about, and led Lock and the two Indians up into the heart of Amara.

The dust-choked streets of the town were crowded with the Arab inhabitants all looking on in excited awe as Lock and the others marched by. Lock kept his shoulders back and his head high, but inside his stomach was churning. This was insanity, yet it was happening like a dream. Why the Turks and the Arabs of Amara had so readily surrendered, he just couldn't fathom. The British were outnumbered by at least fifteen thousand to one. But the bluff was holding. He just hoped Townshend and his crazed regatta was close by.

Faces young and old, male and female, watched as Lock marched on. He caught many an eye as he scrunched up the wide, dusty street feeling slightly otherworldly. But he just nodded affably, saying the odd '*As-salaam alaykum*', and strode on.

The town itself appeared to be well maintained, with street lamps and telegraph lines, and rows of four-storey buildings that were just as impressive and of a similar design to those in the older parts of Basra.

Soon the barracks loomed up ahead. It was a great block of four houses with a common courtyard in front. They passed through the stone arched gates into a vast cloistered yard edged by verandas of little inner courts, and with a bare flagpole in the centre. Waiting for them, like a battalion ready for inspection, were about 500 Turkish soldiers all standing to attention in orderly military rows, with rifles presented. At their head stood the officers, smart and erect in their service uniforms.

Lock gave Singh an uneasy glance, then with his chin held high, strode towards the senior commander.

The officer, a *binbaşi*, was dressed in the same khaki green as the rest of the Ottoman troops in Amara, but their uniforms bore the distinctive Firemen Regiment badge, a brass fireman's helmet on a green collar. They also wore steel peakless helmets with a flame-proof cloth hanging down over the back of the neck. The men's helmets were completely lacquered in red, with a brass Order of the Orta crescent badge in the centre, while the junior officers' had a polished brass brow, while the senior officers' were in solid polished brass. They all wore brown leather halter straps, and the men also wore hatchets attached to their belts.

The *binbaşi* had an angular face, with a strong nose above a deep black and neatly manicured, upturned moustache. He was slightly shorter than Lock, standing at a little under five foot ten, but his body looked lean and athletic under the well-tailored uniform. He can't have been much older than Lock, either, maybe just thirty at the most. His green eyes peered back with an intense glint, then briefly danced around Lock's appearance, noting the holstered Beholla, the bullet hole in the left breast of the tunic, the Australia shoulder flashes, the slouch hat, before eventually coming to rest on Lock's eyes. They flicked from one to the other, and Lock noted the gentle raise of a curious eyebrow.

'*Monsieur le Capitaine,*' the *binbaşi* said in perfect French, '*I would like to offer you our unconditional surrender.*'

He clicked his heels together, bowed his head and held out his Mauser M1910/14 pistol, butt first.

'*Please, Binbaşi, keep your weapon,*' Lock replied in Turkish, holding his palm up.

The Turkish officer looked Lock in the face with initial surprise, then he nodded, and reholstered his pistol.

'*Thank you, Yüzbaşi. I am Binbaşi Esad Čuvidina. These are my men,*' he said with a flourish of his hand. '*They are all honourable, good soldiers. And loyal. I have surrendered, therefore they have surrendered. You will have no trouble from them, I give you my word.*'

345

He clicked his boot heels again and gave another little bow of his head.

'*I know who you are, Esad Čuvidina Bey. I saw your troops parade in Constantinople before the war,*' Lock said. '*Fine men.*'

'*You honour us, Yüzbaşi . . . ?*'

'Lock, Kingdom Lock. *But no, Binbaşi Bey, you honour us with your surrender,*' Lock said, giving a little bow of his head in return. '*However, I would request that your men surrender their weapons.*' He glanced over to the far side of the courtyard and to what appeared to be a heavy iron door. '*Is that a storage vault? Do you perhaps have the key?*'

'*Onbaşi Akşener, keys,*' *Binbaşi* Čuvidina barked.

A corporal broke from the ranks, trotted over, and saluted. He handed out a large bunch of heavy iron keys. *Binbaşi* Čuvidina nodded over to the large iron door, and the *onbaşi* saluted again, ran over to the doors, unlocked them, pulled them open, and then ran back. He snapped to attention again. The *binbaşi* took the keys from him and passed them to Lock.

'*Thank you,*' Lock said. 'Sid,' he called, and tossed the keys over to the big Indian. 'Have the weapons piled up in that vault and then lock them away. Don't want the locals getting any ideas, do we?'

'Sahib,' Singh called.

Lock turned back to the Fire Brigade's commander. '*If you would, please, Binbaşi Bey, we shall march down to the Customs House at the quayside, where the rest of your fellow officers are, along with the governor.*'

'*I hope, Yüzbaşi Lock, that all your commanding officers are as learned and courteous as you,*' the *binbaşi* said.

'Some, Binbaşi Bey. But not nearly enough.'

The Turk officer snorted lightly. '*It is the same in our army. I fear it is the same the world over.*' He gave Lock a smart salute, then turning to the *yüzbaşi* to his right, passed the order for the men to hand in their weapons. The Turks circled in an orderly fashion, piling their rifles and hatchets inside the storage vault under the watchful eye of Singh and Ram Lal, and turned back to form orderly lines in the courtyard once more.

A *başçavuş*, sergeant major, holding a large brass parade torch, clearly a symbol of great honour for the regiment, stepped forward a pace. He stamped to attention, and the men behind him all shouted in unison,

Yangın var! Yangın var!
Ben yaniyorum
Yetişin a dostlar
ben yaniyorum.

Lock glanced over to Singh, who was just finishing locking the storage vault shut. He turned and gave a thumbs up, then with Ram Lal at his side made his way over to the gate. Lock moved off with the *binbaşi* walking regally beside him. The *başçavuş* came next with the parade torch held aloft and then, marching two abreast, followed the troops of the Constantinople Fire Brigade.

Lock gave Singh and Ram Lal a reassuring wink as he passed back through the stone arch entrance. 'Bring up the rear, Sid. Make sure nobody strays.'

'Very good, sahib,' Singh said, and waited, watching as the Turks filed by.

The crowds of Arab inhabitants were still lining the streets. Lock and his Turkish prisoners marched back down towards the shimmering Tigris; there was a hushed silence as if the populous could not quite believe that their time under Ottoman rule had come to such an abrupt and peaceful end.

A low murmur started up somewhere to Lock's left, that quickly spread through the crowd like wildfire, and soon the men, women and children alike were shouting and clapping and singing and calling out Allah's name in joyous celebration.

CHAPTER TWENTY

By the time Lock had made it back to the river front, the *Comet* was docked along the foreshore. With her were the armed tugboats the *Samana* and the *Lewis Pelly*, both with a horse-boat containing a mounted 4.7 gun on tow. The Turkish dignitaries were no longer out on the quayside and there was no sign of Major Ross. The Union Jack that Singleton's men had taken up to the roof of the Customs House was now flapping gently in the dry, hot breeze. Perhaps they were all inside. Lock was about to go and find out when a marine approached. He was wearing the dark-blue underdress uniform with the distinctive peakless 'Broderick' cap, and his trousers, with their red seam down the outside, tucked into brown laced-webbing gaiters and black laced boots, made Lock think of the Red Caps. It gave him an uneasy feeling, and he suddenly regretted leaving Ross to take the surrender, when Singleton would have been perfectly capable of doing the task.

'Captain Lock, sir,' the marine saluted. 'If you will follow me, I'll show you where the prisoners are to be taken.'

Lock nodded and led the prisoners further on down the quay. They marched on, passing the vast open courtyard of the bazaar, its rib-vaulted domed ceiling like that of the inside of a cathedral. Outside, in front of rows and rows of crates, fishermen were working at repairing their nets, others sorting through the day's catch. Lock could see baskets full of a carp-like fish, some as big as 70lbs. His mouth watered at the prospect of sitting down to eat one of the monsters.

'Captain Lock, sir, this way.'

The marine led Lock and his prisoners down some greasy wooden steps and onto the muddy foreshore where local children were crying and laughing as they ran in and out of the water.

'Where exactly are we taking them?' Lock said.

'There, sir.'

The marine pointed to a big iron lighter that was anchored out in the middle of the river.

Look stood with Singh and Ram Lal, watching the transfer of men as gulls screeched and swooped overhead in the morning haze. Two able seamen from the *Comet* were ankle-deep out in the water, helping to steady the launch, while under the suspicious glare of the marine, the men of the Constantinople Fire Brigade lined up quietly, ready to climb aboard. The launch then sped off to the lighter, unloaded and returned, where the process was repeated.

Lock was thinking about finding a cafe someplace and ordering a good hot meal and some strong coffee, when his mood was broken by a familiar figure slipping and splashing towards him across the mud.

'Sir, sir . . . there's trouble,' Elsworth gasped, catching his breath.

Lock glanced back along the muddy foreshore towards the Customs House.

'What is it, Alfred?'

'Captain Bingham-Smith . . . and the colonel, sir. I overheard them arguing . . . with Major Ross, about you . . . sir. Something to do with . . .' Elsworth hesitated.

'Go on, Alfred. I think I know what you're going to say.'

'Lieutenant Harrington-Brown, sir . . . He's dead. Only they're . . . saying it's murder, sir.'

'Sahib,' Singh said leaning close to Lock's ear, 'I would very much advise you to get out of here.'

'Make a run for it? From Bingham-Smith?' Lock shook his head. 'Never, Sid. It was self-defence, and the major knows it.'

Singh shifted uneasily on his feet, throwing glances up towards the Customs House. Lock had never seen his Indian friend look so concerned, so doubtful, before.

'Look, Sid,' Lock said, putting a reassuring hand on the big Sikh's shoulder, 'I'm not stupid. I know they're after my blood, but this war's bigger than any of us, and if they ca—'

'Captain Lock?' a voice called from behind.

Lock turned to see three armed marines standing at the edge of the quayside. They didn't look friendly.

'You're to come with us, sir,' the burly NCO at the front called, as they descended the wooden steps leading down to the muddy foreshore.

'Oh? On whose orders?' Lock called back, standing with his hands on his hips waiting for the three marines to get closer.

The rifles the two junior men carried were the older

Navy issue Charger-Loading Lee–Enfields. The NCO wore a holstered Webley at his hip, although Lock noted the holster was unclipped.

'General Townshend's, sir,' the NCO said, as he approached.

'Bugger,' Lock said. 'Very well, Sergeant. Lead on.'

'And you're to hand over your weapon, sir.'

'I shall do no such thing.'

The NCO put his hand to his holster and the two marines with him raised their rifles a touch.

'Sir. It's not a request, sir. Sorry,' the NCO said.

'Listen you—' Elsworth said, a surprising level of anger in his voice, as he stepped forward.

Lock held up his hand to stop the young sharpshooter making trouble for himself.

'It's all right, Alfred. Just a misunderstanding. Here.' He unclipped his holster and removed the Beholla, but handed it to Singh and not to the NCO. 'Look after it for me, Sid.'

'Sir, that's not—' the NCO started to protest, but Lock turned a steely glare on him. The NCO thought better of it, his eye dropping to the bullet hole in Lock's left breast pocket, then back up to Lock's face. He cleared his throat. 'If you'd accompany us back to the Customs House, sir,' he said.

'Very well, Sergeant.'

Lock splashed on up the foreshore, with the two marines flanking him and the NCO leading the way. Singh and Elsworth followed, leaving Ram Lal with the two able seamen and the first marine to watch over the transfer of the last of the Turkish prisoners.

* * *

Lock was sat on a hard chair to the left of a closed, heavy wooden door in the foyer of the Customs House. It was a bland, soulless space, vast and full of echoes. A sweeping staircase curved up from the left leading to a mezzanine level above. Two Tommies, one on a stepladder, the other leaning down precariously from the balcony above, were removing the only form of decoration in the foyer. It was a huge imposing portrait of Enver Pasha, framed by the Ottoman and the German flags, hung just below the balcony. It was the first thing you saw when entering the Customs House, and Townshend wanted it gone. The only other presence in the foyer was an armed marine guard. He was standing on the opposite side of the door to Lock, but his eyes were keeping a close watch on him.

From behind the heavy wooden door, Lock could hear raised voices. He couldn't make out exactly what they were saying, but as Townshend, Ross, Godwinson and Bingham-Smith were in there, Lock was confident that he was the subject of their heated debate.

Lock crossed his leg over his knee, sighed, and began to pick at the loose stitching on the brim of his slouch hat held in his lap. He licked his lips and tried to ignore the dryness of his throat. How long had it been since he'd had a decent drink? Christ, he could use a smoke, too.

'I wonder . . .' Lock started to ask the marine guard, before a sudden voice echoing around the foyer interrupted him.

'I might have known you'd be the cause of all this fuss.'

Lock looked over to the main entrance. Standing in the threshold, leaning against the door jamb, with sun streaming in behind her, was the silhouette of a woman.

Lock grinned, recognising the voice. 'Pretty Officer Boxer, what brings you to this desolate part of the world?'

'You do,' she said striding forward, her shoes click-clacking against the stone floor.

'I'm honoured.'

'I wouldn't be,' she said, pulling a cigarette from between her lips, and blowing a smoke trail behind her like a slow-moving locomotive.

Lock got to his feet, a move that unnerved the nearby marine guard, who took a step towards him, rifle raised.

'Easy, tiger,' Betty snarled to the guard. 'He ain't goin' nowhere.'

The guard scowled back at her, eyes dropping to the three chevrons on her sleeve. He frowned, then took a step back to his post, having made the decision to leave be.

Lock couldn't help but run his eye up and down Betty as she walked closer. She was no longer dressed in the heavy blue serge uniform, but had swapped it for more sensible summer whites. She had on a single-breasted Norfolk-style coat, decorated with gilt buttons and a rating badge on her left sleeve. The skirt was hemmed to no more than four inches above her slender ankle and her shirt was open at the neck with a standard Navy neckerchief completing the look. She was hatless and her lightly curled, thick raven hair was hanging loose to just above her shoulders. It bounced, as did the rest of her, in time with her movements.

She came to a halt a mere step from Lock, and stared up at him through narrowed dark-brown eyes.

'What happened to that ridiculous straw hat?' Lock said.

Betty scoffed and took the cigarette out of her wide mouth

again. She held it up and raised a slim eyebrow. 'From Cairo.'

Lock took the offered cigarette, noted the pale lipstick mark, then put it between his own lips, and inhaled deeply. He closed his eyes and let the sweet Egyptian tobacco coat his mouth and tongue.

'God, that's good,' he sighed. 'Thanks. So, why are you here?'

'I'm escorting *you* back to Basra. Doesn't look good, you know, about this assassination thingy.'

Lock shrugged. 'I may be up for more than that now.'

Betty gave Lock one of her lopsided, wry smiles. 'Such a bad boy.'

'So are you taking me back all on your own?'

'Hell, no,' Betty snorted lightly. 'You ain't to be trusted. I bought some of the Red Cap boys with me. They're hanging around outside,' she said, jerking a thumb over her shoulder.

Lock smiled and continued to smoke.

'We had to let Grössburger go,' Betty said.

'Why?'

'Pressure from APOC and the Swiss consulate. He's got some powerful friends.'

'Don't they all,' Lock scoffed. 'Tell me, how did you get here?'

'Boat. Same as you.'

'No chaperone?' Lock mocked.

Betty gave him a withering look. 'I had some nurses for company. General Nixon was so confident of victory that he arranged for medical staff to be ready to set up a hospital here. I'm thinking that the Brits want Amara to be their new administrative centre before long.'

Lock nodded. 'Nurses, hey?'

'That's right. Mind you, I've heard that you didn't have too many casualties.'

Lock had drifted off into thought. Could Amy be among the nurses?

'I was saying,' Betty said, 'not too many injuries.'

Lock focused on Betty again. 'What? Oh . . . no . . . nothing like Shaiba. Incredible really. Tell me, Bet . . . Petty Officer . . . was a Miss Townshend one of the nurses?'

'Shoot, I don't know,' she said with a touch of irritation. 'Why, she your sweetheart?'

Lock shrugged. 'Was.'

'Uh, huh,' Betty said, nodding slowly. 'Sounds as if you don't like the situation.'

Lock was about to reply, but his answer was cut short by the door behind him suddenly opening. The guard snapped to attention and Lock turned to see Ross staring back at him. The major gave a brief nod to Betty, then beckoned for Lock to come in.

'Excuse me,' Lock said to Betty, tipping his forelock mockingly and passing her back the cigarette.

Ross held the door open wide for Lock, then shut it firmly behind him.

The office was a surprisingly tranquil room, not at all militaristic, and reminded Lock of the headmaster's study he had stood in once too often when he was a child. Huge French windows were open at the far end, and Lock could see an invitingly cool courtyard outside with a lone palm tree in its centre offering ample shade. The only sound was the soft chirruping of birds and the gentle patter of water from some unseen fountain. In front of the French windows was a desk, behind which sat a stony-faced General Townshend. He didn't look at all well to Lock, his skin grey and taut, his eyes bloodshot and watery. The desk was bare except for a single candlestick telephone, the cardboard file of documents he had taken from the *liva amiral* and then later given to Bingham-Smith, and a Webley. And something . . .

Oh, bugger, Lock thought. His knife.

There were two more chairs lined up to the left of the desk. Colonel Godwinson, legs crossed, cane tap-tapping lightly against his boot, was sat in one, Bingham-Smith, with his usual smug smirk written across his face, was sat in the other. Lieutenant Singleton was standing, smoking a cigarette, on the far side of the room in front of a large, empty stone hearth cut into the wall. Major Ross crossed the room to join the Royal Navy commander. Beneath the tobacco and leather, the room smelt faintly of mint tea.

Lock, slouch hat in his hand, stood to attention in the middle of the Herati-patterned Persian rug that dominated the room, and waited.

'Bloody fellow doesn't even shave,' Godwinson grumbled, his blue-grey eyes boring into Lock. 'Never seen him with a smooth chin. A damned disgrace.'

Townshend coughed lightly and Godwinson fell silent.

'Sir, I . . .' Lock started to say, but the general just glared back at him. Lock snapped his mouth shut.

'Two things, Lock,' Townshend said. 'One. Did you disobey a direct order from your commanding officer and refuse to transfer a valuable prisoner to the command vessel, the *Espiegle*?'

'No.'

'Rot!' Godwinson spat. 'Casper . . .' He paused, clearing his throat to correct himself. 'Bingham-Smith is your superior officer and after he led the assault on One Tree Hill he discovered that there was an important Turkish officer—'

Lock began to laugh.

'What the devil?' Godwinson spluttered, turning to Townshend. 'See? This man is not fit to lead men!' He turned back to Lock, rising from his seat, his face a deep crimson, eyes bulging with fury. 'This is not a joke, you nasty little colonial . . . blaggard. How dare you?'

Lock was shaking with the effort of trying to hold in his laughter. But it was no good, for the more he tried, the more Godwinson bleated and blustered, and the more Lock found it hilarious.

'Stop it! Stop it, I say.' Godwinson lunged forward, his cane raised.

There was a vicious snap as the cane sliced through the air. But Lock's hand shot straight up and caught it just inches away from his face. He gripped it tightly and glared back at the colonel, all his laughter evaporated.

'Uncle . . .' Bingham-Smith was standing, his hand on Godwinson's arm in an attempt to calm him.

Godwinson shook him off irritably. 'Keep out of this, Casper.'

'Sit down. Please, Colonel,' Townshend said calmly.

Lock let go of the colonel's cane, with a forceful shove. Godwinson glared back, the colour high on his neck, but he stepped away and sat himself down again.

'You had two points, sir,' Lock said, turning his gaze back on Townshend. He could hear Ross's sharp intake of breath, but he no longer cared at what these men thought. They had already decided his fate. That much was clear. There was nothing left for him to do but get this over with and get the hell out.

Townshend narrowed his eyes and his mouth took on a hardness Lock had never seen before. The general took a deep breath through his nostrils.

'Two. Did you kill Lieutenant Harrington-Brown?'

'Yes.' Lock didn't even hesitate to reply.

Townshend sighed and slumped back in his chair. He stared at Lock long and hard and gave a barely detectable shake of his head.

'I note with interest the engraved words on this dagger,' the general said eventually, leaning forward and picking up the blade from the desk in front of him. '"For Kingdom and Country".'

He raised his eyes and fixed Lock with a steely glare. 'There's no room in this war for selfish acts, Lock. You've disobeyed orders once too often.'

Bingham-Smith snorted, but fell silent when Townshend shot an angry glance his way.

'You took matters into your own hands,' the general continued, 'and all you have to show for it is this file of useless documents and the blood of one of your fellow officers on your hands. I know you need to operate in a somewhat unorthodox manner, Lock, but murder?'

Lock remained silent, staring back at the general, using all his will power not to look at Bingham-Smith and the colonel.

Townshend gave a long, heavy sigh and passed his hand through his neatly combed hair. 'I wash my hands of you, Lock. For King and country is how one should act, not for self, not for . . .' He held up the knife, '. . . Kingdom and country. You will be escorted under guard back to Basra where you will face court martial. I'm sure you can guess what the inevitable outcome will be.'

Look stood still and didn't show any reaction to what the general had just told him.

'Well?' Townshend said.

'Sir?' Lock said.

'Have you nothing to say?' Townshend blurted out, spraying spittle across the desk, his impatience getting the better of him.

'I like the courtyard,' Lock said, nodding past the general's shoulder.

Townshend smashed his palm down on the table. 'Ross! Get him out of here!'

The major indicated for Singleton to follow and made to leave. Lock put on his slouch hat, gave the general a smart salute, and turned on his heels, ignoring the gloating face of Bingham-Smith, and marched out of the door, with Ross and Singleton close behind.

Outside, Ross pulled Lock angrily back. There was a deep-set fire of anger in the major's eyes, but Lock was beyond caring now.

'This isn't a game,' Ross snapped. 'What the hell do you think you are playing at?'

'Oh, come on, sir. It's all bullshit. You know it. Christ, even the old man knows it.'

Ross glared back at Lock, nostrils flaring, his face taut with anger.

'What exactly do you bastards want of me?' Lock said. 'You set me up with this commission in the AIF, you employ me as a White Tab agent, and you tell me there's a German spy – hell, a whole network of spies, working against us, and that you want me to put a stop to it. But every time I get somewhere, I find obstacles put in my way by the men on my own side. I followed Wassmuss's trail

360

on your lead, sir, and Harrington-Brown was in the way. He's the rat and now he's gone. One less obstacle.'

'But we're no closer to catching Wassmuss or the people behind him, are we?' Ross said. 'You killed a major suspect who probably had answers. He's dead, so now we can't interrogate him, and you can't prove who he really was.'

'But you know!'

'What does that matter? Those men in there,' Ross said jerking his head back towards the closed office door, 'Christ, most of the bloody British command, think you're a killer, Lock, an animal that needs to be not just neutered, but put down.'

Lock took a step closer to the major, their noses almost touching.

'Do you know something, Major? Not only are you a cold bastard, but you're a manipulative using backstabbing bastard, too. If you hadn't secured my release from that prison in Van, if you hadn't then recruited me to the bloody White Tabs and sent me off to China, then none of this would be happening. I would never have met Mei Ling, I would never have met Amy, and I would never have lost them both.'

Lock's chest was heaving, and Ross opened his mouth to interrupt, but Lock wasn't ready to stop.

'You bloody well arranged my arrest in the first place, didn't you?' Lock added. 'In Turkey, just so you could use me, so you could manipulate me like you do everyone around you. Hell, it wouldn't surprise me if Harrington-Brown was spying for Wassmuss under your orders. You could support me. You could insist that Harrington-Brown was a traitor and that I had no choice in killing him. You have shaped me into a weapon that you

361

wished you had the guts to be yourself. But you can't, can you? Because you're just the same as those fuckers in there, a yellow manipulative, self-serving coward.'

Ross slowly pulled out his pipe and tobacco pouch. He didn't say anything in response to Lock's tirade, he just calmly went about the ritual of filling his pipe. Only he wasn't calm, Lock could see that, he was angry. The major's colouring hadn't changed, but there was a rage emanating from him, and his hands were ever so slightly trembling. A clump of tobacco fell to the floor. Lock's eyes watched its progress and when it hit the ground, he looked up and Ross was staring back at him.

'Petty Officer Boxer,' the major said softly, 'escort Captain Lock here back to Basra, if you'd be so kind.' He then dropped his eyes again and continued filling his pipe.

'Pleasure, sir,' Betty said. 'Come on, Captain, we've a long journey ahead of us.'

Lock glared back at Ross waiting for him to deny his suspicions, to answer his accusations, but the major didn't look up again. Lock swore and turned away.

Outside on the steps to the Customs House, three Red Caps were standing idly by smoking and talking quietly amongst themselves. They didn't even look up when Lock emerged, blinking into the blazing sunlight, or when the American girl came out moments later. A fourth figure, who was sat a little apart from the Red Caps, did notice Lock and Betty, though. He got to his feet and sauntered over to them.

'Still alive, Sergeant Major?' Lock said, a touch of disappointment in his voice.

'You in the shit again? Sah.' Underhill said with a twinkle of glee in his eye.

'How ever did you guess?'

Underhill stood with his back to the Red Caps, blocking them from Lock's view.

''E was a pompous prick,' the sergeant major sniffed, glaring up at Lock, 'that 'Arrington-Brown. Never trusted 'im, never liked 'im.'

Lock stared back at Underhill in surprise, and then glanced at Betty.

'You go easy, sah. And I'll see you soon. Unless you go and get your bleedin' 'ead blown off,' Underhill smirked. 'Now there's a thought, eh?'

Lock frowned, totally at a loss to what the sergeant major was playing at.

'I . . . I'll try . . . Sergeant Major,' he said warily.

Underhill nodded to Betty. 'Go careful, miss.'

She gave the sergeant major a casual salute, then pulled Lock after her.

Lock hesitated, looking back at Underhill. 'Why?'

Underhill glanced over his shoulder at the three Red Caps, who were still minding their own business, then he stepped a little closer to Lock.

'White Tabs, innit,' he hissed, and tapped his nose.

'What the hell's that supposed to mean?'

The sergeant major shrugged. 'Orders, sah. Ain't cus I like you,' he spat, then grinned. 'We both knows that. But can't be 'avin' no court martial ending yer life now, can we? That's gonna be my pleasure. Some day.'

Lock narrowed his eyes. Was Underhill joking? He didn't joke. He was a sly, cunning bastard. No, he was up to something. Perhaps he was going to shoot him the moment he turned away, saying that he had tried to escape. Lock licked his lips.

'Go on, then. The Yankie bint's waitin',' Underhill sneered, jutting his chin over towards Betty. 'I ain't gonna shoot you in the back, if that's what yer thinkin'. 'Onest to God.'

Lock nodded and backed away a few paces. Underhill was watching him, a curious expression across his pug-ugly face, but the three Red Caps were still paying them no attention. Lock glanced at the open doorway to the Customs House. Empty. No sign of Ross or the sentry. He gave a curt nod to Underhill, then turned and ran.

There was a narrow alleyway that passed down the side of the Customs House. It was in deep shadow, cool, but stank – like all alleyways did – of fecal matter. Lock breathed through his mouth, keeping close behind Betty.

'What a charming aroma.'

'Shut it, bud,' she growled over her shoulder.

They came out onto an open stableyard and Betty made her way quickly across to a pair of large barn doors. Lock followed and helped her slide them open. Inside, there was a parked automobile. It was a civilian touring car that had been converted into an armoured vehicle. The rear sedan seat had been removed and replaced by a platform, upon which a Hotchkiss M1900 8mm machine gun with an armour plate shield had been mounted. The platform was surrounded by a bulwark, so, apart from the gunner, there was only room for a driver and a passenger to sit cramped under a small rain cover roof at the front.

'Get in,' Betty said, and she began to crank-start the motor.

'How did you know about this?'

'Until . . . recently . . . it was . . . the pride . . . and joy . . . of the governor . . . of Amara,' she said, in between hard jerks of the cranking handle.

'Let me do—'

The engine backfired, then coughed into life with a spew of black exhaust smoke. Betty straightened up, brushed her hands, and grinned at Lock. The motorcar began to vibrate from side to side, making a gentle tock-a-tock-a-tock noise as it idled.

'I think we'd best go before it shakes apart,' Lock said, climbing into the driving seat.

'Hey, shift,' Betty said, hitching up her skirt a little as she climbed up the same way. Lock scooted over, and Betty plonked herself down behind the wheel. She released the handbrake and, with a loud crunch, engaged the gears and the car chugged off.

Lock held on tight as Betty swung the motor vehicle out of the stableyard and onto the side street that ran north away from the Customs House.

Lock leant out and glanced back the way they had come. The road was empty.

'We being followed?' Betty shouted over the engine and the rushing wind.

'Doesn't look like it,' Lock said, sitting back in his seat. 'Do you think there's ammo for that?' he jerked his head at the mounted machine gun above them.

Betty shook her head. 'Didn't find any.'

'Pity.'

They were doing a steady 10mph now, heading west away from

the Tigris. The motor vehicle bounced and shuddered along, Betty doing her best to steer them away from the potholes in the rough, hard, dusty streets.

'Are you deliberately aiming for those holes?'

Betty ignored the remark and then suddenly jerked the wheel to the side and they crashed and bounced in and then back out of a particularly nasty hole.

'Like that one?'

'*Touché*.'

They rattled on, passing through a row of low storerooms and into a deserted railhead. Betty swung the automobile to the left and they juddered over the single rail tracks to head west. The depot looked empty, with not a soul about that Lock could see. There were no locomotives, either, or sidecars, just a lone carriage parked under a thin line of palms to the right. It too looked abandoned.

'He's OK that SM,' Betty said after a while.

'He's a shit.'

Betty glanced at him and gave another one of her lopsided grins. 'You were pretty hard on the old man.'

'The general?'

She shook her head. 'The major.'

'I said it like it is.'

They swung out onto another road, larger and busy with mostly pedestrian traffic. Betty gave a toot of the horn and swerved skillfully, narrowly missing a team of camels laden with sacks of grain. The Arabic abuse shouted at them was instantly lost as they trundled past in a cloud of choking dust.

'It's all true,' Lock said, eying Betty. 'He's a using bastard, don't you forget that.'

'Uh-huh. That's what my mom says.'

Lock adjusted his position in the hard leather seat so he could watch Betty as she wrestled with the steering wheel, twisting it hard from left to right as she avoided the many native hazards wandering about on the road in front of them.

Lock smiled to himself. He liked this girl, he thought, the confidence that oozed out of her, the way she carried herself. He especially liked the way she bit her lower lip when concentrating. He decided he was going to ask her something, something profound. But he changed his mind and let the question hang.

'Here's your ride,' Betty said, breaking Lock from his thoughts.

He looked up as the automobile skidded round a corner.

They were now on the outskirts of Amara and had arrived at what looked to be a playing field of some kind. There was a stretch of scrub grass and a covered spectator stand over to one side. Beyond that the flat, desolate desert stretched out to the horizon, bleak and empty. In the middle of the field, parked facing south, was the aeroplane Lock had seen a number of times over the past few days, but always up in the sky. Now, up close, on the ground, it looked frighteningly fragile.

Betty slowed the automobile, and pulled up with a juddering halt about twenty feet away from the aeroplane.

A tall man dressed in khaki overalls was tinkering with the engine by the rear-facing propeller. He straightened up and shouted something to the pilot who was leaning down from the cockpit up above him.

Lock and Betty jumped out of the automobile. She made her way to the back, and returned with a bulky haversack in her arms.

'Here, this is for you,' she said, tossing it to Lock.

The haversack landed with a dull thud against his chest as he caught it.

'And you'll be needing this,' Betty said, handing him his Beholla automatic and holster. 'A big Indian fella insisted I take it and give it to you.'

'Sid,' Lock smiled, nodding his head.

They stood facing one another in silence, and Lock felt a twinge of desire as he stared back into Betty's deep brown eyes.

'Thanks,' he said.

'Don't thank me. Thank Major Ross.'

Lock raised a questioning eyebrow.

'Aw, come on. You don't think he'd abandon you, do you?'

Lock stared back at her, but didn't say anything.

'Who d'ya think arranged all this?' Betty gave another of her lopsided smiles.

'Hurry up, mate,' the mechanic shouted and beckoned over to them.

'I think it's time for you to get going.'

'I guess so.'

But Lock couldn't drag himself away from her stare. Pull yourself together, Kingdom, he thought with a smile, and made to move away.

Betty grabbed his sleeve and pulled him back. They hesitated, eyes searching each other's faces, then Lock felt an electric current race through his veins as their lips met. He felt her tongue dart into his mouth and suddenly all of his tensions and worries evaporated. He was falling, falling deeper and deeper inside of her.

Then Betty pulled her head away and opened her eyes.

'Get going, handsome,' she said huskily, and gave him a gentle shove.

'I'll be back.'

'Sure, just make damned certain you got that Feyzi fella with you. Otherwise the major says don't bother coming back at all.'

Lock grinned and moved off towards the waiting aeroplane.

'Tell him he's a nasty Scot's bastard,' he called over his shoulder.

'I can't do that,' Betty called back.

'Why not?'

'He's my pa,' she said.

'What? What did you say?' Lock stalled, and turned back to face her, but the pilot was shouting at him now to get a bloody move on.

'Well, bugger me . . .' Lock said.

He turned to the man in the khaki overalls who was standing by the propeller.

'Here, put this clobber on, mate.' The Australian mechanic handed Lock a leather pilot's cap.

Lock stuffed his slouch hat inside his tunic, and pulled on the cap. It was a snug fit.

The mechanic gave him a wink. 'Beaut', mate,' he said, and then thumbed for Lock to climb up into the observer's seat at the front of the nacelle.

The mechanic cupped his hands together, stooped down and gave Lock a bunk up.

Lock pulled himself up onto the wing, haversick hitched over his shoulder, and scrambled past the pilot and into the front section of the nacelle. He squeezed himself into the tiny, hard seat, strapped himself in, and sat for a moment breathing in the heady stench of hot oil and leather. He then twisted round and shook hands with the pilot, a tanned young man with piercing pale-green eyes and an easy smile.

'Captain Henry Petre,' the pilot said, introducing himself, accent thick with an easy Australian drawl. 'Welcome to Aussie Mesop Airways,' he grinned.

'Glad to meet you, Captain. Name's Lock, Kingdom Lock.'

Petre nodded, then turned and called down to the mechanic. 'Right-o, Bluey.'

Lock peered down to see the mechanic grab hold of the propeller and give it a spin to catch the magneto. He dodged away, and after a few splutters, the engine caught, and with a cough of blue-white exhaust, began to turn over.

'Ever flown before, Lock?' the pilot shouted above the engine as he adjusted his pedals and readied himself for take-off.

'Yes. In Tsingtao. Last year,' Lock called back.

'Bet it wasn't in one of these crates, though?'

Lock shook his head. 'A German Taube.'

'Fancy. Well, this ain't no Mercedes engine, it's Frenchie, a Farman MF.11. But if we're lucky, we won't crash. Unless we run into the bloody *shamal*.'

'The what?' Lock shouted back.

'The desert wind. This bucket can't cope. Wasn't built for this climate.'

'Then why are they here?'

'Why the hell are we all bloody here?' Petre shouted back and patted Lock on the shoulder. 'Right-o, mate, here we go.'

The aeroplane's engine roared even louder as Petre opened the throttle, then when the entire aircraft was vibrating and Lock felt certain that his teeth would rattle loose, let alone the bolts and rivets holding the winged death trap he was sat in together, they began to taxi forward.

'Where to?' Petre shouted.

'You got enough fuel to get us back to Oz?'

He could hear Petre's laugh above the howling engine. 'You think I'd still be here if I did?' the pilot shouted.

'South. I need to get to Nasiriyeh, beyond Hammar Lake, some eighty miles west of Basra. On the Euphrates,' Lock shouted back.

Petre patted him on the shoulder again in confirmation. Lock focused forward as the aeroplane picked up speed. It pitched and bounced across the grass, then all of sudden Lock felt his stomach drop as the aircraft lifted. As they rose, he craned his neck over the edge and peered back down at Betty. She was standing beside the motor vehicle watching them climb with a hand shielding her eyes. The mechanic was with her now, looking up also. Lock gave an exaggerated salute and Betty waved back. Then the aeroplane banked to the left and headed out towards the river.

Lock was amazed at how calm and still the Tigris looked from above, as it snaked off into the hazy distance, such a contrast to the raging current and the stifling heat that he'd endured over the past few days when actually down there, on it and in it. Disturbed by the passing shadow of the aeroplane, a flock of birds rose up from the muddy foreshore. They kept formation with them for a while, then turned as one and glided back down to the water. Lock's eye followed their movement, then it was drawn to the vast amount of shipping steaming northwards towards Amara.

Townshend's Regatta had been a resounding success, there was no doubt about it. The Turks had barely put up a fight. But the war was far from won. This mission had been a failure for

Lock personally. He hadn't gained any ground, or made any progress in getting closer to solving who had shot him outside the brothel in Basra.

Ross and Betty's investigation had come up with nothing new, either. Could the answer lie in Nasiriyeh?

When Lock had told Ross that he thought Wassmuss was more than one man, that 'he' could be a group, the major had been encouraged by the idea. And the more Lock thought on it, the more he believed the theory to be right. Grössburger, Harrington-Brown, Bombegy, the dead German officer on the *Marmaris* that Harrington-Brown had silenced . . . So many were involved. And what about Godwinson's name being on that list? Was that the reason why the colonel was so keen to see him fall? Because of the threat of exposure? There was also the man who Lock had thought was 'Wassmuss', the blue-eyed chameleon who had kidnapped Amy and nearly killed her. Was he this Brugmann, Ross had mentioned? And finally there was the mysterious 'G'. Was he the paymaster general? The commander? The real Wassmuss?

Lock cursed and closed his eyes, trying to block out all the tumbling thoughts. His head hurt with the questions and he was beginning to feel dizzy. It was an infuriating puzzle.

'How long before we land, Captain?' Lock called over his shoulder.

Petre held up two fingers.

Lock nodded and turned back to face the direction of travel.

The aeroplane jolted suddenly as it hit a pocket of cooler air and banked once more to head south. Lock peered down at the Tigris for a final look at Amara before they left it behind.

There was a steamer with a huge red cross daubed on its funnel anchored in the middle of the river. Lock wondered if Amy was on board and then he swore softly. Had he truly lost her? Was it time to let her go, let her make her bed with that fool Bingham-Smith? He put his fingers to his lips and smiled, remembering the strong kiss he had just shared with Betty Boxer. Perhaps it was time to move on?

'Officers' daughters, Kingdom,' he said to himself and smiled wryly. 'It'll end in tears.'

CHAPTER TWENTY-ONE

Lock awoke with a start. He was cold and stiff, the wind chill having crept in through his clothing as he had dozed. His mouth tasted sour and he was thirsty. But, to his surprise, he didn't feel groggy, he felt invigorated.

'Hey, Lock. Down there,' Petre shouted from over his shoulder.

Lock twisted in his seat. Petre was pointing down to their left. Lock waved in acknowledgement.

Below was the sparkling Euphrates River, snaking off to the bleak horizon both to the east and the west. The ground to the south was no longer awash with floodwater but was dry, flat, desolate desert.

The aeroplane banked into the afternoon sun and spluttered lower. Lock could now see a series of mounds breaking up the otherwise bleak landscape.

'Where are we?' he shouted back over his shoulder.

'Ten miles south of Nasiriyeh,' Petre hollered over the engine, 'place called Ur . . . Nothing here now, except Ziggurats . . . ancient ruins . . . Meant to be the birthplace of Abraham . . . according to the Book of Genesis . . . Gonna put her . . .' But the rest of Petre's words were snatched away by the wind as the aeroplane dipped and bobbed.

Lock watched the landscape get closer and closer, as Petre searched for a suitable spot to put down. There was a thin, dusty trail stretching off into the desert haze in both directions that ran parallel to the strange mounds. Lock caught sight of a small black dot of movement and, as they dropped lower still, it soon transpired to be a single man leading two camels.

There was a tap on his shoulder, and Lock turned to see Petre jabbing his finger downwards again and then giving the thumbs up. He was going in.

The aeroplane swooped low over the figure and the camels, banked, then slowed and began its descent. As the ground rushed up towards them, Lock could now see that it was a well-worn track and would make for a perfect landing strip. The desert either side was rocky and treacherous.

They spluttered lower and lower passing over the Arab once more, who was now standing still, gawping up at them. His camels flicked their heads nervously and opened their mouths in complaint, a sound lost in the aeroplane's noisy engine.

The Farman MF.11 dropped, bounced once, twice, then with a swing to the left and a corrective jerk back to the right, met the ground and was down bumping and juddering along the track, throwing up a choking cloud of dust. The aeroplane came to a standstill, coughing and spluttering as it turned, and taxied back round the way it had come in.

Lock loosened his safety harness, grabbed the haversack Betty had given him from beneath his feet, and dropped it over the side of the nacelle. He climbed out onto the wing and jumped down to the desert floor. The ground was hard and Lock could feel the stifling heat radiating up through the soles of his boots already. He glanced up along the track. The Arab with the camels was about 500 yards away, heading slowly in their direction.

Lock quickly unfastened his Sam Browne belt and cross strap, pulled his jacket off and snatched the pilot's cap from his head. He removed the holstered Beholla, putting it to one side, then making sure that his slouch hat was still stuffed safely in the inside pocket of his jacket, he tied the whole thing up with the belt. He gathered the bundle up, scrambled back up onto the wing, and handed the pilot's cap and then the bundle to Petre.

'Keep these safe for me?' Lock shouted over the idling engine.

'Will do, mate,' Petre said, stuffing the bundle down under his seat.

'Thank you, Captain,' Lock said. 'You'll get back all right?'

The two shook hands.

'No worries. I've enough fuel to get to Shaiba. Good luck, Captain Lock.' He gave a grin and a thumbs up.

Lock returned the gesture and jumped back down to the ground. He scooped up the haversack and scampered out of the way, turned and waved.

Petre gave a quick salute, let the throttle out, and taxied forward. The aeroplane picked up speed, and just as Lock thought it would plough straight into the Arab and his camels, it shot up into the air and was on its way south.

Lock stood watching until Petre's Farman MF.11 was a tiny speck glinting in the sun, then he crouched down and opened up the haversack Betty had given him. Inside was a water canteen, a bag of dates and a hunk of bread. There was a tin mug, inside of which, wrapped in a piece of cloth, was a small piece of mirror, a cut-throat razor, a cake of soap and a shaving brush. Lock rubbed his stubbly chin.

'Good thinking, Betty,' he smiled. He hadn't the growth to fashion a traditional Turkish moustache, so he'd best be clean-shaven if his ruse was to work.

Underneath a layer of newspaper was a neatly folded Ottoman Imperial Navy officer's uniform in dark blue. The shoulder boards were gold and red for engineering and the cuff insignia indicated the uniform was that of a *korvet kaptani*, a lieutenant commander. There was also a traditional red fez with black tassel, a belt with anchor insignia, leather gaiters and black shoes.

Lock glanced up to check the progress of the Arab, then pouring a little water into the tin mug, he took up the cake of soap and the brush and began to lather his face. He held up the mirror at such an angle that, as he shaved, he could also keep an eye on the trail behind him. The Arab was still a good distance away.

When he had finished, Lock checked his smooth jaw, and satisfied, wiped the excess soap off with the cloth. He stood up and stripped naked. The afternoon sun felt good on his skin and there was a little breeze now. Even the incessant flies weren't bothering him. He closed his eyes momentarily, wishing he were some place else.

'Time to get ready, Kingdom.'

He set about putting on the Turkish uniform. It was a snug fit, but at least the shoes didn't pinch. He gathered together the shaving implements and the tin mug, tossing away the dirty water, and cleaning it out with sand. Then he rolled up his own khaki breeches, and stuffed them along with the shaving kit and his old boots in the haversack. He took a sip of water from the canteen.

'Nasty stuff,' he mumbled, replacing the stopper.

He got to his feet and pulled at the hem of his jacket, straightening out the creases and patting the pockets.

'Bless you, Betty Boxer.'

Lock pulled out a packet of Fatima brand Turkish cigarettes and a book of matches. He lit one and let the strong flavour envelop his mouth. He slipped his left hand in his pocket and pulled out a handful of coins, all German marks. He put them back in his pocket and stood, smoking contentedly, waiting for the Arab to catch up.

The afternoon sun was lower now, but its heat was still intense as it burnt into Lock's back. Already sweat was trickling down from under his arms and down his spine. He finished his cigarette, crushing it out with his shoe, and looked along the trail.

He could smell the heady mix of piss, shit and rank fur of the camels long before the creatures got anywhere near. Then the single-humped dromedaries let out a long gurgling, guttural cry as if to warn their master of danger up ahead.

'*As-salaam alaykum*,' Lock called, swinging the haversack up onto his shoulder and stepping forward, raising his hand in greeting.

The Arab was an elderly man, very short, lean, with a face as blotchy, lined and cracked as the desert floor around his sandalled feet. He had a dirty white beard and wore a black aba and kufiya. But the most interesting thing to Lock about the Arab's appearance was the fact that he wore a black patch over his left eye. That was something that would come in very handy. The Arab was carrying

379

a wooden staff and leading his two camels, both laden with goods, by a line of rope, one behind the other. Now, Lock was up close, he found it hard to determine who smelt the worse, the man or his beasts of burden.

The Arab nodded a greeting in return, but did not break his stride or slow down, as if seeing an aeroplane land and deposit a lone man in the middle of the desert was an everyday occurrence to him.

Lock fell into step beside the elderly Arab.

'*Do you mind if I walk with you?*' Lock asked in Arabic.

'*Ensha Allah,*' the Arab croaked, his voice as dry as dust.

They walked in silence, the camels plodding languidly behind them, every now and again snorting in complaint. Lock pulled out the pack of Fatimas and offered one to the Arab.

'*Shokran jazeelan,*' the Arab nodded and smiled a gummy smile. His bony fingers eagerly snatched one of the cigarettes and put it between his thin, cracked lips. '*Shokran, shokran. Jayyed, jayyed,*' he said as Lock struck a match for him.

They walked on, and Lock considered the packet of Fatimas. He took four out for himself, then handed the rest of the pack to the Arab. '*Tafadal.*'

The old man nodded, hid the packet quickly away within the folds of his aba should Lock change his mind, and carried on walking, smoking in silence.

Lock turned his attention to the huge mounds off to their right, the highest heap now looking more like a truncated pyramid the closer they got. Lock could just make out the niched brick casing of its construction poking through the drifted sands. They were indeed eerie monuments to an ancient civilisation half-buried and forgotten, and he wondered what they would look like if someone took the time to clear away the sand. He cast his eye over the surrounding rocky, dusty plain. There was nothing. No vegetation, no animals, not even a bird in the cloudless sky. Just him, the Arab and the two camels. The war was a million miles away, and Lock felt at peace. He smiled.

'*Are you walking to Nasiriyeh?*' he asked the Arab after what seemed like an age.

The Arab nodded.

'*The market?*'

Again the Arab nodded his head.

'*I would like to make a trade.*'

The Arab carried on walking without hesitation or question.

'*With you. Your eyepatch. For . . . this blade.*' Lock fished out the cut-throat razor from the haversack, and offered it out.

The Arab gave the razor a cursory glance, stroked his beard as if to say what need had he for a razor, and continued putting one foot in front of the other without comment.

Lock opened the haversack again and fingered the riding boots. He was reluctant to give them up and cursed himself for not having left them with Petre along with the rest of his Aussie uniform. But he knew he couldn't carry them with him into Nasiriyeh.

'*. . . and these boots.*'

The Arab stopped, turned to Lock and narrowed his one grey eye.

Lock held out the boots.

The Arab softly cackled and removed his patch. Underneath, the eye was opaque and blind. He kicked off his tattered leather sandals, sat himself down on the ground and pulled on the boots.

They looked far too big, but he appeared delighted. Lock helped him back up onto his feet.

'*Here, you may as well have this, too.*' Lock handed out the haversack.

The old man peered inside and pulled out the khaki breeches and then the shaving items. He nodded, grinning up at Lock, then bending to pick up his old sandals, stuffed everything in the haversack and plodded over to the first camel. He stashed the haversack away, and then began to rummage around in the packages and boxes tied to the animal's hump.

Lock removed his fez, and tied the patch in place to cover his grey-blue eye. Now his disguise was complete. He couldn't be walking about behind enemy lines as *Kedisi*. He didn't want to stand out and he couldn't afford to be recognised, obviously, before he found Wassmuss. Now he was just a one-eyed naval officer.

He checked his watch. It was a little before 4 p.m. He estimated that it would be a good three hours before they reached the town. The sun would set near to 7 p.m., so if he was lucky they'd be there just before dark.

Lock lit one of his remaining cigarettes and waited for the old Arab to finish whatever it was he was doing amongst his packages. A minute later the old man came back, a paper bundle held in his hand. He opened it up to reveal a cooked fish that had been picked at a number of times already.

'*Masgouf,*' the Arab said holding out the fish with his right hand, wafting the curious flies away with his left. '*Tafadal.*'

'*Shokran,*' Lock said, pulling off a piece of the cold fish with his right hand. He placed it in his mouth and chewed. It was surprisingly smoky, succulent and quite delicious. He nodded his appreciation, and pulled off another piece of the flaky fish.

'*Wa howa ka-zaalek,*' Lock said.

The old Arab nodded and grinned and tore off a piece of the fish for himself. He stuffed it in his mouth, then folded the rest away and this too was hidden away within the folds of his aba.

On they walked, the desert scrunching underfoot, while the sun beat down and the camels gurgled and snorted behind them.

By the time the sun had become a hazy orange orb low on the horizon in the misty eastern sky, turning the sand of the track underfoot a deep red, the desert around them had begun to show signs of life. There was more and more scrub grass to see and Lock even spotted a far away bird of prey circling slowly. Then, with their shadows stretched far into the dusk, they came to the outskirts of Nasiriyeh itself.

Lock stayed with the Arab as the desert floor became a carpet of green until, passing through a cluster of date palms, they finally hit a more established road. The air was fresher here, as the road ran parallel to the nearby Euphrates River, but the mosquitoes were out in droves. Lock waved his hand in front of his face over and over, but the act was futile.

Buildings came into view, their rooftops taking on a deep orange hue in the setting sun. There were a few people about, all native Arabs, but no one gave Lock more than a cursory glance. This was, after all, Lock thought, occupied Ottoman territory. At the end of a small row of mud-brick hovels was a checkpoint. There was a wooden pole stretched across the road, and beyond that, a sentry hut. Lock could see a telephone wire running from the roof of the hut up to the string of telegraph poles that lined the street. A lone street lamp, a beacon for hundreds of moths and insects, was throwing a pale pool of yellow light over the queue waiting to be admitted to the town. Three Turkish *nefers*, privates, and their officer were meticulously scrutinising each person and checking through their baggage.

Lock felt a moment's hesitation in his stride. Surely they weren't looking for him? And then he dismissed the thought as ridiculous. Nobody knew he was here except for Betty and Ross, and Captain Petre, and they were all miles away in the opposite direction. Still, he had no papers and his uniform was suspiciously dusty from the trek through the desert. He pulled up and felt for a cigarette. Then he remembered that he had already smoked the few he had taken before handing the pack to the Arab.

'Bugger,' he muttered.

The Arab stopped and turned. He looked Lock up and down and seemed to be reading his mind. Once again he moved to the first of his camels and began to rummage about amongst the pack tied to its hump. He returned momentarily brandishing a stiff brush in his bony hand. He pushed Lock's arms up and began to vigorously groom the dust from the uniform. Lock tried to protest, but the Arab refused to stop, muttering under his breath as he worked. He then stepped back and nodded as he ran his good eye over Lock's appearance.

'*Afdal be-katheer*,' the Arab smiled.

Lock glanced down at himself and had to agree. He did look much better. He looked up over towards the sentry post. 'What to do?' he thought. He could slip away, down to the water's edge, find a boat, then row into town under the cover of darkness. Or he could just bluff and bluster his way through this sentry post.

The Arab pulled out the pack of Fatimas and offered one to Lock. Then he took one for himself, and Lock lit them both.

Lock glanced again at the sentry post. 'Sod it,' he muttered. He held his hand out. '*Maa as-salaamah, my friend.*'

The Arab shook Lock's hand, nodded and grinned. '*Wa-alaykum as-salaam.*'

Lock gave a short nod back, patted the elderly Arab on the shoulder, then turned and strode towards the sentry post. He held his head up, puffed his chest out, and began to scrutinise the line of waiting Arabs as if he were searching for someone.

The three *nefers* were busy with one particular tradesman, a carpet seller, who was angrily complaining about how his wares were being tossed about during the search of his cart.

'*Kes sesini!*' the junior officer growled at the Arab tradesman, as his men continued to throw the carpets aside peering underneath them.

Lock walked on towards the barrier.

The junior officer glanced up as Lock approached. But instead of challenging him, the officer snapped to attention and threw out a smart salute. Obviously Lock looked smarter and more pissed off than he had hoped.

'*Korvet Kaptani,*' the junior officer said, with a trace of alarm in his high-pitched voice.

Lock was pleased to see that the officer was actually a *başçavuş muavini*, an assistant sergeant major, notable by the two cross bars on the shoulder boards of his khaki uniform, and not some pompous *yüzbaşi* angry at being assigned to such a tedious duty. It should be easy to pull rank now and bluff his way through.

Lock gave a stiff nod and glanced back along the line, taking a puff on his cigarette. '*What is all this, Başçavuş Muavini? I was out for a quiet stroll along the river and heard the commotion.*'

'*Merely routine, Korvet Kaptani Bey.*'

'*No trouble, I hope?*'

'*None, effendim. All very quiet.*'

Lock snorted. '*Not quiet enough.*'

He gave the junior officer as steely a glare as he could with his one uncovered eye. A trickle of sweat had run down under the patch and the eye underneath was stinging like crazy. He waved his hand irritably at the barrier blocking his path.

'*Oh, I am sorry, effendim.*' The *başçavuş muavini* rushed over to lift the barrier himself.

Lock passed underneath and turned back. The *başçavuş muavini* dropped the barrier down again and stood stiffly to attention. Lock jutted his chin down the line at the elderly Arab he'd walked in with.

'*I know that man. At the back. He is a good friend of Binbaşi Feyzi. I'd advise you not to delay him.*'

The *başçavuş muavini* glanced down the queue of Arabs and nodded eagerly. '*I understand, Korvet Kaptani Bey. He shall not be held up.*'

'*Do it now, Başçavuş Muavini,*' Lock said coldly.

'*I . . .*' The *başçavuş muavini* hesitated, then snapped a quick salute and scurried off down the line.

Lock quickly pushed his finger under the patch and wiped the stinging sweat from his eye. He swore and grimaced, then adjusted the patch so that it was a tighter fit over his eye socket. He watched the *başçavuş muavini* gesticulating as he tried to direct the elderly Arab to move out of line with his camels, and to follow him.

'So,' Lock thought, as he took a final puff of his cigarette and then tossed it aside, 'the name Feyzi is known even to a humble *başçavuş muavini* on sentry duty. Which means he's here. Somewhere.'

The *başçavuş muavini* was shouting at the elderly Arab now and had drawn his pistol from his holster. Lock was about to intervene, when the Arab took the hint and finally stepped out of the line with his camels in tow. The *başçavuş muavini* waved his pistol and marched back towards Lock with the Arab trotting after him. He lifted the barrier once more, and Lock stepped aside as the elderly Arab and his gurgling camels were hurried through.

'*Hizlan, hizlan!*' the *başçavuş muavini* said impatiently.

Lock gave the elderly Arab the briefest of nods and watched until he and his camels had made their way down the street and had been swallowed up by the gloom. He turned back to the junior officer.

'*Thank you, Başçavuş Muavini*,' he said with a watery smile. '*Ours not to know the reasons why some men are favoured.*'

The *başçavuş muavini* smiled appreciatively. '*Yes, effendim. Thank you, effendim.*'

'*Well*,' Lock said, pulling at the hem of his jacket, '*duty calls. Good night.*' He gave a quick salute, turned on his heels and headed off down into the town.

'*Good night, effendim*,' the *başçavuş muavini* called after him.

CHAPTER TWENTY-TWO

Lock followed the line of illuminated lamp posts, catching and passing his shadow over and over, as he made his way through the increasingly populated streets. There were a lot of people out and about, and turning a corner, Lock suddenly found himself in a busy area where beggars and German officers, tinkers and traders, camels and open-top *Gräf und Stift* staff cars, jostled with one another for space. Off-duty Turkish soldiers and officers were perusing the various shopfronts and stalls that were selling everything from onions and dates to brass trinkets and what appeared to be pieces of stone. The pavement cafes were doing a roaring trade, and Lock's stomach grumbled as he strode by, the enticing smells of fresh coffee, cooked meat, grilled fish and overripe fruit assaulting his senses. It was tempting to pull up a chair, but he had to find Wassmuss and make it back to the British lines. But where to find him? Staff headquarters would be the best bet, but he couldn't very well ask for directions without raising suspicion.

In the near distance, Lock could see the tall minarets and domes of a nearby mosque jutting up above the surrounding trees and rooftops, their brickwork and tiles tinged deep orange against the darkening sky. But no telltale flagpole. He checked his watch and then stopped dead in his tracks.

Someone collided into his shoulder, and Lock turned to see an irate German officer glaring back at him through a monocle.

Lock stepped aside and saluted. '*Guten Abend, Herr Major*,' he said, hoping the officer wouldn't say too much in return, as his knowledge of the German language was limited to but a few pleasantries.

The German, a major on the general staff judging by his crimson collar patches, narrowed his blue eyes and Lock was momentarily taken aback. Then he quickly collected himself. This man was tall, at least six feet, and very slim, with smooth skin and baby-blond hair just visible under his peaked cap. He wasn't Wassmuss.

The major's blond moustache twitched, and he gave a stiff nod. '*Korvettenkapitän*,' he grunted, and pushed on.

'Jesus, Kingdom,' Lock hissed to himself, 'calm down. Wassmuss can't be every blue-eyed German you meet.'

He pulled at his collar and straightened the hem of his tunic, but couldn't help thinking what a strange feeling it was being up close to so many German officers.

If only he had one of Pritchard's jam-tin bombs, he thought as he looked about at the busy cafes and stalls, and at the laughing faces of so many enemy officers.

'Just think what I could do for the war effort by taking out all these Boche officers,' he muttered. 'Still . . . Oh, shit.'

Lock remembered why he had pulled up so suddenly. His watch. It was a British trench watch. Not noticeable from afar, but it could be awkward if seen close up, or someone happened to ask him for the time. Lock pulled his sleeve down to cover the timepiece and turned his attention back to the road ahead. He soon spotted the German officer who had bumped into him, quickly darting across the road and disappearing up a side street.

'You seem in rather a hurry, *Herr Major*.'

Lock skipped across the road making after the German officer. He dodged by a team of camels and narrowly avoided being struck by a toot-tooting staff car. A bewhiskered Austro-Hungarian *generaloberst* was sat stiffly in the back seat, a tall shako jammed on his head. His eyes momentarily met Lock's, and the car sped by in a cloud of dust. It too turned down the road after the German *major* with the monocle.

'Two Big Noises in rather a hurry . . .'

Lock made his way down the same side street and caught the rich and earthy smell of the nearby river again, carried on the light breeze blowing towards him. A troop of Turkish infantrymen led by a painfully fresh-faced *mülazimi sani*, a second lieutenant, was marching towards him on the other side of the road. The soldiers looked to be well equipped and well dressed, with German-style packs on their backs and standard issue Ottoman Mauser M1893 rifles at their shoulders. The *mülazimi sani* gave Lock a smart salute as he and his men trudged past.

A shrill tinkle of a bicycle bell warned Lock to step aside just as an Arab messenger cyclist swerved by and disappeared around the corner up ahead. There were two staff officers walking a few paces in front of Lock on his side of the road, and so Lock slowed his pace down, not wanting to catch them up. But he needn't have bothered for the German *hauptmann*, captain, and the Turkish *mülazimi evvel*, a first lieutenant, barely registered their surroundings, so deep were they in conversation. They turned the corner and Lock paused, before following on.

He found himself stepping out into a pleasant, tree-lined square. The white brick, flat-roofed buildings on two sides were of two storeys, with the ground floor being a series of open archways, and the floor above being one long open terrace. The larger building over to the left was a grander affair of three storeys. Jutting out from the top of the latticed balcony on the second floor was a flagpole from which, flapping limply in the breeze, hung the red and white crescent moon and star of the Ottoman Empire. It had to be the Command Headquarters.

The entrance, a large, studded wooden door, was at the top of some stone steps lit by a pool of yellow light from a lamp suspended from an iron arm above. Lock could also see various other lights shining from behind the latticed windows on either side of the building. The German *hauptmann* and the Turkish *mülazimi evvel* had just crossed the square in front of Lock and were now mounting the stone steps. The *nefer* on sentry duty snapped to attention as the officers passed into the building, then relaxed again.

Lock glanced behind him, then set off at a brisk pace across the square. Four automobiles were parked in a line to his right, their drivers standing together, smoking and chatting, voices rising and falling in whispered conversation. Three cars were *Gräf und Stifts* and each had a different marking on the rear sedan seat doors; a red circle and white star and crescent badge for the Ottomans, a German eagle, and the double-headed eagle of the Austro-Hungarian Empire. Lock slowed and squinted his one eye. The fourth vehicle parked was a British Crossley 20/25 touring car. Unlike the others, its roof was up, and on its passenger door the words Anglo Persian Oil Company were written in a semicircle above a palm tree emblem in white on a black square. Lock also noticed that the motor car had twin rear wheels and that there were a couple of extra jerrycans attached to the running-board. Ready for a long journey?

Lock hurried on, passing the rustling ancient fig tree to the left of the entrance, and throwing a quick salute to the *nefer*, as he bounded up the steps two at a time.

Lock opened the door to reveal a long, dimly lit and cool inner corridor. There was a large portrait of Enver Pasha on the wall to the left, with two hard-backed chairs and a potted palm underneath. Opposite, was a rather glum painting of Kaiser Wilhelm II. Various doors led off the corridor, but Lock ignored these and continued on down towards a desk he could see at the far end. There was a soldier sat there, half in shadow, half in the stark light thrown out from the table lamp at his elbow. Lock's shoes echoed loudly as he approached, and soon he could make out the distinct sound of muffled chatter, laughter and the clink of glasses and crockery. A party?

The man sat at the desk was a military clerk, with the rank of *mülazimi sani*, distinguishable by his purplish-brown collar and plain gold shoulder boards. On hearing Lock's footsteps, he looked up from the papers he was reading.

'*Good evening, Korvet Kaptani*,' he said. '*Are you here for the briefing?*'

'*Yes, with Binbaşi Feyzi. I'm a little late. Automobile trouble*,' Lock bluffed, hoping it was Feyzi holding the meeting.

The *mülazimi sani* smiled the way all jaded junior clerks do when listening to lame excuses from superior officers. '*Do not worry. As you can hear they are still toasting the binbaşi's promotion.*'

'Promotion?'

'*To miralay. Please, go in.*'

Lock nodded and walked on past the clerk. He quickly wiped the sweat from his top lip and made his way to the slightly ajar door from beyond which the sound of voices wafted out. So Wassmuss's Feyzi had made colonel. To what ends? Was he in command of the garrison at Nasiriyeh now? Lock paused at the threshold of the office, his own reflection staring back accusingly from the brass nameplate screwed to the outer door. He mouthed the name, *Miralay Erkan Feyzi*, while his mind screamed at him to turn and leave, that this was a terribly foolish thing to do. He couldn't step into that room! What was he thinking? He had no idea who was in there with Feyzi, and he didn't believe for a minute that if Feyzi was indeed Wassmuss that he wouldn't recognise him instantly, and call the guard and have him arrested. Or shot on the spot.

'This could be a very short kidnapping attempt indeed,' Lock muttered to himself. 'Bugger.' He pulled his hand back from the handle and glanced over his shoulder. The clerk was still sat at the desk, but facing the opposite way.

Lock swiftly moved from the office door and made his way further down the gloomy corridor. He tried the door to the room next to Feyzi's. It was unlocked. He glanced back at the clerk, then slipped inside.

Thankfully the room on the other side was empty and in darkness. Lock stood with his back to the door, letting his one uncovered eye adjust to the gloom. He appeared to be in a small office and could make out a desk and a couple of chairs over to the left. There was a large window at the far end. It was shuttered, but he could see thin strips of faint light shining through the slats. He moved towards it and his shin struck something heavy. There was a scrape and a crash as something fell to the floor. Lock froze, ears peeled, ignoring the sharp pain in his leg. Nothing. He moved on to the window. He felt around, found a latch, and slowly lifted the lower panel. It made a high-pitched squeal as wood scraped against wood. Lock cursed and froze again, feeling the sweat trickle down from under his arms as he listened intently to the muffled conversation from the room next door. They didn't stop or hesitate. Somebody laughed.

Lock gently pulled and lifted the lower window towards him. This time its action was smooth. He pressed his palm against one shutter and gave a gentle push. It gave. That was good. It meant that they weren't fastened from the outside. He pushed the left side open a crack, just enough for him to be able to see out to the right.

An intense aroma of jasmine suddenly tickled Lock's nose, and he sniffed away a sneeze. He could smell the earthy rot of the Euphrates under the scent of the flowers. He pressed his face to the gap and peered out. It was dark outside, but light was spilling from the office next door where Feyzi and his guests were gathered. Lock could make out that there was a tranquil park-like garden beyond the window, resplendent with flowering bushes and lush palm trees. There was nobody outside from what he could see, so, cautiously, he pushed open the shutters on both sides. He paused and listened again.

Beneath the continual murmur of conversation from Feyzi's office, Lock could hear the constant buzz of tiny unseen insects and the soft flutter of moths dancing in the artificial light. There was the gentle trickling of a nearby water feature and in the distance the cough and splutter of an outboard motor. Then a harsh human laugh broke the spell of calm once more.

Lock poked his head outside. There were beds of managed bushes and plants running along the walls underneath the window, then a gravel path and then, to his surprise, a lush lawn with palm trees and fig trees beyond. It was like something he would expect to see in a European stately home, not a Middle-Eastern town. Satisfied that the coast was clear and that the garden was empty, he eased himself out of the window.

Lock had to stretch his legs far to avoid the low bush directly below the sill. He stepped out onto the gravel path. It scrunched softly underfoot. He leant back and pushed the shutters closed, then turned and stepped off the path and onto the lawn. The grass was surprisingly spongy and Lock was filled with a sudden irrational desire to pull off his shoes and feel the cool, soft grass on his bare feet. The sound of gently trickling water was indeed coming from an ornate stone-carved water fountain. It was placed directly in front of the open French windows to Feyzi's office.

The light spilling out from the room only went so far, and Lock was able to keep in the dark shadows, thankful that the uniform Betty had supplied him with was the dark blue of the navy and not the summer whites of the artillery. He moved around the outside of the fountain until he had a clear view of the office interior.

Lock counted ten men. Some held champagne glasses in their hands, others china cups and saucers. There were three German staff officers, taller than everyone else, all senior men wearing tailed uniforms of field grey and breeches with crimson piping. One was an *oberleutnant*, the other a *major*, the same monocle-wearing *major* whom Lock had collided with outside of the cafe. The third was the bewhiskered Austro-Hungarian *generaloberst* that had sped by Lock not fifteen minutes earlier. Without his shako on, Lock could see that the *generaloberst* had a head of thick snow-white hair. He was wearing a distinctive sky-blue uniform with gorget patches of three silver stars on a gold balloon.

On the other side of the room, speaking amongst themselves, were two Turkish staff officers dressed in green with red collars and piping on their breeches, and a man whom Lock presumed was a pro-Ottoman Arab. He was wearing a Turkish *birinci ferik*'s, a general's, uniform with gold epaulettes and a ludicrous amount of medals on his chest, as well as a pair of white gloves. Flitting between the two groups, clutching a bottle of champagne, was a Turkish naval officer, a *yüzbaşi*. Feyzi's adjutant perhaps?

The other three men in the room were standing near to the open French windows. Two were civilians, dressed in dark business suits. Lock couldn't see their faces clearly as they were masked by the final man in the room, the man standing with his back to the French windows. But Lock knew who he was. It was Wassmuss, or Feyzi, and he was very distinctive, indeed, dressed in a blue tunic with red collar and cuffs, a full dress uniform usually only worn by *birinci feriks* at Headquarters.

'Only a colonel, but dressed like a general?' Lock snorted to himself. 'Tisk-tisk, Wilhelm, you really are a snob, aren't you?'

And then Lock caught his breath and stared, slacked mouth into the room. Wassmuss had leant forward momentarily to pick something up from the desk beside him, and Lock had a sudden clear sight of the two businessmen. One was Grössburger, the fat Swiss whom Lock had last seen tied to a chair in a prison cell in Basra. But he wasn't really surprised that he was here, after all

Betty had said that they'd had to release him following pressure from the Swiss consulate. But it was the second businessman, the thin, grey, sallow-faced man wearing round spectacles perched on a straight nose, that was a shock to see. He was a man whom Lock was convinced was dead, a man whom Lock had seen lying on the floor of Ross's cabin on the *Espiegle* two months ago, with a stab wound to the heart, face fixed in a grimace of surprise.

'Lord Shears?' Lock gasped.

The tink-tink-tink of a knife tapping against glass called the room to order and the conversation quickly died down.

Lock was fingering his holstered Beholla. He had a full clip. Seven rounds. Tempting . . . He had to get closer, he had to hear what was being said in that room.

Circling round the fountain, and keeping to the shadows, Lock made his way back to the window he had climbed out of earlier. He crept past the bushes until he was able to press himself up against the wall just to the left of the open French windows.

'*Zum Wohl!*' came a toast from inside. That was Wassmuss's voice, no mistaking.

'*Herzlichen Glückwunsch!*' one of the German officers said throatily.

There was a murmur of approval and then a moment of silence while the men took a drink. A glass clinked as it was placed down on a surface.

Much to Lock's irritation, the overheard conversation that followed was in German. But he made a mental note of a few words and names that he recognised, especially one name: 'Djavid'. He was the Turkish Minister of Finance. A small argument broke out when the name 'Metternich' was mentioned two or three times, followed by the German word '*trottel*', and then by two words Lock knew, '*Zaptielis*', the Turkish Military Police, and '*khafiyeh*', the Turkish word for spy. These seemed to calm things.

Lock's ears then pricked up when 'Godwinson' was mentioned, followed by laughter and a spit once again of the word '*trottel*'. Another name was mentioned that Lock didn't quite catch. There was a pause.

'*Verstehst Du?*'

'*Ja, ja.* Townshend. Amy Townshend.'

Lock's heart skipped a beat. Why were they talking about Amy? He cursed his lack of understanding. Why can't you bastards stick to Turkish? he thought.

There was another burst of laughter and then shifting movement and a buzz of murmured *Auf Wiedersehen* and *Hoşça kahn*. It would appear the briefing was over.

Lock risked taking a peek through the crack in the door where the hinges met the frame. The men were collecting their various caps and hats from a table in the far corner and nodding farewell to Wassmuss. He was standing, arm outstretched, subtly herding them out, while the Turkish naval adjutant stood holding the door open.

'*Kommen Sie gut nach Hause.*'

'*Danke.*'

'*Gute Nacht.*'

'*İyi geceler.*'

Lock could hear the soft click of the door closing, then footsteps returning across the carpet. There was a pause, followed by a rustle of fabric, the sudden jangle and turn of a key in a lock and then a tiny creak like a cupboard opening. Silence again, and then what sounded like the jangling of beads, followed by some shuffling of papers and the dull thud of a number of items being placed down on a wooden surface. A sigh of satisfaction was followed by the hack of a throat being cleared, then the clink of a glass and the glug-glug-glug and fizz of champagne being poured. A pause, then a slurp, followed immediately by a sharp hiss and a curse.

'*Sheiße. Dieses Glas hat einen sprung.*'

Lock drew his Beholla and stepped out from his hiding place and into the threshold of the French windows.

'*Guten Abend, Herr Wassmuss,*' Lock said.

Wassmuss was standing, glass in hand, while his other was a few inches from his mouth. There were spots of blood on his fingertips and a bleeding cut on his bottom lip. He was frozen to the spot, eyes wide, a look of bafflement on his face.

Lock stepped into the room and smiled wryly. 'Or should I say *Binbaşi* . . . Sorry, *Miralay* Feyzi?' He spoke in English.

Wassmuss glanced at his fingertips, put them in his mouth and sucked. He tut-tutted and placed the champagne glass down on the desk to his right.

Lock took a step forward, gun raised. 'Hands flat on the desk. *Bitte.*'

There was a pinpoint flame of anger in the intent blue eyes, and then it was gone and Wassmuss, placing his hands flat on the desk in front of him, blinked calmly back.

'Herr Lock,' he said. 'Good evening.'

Lock felt his finger twitch on the trigger of the Beholla. He vowed to shoot this man the next time he saw him and yet here he was unsure of the best thing to do. There were too many unanswered questions, there were too many lives at stake, his own included. He eased off the trigger, but didn't lower the gun.

'Surprised to see me?'

Wasmuss shrugged. 'If I had known you were coming I would have asked for an additional glass. Though your get-up did, I admit, confuse me momentarily. However,' he smiled thinly, 'I do like the eyepatch. Most fetching.'

'It's the best I could do at such short notice.'

Wassmuss parted his fleshy lips and flashed his white teeth. 'Well, I had planned for you to be halfway up the Tigris on a . . . How do you say it? Wild duck chase?'

'Goose.'

'*Ja*, "goose",' Wassmuss chuckled. 'But I underestimated your determination to track me down, Herr Lock.'

'Perhaps if you hadn't tried to have me killed . . .' Lock said.

Again Wassmuss shrugged. '*Ja*. Perhaps . . .'

The two men stared back at one another in silence for a moment. Wassmuss's face was, Lock noticed, covered in tiny little scars.

His eyes dropped to the desk in front of the German. There was a pair of kitchen scales, iron weights and a number of drawstring cloth bags. Very similar bags, in fact, to the one he had found in the possession of the *liva amiral* back on the tiny sand island next to One Tower Hill.

'So, not only Grössburger, but Lord Shears and, I imagine, the entire board of APOC are part of your network, too?' Lock said.

Wassmuss didn't say anything in return, but just stared back at Lock defiantly.

'We're closing in on your operations, Herr Wassmuss. Grössburger, Brugmann, Harrington-Brown, Godwinson . . .'

Wassmuss gave a snort of derision. 'You really have no idea, do you, Herr Lock?'

'You will talk. I'm taking you back with me to Basra.'

Wassmuss started to chuckle. 'And just how do you propose to do that, Herr Lock?'

'In your launch, down by the river.'

Wassmuss frowned. 'How do you kn—'

He cut his question short, realising his mistake. He'd just gone and told Lock that he did have a launch.

Lock gave a wry smile. 'And when we get back to Basra, I know a certain sergeant major who'd like to make your acquaintance. He's also extremely good at extract—'

The door at the far end of the office opened and closed, and the Turkish naval adjutant entered, his nose buried in a sheet of paper.

'*Excuse me, Miralay Feyzi Bey, could y—*'

The adjutant's eyes lifted to meet Lock's, and he froze on the spot, the paper fluttering from his hand.

Wassmuss took advantage of the split-second distraction and flung the chipped champagne glass at Lock with a swipe of his hand. Lock put his arm up to dodge the glass, and it bounced off his elbow and smashed on the edge of the desk.

'*Guard! Guard! Assassin! Spy!*' the adjutant shouted, as he turned and wrenched at the door handle to make his escape.

Lock felt the Beholla kick back in his hand as he pulled the trigger once, then again.

The adjutant collapsed against the door, slamming it shut, and crumpled to the floor. Wassmuss yelped, stumbled back, and crashed back against one of the chairs to the left of the fireplace. He gasped and slumped down onto his backside, hand pressed to his neck. Blood was pulsing through his fingers and down over his hand, staining the cuffs of the white

402

shirt that protruded from the sleeve of his blue tunic.

There was a commotion of running footsteps from the corridor outside and then a frantic banging on the closed office door.

'*Miralay? Miralay? Are you all right?*' came a shout from the other side. The handle was jerked up and down. But the door was jammed shut by the body of the adjutant. He was lying at an impossible angle, his face twisted up towards Lock, brown eyes staring back at him, lifeless and dull.

Wassmuss gurgled, but could form no words. Lock stepped over and crouched down beside him. He pulled Wassmuss's hand away from the neck wound. It was deep and the bullet had nicked the artery. Blood was pulsing out at a steady beat. Lock pressed Wassmuss's hand back to the wound.

'Bugger,' Lock said softly.

A flurry of voices was arguing from out in the corridor. Then came a heavy bang as someone began to try to kick the door in. Lock put two more bullets through the door.

The banging stopped.

Lock knew that he didn't have long before the men on the other side decided to come round through the garden. He looked down at Wassmuss. The German's eyes were flickering and the colour was draining from his face.

'What were you planning with APOC? Why was Shears here? Is he part of your network?'

Wassmuss grimaced up at Lock and shook his head.

'Tell me one thing before you die,' Lock said coldly. 'What does the list mean? The *Braut* and *Bräutigam* list . . .'

There was a flicker of surprise in the blue eyes staring up at him.

'Is it a death list? People marked for assassination? Is Amy Townshend in danger?'

Wassmuss suddenly convulsed, but Lock couldn't tell whether the grimace that stretched across the German's face was in amusement or pain.

'Are you really even Wassmuss?' Lock said.

The German's eyes narrowed. He coughed once. A trickle of blood oozed from his mouth, and then he was still.

Lock grabbed the lapels on Wassmuss's uniform and pulled the German towards him. 'Answer me, you bastard,' he spat, giving the German a shake. 'What are you planning to do with Amy? Shit!'

Wassmuss's lifeless eyes just stared back at him. Lock wasn't going to get any more answers from this man. Ever.

Lock shoved the German back against the fireplace and stood up. He glanced up at the door just as an axe blade came splintering through the top panel, then back down at the still German.

Raising the Beholla, Lock put a bullet between Wassmuss's eyes. A halo of red bloomed across the wall behind the German's head.

'Now I know you're dead.'

Lock turned and hesitated. Behind the desk, in the wall next to the French window, was an open safe. There was a portrait propped up on the floor just below that of Enver Pasha. The axe splintered the door panel a second time. Lock moved to the safe. Inside were a number of files, a wooden jewellery box stuffed full with drawstring bags of pearls, and a very familiar leather-bound notebook held together with string – Wassmuss's notebook. Again the axe crashed into the door panel. Lock pulled out the jewellery box, stuffed the notebook in his pocket, turned to the table and pocketed the rest of the drawstring bags of pearls. And then he ran, out through the French windows, past the water fountain, and into the darkness, heart pumping, feet pounding. He ran on across the lawn, through the trees, leaves and branches scratching at his face, and down towards the river. He could hear whistles and shouts of '*Khafiyeh*' far behind him now. Then a sudden sense of calm washed over him, and he slowed, realising that the two men who had seen him in that office back there were dead, and that the clerk at the desk in the corridor would perhaps not even associate the one-eyed naval officer with the killer. Still, Lock thought, it would be foolish to hang around. There was a weak light up ahead and when he reached the river's edge, Lock could see that it was a lamp post illuminating a small wooden jetty. Tied at the end of the jetty was a lone motor launch.

'Thank you for your predictability, Wilhelm,' Lock smiled to himself. He holstered his Beholla, glancing up and down the high, grassy bank. There were plenty of other tied vessels there, but Lock could see no signs of life, and the river itself was dark and still. He strode purposefully out onto the jetty, unfastened the tie ropes, and climbed aboard.

It was a small wooden motor launch, about twenty-five feet long and fashioned in mahogany. The cockpit was situated behind a curved windscreen, itself above the forward cabin that was accessed through a pair of solid mahogany doors set in the forward bulkhead. Next to this, the wheel and throttle. A Turkish flag hung limply from the mast at the stern. Lock checked the cabin just to be sure. It was empty. He glanced back along the jetty and up the long garden that rose to the building of the Command Headquarters of Nasiriyeh's garrison. He could just make out the light from

Wassmuss's office through the trees. There were torchlights now, dancing and cutting through the dark. Voices called and shouted to one another. But nobody had run down to the river. Yet.

The petrol engine fired up first time, gently purring as it idled. Lock placed the box of pearls at his feet, engaged the throttle, spun the wheel and puttered away from the jetty, heading east.

'Bugger it all,' he cursed. He really was in trouble now. Wassmuss was the one person who could have cleared his name. So now, not only was he still accused of being an assassin by the Turks, but he was a fugitive from the British, too.

Unless . . .

Lock let the boat putter to a standstill, and glanced back over his shoulder. It was a slim chance. But any chance was better than no chance at all. There was something he could do after all, a possibility of reconciliation, of returning to General Townshend and Major Ross triumphant and vindicated. He glanced at his watch. How long had it been since the briefing had broken up? Since he had killed Wassmuss? Ten minutes? Fifteen? Would he catch them? Sod it, what did he have to lose? He punched the throttle back in and puttered forward, scanning the bank for an access road that would lead back up to the edge of town.

CHAPTER TWENTY-THREE

The bank of the river changed after just a few yards, becoming more and more commercial, with stone embankments and steps leading up from the water to the quayside. Lock puttered along trying to estimate how far he needed to travel before he should go ashore. Then it would only be a matter of heading inland and making for the same checkpoint where he and the elderly Arab had first entered Nasiriyeh.

The embankment was surprisingly busy with fishermen preparing their nets, and dockhands loading a low barge with what looked like sacks of grain. Artificial lights burnt brightly from the open doorways of the various stores and warehouses, and from a string of lamp posts that lined the quayside.

Lock slowed the motor launch when he came to a large steamer that was docked along the quay with a lighter attached. A troop of soldiers were mustering, ready for transportation.

Lock carried on a little further and then caught sight of a berth at the foot of some stone steps, in between a lenj fishing boat and a row of dhows. He cut the engine and glided the motor launch in. A dockhand was sat at the quayside edge, feet dangling over the water.

'*Hey, you! Grab this!*' Lock shouted in Arabic, throwing the dockhand a mooring line.

The dockhand scrambled up, caught the rope, and tied it down. Lock leapt off the motor launch and bounded up the steps, the box of pearls tucked safely under his arm. He gave the dockhand a coin and nodded his thanks, then made his way back along the quayside towards the assembled troops. There was a flustered *çavuş* directing the men towards the barge, but no senior officers that Lock could see. He elbowed his way through the troops, noting that they were all well attired and well equipped. He reached the line of storehouses, all one-storey wooden buildings with latticed shuttered frontages. There were a couple of dock officials sat on wicker armchairs outside one entrance. They were smoking and drinking coffee, oblivious to the insects that danced and flitted above their heads in the veil of light thrown down from a single electric lamp. An Arab messenger cyclist was standing nearby, deep in animated conversation with a scrawny native dressed in a grey, oil-stained suit jacket. There were two bicycles propped up against the side wall to the storehouse. Lock casually strolled by the two men, grabbing one of the bicycles as he passed, and wheeling it along with him. He continued walking in a straight line for a few yards waiting for a shout of protest. But none came, so he picked up speed, threw his leg over the crossbar, and with a shaky, unsteady wobble, pedalled away.

With the box of pearls balanced precariously between his wrists across the handlebars, Lock weaved through the last of the shuffling troops and turned south at the first junction he came to. He bumped and shook and creeked his way up a quiet side street of dark warehouses, eventually coming out onto the road he had walked up a few hours earlier. He recognised the pavement cafe, now closed up, where he had been tempted to stop to take refreshment before the German *major* had collided into him. The road ran down towards a distant light, the lone street lamp burning near to the sentry hut. There was no sign of a motor vehicle. He glanced over his shoulder. The road was empty in both directions.

'Bugger,' he muttered. Was he too late?

Lock cycled on down towards the checkpoint and pulled up. A lone *nefer* sentry was dozing on his feet, outside of the closed door to the hut. The sentry didn't stir as Lock climbed off the bicycle and rested it up against the mud-brick wall of the hut. With the box of pearls under his arm again, he approached the door, clearing his throat loudly.

The sentry started, pulling his rifle nervously from his shoulder. '*Halt!*'

The sentry momentarily relaxed on seeing Lock's uniform, then immediately snapped his heels to attention.

'*Relax, nefer,*' Lock said with a smile. '*Is the başçavuş muavini in?*'

'*Effendim. Yes, effendim. Sorry, effendim.*' The *nefer* opened the door, and stood aside.

Lock stepped inside and closed the door behind him.

The hut was a barren affair, four plain walls with a hard-earth floor, a single electric bulb dangling down from the flyblown ceiling, and a bare window looking north up the road. The only furniture was a desk and three chairs, and a black pot-bellied stove in one corner. There was a pot of strong-smelling coffee boiling away on top. Sat opposite the stove were two more *nefers*, and over behind the desk was the young *başçavuş muavini*. He rose to his feet on seeing Lock enter, and saluted.

'*Korvet Kaptani, good evening.*' He snapped his fingers for the two dozing *nefers* to get to their feet.

Lock held his hand up. '*Stay where you are, lads. This isn't an official visit.*' But the stern look he was projecting to the *başçavuş muavini* said otherwise.

The two *nefers* glanced at the *başçavuş muavini*, and he gave a subtle jerk of his head. The *nefers* gathered up their rifles and shuffled outside.

'*Can I get you some coffee, Korvet Kaptani?*' the *başçavuş muavini* said, moving out from behind the desk.

'*That would be most welcome.*' Lock said, removing his fez. He put the jewellery box inside, and placed the fez on one of the chairs.

'*Cigarette?*' The *başçavuş muavini* held out a packet of Fatimas.

Lock took one. The *başçavuş muavini* struck a match for him, and then went to the stove and poured out a cup of coffee.

'*Tell me, Başçavuş Muavini, has an automobile passed through this evening?*'

The *başçavuş muavini* paused for a moment, thinking, then he shook his head.

'*No, Korvet Kaptani.*' He handed the cup of steaming coffee to Lock. '*May I ask why?*'

Lock took a sip of the coffee and pulled his lips away sharply. It was scalding. He blew on the dark-brown liquid.

'*We have reason to believe that one of the chauffeurs for the officers*' who attended the briefing at Command Headquarters this evening is a spy. I would ask that you are meticulous in checking all travel documents, particularly those of the drivers.'

'I assure you, effendim, I am always meticulous,' the başçavuş muavini said, a touch of annoyance in his voice.

Lock nodded. 'I do not doubt it, Basçavuş Muavini. I have been most impressed with your attitude, thus far. As has Binbaşi Feyzi. That is to say, Miralay Feyzi.'

The başçavuş muavini puffed out his chest a little in pride. 'But no automobiles have passed this way all night, effendim.'

Lock rubbed his chin. 'Well, then let's hope none do. This is excellent coffee, Basçavuş Muavini, excellent,' he lied, taking another sip, and resisting the temptation to wince. It was truly foul.

The başçavuş muavini smiled sadly. 'I regret to say that we have plenty of time on our hands to make good coffee, effendim.'

A light suddenly shone through the window, and Lock and the başçavuş muavini turned to see a flaring set of headlights approaching.

'Perhaps this is your man, effendim?' the bascavus muavini said, taking his kabalak from a coat hook on the wall. 'If you would excuse me a moment?'

Lock nodded and pulled hard on the cigarette, trying to rid his mouth of the taste of the rank coffee. The başçavuş muavini stepped outside, closing the door behind him. Lock heard the squeal of the automobile's breaks and then a brief, muffled exchange of words. A car door opened and closed, and then the başçavuş muavini came back into the hut, closely followed by a flustered-looking Persian chauffeur. Lock glanced out of the open hut door. He could clearly see the rear passenger door of the automobile, decorated with the palm tree emblem he'd seen earlier.

'. . . *it is merely routine, you understand?*' the *basçavuş muavini* was saying as he moved behind the desk. He had the chauffeur's travel papers in his hand and was frowning down at them. '*Please sit.*'

Lock put the coffee mug down, picked up his fez and the jewellery box, and casually made his way out of the hut, cigarette dangling from his lips, hand in pocket.

The automobile, the same Crossley 20/25 touring car with the raised roof that Lock had seen parked outside of the Command Headquarters, was idling softly. There was a trail of blue tobacco smoke seeping out from the open sides, and Lock could just make out the lower torsos of two men sat in the back. They were chatting quietly, but the voices were unmistakably those of Grössburger and Shears.

'. . . do not trouble yourself, Günther,' Shears was saying. 'The quota of pearls you have distributed more than compensates for the stutter in oil production. For the moment. But we are back on track. And with this next push, the British government will be forced to consider their options.'

'I hope you are right. But I do not like the way that these Ottomans are handling the situation on the Tigris,' Grössburger grumbled. 'It has be—'

Lock sauntered on, heading the few yards up towards the barrier where the three *nefers* were huddled together, smoking and talking in low tones. One turned on hearing Lock's footfall, shielding his eyes against the bright headlights of the Crossley. He nodded, and Lock gave a nonchalant wave of his hand in return. Just before the beam from the headlights would reach his face, Lock stopped and turned back. He continued strolling and smoking his cigarette, making his way casually over to the driver's side of the Crossley. That side of the motor car was in complete shadow. Lock walked slowly by, kicking his feet in the dust, head down.

'. . . the British are getting worryingly close to Baghdad, I am thinking,' Grössburger was saying.

'Nonsense, Günther. Nonsense,' Shears said. 'You must have faith. And faith, my dear fellow is a very powerful weapon, particular in this part of the world. One that we will continue to use and corrupt.' He gave a soft chuckle, before continuing. 'Besides, the British have a surprise in store, mark my words. And our Russian friends will be adding to their worries soon. No, things have been . . . difficult, but . . .'

Lock glanced across the roof of the car, through the open door of the office. The *başçavuş muavini* was still interrogating the chauffeur.

It was now or never.

Lock tossed his cigarette aside, and quickly pulled open the driver's door and slid in behind the wheel. He was sat in total shadow.

'Everything in order?' Shears asked from the back seat.

'Yes, sayyid,' Lock replied, giving his voice a heavy Persian accent.

'Then let's be going.'

Lock tossed the jewellery box onto the seat next to him. He shoved the car into gear, released the brake, and stamped his foot down on the accelerator. With a scrunch of dust, the Crossley shot forward, skidded and sprayed the wall of the sentry hut with gravel, making a sound like machine gun fire. The three *nefers* had a split second to dive out of the way, blinded by the beams of the headlights looming up on them. There was a terrific crack of splintering wood, and of breaking glass, as the Crossley smashed through the barrier. Lock wrestled with the wheel as the Crossley swerved and skidded away. He glanced in the wing mirror to see the *basçavus muavini* and the chauffeur running out of the sentry hut and the three *nefers* picking themselves up.

'What do you . . . ?' Shears gasped from the back seat.

There was a ping of a bullet ricocheting off the Crossley's wing, but Lock just pressed his foot down as far as it would go, sending the car chasing after its own headlight beam that stretched out into the darkness ahead. Lock remained tense, his shoulders hunched, until the light of the checkpoint behind him was but a speck in the wing mirror.

'Farrokh!' Shears shouted.

'*Was ist . . . ?*' Grössburger blustered, but the car was swinging and bumping and crashing so violently that the two men in the back seat couldn't string a sentence together, let alone attempt to grab a hold of Lock.

Every now and again a hand would manage to snatch at his shoulder, but Lock just wrenched the wheel to the left or right, and the oilmen would be thrown back again in a spit of curses.

'*Halt! Halt!*' Grössburger shouted.

'Just what in God's name has gotten into you, Farrokh?' Shears growled.

Lock pushed the accelerator down harder still, until the oilmen's protests were drowned out by the wind that whistled in past the windscreen and through the open sides of the Crossley. On and on Lock drove, until the large Ziggurat mounds of Ur loomed up ahead and he realised that he had reached the same stretch of track that Captain Petre had landed on some eight hours earlier.

Suddenly the Crossley coughed and backfired and jolted. Lock guessed that it needed refuelling, but he wasn't concerned, remembering the extra jerrycans he had spotted attached to the running-boards of the car. He eased off the accelerator, swung the car about by forty-five degrees, and slammed on the brakes. Shears and Grössburger were thrown forward in their seats and then violently back again. Lock turned off the engine and sat for a moment, hands gripping the steering wheel, listening to the heaving breathing of the two oilmen behind him over the ticking of the cooling metal of the bonnet.

One of the oilmen lurched forward and made another grab for him, but Lock snatched the clawing hand, twisted it until there was a squeal of pain.

'Touch me again and I'll break your arm,' Lock growled. He let go of the hand.

'Wh . . . what do . . . you want? Wh . . . who are you?' Grössburger gasped through his pain.

'Get out,' Lock said. 'This side. Hands where I can see them.' He opened the driver's door, pulled out his Beholla and went to stand a good distance away from the car, keeping out of the faint glare from the headlight.

The passenger door swung open and Grössburger struggled to pull himself out. Shears followed.

'In the light. Move,' Lock said, waving his gun in the direction of the front of the car.

Grössburger stumbled, cradling his bruised wrist, and Shears helped to steady the fat Swiss as they walked forward into the single headbeam of the Crossley. Lock took a step after them and glanced at the front of the car. The left-hand headlight was smashed and twisted back, the wing crumpled and hanging loose. But thankfully that looked to be all the damage there was from ramming through the checkpoint barrier.

'Far enough,' Lock said.

The two oilmen shuffled about, squinting and averting their eyes from the glare of the beam. Lock could see that Grössburger's face still bore the marks of Sergeant Major Underhill's interrogation. His left eyebrow was swollen and there was bruising around his jawline. Shears must have hit his head in the back seat at some point during their escape, as he had a fresh cut above his left eye, and the left lens of his spectacles was cracked.

'Wh-who ar-are you?' Grössburger asked, his voice shaky with nerves.

Lock glanced up at the sky. The cloud cover was breaking and there were some stars out, but the moon was yet to rise. He removed the fez and lifted the patch from his eye, glad to feel the air rush to the itching socket. He patted his pockets and cursed, remembering he had no cigarettes. And then he raised his eyes and focused on Lord Shears. The oilman, he remembered, always had a steady supply of cigarettes.

'Give me a cigarette,' Lock said.

'Certainly,' Shears said, hurriedly reaching into his pocket.

Lock let off a quick shot, firing into the ground only inches from Shears' boot.

'The next one will go right between your eyes.'

Shears froze, hand halfway in his right-hand pocket.

'Toss it here.'

Shears slowly pulled a P.08 Luger pistol from his pocket by the barrel and threw it over to Lock.

'You. Fat man? Do you have a gun for me as well?'

Grössburger shook his head vigorously. '*N-nein, n-nein*,' he stuttered.

Lock crouched down, picked up the Luger and stuffed it in his pocket. 'Now for that cigarette,' he said, standing straight again, and holstering his Beholla.

Shears nodded and cautiously put his hand in his left-hand pocket and pulled out a packet of Pall Malls. He held the packet out, seemingly unsure whether he should approach.

'*A* cigarette, I said.'

Shears took the hint, opened the pack, and started to walk towards Lock, squinting in the glare of the headlight.

Lock waited until Shears was just at the edge of the beam, then stepped forward out of the shadows.

Shears stopped dead in his tracks. His eyes met Lock's and they widened with shock. 'Lieutenant Lock?' he whispered.

'*Was? Was . . . Was hast du gesagt?*' Grössburger gasped, lifting his chubby hand to shield his eyes.

Lock helped himself to one of Shears' cigarettes. The oilman put the pack away in his pocket, pulled out a book of matches, and struck a light. Lock steadied Shears' shaking hand and leant into the flame, his eyes burning through the oilman's glinting lenses.

'No, my dear Lord Shears,' he said, letting out a sigh of tobacco smoke, 'it's captain now.'

'Very well, *Captain* Lock. Now what? Do you plan to drive us all the way back to Basra?' Shears said with a touch of arrogance.

Lock stared back at the oilman letting the silence stretch out. When he could see that Shears was getting uncomfortable, he spoke. 'There's extra jerrycans there,' he said jutting his chin back towards the automobile. 'More than enough for a long journey.'

Shears remained tight-lipped. Grössburger glanced at his colleague nervously.

'But you were setting off at night,' Lock continued, 'and I doubt you were driving all that way.'

Lock finished his cigarette and stamped out the stub. A boat? No, he thought, if they had a boat it would be in Nasiriyeh. Besides, these two wouldn't be heading back to Basra. Shears was 'dead' and Grössburger under suspicion by the British authorities. So where? Then Lock smiled. Of course. They would be going back to Persia, to Ahwaz and the oil refinery, or perhaps Abadan Island at the mouth of the Shatt al-Arab. That was a long way, though.

He strode back over to the automobile and opened the driver's door, struck a match and peered inside. Under the box of pearls on the front passenger seat was a map. Lock reached in and pulled it out. He tossed the match aside and went to stand near the headlight. He glanced over his shoulder.

'Back to the fat man, Lord Shears. If you please.'

Lock waited until Shears had gone to stand next to his colleague again.

'Sit down. Both of you.'

The oilmen sat themselves awkwardly down on the desert floor.

'C-Cap-Capitan . . . Lock,' Grössburger stuttered, 'I ass-assure . . .'

'Shut your fat mouth,' Lock snarled. 'I won't ask again.'

Grössburger blinked back through the headlight beam, then

dropped his head and mumbled something to Shears.

Lock opened up the map and ran his eye over its detail. The road they were on, for want of a better word, was marked, and it followed the length of the Euphrates all the way to Hammar Lake. The first town they would pass was Suq ash Shuyukh, which rested on the edge of a smaller body of water called Lake Hokeike. Beyond that the road would, Lock imagined, become impassable as they would hit floods and reed marsh. To continue to Basra by automobile, they would have to circle south, deep into the Shamiya Desert, and he just couldn't see that happening. They hadn't the water. Unless the plan was for the oilmen to rendezvous with a team of horses or camels?

Lock folded the map away again and stumped out his cigarette. 'All right, gentlemen, back in the motor car,' he said, opening up the rear passenger door for them.

Shears and Grössburger glanced uneasily at one another and pulled themselves stiffly to their feet. They shuffled warily over to Lock, hesitated, then climbed into the back seat. Lock slammed the door shut on them and slipped in the front behind the steering wheel.

'What's waiting for you at Lake Hokeike?' he said, twisting round in his seat.

He was met by stony silence.

'Very well.' Lock leant to his side and turned back again with Shears' Luger in his hand. He pulled the trigger in the same second. There was a terrific crack, a flash that illuminated the terrified faces of the two oilmen, followed by a soft splintering of glass as the bullet punched its way out of the rear window.

The smell of cordite and fear was almost overwhelming in the confined interior of the automobile.

'We have an aeroplane! We have an aeroplane!' Grössburger blurted out.

'At Suq ash Shuyukh?' Lock said.

'*Nein, der see*. The lake. On the lake,' Grössburger whimpered.

'*On* the lake?'

'*Ja, ja*. It is . . . flying boat.'

Lock turned back in his seat. 'Well, well. Whatever will they think of next?' He struck a match and checked his watch. He estimated there was some four hours left until sunrise.

'Get some sleep,' he said and switched off the headlight. They were suddenly plunged into darkness.

Slowly Lock's eyes adjusted to the gloom and he lay back across the front seats, the Luger resting on his chest. He stared up out of the windscreen at the stars in the night sky. The clouds cleared and the waning gibbous moon suddenly brought a silvery glow to everything.

As Lock lay there thinking, not for once of Amy, but of Betty and that kiss, he was vaguely aware of the two oilmen fidgeting about until finally there was stillness. After a while one of them began to snore softly. Grössburger. Shears would be wide awake, Lock knew, his mind no doubt working overtime as to how he was going to worm his way out of this predicament. Or perhaps he wasn't, Lock thought. Perhaps the oilman already knew what would happen.

Lock lifted the Luger up and looked it over. It was a nice gun, not as graceful as his Beholla, but he could see why so many British officers liked them compared to the bulky Webley. Maybe he'd give it to Ross as a gift. Or keep it for himself. After all it used the same 7.65 parabellum round that . . . Oh, but of course, he suddenly thought. What an idiot I am.

'You're a most appalling shot, Lord Shears,' he said.

There was a snort of derision from the back seat.

'You owe my friend an apology,' Lock said.

'Why on earth should I apologise to that Indian fool?' Shears said.

'For the pain you gave him,' Lock said. 'His ribs ache all the time. He hides it, but I can see it on his face. Now me . . . I don't expect an apology, I can understand you just wanted me out of the way.'

'It was nothing personal.'

'A professional matter? I see. Then, I suppose Singh was just unlucky.'

'You could say that.'

'But what I don't understand is . . .' Lock paused, sitting himself up. He stared back at Shears' face illuminated by the moon, his lenses two discs of white light, '– why you pulled the trigger yourself?'

'Did you know dear Günther here was there that night? At the brothel?' Shears said.

'No.'

Shears scoffed and glanced at Grössburger, snoring softly in the seat next to him. 'He has a soft spot for the ladies—'

'Hardly soft.'

Shears turned his face back to Lock and gave one of his withering smiles.

'Quite. But he was late, as usual, for a meeting. And I had no choice but to go and fetch him myself. Fortunately Jalal Al-din Bahar is a most discreet host, so I was not afraid of him seeing me. But when you suddenly stepped out of the door and struck that match, I panicked.'

'Now I know you're lying.'

Shears shrugged. 'I am not a soldier, Captain. I don't like guns.'

'Guns are neutral,' Lock said. 'It makes more sense to detest the man who holds it.'

'Very profound.'

'I have my moments.'

Shears stared back at Lock for a moment, then continued. 'I presumed that you were one step closer to discovering that I wasn't dead. I was rash and foolish.'

'Were you?' Lock didn't believe the oilman. He knew there was more to it than that.

Shears smiled thinly again. 'I realise now that you had no idea that I was still alive. Why would you?'

Lock yawned and rubbed the back of his neck. 'Give me one of your gaspers, will you?'

'Certainly.' Shears offered the pack of Pall Malls to Lock. 'May I join you?'

Lock waved his hand. 'Go ahead, they're your cigarettes.'

Shears took one for himself and Lock lit them both. The two men then sat smoking in silence, alone with their thoughts.

'What do you plan to do with us?' Shears eventually said.

'Take you to Major Ross.'

Shears nodded through a cloud of tobacco. 'I see.'

'You don't seem overly troubled.'

'I'm not.'

'You're a traitor, sir. Do you know what they do to traitors?'

Shears just continued to smoke in silence.

Lock sighed and glanced at his watch again, twisting his wrist until the face caught in the moonlight. It was a little after three now. He estimated that it was no more than an hour's drive to Lake Hokeike. If they set off in half an hour, they'd arrive at dawn.

'Is this flying boat easily accessed?' he said.

'There is a jolly boat on the shore. Our chauffeur was to row us out to the flying boat.'

'And the crew?'

'They stay with the craft at all times.'

Lock pulled himself upright, opened the door on the passenger side and climbed out. He stretched, felt his knee crack, took a final draw on his cigarette and flicked it out into the silvery desert. It bounced once in a sprinkling of sparks and was gone. Lock unstrapped the jerrycan from the running-board and carried it to the back of the automobile. He unscrewed the filler cap and began to pour in the petrol. The fumes wafted up around his face and he turned his head away suddenly feeling nauseous. While the petrol glugged and sloshed into the tank, Lock kept glancing back through the rear window to check on the two oilmen. The last of the petrol dribbled out into the tank, and Lock tossed the jerrycan away into the gloom. It made a hollow clang as it landed causing Shears to jerk his head to the left.

Lock brushed his hands and walked back to the driver's side of the automobile. He opened the door and leant in to turn the magneto on. There was a dull electric buzz that made Grössburger suddenly stir from his slumber with a snort.

'*Was ist . . . ?*' the fat Swiss yawned.

Lock set the throttle lever up, pushed the spark advance to slow, then walked to the front of the automobile. He glanced up. Shears and Grössburger were sat watching him through the windscreen.

Lock bent down, pushed the hand crank lever in and then, with his left hand, gave it a single, but forceful, turn to the right. The engine coughed, spluttered and kicked into life. Lock moved back round and slipped in behind the steering wheel once more, closing the door after him. He flicked on the headlight, adjusted the spark advance until the engine was purring smoothly, then released the handbrake, and with a scrunch of loose stones, they drove off.

CHAPTER TWENTY-FOUR

By the time they neared the settlement of Suq ash Shuyukh the first signs of dawn had turned the sky to their left a magnificent hue of red and orange. Lock steered the Crossley away from the town to avoid any curious approaches. There wouldn't be a large Turkish garrison here, more likely a small outpost, but he still didn't want to run the risk of having to show transit papers, despite the fact he still wore the Turkish naval uniform. Eventually the shimmering pink and blue waters of Lake Hokeike appeared up ahead. Lock drove on. There were a number of boats, mostly the lenj fishing vessels, but fortunately there were no fishermen about just yet. Out on the water Lock could see a bulky silhouette edged with an orange halo of light. The flying boat. He'd never seen one before, although he had heard of them, and indeed they did look just like a boat with wings and a tail attached. How on earth could that fly, he wondered?

'There,' Shears suddenly said from the back seat, pointing forward.

Lock spotted a small dinghy up on the shore. He steered the automobile as close as he could get, then stopped and switched off the headlight and the engine. He twisted round in his seat, Beholla raised.

'All right, gentlemen, in the boat. Shears, you'll be rowing.'

The two oilmen shuffled out of the same door and Lock quickly followed. They scrunched down the gravelly foreshore and Lock stood by as the two oilmen dragged the dinghy down to the water.

Grössburger moved awkwardly to the bow, while Shears sat facing the rear with the oars in his hands. Lock pushed them off, then clambered in and sat down at the tiller, his Beholla covering Shears.

'Off we go.'

It took them less than five minutes to row out to the anchored flying boat, with not a sound around them but the gentle rhythmic splosh of the oars passing through the water. In that time, the sun gradually crept up over the horizon, shooting its orange warmth across the choppy water and burning away the last of the shadows concealing the details of the aircraft.

It looked very impressive as they moved steadily closer, sat in the middle of the lake like a giant seabird at rest. It was a pusher type like Petre's Farman MF.11, but this aeroplane had two engines with rear-facing propellers, a large boat body and a fully enclosed cabin. The name *America* was written on the bow, and the APOC palm tree emblem was daubed on the tail rudder, yellow on black.

'What is this?' Lock said.

Shears craned his neck over his shoulder. 'It is a Curtiss . . . Model

H-4 . . . flying boat . . . Lock . . . A very . . . interesting . . . craft, don't . . . you agree?' the oilman said breathlessly, between strokes. 'APOC . . . acquired a . . . couple of . . . them at . . . the beginning . . . of the year . . . From the United . . . States.'

'How many can she carry?'

'Crew of . . . three, four . . . passengers.'

'Fortunate for Grössburger,' Lock said.

Shears was about to ask why, then he just turned his gaze away.

Lock gave a shallow snort of amusement at the oilman's reaction.

The flying boat was still and silent as they came alongside. Grössburger grabbed hold of the lower wing and Shears clambered unsteadily out of the dinghy. He gave a hand to Grössburger, and Lock, his Beholla still trained on the two oilmen, leapt out onto the wing himself. The dinghy began to drift away on the current.

'Well, gentlemen,' Lock said with a sly grin, 'we best wake the aircrew and get underway.'

A cramped, mentally draining two hours later the civilian pilot, a gruff Afrikaans with hateful, dark eyes and a scar down his left cheek, shouted back across the noisy, stuffy cabin that Amara was in sight. Lock closed up Wassmuss's notebook and put it away in his breeches pocket. He'd removed the naval jacket and the fez, and was dressed just in his shirtsleeves now. He peered bleary-eyed out through the window and down at the shimmering Tigris snaking its way north-west.

Amara was little different from twenty-four hours earlier, Lock thought, just a lot more boats on the water. The rest of Townshend's Regatta had evidently arrived.

It had been easy enough to disarm and encourage the three sleepy members of the flying boat's aircrew to get their craft ready and up into the air. Lock spotted the odd conspiratorial glance between Shears and the Afrikaans pilot, but nothing happened and the flight was uneventful. Lock settled at the very back of the cabin and, with one eye on the crew and the oilmen, he overcame the overwhelming desire to sleep by studying Wassmuss's notebook.

The Curtiss H-4 spluttered down towards the river like a giant, egg-laden pelican searching for a nesting sight. They turned and slowly dropped down, passing low over the damaged bridge of boats, which Lock could see was now busy with engineers going about repairs. The flying boat skimmed the choppy surface of the Tigris, bounced, shuddered and finally sighed as it settled on the water. The pilot eased off the throttle and glided the craft towards the main quay and the Customs House. Already there was quite a crowd standing on the river's edge and out on the muddy foreshore staring and pointing out at the strange boat with wings.

'Thank you, gentlemen,' Lock said to the aircrew as he got to his feet. 'Lord Shears, Herr Grössburger and myself shall be leaving you now.'

'What about us?' the Afrikaans pilot growled, twisting round, his knuckles white as they gripped the back of his seat.

'I'm a man of my word,' Lock said. 'You are free to do as you wish. You're civilians. Fly off or stay, it makes no difference to me. Unless you try something stupid that is.' He raised the Beholla to make it clear how serious he was.

The pilot's eyes dropped to Lock's pistol and he licked his lips. 'You'll have no trouble from us.'

'Good.'

'I imagine we will be needed before long,' the pilot added, glancing at Shears.

'As you wish,' Lock said. 'I'd just ask that you stay here until we have safely reached the shore. Just so there's no misunderstandings.' He smiled. 'You,' Lock said, pointing to the navigator, 'open the hatch.'

The navigator, a slim man with an acne-scarred complexion, glanced uncertainly at the pilot.

'Go ahead,' the pilot said, 'let some air into this stinking box.'

Lock stepped back and watched as the navigator climbed the ladder at the back of the cabin, and opened up the rooftop access hatch. He climbed back down, and returned to his seat.

Lock picked up the jewellery box, climbed up the ladder himself and out of the access hatch. A warm breeze hit him in the face and it was a welcome relief from the stuffy cabin. He waved his arm, signalling to the shore, and soon spotted a flurry of movement along the quayside. A moment later a motor launch was bouncing its way towards him across the water. Lock stood to one side and called down into the cabin.

By the time Shears and Grössburger had climbed up out of the cabin and stepped down onto the wing, the motor launch, manned by a single marine, a corporal with a black beard, had reached them. The marine corporal skillfully glided close to the wing, and Lock steadied the launch while Grössburger and Shears climbed in.

'Captain Lock, with two prisoners.'

'I know who you are, sir,' the marine corporal said, with a nod. 'There's a Major Ross on the quay waiting for you.'

'Good. Let's get going.'

'Never seen one of these before, sir,' the marine corporal said, running his eye over the flying boat. 'Thought you were going to crash when we saw you dropping down to the water.'

Lock jumped down from the wing into the launch. 'It's the best of both worlds, Corporal,' he said. 'Albeit a little cramped.'

The marine corporal smiled, then opened up the throttle and, in a spray of water, spun the launch about and sped off back towards the shore.

Major Ross was standing, arms folded, pipe clenched between his teeth, a pair of binoculars dangling from his neck, waiting on the quayside. There were two Red Caps at his side, rifles slung across their bellies, and a small crowd of curious natives and off-duty soldiers, all chatting and pointing out towards the flying boat. The aircraft had evidently caused quite a stir.

The marine corporal steered the launch up to a wooden jetty where a native dockhand was ready to tie the boat off. Lock waved his Beholla directing Shears and Grössburger to climb out, and he then prodded them towards the wooden steps.

The two Red Caps immediately stepped forward to take the oilmen in hand.

'To the detention cells,' Ross said. He didn't even look at Shears.

Lock holstered his Beholla and passed a hand through his damp hair.

'I thought for a minute those Red Caps were for me,' he said, nodding after the two provosts as they marched Shears and Grössburger towards the Customs House.

'Aye, laddie, they very nearly were,' Ross said, taking his pipe from his mouth. 'And then I saw who you had for company. I nearly fell off the quay in shock.'

'A dead man and a fat man,' Lock grinned, looking about. He spotted what he was after. 'Hey, Private,' he called to one of the Tommies standing nearby, 'can I bum a smoke?'

The private fished out a pack of Navy Cut. 'Sure. You look like you need one, pal.'

Lock nodded his thanks. The Tommy struck a match for him and then stepped away again.

'So no Feyzi? No Wassmuss?' Ross said.

Lock shook his head. 'Dead.'

'Are you certain?'

'*Coup de grâce*,' Lock said through a sigh of tobacco.

'Pity.'

'Not so, sir,' Lock said. 'Those two,' he nodded in the direction of Shears and Grössburger, just as the two oilmen entered the Customs House and disappeared from sight, 'were with Feyzi, Wassmuss, whoever he bloody was, and a bunch of senior enemy officers. APOC are involved in some serious shit, sir. Colluding with the enemy, taking bribes, paying bribes. Who knows what exactly.' He paused and put his cigarette between his lips. 'But I did retrieve this,' he mumbled, taking Wassmuss's notebook from his pocket and handing it to Ross. 'Makes for very interesting reading. Most of it's in code, as we know, but there's a list of names at the back very similar to that list I gave you mentioning payments and locations and names relating to that pearl company. Only this list has sub-lists, and Harrington-Brown's name is among them . . .'

Ross was flicking through the notebook with a frown of concentration etched upon his face. He looked up realising Lock had stopped talking. 'I see.'

'You see?'

Ross nodded and closed the notebook up, putting it away in his pocket. He steered Lock away from the quayside and they walked side by side towards the Customs House.

'What about the investigation?'

'Investigation?'

'The assassination, this Turk officer I'm supposed to have murdered in cold blood.'

'Oh, that. Don't let it bother you, laddie.'

'What?' Lock pulled Ross to a halt. 'Don't let it bother me?'

The Major smiled. '*Kaymakam* Süleyman Askerî Bey committed suicide. At least that's the official line coming out of Constantinople now.'

Lock just gaped back at Ross at a loss for words.

The Major took him by the elbow, and pulled him on. 'Politics, laddie.'

Lock grunted and they both continued walking in silence. More mind games, he thought. Would they ever end?

'I worked out who shot me, by the way,' Lock said after a while.

'Oh?'

Lock pulled the Luger from his waistband and gave it to Ross.

'Wassmuss,' the major said, turning the gun over in his hand. 'I thought so.'

'No, sir,' Lock said. 'That belongs to Shears. It seems I was just in the wrong place at the wrong time. He was on his way to fetch Grössburger from the brothel. When I stepped out with Singh, Shears panicked. Or so he says.'

As they arrived at the foot of the steps running up to the Customs House entrance, Ross paused and glanced back out across the water towards the anchored flying boat.

'Interesting. I know the Admiralty are looking into those flying boat contraptions for use over the North Sea. But as far as I was aware, they were still in the developmental stage.'

'Shears told me that APOC had obtained it from America,' Lock said. 'It would seem that the oil company are better equipped than the British forces.'

Ross snorted and his gaze fell on the jewellery box under Lock's arm. 'What's that?'

Lock pulled the box out and considered it for a moment. 'Oh, this. Just my shaving kit, sir. Supplied by Bet . . .'

'Well you best go use it,' Ross said. 'You have a party to attend this evening.'

'A party? I'd rather not, sir, if it's all the same to you.'

'All the officers are expected to attend, laddie,' Ross said, pulling his pipe from his mouth and jabbing it towards Lock. 'No exceptions. The general's throwing it to celebrate our victory. Besides, I think it best you are there, to show certain . . . persons that you're back in the fold, as it were, all forgiven.'

'But what about the general, sir? The last time I saw him—'

'He's the one who insisted, Lock. He knows what you've done, what you've been doing. Most of that . . . bluster the other day about murder and court martial was for show, for the benefit of Colonel Godwinson.' Ross shrugged. 'Like I said, politics. You know?'

Lock nodded and stamped his cigarette out. 'I'm beginning to, sir.'

EPILOGUE

Lock hated parties. He just felt so out of place and uncomfortable. He'd rather be with Singh and the others. But orders were orders and, besides, Amy was to be in attendance. Singh had told him so when he'd left Ross and trudged up to the barracks, the same barracks where he'd recently taken the surrender of the regiment of the Constantinople Fire Brigade. That's where he'd found his men, in their new digs, all sat around cleaning their rifles, reading letters, dozing, and all under the stern, watchful eye of Underhill.

'Back is ya', sah?' was all the greeting he got from the sergeant major.

But the others were all there, Elsworth, Pritchard, Ram Lal and the rest of the sepoys, Jawad Saleem, and even the dog. And they were, at least, pleased to seem him. But, more than that, Lock was delighted to find that Green Platoon had suffered not one casualty during the advance up the Tigris from Qurna. Apart from Harrington-Brown, of course.

After a welcome meal of chicken and flat bread washed down with strong coffee, Lock had retired to the room Singh had made up for him. He'd slept on the small bunk there for six hours solid and following a hot bath, had shaved and dressed in his own uniform. It had been waiting for him, hanging on the back of the door, cleaned and pressed. There was even a fresh pair of leather riding boots at the foot of the bed.

'An Australian pilot dropped your uniform off, sahib, along with the battalion mail,' Singh said.

'Good old Petre,' Lock said.

'I managed to find the boots, sahib, in the stores. I think they are German. And this carton of cigarettes, sahib.'

Lock grinned at Singh and gave him a friendly whack on the arm. He tore open a fresh pack of Fatimas. 'Pass the rest around the lads.' He gave the carton back to Singh and lit himself a cigarette.

'How are the ribs, Sid?'

'They are fine, sahib. They only hurt when I laugh now.'

Lock then checked himself over once more in the grubby, spotted mirror that was propped up against the wall. Satisfied, he pulled on his slouch hat.

'How do I look, Sid?'

Singh nodded his approval. 'Very fine and smart, sahib. She will not be able to resist you.'

'She?'

'Memsahib Amy, sahib,' Singh said. 'She is here. Arrived on the hospital ship with many, many nurses, sahib, and the Memsahib Lady Townshend.'

'Bugger. Then they'll both be there tonight,' Lock said, straightening his tie. How he hated wearing the things.

'Sahib?'

'At this bloody party, Sid. It's the last thing I want to do. But . . .'

'Orders is orders, sahib,' Singh grinned.

It was a more intimate affair than the last party he'd attended of Townshend's, and was being held outside in the courtyard garden of the Customs House. The sun had gone down and the sky above was clear and full of bright stars. It was a warm, but comfortable evening. There was a buzz of insects, but thankfully the mosquitoes were few and far between. Light was spilling out from the open French windows of Townshend's office, and there were candles dotted about amongst the potted plants and around the edge of the water fountain. An unseen gramophone was playing light classical music. The whole set-up looked eerily similar to Feyzi's office back in Nasiriyeh, down to the murmur of conversation and the gentle tinkle of glasses. Four or five marines in white jackets were acting as waiters, weaving in and out of the guests with trays of drinks and canapés in their hands.

The guests were mostly high-ranking officers, those men who had led the various attacks from Qurna, and a few senior nurses. Godwinson was there, deep in conversation with the artillery commander, Brigadier General Smith, and the commander of the 22nd Punjabis, Lieutenant Colonel Blois Johnson. Captain Nunn and a portly lieutenant colonel, whom Lock didn't recognise, were standing at the far end of the garden, near to a wrought iron gate that was set into the high wall. Lock could see the stableyard beyond. The officers were sharing a joke with Lady Townshend, who was dressed in her Sister's uniform, and another middle-aged matron. Nunn caught Lock's eye and gave him a brief nod of recognition. Lock's gaze passed over the rest of the guests and eventually fell on

Amy. She was in her nurse's uniform, too, and was standing over by the water fountain. Bingham-Smith was at her side, his hand resting on the small of her back. The couple were talking with Major Winsloe of the Engineers, and Lock's former company commander, Major Carver.

'Pink gin, sir?'

A waiter was offering out a tray of drinks.

'Thank you.' Lock took a glass. He sniffed the contents and had a wary sip. He grimaced at the spicy taste. 'Christ, I'd rather drink my own piss.'

'My sentiments, exactly.' Ross had come up alongside him. 'I have some decent whisky in my pocket if you'd rather, laddie.'

Lock dumped his pink gin out into a nearby plant pot without hesitation, and held his now empty glass out. Ross poured him a good measure of whisky from a hip flask.

'Hello, handsome.'

Lock turned to see Betty sauntering over, looking very smart in her white uniform.

'Father,' she nodded to Ross.

The major cleared his throat and shifted uncomfortably on his feet.

'You made it, then?' Betty said to Lock.

Lock was about to offer some witty response, when another familiar voice called out from across the garden.

'There you are, Lock.' It was General Townshend.

Lock nodded affably at the general as he approached and was then suddenly rather taken aback. Townshend was as white as a sheet and had dark rings under his eyes, and there was a thin film of sweat across his brow that glistened in the candlelight.

'Good evening, sir,' Lock said.

'It appears I . . . we all' – Townshend said, raising his voice slightly above the general murmur of conversation – 'owe you an apology, my boy.'

'That's really not necessary, sir,' Lock said, knocking back his whisky.

'Nonsense. You've been treated in the most ghastly manner,' Townshend said. 'So please, accept my hand in gratitude and respect. I am sorry to have doubted you.'

Lock took the general's hand in his. 'Just glad to be of help, sir.'

'You're a good sport, Lock,' Townshend smiled, 'a good sport. I . . .' The general broke into a coughing fit.

'Are you all right, sir?' Lock said, putting a reassuring hand on the general's shoulder.

Townshend waved his hand as if to say he was fine, but the coughing continued, and then suddenly his legs gave way and he collapsed to the floor. There was a gasp of concern from those nearest, and Lock knelt down immediately, pulling the general over onto his side. He was alive, but unconscious, and the breath was rasping in his chest.

'Charles! Charles!' Lady Townshend came rushing over. '*Mon dieu!* Charles.'

'He just collapsed, Lady Alice,' Lock said.

Lady Townshend felt her husband's pulse and then put her hand to his forehead. 'We must get him to the hospital.'

Ross clicked his fingers and two of the waiters put down their trays and hurried over.

'Carry the general outside and summon his staff car,' Ross said. 'Get him to the hospital at once.'

'Yes, sir.'

'I will come with you,' Lock said, getting to his feet.

'That will not be necessary,' Lady Townshend snapped.

But Lock wasn't to be brushed off so easily. He stood above her, and after a moment's hesitation, Lady Townshend reluctantly took his hand in hers and let him help her up.

'*Maman, qu'est-ce qui se passe? Qu'est-ce qu'il a?*' Amy said, pushing through the concerned guests. She glared at Lock as if it was his fault.

'It is a fever,' Lady Townshend said. 'Do not worry child. I shall take care of your father. You must stay and attend to our guests.'

'*Mais, maman . . .*'

'*Non*,' Lady Townshend snapped. Then she smiled and put her hand lightly to her daughter's cheek. 'He will be all right, *ma fille.*'

The two waiters lifted the general between them, and the guests parted to let them carry the stricken commander out of the garden and back through the French windows. Lady Townshend gave a curt nod to Lock and hurried after the waiters. The music had stopped, and there was now just the click-whirr-click of the gramophone needle caught in the final groove of the record drifting out from the office.

Once Lady Townshend had disappeared into the depths of the Customs House, the garden became a sudden buzz of excited and concerned conversation.

'Gentlemen, ladies,' Ross said, holding his hand up, and raising his voice above the chatter. 'Please don't concern yourselves. The general has taken ill. A touch of the Mesop Trot, I fear.'

There was a titter and murmur of understanding, followed by knowing nods.

'Lady Townshend has requested that you carry on with your drinks,' Ross added. 'She will return shortly.'

'Thank you, Major,' Amy said.

'He'll be fine, miss. Just overdoing things. You know your father.'

'I hope you are right, Major,' Amy said, glancing back through the French windows. Captain Nunn was inside the office turning the handle of the gramophone. Music started up again, this time a Billy Murray ragtime tune.

'What the bloody hell are you up to now, Lock?' Bingham-Smith said as he strode over to Amy's side. 'Upsetting my fiancée are you?'

'Smith, what a great displeasure it is to see you again,' Lock said.

'I've a good mind to knock you out, Lock,' Bingham-Smith said, puffing his chest out. 'What the devil did you do to the general?'

'Stop it, Casper,' Amy said, pulling at Bingham-Smith's sleeve. 'Father has taken ill. A fever. *Maman* has gone with him to the hospital.'

'Rot!' Bingham-Smith said. 'It's this bothersome colonial oik, I'll wager.'

'You lookin' for a bust in the chops?' Betty suddenly interjected, stepping forward.

Bingham-Smith stared down his nose at Betty, a look of distaste written across his face. 'And who the dickens are you?'

'I'm with him,' Betty glared back, throwing a thumb at Lock.

'Enough, Casper. Please,' Amy said. 'Come along.' She pulled Bingham-Smith away, glancing from Lock to Betty and back again with a frown. There was a look of confused hurt in her eyes.

'You wanna learn some manners, bud,' Betty called after them.

'And you want to learn to speak the King's Eng—'

But Amy had dragged Bingham-Smith off before he could finish his sentence.

'What a heel,' Betty said, turning away and putting a cigarette between her lips.

Ross pulled out the lighter Lock had given him and passed it to Betty.

'When I was spying on Feyzi and his military guests, Amy's name was mentioned in conversation, sir,' Lock said. 'As to what context,' he shrugged, 'I couldn't make out. But I think she's still in danger.'

Betty scoffed. 'Boy, she's in danger all right, hanging out with that goof. Does he always get so steamed up?' She lit her cigarette, handed it to Lock, and lit a second for herself.

Lock nodded his thanks. 'Always.'

'We'll keep an eye on her, laddie,' Ross said, taking a sip of his whisky.

Lock was still staring after Amy, watching her engaged in a heated conversation with a clearly still agitated Bingham-Smith.

'She's a doll, I'll give you that,' Betty said through a cloud of tobacco smoke. 'You got the blues over her, Kingdom?'

Lock gave a thin smile. 'No. I did. But not any more. They're getting married soon. She's having a baby.' He let out a sigh of smoke. 'She knows what she's doing.'

'Uh-huh,' Betty said, with a gentle nod. 'Not his, I'll bet.'

Lock glanced at Betty's profile, but she didn't turn to look at him.

'I've got a fine single malt back at my digs,' Ross said, as he drained his glass and put it on the tray of a passing waiter. He took his pipe and tobacco pouch out of his pocket and began to fill the bowl. 'What say you both that we, in the words of Elizabeth here, "blow this joint"?'

'Now you're talkin', Pops,' Betty said with her customary lopsided grin.

Lock glanced over at Amy one final time, then followed Ross and Betty as they pushed their way through the guests towards the wrought iron gate at the end of the garden.

Godwinson stepped out from the small group of officers he was chatting with, blocking Lock's path.

Lock paused and ran his eyes over the colonel's face.

Godwinson's nose twitched and he rubbed nervously at his moustache, before clearing his throat. 'Lock, glad I caught you. I . . . er . . . That is to say . . . I owe you an . . . er . . . apology, too, Lock. Er . . . the general informed me of . . . er . . . what you did. Nailing the . . . er . . . spy . . . and capturing this traitor chap . . .' His words dried up and he stood staring back at Lock waiting for some response.

Lock glanced over the colonel's shoulder to see Betty and Ross open the garden gate and step out into the stableyard. Godwinson held his hand out in offering.

'So does this mean I get a Company? Sir.'

Godwinson's face fell and he spluttered and mumbled something incoherent about procedure and dates.

Lock stared back at the colonel, but he knew he wouldn't get an answer, not yet. He drew on his cigarette and blew a slow trail of tobacco smoke out of the side of his mouth. Then he gripped the colonel's hand in his. It was limp, but he shook it all the same.

'Good of you, Lock. Well, no hard feelings,' Godwinson nodded, and without another word, he returned to the group he'd been talking with.

Lock glared at the colonel's back for a moment, already regretting having accepted his apology, then he walked over to the gate. He paused, turned to face the garden once more.

'The net's tightening,' he said loudly.

A number of bemused faces broke from their conversations and looked over towards him.

'What? What was that?' Godwinson said, brow furrowed.

'Traitors,' Lock said. 'They're always where you least expect them.'

'What the deuce is that fellow going on about, Godwinson?' the portly lieutenant colonel standing nearby said. 'Who the devil are you, sir?'

Lock took a final draw on his cigarette, dropped it to the floor, and ground it out with his heel. He raised his eyes and glared back at the two officers.

'My name is Lock. Sir,' he said. 'Captain Kingdom Lock.'

AUTHOR'S NOTE

A note on the languages used in this book

On many occasions a translation is provided within the text. The Arabic words and phrases are interpreted in familiar Roman letters and follow an imitated-pronunciation system. For consistency, the main source of reference was the Dorling Kindersley *Eyewitness Travel Guides Arabic Phrase Book* (2003).

I. D. ROBERTS

ACKNOWLEDGEMENTS

History is inspiring and where fiction and fact merge, that's where an adventure like *Kingdom Lock* is born. Some things are true, some are made up, but everything that is written has been done so to entertain. And none of this would have been possible without the help, guidance, and support of many people. So I'd like to thank, in no order of preference:

Robert Dinsdale, Kirstie Imber, Sophie Robinson, Susie Dunlop and all at Allison & Busby, the meticulous Fliss and Simon Bage, James Sharp for his German skills, Di Pearce for her French skills, Lydia Riddle, Ben Kane, Helen Hollick, Elisabeth Storrs, Sean Ryan, Di Roberts, Kenneth Dunmore, Jesse James, Hergé, John Buchan, Ian Fleming, and, of course, Major General Sir Charles V. E. Townshend whose memoirs are a constant source of fascination and inspiration.